THE CURSE OF
KHAINE

The end of the world is coming, and few realise it. Amongst the elves, a small number of individuals are being guided by their dying gods, pushed towards destinies that might help them to avert the triumph of Chaos. Chief amongst these are Malekith, the Witch King of Naggaroth, who plans his greatest – and last – attempt to claim his birthright and unite the elves under his leadership. He is aided by Teclis, greatest of the asur loremasters, who has seen what must come to pass if the world is to be saved. But ranged against them are the armies of Ulthuan, led by the one warrior Malekith fears – Teclis's brother Tyrion. The scene is set for the greatest battle since the Sundering, and one that will decide the fate of not only the elves, but the entire world.

WARHAMMER®
THE END TIMES

SIGMAR'S BLOOD
The Prequel to the End Times
Phil Kelly

THE RETURN OF NAGASH
Book One of the End Times
A novel by Josh Reynolds

THE FALL OF ALTDORF
Book Two of the End Times
A novel by Chris Wraight

THE CURSE OF KHAINE
Book Three of the End Times
A novel by Gav Thorpe

THE RISE OF THE HORNED RAT
Book Four of the End Times
A novel by Guy Haley

GOTREK & FELIX: KINSLAYER
Book One of the Doom of Gotrek Gurnisson
A novel by David Guymer

GOTREK & FELIX: SLAYER
Book Two of the Doom of Gotrek Gurnisson
A novel by David Guymer

DEATHBLADE
A Chronicle of Malus Darkblade
A novel by C L Werner

Visit blacklibrary.com *for the full range of Warhammer: The End Times novels and Quick Reads, as well as digital versions of the Warhammer: The End Times campaign books to use in your games of Warhammer.*

WARHAMMER®
THE END TIMES

THE CURSE OF
KHAINE

GAV THORPE

BLACK LIBRARY

This book is dedicated to Shaun. I can't believe it took me this long to thank you – for being the first gatekeeper, who guided me into the worlds of SF and fantasy and showed me the way to Warhammer and role-playing. I owe you so much.

A BLACK LIBRARY PUBLICATION

First published in 2014.
This edition published in 2015 by
Black Library,
Games Workshop Ltd.,
Willow Road,
Nottingham, NG7 2WS, UK.

10 9 8 7 6 5 4 3 2 1

Cover and internal artwork by Paul Dainton.
Map by John Michelbach.

See Black Library on the internet at

blacklibrary.com

Find out more about Games Workshop
and the world of Warhammer at

games-workshop.com

Printed and bound by CPI Group (UK) Ltd, Croydon, CR0 4YY

The world is dying, but it has been so since the coming
of the Chaos Gods.

For years beyond reckoning, the Ruinous Powers have coveted
the mortal realm. They have made many attempts to seize it, their
anointed champions leading vast hordes into the lands of men,
elves and dwarfs. Each time, they have been defeated.

Until now.

In the frozen north, Archaon, a former templar of the warrior-god
Sigmar, has been crowned the Everchosen of Chaos. He stands
poised to march south and bring ruin to the lands he once fought
to protect. Behind him amass all the forces of the Dark Gods,
mortal and daemonic. When they come, they will bring with them
a storm such as has never been seen.

Already, the first moves have been made. Valkia the Bloody led
the hosts of Khorne into Naggaroth, homeland of the dark elves,
laying waste to the north of the realm and bringing war to the great
cities of Naggarond and Har Ganeth. Ominously, the tower of
Ghrond, home of the sorceress-queen Morathi, gave no warning
of this attack. Only the return of Malekith the Witch King saw
Valkia cast down and Naggarond saved.

In Ulthuan, daemons have run rampant across the lands of the
high elves in numbers unseen since the time of Aenarion seven
millennia ago. The Phoenix King is locked away in his great tower
in Lothern, so Prince Tyrion, the greatest warrior of the age, has
taken command of the asur armies and, with the aid of the magics
of his brother Teclis, driven back the daemons.

Now the destinies of Malekith and Tyrion will be drawn together,
for the war of the gods is repeating and they will act through
mortal avatars. And when they are done, the world will be forever
changed. A darkness is coming for all the elves.

These are the End Times.

PROLOGUE

This is where it all began, before history was recorded. A forest raised from sacred ground by the gods themselves, seeded by the Great Powers that shaped the world. Beneath jade and golden boughs, the elves were taught how to manipulate the energies that permeated the world and its surrounds: they learned magic.

A matriarch ruled over them, and in time she became known as the Everqueen, her immortal spirit reborn into her offspring with each passing generation. These were times of accord, of peaceful bliss and innocent harmony.

Let us be honest and call it what it was: grave naivety.

There were other powers, far older and greater than the tutors of the elves. They had been wronged, their domains trespassed upon, their authority stolen by upstarts. In their anger they laid low the Old Ones and staked their claim to the world.

Mighty was their anger and terrible were the hosts they poured forth to conquer the lands crafted by the usurpers. The pure magic of the timeless aeons was broken, split into the Eight Winds, and the gods of the elves were laid low, exposed as powerless figments. One power ruled, and one power alone: Chaos.

The daemons were their servants. The elves suffered the daemons' wrath more than any, for the elven isle, the realm of Ulthuan, was steeped in the magical energy that sustained the avatars of the Chaos Powers. Great was the torment and slaughter visited upon the Everqueen and her followers, and in the strife of the elves the Great Powers drank rich from despair and hope, fear and rage.

Yet the dominion of Chaos was not to be.

Not then.

Aenarion, spear-wielder, scale-clad, dragon-rider, united the elves and fought the daemons. Sacrificing himself in the flames of Asuryan, Aenarion was reborn as a figure of myth, the Phoenix King, and his presence was anathema to the daemons.

Even so, Aenarion's defiance was not enough. Still the daemons came.

Caledor the Dragontamer, magic-wielder, mage-lord of the southern mountains, allied his cause with Aenarion and the two great leaders of the elves stemmed the tide of Chaos for a millennium.

And this was not enough.

Already imbued with the power of one god, Aenarion sought the aid of another when his beloved wife Astarielle the Everqueen was slain, and he believed his children dead also. Aenarion took the Sword of Khaine from its bloodstained altar upon the Blighted Isle. The Widowmaker, the Bane of Gods, the Deathshard. Nothing, not mortal or daemon, could stand before his ire.

But bloodshed alone could not defeat the power of Chaos. Strife is their fodder, war their platter. It was Caledor Dragontamer that devised the true path to victory. He constructed a network of standing stones upon Ulthuan, making a pattern of monoliths and lodestones that created a magical vortex, siphoning the energy of the daemons out of the mortal realm.

At the end of the war, Caledor and his mages were trapped within the vortex they had created and Aenarion was mortally wounded as was his dragon, Indraugnir. The Phoenix King's final act was to return the Sword of Khaine to its shrine upon the Blighted Isle, but neither king nor faithful steed was seen again.

So the victory of the elves should have been. The daemons were banished, trapped in the Realm of Chaos and the Northern Wastes. The elves should have claimed dominion over the world and ruled benevolently as the inheritors of the Old Ones and Chaos would have been thwarted.

Chaos is not so easily defeated.

What they could not win with war, the Old Powers sought with guile. The whispers of the Chaos Gods polluted the counsel of the elves as they sought to choose a successor to Aenarion.

The princes met in the Glade of Eternity, a great amphitheatre of trees at the centre of which stood a shrine to Isha, the goddess of nature, matron of the Everqueen. Grown of twining silver roots and branches, with emerald-green leaves festooned with blooms in every season, the Aein Yshain glowed with mystical power. By the light of the moons and the stars, the First Council convened, bathed in the twilight of the open skies and the aura of the blessed tree.

Morathi and Malekith were there. Dark-haired and coldly beautiful, the seeress wore a dress of black cloth so fine that it appeared as a diaphanous cloud that barely concealed her alabaster skin. Her raven hair was swept back by bands of finely-woven silver threads hung with rubies, and her lips were painted to match the glittering gems. Slender and noble of bearing she stood, and bore a staff of black iron in her hands.

Malekith was no less imposing. As tall as his father and of similarly dark eyes, he wore a suit of golden mail, and a breastplate upon which was embossed the coiling form of a dragon. A long sword hung in a gold-threaded scabbard at his waist, its pommel wrought from the same precious metal, a dragon's claw grasping a sapphire the size of a fist.

With them came other princes of Nagarythe who had survived the fighting on the Isle of the Dead. They were dressed in their fine armour, and wore dark cloaks that hung to their ankles, and proudly bore the scars and trophies of their wars with the daemons.

The sinister princes of the north were arrayed with knives, spears, swords, bows, shields and armour wrought with the runes of Vaul, testaments to the power of Nagarythe and Anlec. Banner bearers with black and silver standards stood in attendance, and heralds sounded the trumpets and pipes at their arrival. A cabal of sorcerers accompanied the Naggarothi contingent, clad in robes of black and purple, their faces tattooed and scarred with ritual sigils, their heads shaved.

Another group there was, of princes from the lands founded by Caledor in the south, and from the new realms to the east – Cothique, Eataine, Yvresse and others. At the fore stood the young mage Thyriol, and golden-haired Menieth, son of Caledor Dragontamer.

In contrast to the Naggarothi these elves of the south and east were as day is to night. Though all had played their part in the war against the daemons, these princes had cast off their wargear and instead carried staves and sceptres, and in the place of war helms they wore golden crowns as symbols of their power. They were clad predominantly in white, the colour of mourning, in remembrance of the losses their people had suffered; the Naggarothi eschewed such affectation even though they had lost more than most.

'Aenarion has passed on,' Morathi declared to the council. 'The Godslayer, the Widowmaker, he returned to the Altar of Khaine so that we can be free of war. In peace, my son wishes to rule, and in peace we would explore this new world that surrounds us. Yet, I fear peace now is a thing of memory, and perhaps one day to be nothing more than myth. Do not think that the Great Powers that now gaze upon our world with hungry, immortal eyes can be so easily defeated. Though the daemons are banished from our lands, the power of Chaos is not wholly exiled from the world. I have gazed far and wide this past year, and I have seen what changes the fall of the gods has wrought upon us.'

'In war, I would follow no other king,' said Menieth, striding to the centre of the circle formed by the princes. 'In Nagarythe is found the greatest strength of arms upon this isle. The war is over, though, and I am not sure that the strength of Nagarythe lies in tranquillity. There are other realms now, and cities where there were castles. Civilisation has triumphed over Chaos on Ulthuan, and we shall take that civilisation across the seas and the elves shall reign where the gods have fallen.'

'And such arrogance and blindness shall see us humbled,' said Morathi. 'Far to the north, the lands are blasted wastelands, where creatures corrupted by dark magic crawl and flit. Ignorant savages build altars of skulls in praise of the new gods, and spill the blood of their kin in worship. Monstrous things melded of flesh and magic prowl the darkness beyond our shores. If we are to bring our light to these benighted lands, it shall be upon the glittering tip of spear and arrow.'

'Hardship and bloodshed are the price we pay for our survival,' argued Menieth. 'Nagarythe shall march at the forefront of our hosts and with the valour of the Naggarothi we shall pierce that darkness. However, we cannot be ruled by war as we were when Aenarion strode amongst us. We must reclaim our spirits from the love of bloodshed that consumed us, and seek a more enlightened path towards building a new world. We must allow the boughs of love and friendship to flourish from the roots of hatred and violence sown by the coming of Aenarion. We shall never forget his legacy, but our hearts cannot be ruled by his anger.'

'My son is the heir of Aenarion,' Morathi said quietly, menace in her soft voice. 'That we stand here at all is the prize wrested from defeat by my late husband.'

'But won no less by my father's sacrifice,' Menieth countered. 'For a year we have pondered what course of action to take, since the deaths of Aenarion and Caledor. Nagarythe shall take its place amongst the other realms – great in its glory, yet not greater than any other kingdom.'

'Greatness is earned by deeds, not bestowed by others,' said Morathi, striding forwards to stand in front of Menieth. She planted her staff in the ground between them and glared at the prince, her grip tight upon the metal rod.

'It is not to fall upon each other that we fought against the daemons and sacrificed so much,' said Thyriol hurriedly. Clad in robes of white and yellow that glimmered with golden thread, the mage laid a hand upon the shoulder of Morathi and upon the arm of Menieth. 'In us has been awakened a new spirit, and we must temper our haste with cool judgement, just as a newly forged blade must be quenched in the calming waters.'

'Who here feels worthy enough to take up the crown of the Phoenix King?' Morathi asked, glaring at the princes with scorn. 'Who here save my son is worthy of being Aenarion's successor?'

There was silence for a while, and none of the dissenters could meet Morathi's gaze, save for Menieth, who returned her cold stare without flinching. Then a voice rang out across the glade from the shadows of the trees encircling the council.

'I have been chosen!' the voice called.

From the trees walked Bel Shanaar, ruling prince of the plains of Tiranoc.

One decision, poorly taken, and the defeat of the Chaos Gods was thrown away. One decision and the seeds were sown of a doom that was seven thousand years in the growing.

It is a cruel trick of Chaos that prophecy so often becomes self-fulfilling.

That was how it began.
This is how it ends.

PART ONE

ONE

The Witch King Rises

At some point lost in the depths of time someone had called it the Black Tower. Perhaps it had been black then, and perhaps it had been merely a tower. Now it was the highest pinnacle at the centre of Naggarond. The sprawling fortress had grown hundreds of outer fortifications and buttresses, spawned a warren of alleys and streets, rooftop passages and arcing bridges, becoming a settlement unto itself where the only law was the shifting will of the Witch King, alliances were fleeting and death a constant risk.

Its walls were festooned with the heads and corpses of the thousands that had displeased Malekith over the preceding millennia. Some were hung upon hooks and chains, others in nooses and gibbets. Hundreds were skeletons, preserved by dire magic, but dozens were more recent, mouldering flesh clinging to bones gnawed by the clouds of harpies that circled over the bastion seeking new victims to scavenge.

The Black Tower.

A name filled with more grief and terror than three simple

words could describe, etched into the last memories of the unfortunates upon the wall, burned into the agony of those still writhing in the dungeons that were dug into the bedrock beneath the high walls and banner-wreathed ramparts.

None remembered who had first named it, not even Malekith himself as he sat upon his iron throne in a grand hall atop the tallest keep. He did remember a time when Naggarond had not existed, one of only a handful of beings across the entire world.

He had grown up in the Black Tower, the grim atmosphere overshadowed by the brooding presence of his father, Aenarion, and the wicked, bloody machinations of his mother, Morathi. His opponents had claimed that those decades had laid a similar darkness upon his heart.

The Witch King no longer possessed lips, but the irony of history would have caused them to twist into a cruel smile. A face ravaged by holy fire contorted beneath hot iron in an approximation of humour, the sort of humour that delighted in looking out of the window at the heads of a dozen generals who had failed Malekith during the recent war against the barbarous northmen. He viewed them now, taking satisfaction from the screams that had filled this chamber as their bodies had been split apart by dark magic and heated blades.

He looked out past these tokens of his anger, to the surrounding fortress and the high curtain walls beyond. Past them dark shadows pierced the sky, none quite as tall as the Black Tower, shrouded in the dismal chill mists of Naggaroth.

Naggarond.

But this was not the city of his birth, though the Black Tower had been his childhood home. That honour belonged to a fallen place, razed and raised again and again throughout the turning epochs, built upon the blood-soaked soil of ancient Nagarythe.

Anlec.

Capital of Aenarion, once the strongest city in the world, shaming even Karaz-a-Karak of the dwarfs. Anlec, envy of Ulthuan, which had fallen in battle only once, and that had been to Malekith himself and allies within the walls.

All now was ruin. The Black Tower was all that remained of Anlec. The memory was sharp even though six thousand years old.

The storm-wracked seas crashed against a harsh shore of rock pinnacles, foaming madly. The skies were in turmoil, blackened by dark magic. Through the spume and rain dark, massive shapes surged across the seas, towering edifices of battlement and wall.

The castles of Nagarythe followed in the wake of the largest floating citadel, upon the highest tower of which stood Malekith. The lashing rain steamed from his armour as he turned at the sound of Morathi's voice from the archway behind him.

'This is where we flee to?' she said, anger flashing in her eyes. 'This cold, bleak land?'

'They will not follow us here,' replied the Witch King. 'We are the Naggarothi – we were born in the north and in the north we will be born again. This land, bleak as it is, shall be ours. Naggaroth.'

'To build a new kingdom?' sneered Morathi. 'To accept your defeat and start afresh as if Nagarythe had never existed?'

'No,' replied Malekith, flames leaping from his iron body. 'We will never forget that which has been taken from us. Ulthuan belongs to me. If it takes a thousand years, ten thousand years, I will claim my rightful place as king. I am the son of Aenarion. It is my destiny.'

Time – mortality – was a concern for lesser beings. Millennia meant nothing to the Witch King. The tally of false Phoenix Kings that had been crowned and fallen over the course of Malekith's life could not be numbered on two hands and he had greeted the death of each with little regard.

Sometimes he lost entire days reliving the events of his past, withdrawing into his thoughts when the burning agony of his physical shell became too much to bear. The temptation was in him again to reflect on ages past, not to escape pain, but to alleviate the boredom that gnawed at his wits.

'My king?'

Malekith turned his gaze back from the window and his contemplations. It was Ezresor that had spoken, though it took the Witch King a moment to focus and remember his name. Malekith's oldest agent flinched as the burning stare of his master fell upon him.

'You have a question?' Malekith's voice was a rasp, edged with the scrape of metal and crackle of flames. 'A comment, perhaps?'

'You were about to tell us your will,' said Venil, assassin-turned-advisor, patron of many pirate fleets, still known as the Chillblade.

Fire flared through the cracks in Malekith's armour, reacting to his displeasure, forcing Venil to take a step back, face flushed with the sudden heat.

'Is that so?' Malekith moved his attention to the last of the triumvirate.

Kouran met the flaming stare of his lord without a flicker of movement. Malekith stood more than a head taller than most of his minions, but Kouran was almost his equal in presence. Grim-faced, dark-eyed, he was surrounded by an air of chilling hostility in contrast to the burning iron of his lord. Alone of the three council members, Kouran was armed and armoured – the only individual in the world Malekith trusted with a blade close at hand. The captain held his halberd, *Crimson Death*, to one side, the blade symbolically averted from his king. While Malekith's war plate and scale were wreathed with heat, the black steel of Kouran's armour was like oil, shifting constantly with the trapped souls of sacrifices.

'The prosecution of the war, the pursuit against the one they call Valkia and the hunt for your mother,' Kouran prompted without hesitation. The captain had become perhaps too comfortable with Malekith's lapses of focus, but the Witch King knew that alone of all his subjects Kouran would not use such information against him.

'Why is Ebnir not here? I would hear from the Soulflayer about the state of my armies and the forces opposed to them.'

'He is dead, your majesty,' said Ezresor. 'As I just informed you.'

The spymaster's tone irritated Malekith. Insolence. Not enough to warrant death, that would be wasteful, but in pressing times control had to be total. Censure needed to be swift and obvious. The Witch King gave the slightest of nods to Kouran, who knew well enough what his master required.

The captain smashed a gauntleted fist into Ezresor's face, bloodying his nose and sending him flailing to the floor. Widening his stance ready for a kick, Kouran looked back to his king but received a shake of the head.

'Of course he is dead,' said Malekith. 'He is not stupid. He allowed the watch tower at Vartoth to fall and then compounded the error by leading a host of my warriors onto the glaciers to be slain by these hairy wretches from the Wastes. I am sure when the battle turned against him he threw himself on his own blade, or at least allowed one of the northmen to gut him like a pig, rather than face the fate he knew would await him in my dungeon.'

Ezresor pushed to his feet, uncertain, and shared a glance with Venil. The spymaster wiped the blood from his lip with the cuff of his robe and bowed in apology.

'Hellebron has not answered my summons,' said Malekith.

'She fights in Har Ganeth still,' said Ezresor. Malekith was pleased that his counsellor offered fact rather than unrequested opinion.

'The city is nothing but ruins,' added Venil. 'The temples to Khaine have been thrown down.'

'Pride keeps her there,' said Malekith, understanding the motive of the hag queen better than most. 'She was humiliated and now she salves her embarrassment with the blood of stragglers and the lost. I will indulge her a while longer.'

'Forgive my surprise, majesty, but there are lords and ladies that have refused summons and paid dearly for the affront.' Venil licked his lips and chose his next words with care. 'I would not wish Hellebron to become a bad example to others.'

'Hellebron is too useful to have killed,' Malekith said bluntly. 'I'm not sure there is anyone capable of the feat even if I desired her death, and I cannot spare another army.'

'Shadowblade...' suggested Kouran.

'Is an uncertain weapon at the moment,' Malekith replied. 'He answers to me in this world, but his loyalty is to Khaine, and Hellebron is yet the ranking mistress to the Lord of Murder. There is little to be gained by asking of him such taxing questions at this time. Hellebron will return in time. There is no need to yank the leash just yet.'

'There is division in Ulthuan, your majesty,' Venil said with some glee. 'Prince Imrik of Caledor has quit the court of the absent Phoenix King, having exchanged harsh words with Prince Tyrion about his claim to be regent in Finubar's absence. The Dragon of Cothique, it seems, will not be able to draw upon the dragons of Caledor in his defence of the realm.'

'I am sure Tyrion will prevail, even without the dragon princes,' said Malekith.

'As to the matter of the Hag Sorceress, master?' ventured Ezresor. 'She holds court in Ghrond, perhaps believing that you will not dare confront her in her own convent.'

'Perhaps?' Malekith lingered on the word. It suggested speculation, and in speculating it was possible that Ezresor thought there would be cause for Malekith's mother to believe herself safe from his retribution.

'We have had no direct contact with Ghrond for many years, your majesty,' Ezresor added quickly. 'It is hard to be certain of anything. It is unlikely, but your mother may be dead.'

'No, she is very much alive, you can be sure of that,' said Malekith. 'When death finally catches up with Morathi the world will hear her screams of disappointment, mark my words. Do you not think I will know when she has perished? She gave me her life-force, sustained me in my darkest hour and guided me through the many tribulations that I faced. She is as much a part of me as this armour.'

Venil stroked his chin, his mood contemplative.

'It was not wholly the fault of Ebnir that we received no warning of the northlanders' attack. The loss of one watch tower could have been prevented had the seers at Ghrond foretold the incursion.' He paused, licked his lips again and spoke slowly. 'It seems unlikely that the Convent of Sorceresses would choose to abandon their duties on a whim, so we must be forced to conclude that the oversight was deliberate.'

'Who could command the convent to betray their lord in such fashion?' asked Ezresor.

'Cease this embarrassing performance,' snapped Malekith, slamming a fist onto the arm of his throne, throwing up a shower of sparks. 'If you have an accusation to level against my mother, make it plain to me.'

'Apologies, majesty,' said Ezresor, bowing low with a flicked glance towards Kouran. 'I am certain Morathi deliberately kept word of the Chaos attack, ensuring that we would be poorly prepared.'

'And why do you suppose she would do such a thing?' said Kouran. 'Ghrond cannot stand alone against all that the Chaos Wastes vomit forth.'

'Do not underestimate the nihilism of spite,' said Venil. 'For longer even than our lord she has coveted the rule of Ulthuan. Perhaps she sees some advantage in letting Naggaroth fall to disaster.'

All three advisors turned to Malekith, remembering that they spoke in his presence. None of them uttered a word but cast their eyes down at the floor and fell silent.

'You were speaking of my mother,' Malekith prompted, looking at Venil. 'Continue.'

'Begging your majesty's pleasure, it was wrong to resurrect old arguments and vexatious issues,' said the former assassin, wielding his words as carefully as he once wielded poisoned daggers.

'Ezresor?' Malekith's dark gaze fell upon the spymaster. 'You wish to add comment?'

'Your mother believed you were dead, your majesty. She underestimated you, as have many, but she intended no direct assault upon your power.'

'Without her support, I would have lost Naggarond in the absence of our king,' Kouran growled at the others. 'She erred, and when the error was made clear she did all in her power to protect the rule of Malekith.'

'Usurpers had imprisoned her,' said Ezresor, a sneer twisting his lips. 'She would have sought alliance with a bastard shade born of a harpy if it would have helped her cause. She desires the throne of Ulthuan and has used any means to lay her hands upon it, making them puppets when they believed they were following their own will.'

'Including your king?' Malekith finished the sentiment. Ezresor's pale skin seemed to whiten even further and he took a step back, putting distance between himself and his master, throwing a worried look at Kouran for good measure. Malekith laughed but it did not ease Ezresor's fright. 'Do you think I am so blind to my mother's machinations, Ezresor? You may be the lord of my agents, the master of ten thousand cultists and spies, but do not think I know only that which you tell me. I know very well the manner of creature that spawned me, and the deeds of which she is capable.'

A high priestess, lithe and athletic, presided over the despicable ceremony from a dais littered with corpses and blood. Her white robes were spattered with gore, and a daemonic bronze mask covered her face. Her eyes glowed with a pale yellow light from within, and her pupils were tiny points of blackness in pools of luminescence.

In one hand, she held a crooked staff, wrought from bones and iron, and tipped with a horned skull with three eye sockets. In the other, she wielded a curved dagger still slick with the blood of many sacrifices.

Malekith charged across the chamber, cutting down any cultist who barred his path. He was but a few steps from the dais when the priestess thrust forward the tip of her staff and a bolt of pure blackness leapt out and struck the prince full in the chest. The prince's heart felt like it would explode. With a cry of pain torn from his lips, Malekith faltered and fell to his knees. He was as much shocked as hurt, for he knew of no wizard who could best the sorcerous abilities granted to him by the Circlet of Iron.

He gazed in amazement at the priestess. She stepped down from the dais with languid strides and walked slowly towards the injured prince, the tip of her staff fixed upon him.

'My foolish child,' she sneered.

The priestess let the sacrificial dagger slip from her fingers to clatter in a shower of crimson droplets upon the floor. With her hand thus freed, she pulled off her mask and tossed it aside. Though caked with blood, the priestess' lustrous black hair spilled across her bare shoulders. Her face was pristine, the very image of beauty. In her were aristocratic bearing and divine magnificence combined.

The assembled captains and knights gazed dumbly at this apparition of perfection, ensorcelled.

'Mother?' whispered Malekith, his sword slipping from his numb fingers.

'My son,' she replied with a wicked smile, eliciting from those that looked on lust and fear in equal measure. 'It is very rude of you to butcher my servants so callously. Your time amongst the barbarians has robbed you of all manners.'

Malekith said nothing but simply stared up at Morathi, wife of Aenarion, his mother.

* * *

'Her loyalty extends as far as necessity and no further,' Malekith explained. 'Her attempts to usurp my power, subtly or directly, are not new to me. Of far graver concern is her ambivalence. If she is willing to let Naggaroth drown beneath the blades of the northlanders it is because she deems our lands, our people, no longer of value. Her greatest plans require powerful patrons and large sacrifices. It is very plausible that she has relented of her disdain for the Chaos Gods and now seeks to buy their favour in its entirety, offering up thousands of Naggarothi in return for their boons.'

'A treachery far worse than any she has committed before,' said Venil. 'It is not my place to instruct you, majesty, but I think it is finally time that we were rid of her meddlesome double-dealing.'

'You are correct,' said Malekith. Venil's smug smile faded as the Witch King continued. 'It is not your place to instruct me. I will deal with my mother as I see fit.'

'But you will deal with her?' said Venil, unable to keep silent but cringing even as he uttered the words as though his mouth had betrayed him. He offered obeisance with bowed head and spread hands. 'We have lost too much to allow old wounds to continue to fester.'

'I will think on the matter,' said Malekith, turning his stare back to the window.

He spent a few moments in contemplation, imagining Venil's near-dead carcass dancing on one of the barbed chains on the tower opposite. It brought him only a few moments of pleasure before his desire for cruel punishment was superseded by a colder, more pragmatic need.

'The world is in upheaval,' he said. 'Forces of life and death stir and the gaze of the gods falls upon us all. The winds of magic have not been so turbulent since the last great war against the Dark Gods' servants. The tempest of Chaos obscures unnatural sight, so you must bring me all news from across the globe. I will know what rumour passes in Lothern and Tor Achare. You will tell me what counsel is spoken to the ears of the human kings and Emperor. Armies march, alive and dead, and I would know their disposition and strength. All of this you will bring to me, or you are of no more use.'

'From your will, majesty, to my hands,' Venil said, wetting his lips once more. 'I shall be your eyes and ears, as always.'

TWO

Destiny's Master

Malekith dismissed Ezresor and Venil, and sat down on his iron throne to consider their counsel. At a gesture from his lord, Kouran approached the throne and stood to one side, awaiting instruction.

Malekith looked at the backs of the other two elves for a moment before the huge double doors closed behind them. It was too easy to dismiss their concerns out of hand. Seven millennia had delivered many crises and setbacks to Malekith but he had overcome these disappointments. Recent events seemed at first to be world-shattering, especially to his minions that did not share their king's advantage of such long perspective.

Weighed against the risks of over-reaction was the price of complacency. The barbarians had been at the walls of Naggarond itself, during the Witch King's absence, and that was almost unthinkable. This was not just another incursion by the culture-less hordes of the north, this was a far rarer moment, a genuine mass migration, an expansion of the Chaos Wastes that could signify a great change in the course of history.

None other than Malekith, save perhaps his mother, understood the importance of harnessing the turning points of history to one's own end. He looked at Kouran.

'Destiny,' said the Witch King, 'is a lazy device invented by simpleton philosophers, endorsed by inadequate playwrights and poets, and thrown around by half-blind mages. The gods rarely care to interfere in the life of a single mortal, and the wider universe certainly does not pause in its cycle or shape itself for the betterment of a single person. If one believes in destiny, one forfeits the right to choose a path, giving away all credit and taking no blame for one's actions.'

'I understand, my king,' said Kouran.

Malekith regarded his lieutenant, looking for a sign that this was merely platitude. It was not, and Malekith could tell.

'Of course, my dear captain, there are few better examples of a self-made elf than you. Gutterspawn you were, am I right? Raised in the streets and alleys, orphaned?'

'I was, my king. I fought for food, for survival. The Black Guard took me in and gave me something else to fight for.'

'For a master?' said Malekith, knowing the truth but curious to see if he could tease it from his loyal bodyguard.

'Respectfully, no, my king. Though I am honoured to serve and would give my life for yours, it was not loyalty to you that drove my ascension through the ranks. The Black Guard gave me a chance to earn respect.'

'Do they respect you, or do they fear you?' It was a question Morathi had oftentimes asked of Malekith down the centuries. Malekith had always been ambivalent to the difference but he sensed it meant something to Kouran.

'A mixture of both,' the captain replied with a rare half-smile. 'Those that do not know me, fear me, and that is enough. A few that know me, they respect me. I would hope, my king, that you do not fear me, but that I have your respect.'

Malekith nodded thoughtfully.

'Yes, my dear Alandrian, you have my deepest respect. So few do, these days.' Malekith was in a strange mood and felt like confiding in his companion something he had not shared with any other. 'The truth is, I do not fear you, and perhaps you are the only mortal I do not fear. The others are weak and venal and would strike me down in a heartbeat if given the chance.'

'Surely you are too powerful to be overthrown in such fashion, my king?'

'I can die, despite my longevity. It is not a casual dread, of mortality, but an ever-present knowledge that I am not loved, and those that serve, except for you, serve me out of fear not respect. I wonder, Alandrian, if I should have tried harder to win them to my cause rather than coercing them into servitude.'

'My name is Kouran, my king,' the captain said, his voice edged with concern.

'Yes, I know that,' Malekith snapped. 'What of it?'

'Twice in the last few breaths you called me Alandriàn. One of your earliest lieutenants, I think.'

'Did I really?' Malekith tried to recall what he had said but could not remember misnaming his companion. There was, unusually for Malekith's retainers, no cause for Kouran to lie so the Witch King accepted the correction without doubt. 'Take it as a compliment, *Kouran*. Alandrian was an exceptional commander, an accomplished negotiator and orator, and one of my most loyal servants. He helped me forge the colonies across the water in Elthin Arvan.'

'I recall now, my king. You made him Regent of Athel Toralien. He was Hellebron's father.'

'The past vexes me,' Malekith said suddenly. 'That must be why I was thinking of Alandrian. The past is returning. It repeats itself, coming in cycles, birth and death and rebirth. Ever has it been so, since before my time, until the End Times. The gods rise and fall, are worshipped and cast aside, and the lives of mortals pass like the heartbeats of the world.'

'What about the past particularly vexes you this day, my king?'

'Something is changing. Like a familiar smell, of blood and hot iron, these past days remind me of a time long, long passed.'

'We have fought many wars with the northmen – it is not strange to be reminded of such events when the barbarians come south again.'

'It is not the northmen that I can smell, my dear Kouran. I smell something far older and far deadlier. Chaos in its raw form. The portal opens and the Realm of the Gods expands, polluting the world. The winds of magic are changing. Death shrouds the world.' Malekith took a breath, the flames of his body dimming to ruddy embers as he shuddered. 'Daemons, Kouran. I smell the spoor of daemons. They have come again to Ulthuan – the hosts of the Chaos Gods' minions throw themselves upon the spears of our weaker cousins.'

'Yes, my king, we have received reports that the upstart Tyrion leads the armies of the Phoenix King in defence of our ancestral isle. What does it mean?'

What did it mean? Malekith knew. He had known this time would come for six thousand years.

His glowing hand reached up to the spiked crown upon his head – the Circlet of Iron – and the Witch King's thoughts drifted back across the ages to a strange city in the north, wherein he and his expedition had found a temple unlike any other, and within that temple Malekith had found a prize that promised the world.

Seven figures sat upon low square stools, more opulent versions of the skeletons below with more pearls and brooches of the same dark, black material. Six sat facing outward, each one facing one of the lines upon the ground below as far as Malekith could tell. They had no hoods but instead wore simple crowns, each nothing more than a narrow band about the skull with a black gem that reflected no light.

The seventh figure sat facing Malekith, though he suspected that he would have faced the intruders regardless of from which direction they had approached. His crown was much larger, of a silver-grey metal, with curling, horn-like protrusions, the only organic shape they had seen since entering the city.

'Highness!' snapped Yeasir, and Malekith turned, his hand on his sword hilt. It was only then that he realised that his other hand had been reaching out towards the skeletal king, to pluck the crown from his skull. Malekith had no recollection of having crossed the dais and shook his head as if dazed by a blow.

'We should touch nothing,' said Yeasir. 'This place is cursed, by the gods, or worse.'

Malekith laughed and the noise seemed stifled and flat, with none of the ringing echoes of his earlier shout.

'I think this great king rules here no more,' said Malekith. 'This is my sign, Yeasir. What greater statement about my destiny could I make? Imagine returning to Ulthuan with such a crown upon my head, an artefact of the time before.'

'Before what?' asked Yeasir.

'Before everything!' said Malekith. 'Before Chaos, before the Everqueen, before even the gods themselves. Can you not feel it, the great antiquity that fills this place?'

'I feel it,' growled Yeasir. 'There is ancient malice here, can you not sense it? I say again, there is a curse upon this place.'

'You were willing to follow me to the Gate of Chaos,' Malekith reminded his captain. 'Would you rather we left this treasure here and continued north?'

Yeasir's muttered reply was inaudible, but Malekith took it to be his captain's acquiescence. Not that the prince needed the permission of anyone to take whatever he wanted, from wherever he wanted. Magic had guided him to this place and Malekith knew that there was purpose behind it. Whether it was the gods or some other will that had led him here, it was to stand before this prehistoric king and take his crown.

With a smile, Malekith lifted the circlet from the dead king's skull; it was as light as air and came away with no difficulty.

'You have it, now let us leave,' said Yeasir, fear making his voice shrill.

'Calm yourself,' said Malekith. 'Does it not make me kingly?'

With that, the prince of Nagarythe placed the circlet upon his head and the world vanished.

A kaleidoscope of clashing colours swarmed around Malekith. He was filled with the peculiar sensation of rising high up into the air while at the same time plummeting down towards some bottomless depth. His head swam and his skin tingled with power. He was lost in sensation, his whole being pulsing and vibrating with unknown energy.

In time – moments or an eternity, Malekith could not tell – the swirling colours began to coalesce around him. They formed into a nightmarish landscape above the centre of which floated the elf prince. The skies boiled with fire and black clouds, and beneath him stretched an arcane plateau that stretched on for infinity: the Realm of Chaos.

In one direction Malekith spied an unending garden, forlorn and decaying, filled with drooping willows and sallow grasses. A miasma of fog and flies drifted up from the overgrown copses of bent and withered trees, and rivers of oozing pus flowed between fronds of clinging fungi and piles of rotted corpses. Marshes bubbled and boiled and pits of tar gurgled, spewing gaseous vapours into the thick air.

At the centre of the unkempt morass rose up a mansion of titanic proportions, a grandiose but tottering edifice of crumbling stone and worm-eaten wood. Peeling paint and flaking brick stood upon cracked stone and bowed beams, crawling with sickly yellow ivy and immense black roses. Fumes belched from a hundred chimneys and gargoyle-headed pipes spat and drooled gobbets of ichor across cracked tiles and mouldering thatch.

In the smog and gloom shambled daemons of death and plague:

immensely bloated creatures with pestilent flesh and pox-marked skin, and slobbering beasts with slug-like bodies and fronds of tentacles dribbling noxious emissions. Swarms of boil-like mites scrabbled over the sagging walls and roofs of the manse, while a legion of cyclopean daemons, each with a single cracked horn, meandered about the wild gardens chanting sonorously.

Turning his gaze from the filth and squalor, Malekith then looked upon a mighty citadel made up of glimmering mirrors and crystal. Its surface shimmered with a rainbow of colours, translucent yet transparent, shifting with eddies and swirls of magic. Doors yawned like devouring mouths and windows stared back at the prince like lidless eyes. Fires of all colours billowed from the spires of thin towers, sending fountains of sparks trailing down to the ground below.

All about the bizarre palace was an immense maze, of shifting walls of crystal. The twisting, contorted pathways overlapped above and below, and passed through each other via unseen dimensions. Arcing gateways of flame linked parts of the immense labyrinth together, flickering from blue to green to purple and to colours not meant to be seen by mortals.

The skies about the horrifying tower were filled with shoals of creatures that climbed and swooped upon the magical thermals, shark-like and fearsome. Formless, cackling things cavorted and whirled about the maze, flashing with magical power. Daemons with arms that dripped with fire bounded manically along the winding crystal passages, leaping and bouncing with insane abandon. Malekith felt his eyes drawn back to the impossible fortress and saw that a great gallery had opened up.

Here stalked arcane things with multicoloured wings and bird-like faces, with contorting staves in their hands and robes of glistening pink and blue. One of the creatures paused and looked up at him. Its eyes were like pits of never-ending madness, deep oceans of swirling power that threatened to draw him into their depths for eternity.

Breaking that transfixing stare, Malekith then looked upon a blasted wasteland, surrounded by a great chain of volcanoes that spewed rivers of lava down their black sides and choked the air with their foul soot. Immense ramparts were carved from the mountainsides, huge bastions of dread hung with skulls and from whose jagged battlements fluttered a thousand times a thousand banners of red.

Within the encircling peaks the land was rent by great tears and chasms that welled up with blood like wounds, as if it had been constantly rent by the blows of some godly blade. The skeletons of unimaginable creatures were piled high amongst lakes of burning crimson, and all about were dunes made of the dust of countless bones. Hounds the size of horses with red-scaled flesh and enormous fangs prowled amongst the ruination, their howls tearing the air above the snap and crack of bone and gristle.

At the centre of this desolation grew a tower of unimaginable proportion, so vast that it seemed to fill Malekith's vision. Of black stone and brass was it made, tower upon tower, wall upon wall, a castle so great that it would hold back the armies of the whole universe. Gargoyles spouted boiling blood down its brazen fortifications and red-skinned warriors with wiry frames and bulbous, horned heads patrolled its ramparts. Upon its highest parapet there stood a thing of pure fury: rage given bestial, winged form. It beat its broad chest and roared into the dark skies.

Shuddering, Malekith turned fully about and stood bewitched by a panorama of entrancing beauty. Enchanting glades of gently swaying emerald-leafed trees bordered golden beaches upon which crashed white-foamed waves, while glittering lakes of tranquil water beckoned to him. Majestic mountains soared above all, their flanks clad in the whitest snow, glistening in the unseen sun.

Lithe creatures clad in the guise of half-maidens cavorted through the paradise, laughing and chattering, caressing each other with shimmering claws. Across emerald meadows roamed herds of sinuous beasts whose bodies shimmered and changed colour, their iridescent patterns hypnotising to the elf prince. Malekith felt himself drawn onwards, ensnared by their beauty.

Suddenly realising his peril, Malekith tore his gaze away from the mesmerising vision. He became distinctly aware that he was being watched and could feel the attention of otherworldly beings being turned in his direction. Feeling as if his soul were about to be laid bare and flayed before the gaze of the Chaos Gods, Malekith felt terror gripping him. He sought somewhere to flee, but in every direction spread the domains of the Dark Gods. With a last dread-driven effort, he wished himself away and was surrounded again by the twirling energies of magic.

When his vision had cleared again, Malekith found himself hovering far above the world, as if stood upon the edge of creation itself and looking down upon the realms of men and elves and dwarfs and every other creature under the sun. He could see the jungle-swathed forests of Lustria where lizardmen scuttled through the ruins of the Old Ones' cities. He saw orc tribes massing in the blighted wilderness, carpeting the ground in tides of green.

Over everything drifted the winds of magic, now more clear to him than they had ever been. The prince saw them streaming from the shattered Gate of Chaos in the north and spreading out across the northlands. He saw the vortex of Ulthuan as a great swirl of power, drawing the energy out of the world. He saw sinkholes of darkness and blazing mountains of light.

In that instant it all became clear to Malekith. The whole world was laid out before him, and he saw as perhaps only his mother had before seen. There were torrents of power that swept across the lands untapped by mortal kind. The very breath of the gods sighed over oceans and plains, down valleys and across forests. From Chaos came all magic, whether good or ill. It was stunning in its beauty, just as a storm-tossed sea can enthral those not caught in its deadly grip.

Malekith lingered awhile, now aware of the crown burning upon his head. It acted as some kind of key, some artefact created by the races that had come before the rise of elves, before even the coming of the Old Ones. It would be easy for him to stay here forever, marvelling in the rich, random choreography of the dancing winds of magic. He could spend an eternity studying their heights and depths with the circlet and still not unlock all of their secrets.

Something nagged at his mind however, a sensation deep within his soul that threatened to break his reverie.

Malekith summoned the willpower to master the Circlet of Iron and returned to the mortal world. With the power of the crown, Malekith could see the magical forces binding the skeletons together and the ancient commands that blazed within their empty skulls. It was simplicity itself to order them to stop and then with another thought, the prince bade them return to their eternal slumber. All about him the hall was filled with great golden arches and glittering pillars, unseen to all except him.

Given extraordinary awareness by the circlet he could look upon the magic of the ancient architects of the city, the curving galleries and arching balconies constructed from mystical forces that even he had been unaware of. This was why the chamber had been devoid of other magic, for it contained its own power, far stronger than that of the fitful winds of magic. Just as air cannot pass into a solid object, so too the winds of magic found no room to creep into the enchantment-filled chamber.

Now gifted the insights granted by the crown, there was no telling how acutely the Naggarothi prince might master the power of Chaos. With the circlet to act as his key, Malekith could work such spells as would make the witchery of Saphery seem insignificant. Had he not looked upon the realm of the Chaos Gods itself? Did he not now know their lands, and had he not dared them and survived?

Elation filled Malekith, more majestic than any triumph he ever felt before. His mother had warned that Chaos was the greater enemy; the perils of orcs and the armies of the beastmen paled into *insignificance against those legions of daemons that Malekith had seen. The Chaos Gods plotted and waited, for they had an eternity to ponder their plans and to make their schemes. The elves could not shelter behind the power of the vortex forever, Malekith realised, for he had felt the slowly growing power of the Chaos Gods even as he had stood in their midst.*

It all came together in the prince's mind. The men of the north were vassals of the Dark Gods, and as they prospered and multiplied, so too would the influence of their ineffable masters. There might come a day when the bulwark of the vortex would fail, and again the hordes of Chaos would be unleashed upon the world. Ulthuan was utterly unprepared for such an eventuality. Bel Shanaar could not hope to meet such a threat. It was an apparent truth to Malekith that he alone, with the power of the circlet, now bore the means by which the elves might be protected from this greater doom.

Slowly, with much effort, Malekith took the crown from his head. The great magical architecture faded from his vision and he found himself back in the strangely-angled hall beneath the prehistoric city. His Naggarothi surrounded him, staring at their lord with eyes full of wonder and fear.

Malekith smiled. He now knew what he must do.

'It means,' Malekith said slowly, 'that a time of *destiny* is upon us. An opportunity to shape the future and seal fates presently caught in the balance.'

'You plan to move on Ulthuan once again?'

'Not yet, there is too much turmoil in Naggaroth with the army of that blood-bitch Valkia still roaming my lands, and Morathi haunts Ghrond with further mischief in mind, I am sure. There can be no fresh attack while these matters are yet to be decided.' Malekith stood, the flames from his body erupting into fresh life, so hot that Kouran was forced to take a step back, his armour glittering in the orange and yellow light. 'Assemble my army and call for my generals. Send the word to all that have fought beneath my banner and let them know that I demand their service again. The Witch King marches forth.'

THREE

The March North

A city of tents dominated the high ground, walls and banners flapping in the incessant breeze that brought its icy touch across Naggarond from even more northerly climes. In more comfortable lands it was spring, but the Land of Chill had been well named in the first years after Malekith had arrived with his exiles. Snow covered the frozen ground, broken by patches of hardy grass and low-growing shrubs with tiny leaves and long thorns.

To the west the Iron Mountains heaped steeply from the foot-hills, charcoal against the pale sky. To the east the tips of the Spiteful Peaks could just about be seen, as jagged as their name suggested. The gap was the only way to reach Ghrond, and though for that day the blizzard had paused in its ferocity, many thousands of the Naggarothi host had already succumbed to the ceaseless march and deadly weather. As many again had fallen to northlander blades and mauls, slain during raids and pitched battles that had dogged the army as it had forged north, marching into the night for the daylight hours were far too few, progress slowing as their destination neared and the weather worsened.

Like any settlement the army camp had its distinctive areas and quarters, each with a character of its own. Immediately within the picket of sentries were the cloth-roofed corrals of the dark riders, where patrols and messengers came and went without hindrance. Sturdier stables of timber and chain housed the reptilian cold one mounts of the knights and nobles – the hideous smell of the beasts ensured that only slaves and the most disfavoured druchii held their quarters downwind.

The shamble of bivouacs and rough hide shelters that housed the slaves had grown slightly since the army had left Naggarond, swelled by northlanders that had been foolish enough to allow themselves to be taken prisoner. Though born into hardship in the cold wastes, they nevertheless yammered and howled their torment as icy wind cut through the sparse canopies protecting their lodgings and snow quenched their few attempts to start warming fires.

In slightly better state were the beastmasters, whose mammalian, reptilian and monstrous charges were also kept on the outskirts of the tent city. Few of the greater beasts – hydras, manticores and dark pegasi – had survived the battles of late, but some of these larger animals were bound by chains and staves, their grunts and howls muted by the snow and carried away by the wind. Hounds and smaller hunting reptiles yammered and yowled and hissed in their pens, woken by the dim grey of dawn.

The bulk of the encampment was made up of tent rows in plain black, white and purple, organised by allegiance to the various regiments and noble houses that had answered Malekith's call to battle.

To the south the Khainites had gathered, a great pyre in the centre of their camp, their conical tents strung with gaudy and gory trophies from the preceding battles. The bodies of sacrifices to the Lord of Murder charred in the sacrificial flames and their hearts sizzled in ornate black iron braziers. Their bloodlust sated by the night's revelries the murder cultists slumbered still, their drug-fuelled ceremonies adding to the exhaustion of marching and war.

Closer to the centre of the encampment, a coven of sorceresses still loyal to Malekith had pitched their pavilions. No others had set their tents within three dozen paces of the witches, fearful of the miasma of magical energy that permeated the air. The nights were wracked by otherworldly screams and screeches and each fresh dawn saw a pile of dead acolytes bloodying the snow outside the sorceresses' tents.

The grandest tents belonged to the noble families of Naggaroth, each clustered around their lord's or lady's banner like young sucklings at a mother, feeding off their power and reputation. The peace here was uneasy, the truce between rival dynasties, warring sects and opposing factions kept only by the presence of Black Guard companies patrolling the neutral ground between camps. Even so there had been no few elves that had fallen to ambush and assassination during the long march and ancient hostilities were constantly on the verge of breaking out into open conflict.

At the heart of the druchii camp, glowering down upon all around it, rose Malekith's pavilion, a conglomeration of steel-ringed hide and linen, black-lacquered wood and bare iron that approximated the Black Tower of his capital. It rose far higher than any other, six corners held by ramparted towers that were broken down, transported and assembled with each march, manned by Black Guard under the supervision of Kouran.

A killing ground two hundred paces across separated the rest of the army's lodgings from their ruler, covered by repeater bolt throwers mounted in pits dug into the frozen earth by slaves.

As if these were not barrier enough to any wishing to assail Malekith there was, aside from the malice of the Witch King himself, one final obstacle. Beside the black-walled tent slumbered a beast of such proportion that at first it might be mistaken for a blackened hillock until one noticed the pattern of plate-sized scales and claws as long as bastard swords.

She slumbered, Seraphon the Supreme, but alert to the smallest hint of danger to her master. Progeny of Sulekh, greatest of the black dragons, first honoured mount of the Witch King, Seraphon would allow none to approach that did not brandish Malekith's seal like a shield before them. Her breath spread a bank of mist around the pavilion, tinged with a poisonous gas. A yellow eye opened a slit as shouts broke the stillness.

Beyond this enclave of stillness and dormant power the camp was engulfed by tumult. Riders returned with news of an approaching army, coming south at some speed and seemingly impervious to the blizzard that had trapped the elves upon the ridge for the last five days. The scouts could not state for sure the nature of the foe, for those of their number that approached too close did not return. Of their fate, nothing could be said, but there was rumour of powerful magic and malign influence.

War drums called the companies to muster. Bleakswords, dreadspears and darkshards armed with repeating crossbows fell into rank at the shouted commands of petty nobles and professional captains. Knights and lordlings called for retainers to bring their cold ones while chariots rumbled from the stables to await their masters. The beastmasters whooped and hollered their strange cries, whips cracked and goads struck scaled and furred flesh.

The witch elves and sisters of slaughter roused from their sleep and drank deep of the libations drawn from the cauldrons of the hags that led them. Soon their dismal drug-aches were forgotten as fresh stimulants raced through their bodies and lit their senses. Their battle-screeches and praises to Khaine split the air at the soon-to-commence bloodshed.

About the flag poles and spire-like masts of the Witch King's pavilion dark, winged shapes unfurled themselves like banners. Chittering to one another, a cloud of harpies hundreds-strong launched into the air, startled by the sudden noise.

* * *

'The enemy host approaches, my king,' said Kouran, presenting his halberd in salute as he bowed. There was no carpet underfoot, just weathered hide scorched in many places by the hot tread of his master. 'Do you wish to lead the army into battle?'

Malekith barely heard his lieutenant, just as he was almost unaware of the braying horns and crashing drums. Kouran had proven himself not only a skilled warrior but an adept general. His defence of Naggarond during Malekith's absence demonstrated beyond doubt that he was more than just a blade-wielder.

The Witch King's concern was not set upon the thousands of unwashed, hairy barbarians that were advancing upon his army, but much further afield, beyond this battle, beyond the next battles, to a far grander war. The reclamation of Naggaroth was a necessary distraction, but he would not let such matters intrude upon his longer strategy.

He waved a dismissive hand, indicating that he was content for Kouran and the lower commanders to direct the battle in his stead. Malekith wondered, briefly, if he should have wiped out the humans when he had been granted the chance millennia before they had become civilised. Though they had become a tiresome thorn in his side, they had provided something of a bulwark also, fighting each other as much as they raided the lands of the druchii.

In the end it mattered nothing to him. They were, for the most part, such short-lived, savage creatures it was impossible to know how their fates might have changed. Like the orcs and the halfbeasts and the tunnelling ratmen, the humans had bred and spread across Elthin Arvan in the wake of the great war between the elves and the dwarfs, and but for the tribes of the north had played little part in the affairs of elves until the last few centuries.

Malekith revised his earlier contempt. There were some from the race of humanity that had placed their mark upon history far more deeply than one might have expected, and another had added his name to that roll: Archaon. The so-called Everchosen – the title had spilled from the lips of prisoners easily enough, rendered in the dozens of dialects of the northern tribes – had roused the northlanders in such strength that not elf or man or dwarf had ever seen the like before.

This time was different. Malekith felt it again, the subtle shift of fates uncoiling, history parting from the normal cycle of victory and defeat. The gods were stirring. Old gods, dead gods, coming back to life to meddle in the affairs of mortals once again. His charred skin prickled at the thought.

'Wait.'

The single word froze Kouran at the opening to the Witch King's main pavilion.

'My king?' he asked, turning around, pleased at Malekith's sudden interest. 'You will lead us?'

'Perhaps,' the Witch King replied, standing up. 'If required. I shall watch the battle. You may proceed with whatever preparations you deem fitting.'

'As you command, my king.' Kouran bowed again and left, with considerably more enthusiasm than when he had entered.

'So loyal,' Malekith said to himself. 'So easily pleased.'

His infamous sword, *Urithain* the Destroyer, was already at his hip but his shield hung on a stand behind the throne. He took it up, almost as high as he was tall, emblazoned with runes that seemed like empty gouges in the plate rather than anything forged by mortal hand.

Malekith left his pavilion and called for Seraphon. The black dragon responded swiftly, flying over the outer tents to land a few paces from her lord. She did not share the gift of speech that many of her kin from Caledor possessed, but there was a gleam in her eye that betrayed her desire for battle.

Like a supplicant debasing herself before making petition, Seraphon lowered to the ground and bent down her neck so that Malekith could mount the throne-saddle on her back. At a command from the Witch King she rose up, her wings outstretched, dwarfing all but Malekith's pavilion.

'Up,' the Witch King told her and she bound into the air, carrying Malekith away from the tent city with half a dozen mighty beats of her wings, the downdraught of her strokes kicking up a snowstorm through the tents below.

From on high Malekith could see only a little more clearly. The blizzard was abating and in that he felt magic stirring, the end of the snows not a coincidence. The storm had concealed the Naggarothi for a while, but also it had held them some ten days march from Ghrond, and he suspected his mother of orchestrating the terrible weather. Now its purpose had been fulfilled, delivering the army into the path of the northlander host no doubt.

There was more than just wind-sorcery in the air. Malekith ordered Seraphon to circle while he allowed the circlet upon his helm to reveal the turbulent winds of magic.

Sure enough there was something powerful approaching, but it was not magical, but rather a bottomless pit of anti-magic, a great presence that swallowed the mystical power like a lodestone bending iron towards itself.

The army marched forth, ordering itself to Kouran's scheme, the infantry holding the right and centre with melee units interspersed with the darkshards, while the beasts, chariots and cavalry massed on the left. Dark riders and small pockets of scouts – wicked outcasts from the Blackspine Mountains known as shades – drifted ahead of the army, seeking the foe and testing the treacherous ground for the regiments to follow.

Soon Malekith was not alone in the air. Two manticores swept up from the beastmaster's pens followed by the dark pegasi of a trio of sorceresses. The harpies were drawn to the Witch King's presence, descending in a noisy cloud that was soon driven off by roars and clouds of noxious breath from Seraphon, always ready to jealously guard her master. Disappointed, the harpies drifted down towards the army, alighting between the advancing companies and then lifting off again to slowly circle overhead, waiting for easy targets to present themselves.

Some distance away it appeared as though the land was bleeding. A great column of crimson moved down the pass towards the elven line, which appeared pitifully thin compared to the mass of destruction bearing down upon it.

No mortal host this, Malekith knew.

The smell of blood filled the air, making Seraphon snort heavy draughts while the manticores roared in anticipation of the slaughter. The harpies rose in a flock once more, lashing out at each other with clawed fingers, snarling and biting. A grumble of unease and disconcerted whispers rippled through the army of Malekith.

At the forefront of the daemon army came the flesh hounds – immense beasts with ruddy-scaled hides and scorpion tails, snarling and howling as they led the hunt. Not far behind rumbled chariots of gold and brass pulled by the same, while others, even larger, were drawn into battle by immense juggernauts of daemonic flesh and bronze armour, snorting and bellowing. Horned bloodletters rode on the backs of these chariots, their axes and swords glinting with a light that came not from the storm-swathed sun.

The ground itself trembled at the approach of the infernal host, thousands of clawed and hoofed feet marching in unison to the crash of hellish drums, beating out the doom of their foes. Standards of bone, dripping with gore, rose from carmine ranks alongside tattered banners and skull-adorned icons of the Blood God. Brass trumpets sounded the glorious advance, their sound cutting the air like a whetstone shrieking along a blade.

Rank after rank of armoured minions marched shoulder to shoulder, glaring with dead, white eyes, curling horns splayed from their heads, fangs bared in permanent snarls. The air around them seethed with magic pouring forth from the Realm of Chaos. Their presence melted the snow and caused the ground to crack and blister as they passed, corrupting the soil they trod upon. Their leaders, the heralds, howled challenges on the wind and swore oaths to the Master of War to slay all they encountered in His name.

Daemon princes moved amongst the masses, thrice the height of any elf, some mounted on juggernauts with reins of iron, others borne aloft with wings like bats or pinions covered in raven-black feathers. Porcine, hound-like, human, all manner of faces stared down at the defiant followers of Malekith, seeing nothing but corpses yet to be made.

At the centre of the oncoming host strode a bestial figure greater still than the daemon princes. Its face was a mask of feral rage, tusked and fanged, surrounded by flowing dark hair that spilled between ridged horns that protected its head like a helm, the immense mane spreading down a back humped large with crimson-skinned muscle. From its back sprouted the ragged remnants of two wings, broken and burned.

Its body was clad in brass and bronze, plates and scales marked by savage runes of Chaos that made the eyes ache to look upon. Skulls were woven into bloodied mail, still possessed of their souls, wailing and gnashing their teeth in eternal torment, repeating the words of their killer as it snapped commands. In response the daemons broke away from each other into blood-hungry companies, baying and growling, spreading out to engage the whole of the elven line.

Malekith knew the nature of this beast, one of Khorne's High-handed Slayers, Destroyers of Worlds, Killers of Hope and Lords of Battle.

Bloodthirster.

FOUR

Visions in Blood

The bloodthirster's rage came before it like an aura, sweeping down onto the druchii like a hot wind. Infernal anger seeped into their thoughts. Immortal hatred stirred the blood. Against this daemonic influence the elves had no defence. Mutterings became battle-cries and agitation broke into violence as Malekith's underlings suddenly sought vent for their unnatural fury.

Kouran reacted quickly, leading the host into the enemy from the front of the Black Guard, giving the elves a clear foe upon which to sate their bloodlust. There was no finesse, no manoeuvring for superior position – such niceties were boiled away in their frenzy to spill blood. The druchii line charged down the ridge, meeting the chariots and cavalry surging up towards them. Even the darkshards and shades abandoned their crossbows and set into the enemy with drawn knives and short swords.

The clash was horrendous, bodies churned beneath scythed wheels, warriors decapitated by strokes of bronze swords and axes. Undeterred the elves weathered the impact of their foes, fuelled by the daemon-rage. They quickly surrounded their enemies, tearing into them with sword and spear.

Heedless of the danger, the elves pressed on, swarming past the scant remains of their first victims. Into the teeth of the foe they charged, metaphorically and literally, drawn towards the bloodthirster as moths are drawn to flame and with similarly deadly result.

Both sides hacked at one another without thought, driven mad by the blood-rage of Khorne. Those elves that could not lay weapon or hand upon an enemy fell upon each other, slashing and tearing without relent. Even Kouran and his Black Guard, cold-blooded killers to the last elf, were swept away by the orgy of violent release, cleaving like a dark spear into the heart of the daemonic army. The Khainites were driven beyond even their zealous battle-hunger, and cut themselves to let even more blood flow, glorifying in their own wounds as much as the injuries inflicted on their enemies. Their piercing wails lifted higher than the screeching of the harpies as they fell upon the incapacitated of both sides, sating flesh-famine and bloodlust in equal measure.

The manticores descended like comets of rage, slamming into the daemon regiments with claws and fangs slashing like dozens of swords. Hydras and war dogs matched the baying and screeching of the flesh hounds as they ripped bloody chunks of unnatural flesh from bone and in turn were eviscerated and beheaded.

The bloodthirster smashed through friend and foe alike, a massive rune-axe in each hand that lofted limbs and severed heads high into the air with every swing. Like a mariner wading to shore, the greater daemon stood thigh-deep in the bodies of its victims, pushing on without mercy or pause, a bloody explosion of pure rage.

Malekith watched it all in a detached manner. Seraphon was touched by the blood-thirst too but a growl from the Witch King silenced her protest. He felt the anger pulsing around him, bringing visions of slaughter and victory.

He laughed.

The bloodthirst of Khorne was nothing compared to the hatred and anger that had burned in his heart for six thousand years. The Blood God's promises of conquest and glory were faded temptations, long since outgrown by Malekith's own ambition and towering desire for vengeance. Every day the Witch King fought the need to vent frustration and exact bloody retribution and today was no different.

With a derisive snort, he ordered Seraphon to descend. The battle was going poorly for his warriors, all advantage of superior strategy and skill washed away by the demands of unquestioning bloodlust. There was only one way to even the odds and avoid certain defeat.

The bloodthirster noticed Malekith's descent and, tossing aside the broken body of a manticore, lifted both axes in challenge to the Witch King. Malekith replied with a bolt of pure dark magic that earthed along the unholy blades, sending the greater daemon reeling. Black sparks flew from its iron collar as the power of Khorne dissipated the remaining magical energy.

'It seems your master's protection against sorcery is not all it once was,' Malekith laughed as Seraphon circled the brute, one wingtip almost brushing the ground. The Witch King threw another crackling bolt, but this time the collar earthed its power before any harm was done, spraying the magic away from the bloodthirster in a shower of sable lightning.

'Know that I am thy doom, weak mortal,' the beast roared back, clashing its axes together. 'I am Skarbrand, the Deathbringer, the Corpsemaker, Son of Slaughter.'

'I know of you, Exiled One,' Malekith sneered. 'Shamed, humbled, by the simplest of tricks, abandoned by the Lord of Skulls. And shame again you will know for daring to attack the army of the Witch King, Malekith the Great.'

'Ignoble Malekith, the kinslayer,' laughed Skarbrand. 'Much is the blood that has flowed through my master's domain at your behest. Your skull shall make a fine adornment for Khorne's throne. Fight me, coward, as a true warrior would fight.'

Skarbrand leapt, one of its axes leaving a ruddy trail through the air as it swung towards Seraphon's wing. The old dragon was too wily to be caught by surprise and flicked her wing out of the way, soaring above the bloodthirster's head. Letting forth an enraged bellow, Skarbrand turned in mid-air, the other axe extended for another swing.

Seraphon caught the creature's wrist in two claws, warding away the deadly blow. Striving with fierce growls, she bore the bloodthirster aloft. Before the daemon's other blade could be brought back into play, Malekith struck, driving *Urithain* to the hilt into its eye. The tip of the blade erupted from the back of Skarbrand's skull. Seraphon released her grip as Malekith ripped his sword free and the body tumbled groundwards, crushing dozens of the greater daemon's minions with the impact.

Like a wind suddenly changing and freshening, the aura of death and violence that had emanated from the bloodthirster was swept away by the cold winds of the north. The bloodletters and flesh hounds were thrown into disarray by the death of their general, while the elves recovered a measure of their senses, both sides recoiling from each other in the moments that followed.

The elves recovered more swiftly, still driven by the aftermath of Skarbrand's rage, heeding the commands of Kouran as the elven general issued swift orders to set a proper attack into motion.

As Seraphon lifted Malekith towards the snow-laden clouds, the Witch King considered returning to his pavilion, confident that his servants would know victory after his intervention. He stopped himself from withdrawing a moment later, looking at the broken body of Skarbrand far below.

The mage had foretold this day, in typically cryptic fashion. He had offered several prophecies as evidence that he spoke the truth and indeed was guided by the will of the goddess Lileath. Three visions he had spoken of, three events that would steer Malekith to their common cause.

'I remember when the lords of Saphery ruled from a flying city,' said Malekith, looking around the circular chamber near the pinnacle of the White Tower.

'Beautiful Saphethion,' his host said wistfully, thin fingers tapping together at his chin. 'Destroyed by your ambition.'

'It was not my ambition that brought low your floating city, but the actions of meddling mages,' Malekith replied. 'How little you learn.'

'It is not a scheme of my own devising that I follow, but a divine plan from the watcher of fates herself, Lileath of the Pale Moon.'

'You seek alliance from me?' Malekith shook his head in disbelief, and in doing so caught a glimpse of himself in the silver reflection of an oval mirror set behind the mage's desk. His projection here was as he had been in his early life. No iron-and-fire, no armour of midnight. A tall, darkly handsome elf with lustrous hair and sharp cheekbones regarded him solemnly. But for all that this apparition appeared healthy and hearty, the fires still burned and Malekith felt the pain of his enduring curse. His mood soured swiftly. 'It was you that reawakened that ancient flame in my soul, resurrecting an agony of ages in my heart and bones. You are mistaken if you think I desire anything other than your drawn-out, horrendous death, Teclis.'

'You do yourself a disservice, Prince Malekith,' said the mage. He stood and started to pace the room, hands clasped behind his back. 'There are many things you desire far more than my demise. You would let me live in return for your rightful return to the Phoenix Throne. You would gladly spare me if I released you from the torment Asuryan inflicted upon you so many centuries ago. Your vengeance has never been anything more than a veil for your frustrated ambition.'

Malekith reached out, his insubstantial hand passing through the mage's throat. He tightened his fist regardless, keen to prove his point.

'I do not expect you to trust me, any more than I trust you,' Teclis continued. 'You are called the Deceiver by many with good cause. Nor do I expect you to believe me without proof.'

'You can prove that the End Times are upon us? You have proof that Lileath will guide us to the means by which Chaos can be defeated? Lay it before me now and let me judge how trustworthy your words can be.'

'The power of three is well known to us, and so three dooms my mistress has laid upon you, as maiden, mother and crone, Morai-heg, Ladrielle and Lileath. When they have come to pass, I shall be brought to you again and you will know the truth of what I have told you.'

'Prophecy,' muttered Malekith. 'Some vague declarations that could be construed to mean just about anything. Has not my own doom been prophesied? Is not the curse laid upon you and your twin nothing more than the utterings of a demented seer driven to grief by the rejection of my father?'

Teclis said nothing as he picked up his staff, the image of Lileath at its tip gleaming silver in the moonlight that came through the window. Malekith flinched, for moments before it had been noon daylight, but now he saw a full moon rising above the forested mountains to the east.

Words came from Teclis's lips, but the voice was not his. Mellow and lilting, the female voice slipped into Malekith's thoughts like a lover entwining arms around him, leaving the memory of the words embedded deep.

'In tide of blood it will begin, a crimson fate that covers all. He that fell will fall again, Lord of Battle will fight no more.

'The serpent will come forth, fangs hidden behind the snow, with scales of black and eyes of blood. Its venom shall be the doom of ambition.

'And comes forth the Crippled One's bane, the forgotten maker shall be found. On mercy's anvil shall hope be forged, and godly silence shall be unbound.'

Malekith considered these words carefully as Teclis slumped back into his chair, his face even more wan than usual. His eyes were dull, his hair lank and lifeless. Coughing wracked the mage for a few moments until, with a faltering hand, he drew a phial of liquid from a drawer and took a swift draught. Almost immediately his pallor improved, the light returned to his gaze and he smiled.

'You cannot stop him,' Teclis said. 'Not without my aid.'

'If you think this is the path to anything but utter damnation, you are wrong, my nephew.' Malekith loomed over the mage. 'Believe me when I tell you that I have looked into the abyss where this course of action leads. If you trust anything, trust my experience. I have never been short of spite for those that disowned me, but I will warn you that you will destroy everything you love if you insist on following this road to its end. I have walked it far longer than you.'

Teclis sighed, his look one of regret. 'A wrong six thousand years old cannot be righted in a moment. The time will come when old wounds,' he reached out a hesitant hand and for a heartbeat Malekith's true form was revealed, shorn of glamour and armour, incandescent and scarred for eternity, 'the gravest of wounds even, can be healed.'

Fate was in motion. Morai-heg had foretold this day, but Malekith would not leave to her cruel whim that which he could decide for himself. With a growled command, he directed Seraphon back to the battle. There would be no mistakes this time, no confusion or setbacks or failure by lesser servants.

By his might, the Phoenix Throne would be his again. He was starting to believe.

Teclis had promised it.

The gods willed it.

FIVE

An Unexpected Barrier

It was not long past noon but in the northern reaches of the world the sun was barely a paler disc behind the clouds, the lands of Naggaroth shrouded by twilight. Bearing magical lanterns that burned with cold, blue fire the Naggarothi army appeared like a host of ice statues given life, the bleak light reflected from black enamelled armour plates and silver mail.

A host of knights led the vanguard, five thousand strong, mounted on reptilian cold ones. The stench of the creatures was matched by the steam of foetid breath that rose from their ranks, swathing the riders in a bank of fog that made their appearance even more ethereal.

At their heart rumbled a company of chariots drawn by more of the beasts, twenty of them, flanking the massive war engine of Malekith while Seraphon flew overhead. Malekith's chariot was a construction of black iron, drawn by four cold ones bedecked with barbed armour over their glistening blue scales. The chariot itself was hung with chains and hooks, the wheels spinning with jagged blades to slash the legs from under any unfortunate foe or beast that came close.

The host followed a road of cracked stones, cleared of snow by a legion of slaves driven ahead of the host by whips and hunger. The rag-shrouded corpses of those that had collapsed during their labours were heaped in the snow drifts beside the ancient slabs, faces frozen in pale-skinned grimaces, limbs protruding from the white banks with icicles dangling from splayed fingers.

A lone rider appeared out of the white haze and approached, swathed in a black riding cloak. His horse, also the colour of midnight, was tall and sleek, bred from stock stolen from the fair plains of Ellyrion in generations past, the flanks marked by the brand of Lord Ezresor.

Ezresor's dark steed whinnied and cowered at the stench of the cold ones, almost throwing him as he pulled to a walk a few paces from Malekith's chariot. The high agent dipped his head, sunken eyes betraying nothing as they rose again to meet his king's gaze.

'Your majesty, the riders report that the way to Ghrond is blocked,' Ezresor told the Witch King. The spymaster's steed gnashed at its bit and whinnied, shying away from Malekith. He yanked the reins and dug spurs into the creature's scarred midriff, hauling it in a circle to come alongside the Witch King once more.

'More vagrant northlanders?' Malekith replied. 'Call the captains to arms.'

'No, your majesty, it is not a foe that confronts us,' the spymaster said. He looked perplexed. 'It is... Well, they said we should go and look for ourselves.'

This was a deeply unsatisfactory answer but Malekith could see from Ezresor's expression that no further detail would be forthcoming, regardless of coercion or cajoling. He raised a hand and signalled for Seraphon to descend.

The journey from the van of the column did not take long. Soon the cold one knights were left behind and he saw a group of outriders coming south, riding hard along the road. Ezresor galloped out to meet them and returned swiftly to bring their reports to his master who had landed a short distance behind. The riders departed into the bleak wilderness, moving off the road to give Malekith a wide berth, turning hooded heads to dart looks back to the north.

'They come with a warning, your majesty. Several riders and shades attempted to breach the barrier just before midday,' Ezresor explained. 'They have not been seen since.'

'Barrier?' The Witch King did not mask his displeasure. 'You are being obtuse, Ezresor, and I would know the reason.'

'Your indulgence, for a little while longer, your majesty,' said Ezresor though there was little hint of pleading in his tone. He pointed ahead, to where Malekith could see a darker blur against the white horizon.

'Where is Ghrond?' the Witch King said slowly, looking left and right as though he was lost. 'We should be able to see the pinnacle of the convent by now.'

'That, your majesty, was what we cannot explain.'

Malekith did not press the matter further at that time, but followed Ezresor along the road until the darkness in the distance became clearer. It looked as though a forest had sprung up from the tundra, of black, twisted trunks and stunted branches. It stretched east and west almost as far as the eye could see, and stood many times taller than an elf.

Coming closer Malekith saw that it was not a forest that barred his path but a giant thicket of dead-looking vines, each thicker than his arm, jagged with scimitar-like thorns. The stench of magic contorted the air, undulating as a black and purple aurora.

Malekith studied the barrier for some time, feeling the ebb and surge of the magic sustaining it, watching the lash of mystical wind that caused the thorny extrusions to sway and bend. He barely noticed the clatter of armour as Kouran arrived with a company of Black Guard. Behind them a thousand knights of

Naggarond waited on their cold ones. Several of the dark riders had returned and were riding the edge of the obstacle, not so close that they would be caught, seeking any weakness in the wall of thorns. Other druchii – lordlings and petty commanders – had followed Malekith from the army and waited a short distance away, quietly discussing their own theories on the phenomenon that barred their onward route.

'The Chaos Wastes extend south,' said Malekith, confident of this explanation.

'Not so, your majesty,' corrected Ezresor, his gaze fixed firmly on the thorny growths so as to hide any hint of accusation. 'My riders say that it can be circumnavigated, though it would take us two or more days to do so. It is not daemonic in nature.'

'Morathi.' Malekith growled his mother's name. 'She thinks that this will stop me from reaching her in Ghrond. A girdle to protect her dignity, and as sharp as her tongue has ever been.'

He dismounted to approach the looming barricade on foot. At his approach the thorny growths stirred, moving slowly towards him. A spiked tendril slithered towards his shoulder and he seized hold of it. Fire burned in his fist and the thorny tentacle shook violently, trying to rip itself from his hot grasp. Opening his hands a few heartbeats later he let the charred remnants drop to his feet.

'It would take an age to burn through with sorcery, your majesty, even for one of your puissance,' said Ezresor, keeping his distance and a wary eye on the unnatural hedge.

As he looked more keenly, Malekith saw that the thorns heaped higher and higher, merging with the magical storm overhead, taller than Ghrond itself.

'Seraphon could not penetrate this mass,' the Witch King said to himself. 'And let us not even waste time contemplating digging to the tower.'

'How do we proceed, your majesty?'

Malekith considered his options. Brute force was unlikely to work. Morathi would be wary of any attempt at trickery. There were, however, other types of guile.

'How many sisters of the Dark Convent remain loyal to me?'

'None within Ghrond that we know of, your majesty.' The spymaster shrugged. 'Had any desired to betray Morathi we would have received warning of the northlanders' attack. We must assume that any that attempted as much died before their treachery bore fruit.'

'A shame,' said Malekith, remembering the first time he had been forced to confront his mother in similar fashion. She had usurped rule of Nagarythe and turned Anlec against him. On that occasion princes from House Anar loyal to Malekith had infiltrated her defences and opened the gates to allow entry to his army. He could not expect help from the interior this time. 'I expect that the only course of action left to us is to undo the binding of the enchantment, and that will be laborious work.'

As the last of these words left Malekith's ravaged lips, there was movement in the magical thicket. The vines twitched and curled, parting from each other to reveal a slender, pale-skinned figure standing less than a dozen paces away.

She was garbed in a robe of dark fur, edged with the white pelt of a snowcat. The same trimmed her high boots. Emerald rings glistened on slim fingers, matching the eyes that regarded Malekith from beneath a black shock of hair that was entwined with black brambles that twitched with a life of their own. There were mutterings of approval from the assembled druchii warriors, but Malekith knew that none would be judged worthy of such a prize – not even Ezresor or Kouran.

'Drusala,' Malekith whispered, as the sorceress bowed low, right leg crossed over the left. As she straightened, a fleeting smile passed her lips.

'King Malekith,' said the witch, assuming a demure pose, hands clasped at her waist, head slightly tilted forward, though this made her appear more coy than deferential. Her eyes glittered – literally – as she half turned and gestured along the path. 'My Queen Morathi, beneficent ruler of Ghrond, Eternal Hekarti Reborn, bids you welcome to her demesne and invites you to attend conference at your earliest convenience.'

This caused a different sort of stirring in the elves that heard the declaration. Ezresor moved closer, his voice barely a whisper though Malekith knew that Drusala would hear his words easily enough despite this precaution.

'Morathi declares herself to be divine?' The spymaster wrung his hands, looking more worried by this than any news of rampaging northmen hordes and fallen cities. 'She names herself the goddess of sorcery. There can be only one purpose to such a claim.'

'To cow any further ambition within her sisterhood,' said Malekith. It was a move he himself had used in the past, assuming the mantel of Khaine's avatar to head off the growing power of Hellebron and her bloody cultists. 'Perhaps she is not as certain of her position as leader of the convent as you thought.'

'She would put herself above even you, my king,' snarled Kouran. 'To claim to be Hekarti is an affront to all the Cytharai.'

'My Queen awaits your pleasure,' said Drusala, as if this answered Malekith's doubt.

The Witch King considered rebuffing the invitation, just to remind his mother that she answered to him, not the other way around. He rejected the notion as petty. The real prize was Ulthuan and the longer he delayed at Ghrond the greater the chance that Prince Tyrion and his allies would defeat the latest daemonic intrusion and recover to meet any Naggarothi attack. The season of the sun was just beginning, an ideal time of year for a fresh offensive to reclaim their homeland. If Morathi wanted to play these mind games, Malekith could put aside his pride long enough to gain entry to Ghrond, if not any longer.

'Take me to your queen,' said the Witch King, stepping towards Drusala. 'At my pleasure.'

'Of course, your highness,' replied the sorceress.

SIX

The City of Ghrond

Behind Malekith, the wall of thorns closed, cutting him off from his advisors and army. He did not even turn to look as Drusala led him deeper into the bramble-maze, the path opening up before them, the thorns entwining again when they had passed.

The magical entanglement continued as far as the walls of the city itself, which were unmanned.

'You trust to magic more than the spears of our people?' Malekith said to Drusala.

'Spears are of little use against daemons, your majesty,' replied the sorceress. 'Better that the garrison stays away from the blood-thorns, lest unseemly incidents occur.'

Passing through the great gate beside Drusala, Malekith found the streets empty. Now and then a terrified face appeared at a window or a shutter would creak open, revealing dread-filled eyes for a moment before closing. All was shrouded in near-darkness, the cold light of the sun blocked out by the dome of thorns, broken only by a ghostly green glow that emanated from the pinnacle of the Tower of Ghrond.

The heart of the city was a lone spire almost as high as the tallest pilaster of the Black Tower. A solitary finger of dark rock topped the Convent of Sorceresses, and this tower was tipped with a faceted crystal sphere from which the sisterhood commanded by Morathi would gaze north into the heart of the Wastes, into the Realm of Chaos itself, gauging its moods and movements. The summit of the tower was partly obscured by the wavering miasma of energy sustaining the thornwall.

The atmosphere of dread was as palpable as the dark magic that Malekith felt moving sluggishly through the foundations of the city. The buildings were low and squat for elf construction – barely a tower four storeys high broke the skyline away from the convent. Slate roofs gave the city a grey appearance, broken by the silver and gold of talismans hanging over doorways and windows. Some walls were painted with red or white or pale blue runes of protection, others with names of the Cytharai and many decorated with intricate mural-geometric designs incorporating the name-icon of Hekarti.

'Upon the edge of damnation it is wise to appease all patrons,' Drusala said, noticing the Witch King's stare lingering on these totems. She pointed to his shield. 'The antithetical rune of the supreme witch protects you in battle, my lord.'

'You find judgement where only curiosity exists,' said Malekith, scrutinising Drusala closely. She seemed more defensive than during previous encounters. 'Of more interest to me is my mother's assertion to possess the mantel of Hekarti. It is not the first time in recent memory that one has claimed to me that the gods are ascending and descending to the mortal realm.'

'Really?' Drusala regretted her interested outburst immediately, looking away shame-faced. When she looked at Malekith again she had regained her composure, though there was stiffness in her tone. 'Apologies, your majesty. We are indeed in tumultuous times and the gods themselves will play their part in events to come. Forgive my intrusive demand.'

'It excites you? The possibility that we enter the End Times?'

'There are no endings, your majesty, only beginnings that have not been exploited yet. The world turns upon cycles, and we stand on the brink of a fresh era of growth and dominance.'

'To which 'we' do you refer? The Convent of Sorceresses? The Naggarothi? Mortals?'

Drusala kept her expression neutral when she replied. 'Your people, of course, your majesty. We are all your subjects.'

'Even Morathi?'

'I would not speak for the incarnation of Eternal Hekarti, your majesty, but your mother has long laboured for your power and best interests. Was it not her that aided Kouran in holding together your dominion when you were cast adrift in the Realm of the Dark Lords? If she had desired to usurp your majesty's position, she would have done so then, would she not?'

'My mother does not support me – she fears the reprisals of the princes should one of them ever seize power.'

Drusala clamped her mouth shut, cheeks drawn in as she kept whatever remark she had to herself. It was obvious that Malekith's barbed words had touched a nerve. He was not sure if the sorceress was offended, or upset in some other fashion by his comments. Certainly she held Morathi in very high esteem and it pained her to hear Malekith talk of his mother in such an off-hand fashion.

They continued without speaking. Drusala's footfalls made no noise as she strode along the paved streets, but the impact of Malekith's boots rang hollow from the buildings, each step a knell that announced his passage through the city. More and more faces peered at his approach, some of them now showing curiosity more than fear. Once or twice he caught the expectant gaze of a noble or servant, quickly replaced with fear as his dread gaze fell upon them.

He could imagine the whispered conversations, the rumour. The bloodthorn wall kept out news as surely as it guarded against attack, and perhaps that was Morathi's true purpose. Had the people of Ghrond known that the rest of Naggaroth was being destroyed by the bloodied horde there might have been dissent, even rebellion. He knew his subjects were not overtly loyal to one another, but enlightened self-interest and the risk of total destruction always ensured they would come together against an external foe.

What lies had Morathi and her sisters spun to the military commanders? That it was safe to stay here, waiting for reinforcements that Morathi hoped would never arrive? As time dragged on she would speak of how Malekith had been absent, and how the lords of Naggarond had cared nothing for the people of the other cities. By such half-truths was a new centre of power created, and by such manipulation of events were loyalties shifted.

Drusala was right in one regard. The End Times was an unnecessarily grandiose name for a period of change no worse than any Chaos influx the world had seen before. The magical vortex of Ulthuan ensured that no matter how far the Realm of Chaos expanded, never again would the touch of Chaos corrupt the whole world as it had done during the daemonic invasions that had beset Aenarion. If the latest news from Ulthuan was true, Prince Tyrion was ably impersonating his ancestor in holding back the latest daemon surge.

It was all so repetitive. The cycle of the world, the endless ebb and flow of nations and battles, and here was Malekith again, about to take his mother to task for opposing him, for testing him. He would have hoped that she of all other people would understand the pointlessness of trying to resist his will, but her vanity always urged her to the wrong path at the most untimely moments.

I've been here before, he thought.

Not literally, but the similarity to events in the far past made him wonder if he was an actor in a play being staged again and again with a few alterations to the script between performances.

At the far end of the hall sat Morathi, clad in a draping wind of golden cloth that obscured very little of her nakedness. She held her staff of bone and iron across her lap, her fingers toying with the skull at its tip. Morathi was sitting in a simple wooden chair next to the mighty throne of Aenarion, which was cut from a single piece of black granite, its back shaped like a rearing dragon, of which Bel Shanaar's throne was but a pale imitation. Magical flame licked from the dragon's fanged maw and glowed in its eyes.

Malekith's eyes were drawn to the throne above all other things, ignoring even his mother, for this was the strongest memory he had of this place, of his father girded for war sat upon that immense chair, in counsel with his famed generals.

The memory was so vivid that Malekith could hear his father's soft yet strong voice echoing around the throne room. The prince was but a child, sat in the lap of his mother beside the Phoenix King, and Aenarion would occasionally pause in his conversation and look down upon his son. Always stern was that look: not unkind, yet not compassionate either, but full of pride. For years Malekith had gazed back at those strong, dark eyes and seen the fires that raged behind their quiet dignity. Malekith imagined that he alone knew the sinister spirit that hid within, clothed in the body of a noble monarch, masked against the eyes of the world lest it be recognised for what it truly was.

The soul of a destroyer, the wielder of the Godslayer.

And the sword! There across the Phoenix King's lap lay Widowmaker, Soulbiter, the Sword of Khaine. Even at a young age, Malekith had noticed that only he and his father ever looked upon its blood-red blade, for all other elves averted their gaze and would look anywhere else but directly at it. It was like a secret shared between them.

'Yet you did not pick up the Blade of Murder when it was offered to you,' said Morathi, dispelling the illusion that had so gripped her son.

Malekith shook his head, confused by the enchantment

cunningly wrought upon him by his mother. Truly they were real memories she had stirred, but her spell had made them as tangible as life, if only for a moment.

'I did not,' replied Malekith, slowly, realising that Morathi had seen into his thoughts and learned of his episode on the Blighted Isle, of which he had spoken to nobody.

'That is good,' said Morathi.

She was sitting in stately pose, despite her near-nudity, and exuded regal poise. Not here the barbarous priestess who tore living hearts from the breasts of her victims, not the seductive, wily seeress who wove lies with every word and manipulated all around her into a tapestry to her liking. Here she was as queen of Nagarythe, full of quiet majesty and grandeur.

'The sword controlled your father,' the queen said, her tone hushed, reassuring. 'Since his death, it has yearned for you to seek it out. I was worried that you would be ensnared by its power as well, but I am proud that you resisted its bloodthirsty call. None can truly be its master, and if you are to rule, then you must be master of everything.'

'I would rather the world devoured by daemons than unleash that fell creation upon the world again,' Malekith said, sheathing Avanuir. 'As you say, once drawn it will consume its wielder until nothing but blood remains. No person can become a king with its power, only a slave.'

'Sit down,' Morathi said, waving a hand of invitation towards the grand throne.

'It is not yet my place to sit there,' replied Malekith.

'Oh?' said Morathi, surprised. 'And why is that?'

'If I am to rule Nagarythe, I shall rule it alone,' said Malekith. 'Without you. When you are slain, the army of Nagarythe will be mine again. I shall hold power over the pleasure cults and with them secure the Phoenix Throne.'

Morathi remained silent, looking at her son with ancient eyes, gauging his mood and motive. A sly smile then twisted her lips.

'You mean to slay me?' she whispered, feigning shock.

'While you live, always will your ambition be a shadow upon mine,' said Malekith, angry at his mother's charade. 'You cannot help but be my rival, for it is not in your nature to serve any but yourself. I cannot share Ulthuan with you, for you could never truly share it with me. Even my father was not your master. I would exile you, but you would rise up again in some forgotten corner, a contender for everything that I aspire to.'

'Cannot share power,' Morathi said, 'or will not?'

Malekith pondered for a moment, examining his feelings.

'Will not,' he replied, his eyes full of intent.

'And to what is it that you aspire, my son?' Morathi said, leaning forward eagerly.

'To inherit my father's legacy and rule as Phoenix King,' Malekith replied, knowing the truth of the words even as he spoke them. Never before had he so openly admitted his desire, not even to himself. Glory, honour, renown: all but stepping stones towards his ascension to the Phoenix Throne. The circlet had revealed to him the true nature of the forces that now ruled the world, and he would not stand by while Ulthuan slowly succumbed to them.

'Yes, Chaos is strong,' Morathi told him.

'Stay out of my thoughts,' Malekith snarled, taking an angry step forward, his hand straying to the hilt of Avanuir.

'I need no magic to know your mind, Malekith,' said Morathi, still gazing fixedly at her son. 'There is a bond between mother and son that does not need sorcery.'

'Do you submit yourself to your fate?' Malekith said, ignoring her obvious reminder of their relationship, an attempt to stay his hand.

'You should know better than to ask such a pointless question,' Morathi replied, and now her voice was stern, harsh even. 'Have I not always told you that you were destined to be king? You cannot be king unless you are prince of your own realm, and I will not surrender it willingly. Prove to me that you are worthy of ruling

Nagarythe. Prove to the other princes that the strength within you is greater than any other.'

They came to the great barbican of the convent. The gates were open, and above the portal to the entrance hall blazed a rune of Hekarti, made of polished bones inscribed with smaller rune-shapes that flickered with their own life. Octagonal obsidian tiles paved the floor of the first hall, inset with channels stained dark with dried blood. Walls of granite were painstakingly carved with similar runnels in arcane patterns, the thaumatic geometry spreading up the tower to the sacrificial temples just below the summit. In dire times the whole of the palace could be charged with blood magic, fuelled with death for the mystics to pierce the veil of Chaos or for the sorceresses to take more direct action against a foe.

'Queen Morathi will be with you shortly,' announced Drusala, moving away from the Witch King. She waved her hand towards a spiralling stair. 'In the hall of welcoming.'

The sorceress slipped away through a curtained archway and Malekith was alone, though he could sense the presence of others very close at hand, watching him without eyes. He waited for several heartbeats to see if a new guide would come forth to lead him to his destination, but the palace seemed strangely empty.

Annoyed by the unseemly lack of proper welcome and ceremony, Malekith headed towards the steps, determined that his mother's transgressions would be punished this time.

SEVEN

Mother and Queen

The audience chamber was glorious in its sumptuousness. Golden drapes hung from every wall, and basalt tiles, polished to a mirrored sheen, were barely visible beneath the wine-dark rugs. Marble statues, studies in flawless physique, lined the chamber.

Malekith regarded the statuary with contempt. He recognised a few faces as previous members of his court, who had supported Morathi and in turn been granted her boons, both pleasurable and political.

He had been made to wait for some time, no doubt on purpose. His mother had always been theatrical, and could never resist the opportunity to make a grand entrance. Making him wait upon her pleasure also enforced the notion that she held the power here, not her son. The truth was that Malekith had learned to be above such petty manipulation. There were many that accused him of arrogance, and probably with good right, but such was his towering confidence that he was able to shrug off the minor insults and oversights that drove lesser leaders to rave and punish.

He would never give his mother the satisfaction of seeing her attempts to rile him had succeeded.

A chair was set next to a table before the throne, a ewer of dark wine and a goblet ready for his refreshment, but Malekith barely needed such sustenance these days. It was another goad, for Morathi knew well that the fire that had ravaged his body had all but destroyed his sense of smell and taste as well. The finest meats were as ashes on his tongue and the wine, no doubt liberated from some grand terrace in Ellyrion or Saphery, would be like brackish water.

Wishing to make a point of his own, Malekith stepped past the chair and sat down on the great throne of bloodrock at the end of the hall. He closed metal-lidded eyes and considered what he would say.

The click of heels on tiles and the faintest breeze from the opening door alerted Malekith to a new arrival. He opened his eyes as Morathi entered, and watched as she strode across the rugs, her gaze lingering on a few of the statues that lined the approach to the throne.

A momentary sour look marred her beautiful face as she noticed where he was sitting, an expression of annoyance that was swiftly replaced with a humourless smile. She gave a deep nod of greeting – never a bow, Malekith noted, for that would imply subservience – and crossed to greet her son.

'You have travelled far to speak with me, my child. Should I feel honoured, or afraid?'

'I have yet to believe that either of those words holds any meaning for you, mother,' said Malekith coldly.

'Will you not be seated?' he went on, inviting her to accept his position, the throne, but she would not accede even that.

'I am quite content as I am,' she replied, eyes narrowing. She was weighing up Malekith, trying to judge his mood, but it was impossible even for his mother to know what crossed his mind when his ravaged flesh was hidden behind his helm.

On the other hand, he was well aware of Morathi's mood, though to any other the subtle signs would have been lost. Seven millennia had shown him the slight tension in the shoulders, the merest curl of the lip, were danger signs. She made no overt effort, but subtly the winds of magic were shifting, gathering, funnelling down from the thorn-wreathed sky into the tower of Ghrond and seeping up from the dark rock beneath.

Surely she did not mean to engage in a magical contest? It would be a desperate move. Malekith was not certain he would win such a duel, but neither could Morathi start such a battle with full confidence. It would be a last cast of the bones, and it seemed Morathi was far from cornered and finished. She had tried direct confrontation before, when both of them had been far less experienced.

At some silent command, four figures emerged from the shadows, two to Malekith's left and two to his right. They were sorcerers by their garb, two male and two female, swathed in black robes, tattooed with dark sigils.

Malekith struck out with a blast of magic, materialising as a thunderbolt from his fingertips. Instantly Morathi was surrounded by a shadowy sphere of energy, which pulsed as the bolt struck it. Her adepts unleashed spells of their own, fiery blasts that rushed in upon Malekith in the guise of howling wolf heads, and the prince cast his own shield of darkness to ward them away.

The sorcerers and sorceresses closed in, hurling fireballs and flares of dark power. Malekith protected himself, drawing in more and more magic from the energy seething around the throne room as the spells cascaded towards him.

Morathi sat contentedly upon her chair while her followers unleashed their hexes and curses, watching with interest as Malekith countered each. Churning and bubbling, magic flowed around the hall, growing in intensity as both Malekith and his foes reached their minds out further and further, drawing energy from the city outside.

'Enough,' barked Malekith, letting free the energy that he had pulled into himself, releasing a blast of raw magic not shaped by any spell.

The power blazed, surrounding each of the dark wizards, filling them with mystical energy, more than they could control. The first, a red-haired witch, began to quiver, and then spasmed so hard that Malekith heard her spine snapping as she flopped to the ground. The other sorceress screeched in agony as her blood turned to fire and exploded out of her veins, engulfing her in a tempest of lightning and flames. The third of them flew into the air as if struck, his nose, eyes and ears streaming with blood, his ragged body smashing against the distant wall. The last was consumed by the ravening magic and collapsed in upon himself, crumpled like a ball of paper until he disintegrated into a pile of dust.

'Your followers are weak,' said Malekith, rounding on Morathi. The seeress remained unconcerned.

'There are always more minions,' she said with a dismissive wave of a beringed hand. 'That trinket upon your head gives you impressive power, but you lack subtlety and control.'

Quicker than Malekith's eye could follow, Morathi's hand snapped out, her staff pointed at his chest. He fell to one knee as his heart began to thunder inside his ribs, drowning him with pain. Through the haze of the agony, Malekith could feel the slender tendrils of magic that extended from Morathi's staff, almost imperceptible in their delicacy.

Whispering a counterspell, Malekith chopped his hand through the intangible strands and forced himself back to his feet.

'You never taught me that,' said Malekith with mock admonition. 'How unmotherly to keep such secrets from your son.'

'You have not been here to learn from me,' Morathi said with a sad shake of her head. 'I have learned much these past thousand years. If you put aside this foolish jealousy that consumes you, then perhaps I can tutor you again.'

In reply, Malekith gathered up the coiling magic and hurled it at the queen, the spell materialising as a monstrous serpent. Morathi's staff intercepted it, a shimmering blade springing from its haft to slice the head from the immaterial snake.

'Crude,' she said with a wag of her finger. 'Perhaps you impressed the savages of Elthin Arvan and the wizardless dwarfs with these antics, but I am not so easily awed.'

Standing, the seeress-queen held her staff in both hands above her head and began to chant quickly. Blades crystallised out of the air around her, orbiting her body in ever-increasing numbers until she was all but obscured from view by a whirlwind of icy razors. With a contemptuous laugh, Malekith extended his will, looking to knock them aside.

His dispel met with failure, however, as Morathi's magic swayed and changed shape, slipping through the insubstantial grasp of his counterspell. A moment later and the shardstorm tore through the air towards him, forcing the prince to leap aside lest they rip the flesh from his bones.

'Slow and predictable, my child,' Morathi said, stepping forwards.

Malekith said nothing, but lashed out with his sorcery, a whip of fire appearing in his hands. Its twin tips flew across the room and coiled about Morathi's staff. With a flick of his wrist, Malekith wrested the rod from his mother, sending it skittering across the tiled floor. With another short hand motion Malekith dashed the staff against the wall, shattering it into pieces.

'I think you are too old for such toys,' said Malekith, drawing Avanuir.

'I am,' snarled Morathi, her face contorting with genuine anger.

Something invisible scythed through the air and connected with Malekith's legs. He felt his shins crack and his knees shatter and a howl of pain was wrenched from his lips as he crashed to the floor. Letting Avanuir fall from his grasp, he clutched at his broken legs, writhing and screaming.

'Stop making such a noise,' said Morathi irritably.

Making a fist, she wove a spell that clenched Malekith's throat in its grip, choking him. The pain befuddled his mind, and as he flailed and gasped he could not muster the concentration to counter the spell.

'Focus, boy, focus,' spat Morathi as she stalked forwards, her fist held out in front of her, twisting it left and right as Malekith squirmed in her mystical grasp. 'You think you are fit to rule without me? I expect such ingratitude from the likes of Bel Shanaar, but not from my own kin.'

The mention of the Phoenix King's name acted as a lightning rod for Malekith's pain and anger and he lashed out, a sheet of flame erupting from him to engulf the queen. She was unharmed, but had released her spell to protect herself. Malekith rolled to his side, coughing and spluttering.

The prince was then flipped to his back and he felt a great weight upon his chest. Numbness enveloped him as the weight pressed down harder and harder, and Malekith fought against losing consciousness. As black spots and bright lights flickered in his vision, he thought he glimpsed a shadowy, insubstantial creature crouched upon his chest, a slavering horned daemon with a wide, fang-filled maw and three eyes. Pushing aside the aching of his body, he tried to focus his mind to break the spell, but still his body could not move.

Morathi stood beside her son, looking down dispassionately. She reached down and grasped Malekith's helm in one hand and pulled it from his head. The queen regarded it closely for a moment, her eyes analysing every scratch and dint in its grey surface, her fingers lingering close to the circlet but never touching it. Gently, she crouched beside Malekith and placed the helm behind her, out of reach. Malekith fought back a surge of panic. He felt strangely naked and powerless without the circlet.

'If you do not know how to use it properly, you should not have it,' she said gently. She laid a hand upon his cheek, caressing him, and then placed her fingers upon his forehead as a mother soothing the brow of a fevered child. 'If you had but asked me, I would *have helped you unlock its real power. Without it, your magic is weak and unrefined. You should have paid more attention to what your mother taught you.'*

'Perhaps,' Malekith said. With a shout of pain, he swung his gauntleted fist at Morathi, punching her clean in her face and sending her slamming to her back. 'I learned that from my father!'

Stunned, Morathi lost her concentration and her spell evaporated. Malekith felt the invisible weight lifting from his body. With an effort, he drew magic down into his ruined legs, fusing bone back into place, knotting ruined muscle and sinew together.

Whole again, the prince stood, looming over Morathi. With a flick of his hand, Avanuir jumped from the floor and landed in his grasp, its point a finger's breadth from Morathi's face, unwavering.

His face grimly set, he swung Avanuir over his left shoulder and brought it down in a backhand sweep towards Morathi's neck.

'Wait!' she shouted and Malekith's arm froze, the blade no more than a hand's span from the killing blow.

Here, in her stronghold, the sorceress was far from defenceless, but that did not mean she relished the prospect of testing her skill against that of her progeny. Any such contest would turn Ghrond into a blasted ruin before a winner was determined.

'Why have you come?' she asked, a sharpened fingernail resting on her slender chin.

'You gave no warning of the northlander invasion, as was your duty,' Malekith intoned, savouring each damning syllable. 'Moreover, you have held back from Naggaroth's defence. I should be quite furious with you. Indeed, for a long time, I cherished no thought so well as your broken body beneath the lash.'

The Witch King rose from the throne and began to pace the room, pausing before each statue in turn to gaze into its eyes. Some he recognised, past members of his council, watch commanders and generals that had assisted Morathi in one way or another. He could sense the life energy still trapped within the statues and wondered if any of his mother's favourites had ever escaped her gorgon-like wrath when the relationship inevitably became too much of a burden for her.

'Because of you, Naggaroth is all but fallen.' He did not look at her, but stopped before the image of Cruidahn of Hag Graef, who had been Morathi's consort more than a thousand years earlier. 'Before the year is out, it will be but another ruin in a world already full of them. Yet I find that I feel no sadness for the loss.'

'Pathetic! You disgrace your father's memory.' Morathi spat, unexpectedly flushing with anger.

'Not at all. Indeed, I intend to honour him as never before. Our folk had fallen into weakness and squalor.' Malekith snorted with derision. 'We had grown fat and lazy, a herd of dull-witted beasts no longer fit for the great destiny I shall provide.' He turned to face his mother and spread his hands expansively. 'Now the herd has been thinned, the weak slaughtered by the northlanders' axes. I have you to thank for that, though I am sure you did not intend matters to unfold thus. Those who remain are warriors and survivors all. They will be my army, and Ulthuan's ruin, for they will survive only through seizing the land that is theirs by right. The throne of the ten kingdoms will at last be mine.'

'I have heard you say such things before,' Morathi sneered.

'Before, I did not have aid. The Phoenix King is already slain, betrayed by one of his closest advisors. He died broken and screaming, his last dignity a memory before I choked the life from him.'

'The Five Gates will defeat you, as they have in the past.'

'They will not,' Malekith assured her, 'for I now hold the key to those fortresses, placed in my hand by one of their own. Besides, Ulthuan is as beset as we. While I do not doubt that our cousins will endure, they will not have the good sense to let the times purge their weaklings.'

'If victory is so assured, what do you wish of me?'

'You are my mother and, despite your myriad treacheries, you yet command my regard. Join your armies to mine, and the past will be forgotten. You shall be Ulthuan's queen once more – glorious, regal and beautiful as the night.'

Morathi sighed contemptuously.

'You still think like a mortal, when you should aspire to be a god.'

'You are many things, mother, but you are no goddess.'

'And who is to say that? The power of Hekarti pulses through my veins. As the magic rises, I can be anything I wish, and that is all that matters as the Rhana Dandra begins.'

'You're not the first to speak to me of the End Times, yet I remain somewhat unconvinced.'

'The mage, I suppose,' Morathi said, her contempt clear. 'Did you think I wouldn't hear him whispering to you during your journey? What lies did he tell you?'

'It hardly matters. He serves my goals, whether he realises it or not.'

'Of course,' Morathi mocked. 'You are not one to accept any wisdom other than your own. Look around you. The world cries out in torment, the skies bleed, the twin-tailed comet blazes, and you look for more proof? The Dark Gods are rising, and they will swallow us all.'

'If what you say is proven true, then I shall fight them, as my father once did. I will not be denied my birthright.'

Morathi let forth shrill laughter, bordering on the hysterical. 'You're a fool! These are the End Times. Only those who embrace their true nature will survive. Yours is not that of a victor. Yours is to lose, and to blame others for the loss. Go back to Naggarond. Take what pleasures you may before the tides of Chaos close over your head. I will not waste my strength on foolishness.'

Malekith found himself consumed by a sudden and bitter mirth and matched her insane humour with a mad laugh of his own. 'And your nature is to languish in this ensorcelled tower, I suppose, a jilted princess pining for her love until darkness falls?'

He enjoyed the contorting agony of her features as he revealed his knowledge of her earlier interference with Prince Tyrion and her declarations of affection, unseen and unremembered by all others but revealed to Malekith as he had sought escape from self-banishment in the Realm of Chaos.

'You understand nothing,' Morathi spat. 'He will be mine again. I have foreseen it.'

'How very convenient for you,' Malekith replied calmly. 'And might I ask what you foretell concerning my future?'

There was a long pause. Morathi watched him closely, and could not fail to sense the edge of his anger growing sharper, but equally she could not resist the opportunity to display her superiority. Malekith listened to what she had to say expecting half-truths and outright lies.

'If you go to Ulthuan, you will lose everything,' she proclaimed at last. 'Your realm will fall, your purpose will waver. Everything that makes you who you are – everything that makes you my son – will crumble to naught. Even your name will no longer be your own. I would sooner see you dead.'

'Then it seems that this will be our last farewell, mother,' said Malekith scornfully. He searched for some hint of a lie, but he could find none. He realised that she had not confessed her true reason for allowing Naggaroth to fall into ruin, but he knew now, looking at her, that she would never tell him.

He turned to leave, but could not resist one more jibe. 'Out of fond regard, I grant you one last gift: your life. Your treason is not forgiven, but it will go unpunished. Sit in your tower and rot.'

'My king!'

Kouran's shout caused Malekith to wheel his chariot about, turning to face the company of Black Guard. Behind them the thornwall was rippling with power, first moving like sinewy limbs, the movements increasing to a wild thrashing, as though the enchantment was tearing itself apart.

A huge swathe of the black-thorned barrier lifted and parted, the tearing of mystical tendrils like the scream of tortured children.

Where the thornwall had been now marched a column of armoured warriors, decked in black mail and plate, the regimental standards displaying the scarlet runes of Ghrond. Hundreds – thousands – of soldiers advanced along the old road from the gates of the city within. The warriors eyed the recoiling thornwall with fear and suspicion, many of them no doubt remembering the fate of comrades that had perhaps tried to break free or strayed too close.

The entire army of the north city marched forth.

A cabal of sorceresses led the dreadblades at the vanguard of the army. Mounted on a dark pegasus, Drusala flew over the army, the beat of bat-like wings in time to the drums that marked the tempo of the march.

The sable-skinned beast settled not far from Malekith's chariot, tossing its head in disgust at the stench, spiralled horns embedded with gems catching the dim light. The sorceress bowed in the saddle, her pale skin stark against the dark fur collar of her robe.

Malekith looked at Drusala, not with mortal eyes but the gaze of the Witch King. He could see the winds of magic coiled about her, and the shadow of dark magic that shielded her soul from the mutating effects of the heightened magical power. There was something else in the spirit-gloom, deeper and darker even than the shadow, but Malekith did not know what it was – some power bargained from a daemonic entity no doubt, which would claim her eventually.

As the thunderous tread of the approaching army rang out on the frost-dusted stone of the road Malekith was struck by the scene, reminiscent of the second prophecy of Lileath.

The serpent will come forth, fangs hidden behind the snow, with scales of black and eyes of blood. Its venom shall be the doom of ambition.

Drusala spoke, breaking the chain of thought.

'Queen Morathi, Hekarti Eternal, sends these gifts to her son as acknowledgement of her failings to treat him with due hospitality, and for neglecting her duties in times recent past. She would have it known that she hopes this offering of her host and most favoured coven will make some amends to heal the broken faith of late, and that ever the Witch King is the subject of not only her loyalty but her best intentions.'

Malekith looked at Drusala for some time, not speaking. His stare moved to the column of troops now reaching the Witch King's host and back to the sorceress. Kouran was close at hand, awaiting his master's command. Malekith directed a single, curt nod to his lieutenant, who raised his glaive in salute and turned to issue orders.

The Master of the Black Guard understood his king very well, and directed the garrison of Ghrond to precede the knights and Black Guard. He sent messengers ahead for the rest of the army to break camp and be ready to march by the time the expedition had returned, placing the Ghrondites in the centre of the column, close to the Witch King. This was no honour, as might be taken by others, but a precaution against potential treachery from Morathi's servants.

EIGHT

The Witch King Commands

Turning south and then east, the army of the Witch King left the lands on the edge of the Chaos Wastes and moved back towards Naggarond. Heralds were sent to Clar Karond and Hag Graef, Karond Kar and Har Ganeth, summoning the remaining armies of the druchii to stand ready for fresh conflict. The lords and ladies of these realms were bidden to come to Naggarond to attend Malekith's council – a demand not an invitation, couched in words that left the recipients in no doubt as to the consequences of refusal. Even Hellebron and the hag queens of Khaine realised that they were no longer above retaliation and sent word that they would attend.

While these missives moved back and forth across the breadth of Naggaroth other preparations were undertaken. Through sorcerous means word was sent to the corsair fleets still abroad in the world, raiding distant coastlines and taking slaves from far-flung settlements of many different races. The captains of the fleets and black arks were commanded to return to their cities of berth for a new endeavour. They were likewise offered no alternative when Morathi's sorceresses placed a geas upon the distant seafarers – a curse that filled their minds with tormenting dreams, dusk to dawn each night until they set foot again on Naggaroth's land.

Some thirty days after reaching Ghrond the Witch King was back in his capital and his council brought together. Of the one hundred nobles, slavemasters, city rulers and beastlords that had once attended such gatherings, only a score still remained following the attacks of the northlanders and Malekith's recent purges of any that had shown past disloyalty.

Malekith brought the council together in the great throne room of the Black Tower. Normally this huge hall remained empty, the throne of Aenarion unoccupied. Even Malekith was never so arrogant that he wanted to be measured against his father, but on this occasion, with the announcement he was going to make, comparison would be inevitable and it would be good to remind his subjects that the Witch King's heritage outshone any other elf alive.

The hall was of such vast dimension that its vaulted ceiling and pillared walls vanished into darkness. Massive buttresses, every inch of their surface adorned with intricate carvings, loomed inwards. Stone gods glowered down from the pillars, Ellinill the Lord of Destruction and his wrathful progeny. The eyes of each god were crafted from enormous gemstones, their lustre enhanced by an enchantment that caused them to glow with a smouldering malevolence. Between the buttresses the walls were lost behind macabre tapestries fashioned from scalps encrusted with gore, a silent reminder of the many who had defied the Witch King's authority and the ultimate fate for such defiance.

At the centre of the chamber stood a great circular table fashioned from a single block of obsidian. Glyphs carved into the table's rim denoted each of the noble houses that had been privileged to sit there. Many times a smaller glyph, outlined in crushed rubies, followed the first symbol, noting a house that had been abolished by Malekith and extirpated from both the Black Council and the world of the living.

One hundred seats were set around the table, ghoulish thrones crafted from blackened bones and flayed skin. In many chairs some infamous leader of the dark elves reposed, though not all amongst that assembly were alive. Dozens of the seats were occupied by corpses, some of them fresh and reeking of decay, others withered by time into dried husks caked in dust and cobwebs. The most notorious traitors and disappointments were afforded a permanent position on the Black Council by the Tyrant of Naggarond.

A few paces behind each of the twenty chairs to be occupied stood one of the Black Guard, their halberds gleaming and sharp. Malekith waited on the throne, bathed in shadow, the fires of his curse dimmed by an effort of will so that he seemed an immobile statue of pitted black iron.

The gathering commenced in solemn quiet, with none of the pomp and posturing of previous councils. Not only was the circumstance no cause for celebration, the messengers from the Witch King had made it plain that he expected utter obedience in this testing time and no one was prepared to call undue attention to themselves while Malekith was in such a lethal mood.

The nobles of several cities came first, those of Clar Karond wearing cloaks of sea dragon scales, whips and pendants shaped like goads signifying their accomplishments as slave-takers. Rivals from Karond Kar followed, beastmasters that wore the pelts of manticores and hydras, and bore scarred faces and limbs with pride. They sat upon chairs opposite the Clar Karond delegation, whispering taunts and darting murderous glares that were returned in kind. Lady Khyra arrived shortly after, who took her customary place between the skeletal remains of Drusith Eldraken and the empty seat formerly occupied by Ebnir Soulflayer.

Drusala came next, standing in for the Queen of Ghrond. No

other had ever represented the city before and the feuding city nobles fell silent as the import of Drusala's attendance settled in their minds. They watched her take a seat almost at the foot of the throne dais, her hands neatly clasped in her lap, a chain of silver hung with a pendant of Hekarti wrapped about her fingers. She turned and smiled at the lords and ladies and the atmosphere grew chiller still.

The next councillors to arrive hailed from Naggarond: Ezresor and Venil Chillblade. The spymaster had of late been forced to take up arms himself and there was a raw scar on his cheek from a northman's blade. With the pair came Drane Brackblood and Lokhir Fellheart as representatives of the corsair fleets, having arrived directly from their black arks which now filled a bay not far along the coast from the harbour of Naggarond. Other great citadels of the sea and smaller vessels had clustered into the ports at Clar Karond and Karond Kar, disgorging cargoes of slaves and loot in unprecedented numbers.

A representative for the shade clans, Saidekh Winterclaw, arrived swiftly after. His bald head was tattooed with tribal designs, face pierced and fingers beringed with blood-red metal. He was dressed in fur-lined dark leather armour set with bronze rings, and about his neck hung a necklace of rotting ears and tongues from his latest victory duels with other chieftains of the mountains. The others looked on the highlander with unconcealed contempt as he took his place, returning their looks of disgust with a leer of mutual hatred for the city-dwellers.

Two watch commanders, one male, the other female – the only two surviving watch commanders – had come from far to the east and west, the towers of Shagrath and Drackla Spire, and marched in step down the carpet with helms under their arms, faces raised in haughty disdain for the nobles that had seemingly abandoned them. They glared at their Black Guard escort, unused to such close attention, but sat down without comment.

Kouran arrived next, without ceremony, and took his place beside the throne on the opposite side to Drusala, his magical glaive held upright beside him, within the visor of his helm his eyes moving from one attendee to the next in constant motion, never stopping.

There was a pause until a pair of elves entered, dressed in tabards of red and purple, of a somewhat nervous disposition. They eyed each other and then lifted the clarions they were carrying to their lips. After a further agitated pause they blew a series of rising notes that rang along the length of the hall, disturbing the still. As the last echoes of the peel reverberated into nothing, they lowered their instruments and hailed loudly.

'Presenting the Warpsword, Tyrant of Hag Graef, Daemon's Bane, Lord Malus Darkblade!'

Lips pursed, a strut in his step, Darkblade entered the hall and stopped on the threshold surveying the scene. All eyes turned towards his gauche entrance and there was a shaking of heads and discontented muttering. Seemingly oblivious to his indiscretion Malus sauntered down the carpet and sat next to Kouran, who fixed the Tyrant of Hag Graef with a piercing stare. The captain of the Black Guard gave an almost imperceptible shake of his head and a moment later the two heralds at the door screamed as their guts splashed across the floor.

The two Black Guards that had disembowelled them emerged from the shadow of the doors and dragged the unfortunates away, leaving a trail of gore, their shrieks fading with distance.

'By all the Cytharai, you have chosen to make an enemy of me,' snarled Darkblade, launching to his feet to confront Kouran, who remained seated, though he flexed his fingers on the haft of *Crimson Death*.

Any further protest was silenced by a husky but powerful voice at the doorway.

'Do I smell fresh blood?'

Everyone turned to watch the arrival of the last council member. The Hag Queen of Khaine was in her decrepit phase, her skin a thin veil over wasted muscle and bone, only partially obscured by a robe of flayed elfskin. Hellebron's face was a dreadful mask of sunken flesh, eyes ringed with black kohl that turned them into a shocking glare. Despite this she carried herself without sign of infirmity. Her movements were smooth and assured, and in defiance of her haggard appearance it was clear that she had once possessed outstanding beauty. A wig of white hair stained with bloody smears hung to her waist, kept in place by hooks that bit into the flesh of her forehead, stretching the wrinkled skin. Hands like claws opened and closed like a striking raptor.

She crouched, dipping a curling fingernail into the blood by the door. She licked the fluid from her fingertip and smiled, revealing cracked teeth that had been filed to points, gums bloodless and pale, a tongue stained black by millennia of narcotic abuse flicking between them, savouring the taste of life.

Hellebron had not always been so. All the recent talk of gods incarnating in the land of mortals reminded Malekith of Death Night seven hundred years before, when he had travelled to Har Ganeth for a very special conclave with the witch elves of Khaine.

It was an even choice which grated on his nerves more – the shrieking of the Khainites, the incessant drumming or the smell of burning viscera. The first was like the scrape of a broken blade across his nerves, the second was so monotonous it made him doubt time and sanity and the third was too much of a reminder of his physical condition.

He endured it all as he endured that immortal pain, in silence.

The temple of Khaine in Har Ganeth was an open forum of black pillars with an iron dome across the top hung with decaying organs and bones that swayed and rattled in the thermals of hot air rising from the sacrificial fire and a thousand braziers. In layout it was a good approximation of the ancient site upon the Blighted Isle where the Sword of Khaine rested in its dark stone altar, but considering the heat coming from the sacred fires – heat he could barely feel but had to be near-lethal for the cavorting worshippers – he wondered if the open aspect of the shrine was more practical than symbolic.

Such thoughts amused Malekith as he watched the ceremony continue. Out in the streets of the city, as in all the other cities of Naggaroth and any settlement where there was a shrine to Khaine, the witch elves were celebrating Death Night. The cultists prowled the streets and rooftops, seeking victims for the temple. In times past only those found outside their homes had fallen prey, but as the millennia had passed generations had grown wise to the perils and now in order to meet the bloody demands of their god the Khainites were not above breaking into buildings to snatch away those that could not defend themselves. Across the city howls of grief and the clash of weapons signalled successes and failures in this quest.

The unfortunates were dragged screaming up the temple steps, their bodies already bleeding from dozens of cuts, leaving a trail of blood on the red-veined marble. Hellebron and her coterie of hag queens stood beside an immense cauldron scored with diabolic runes. Wrought from black iron also, hollow with flames burning within, a statue of Khaine was set behind the cauldron, wicked blades held over the magical vessel. There was a fire lit beneath the cauldron, in which a growing pool of blood bubbled and steamed.

The sacrifices were heaved up onto the altar and their arteries opened wide, spilling crimson life fluid into the channels carved into the stone, running down into the dungeon beneath the temple where slaves laboured with cloths and buckets, passing pails of the spilt blood up slick steps to the priestesses in the shrine. Uttering their shrill prayers to the Lord of Murder the witch elves poured their bloody libation into the cauldron for their high priestesses.

Incredibly the victims did not die from this bleeding, but remained as shambling things kept alive by the magic of the temple. That is, until they stumbled into the grim-faced Executioners that lined the columned space, their two-handed draichs slick with blood. Each victim was finished with a single strike and lesser acolytes fell upon the bodies, some to rip out the hearts to toss into the holy flames, others fighting for possession of the heads to flense and gild as trophies. The rest of the remains were dragged away by whip-scarred slaves, to the workshops where they would be rendered down for components used in the Khainites' narcotics and poisons, the remaining organs and body parts illicitly sold on to magical practitioners not willing to draw the eye of the Convent of Sorceresses.

For the whole of Death Night this continued, until just before dawn the Cauldron of Blood was nearly full. Ascending on steps wrought of bones and sinew, Hellebron and her hag queens bathed in the heated blood, laughing and splashing like children in a pool. Malekith watched closely. His unnatural gaze, aided by the Circlet of Iron upon his brow, could see the winds of dark magic binding to the cauldron through ritual and sacrifice. The magic flowed into the blood, energising it, and passed into the hag queens within.

Hellebron emerged as the first rays of dawn shone through the gate-pillars of the temple, her pale flesh bronzed by the sun's early light. She was exquisite, possessed of such youthful vibrancy, her hair lustrous and thick, every limb and feature perfectly proportioned. Malekith knew well why his mother had scorned Hellebron when Alandrian's daughter had asked for favour in the queen's service many millennia ago: simple jealousy. For all her politics and machinations, Morathi was sometimes prone to folly caused by her primal need for superiority. Had she been able to stomach the presence of a maiden more beautiful than her, Morathi *would have made a powerful servant rather than an enemy six thousand years old.*

He snapped himself out of his lustful contemplation, remembering that there was a particular reason he had come to Har Ganeth on this of all nights. Morathi's pleasure cults were growing again, inveigling their way into the courts and armies of Naggaroth as they had Ulthuan in the time before the oceans had swallowed Nagarythe. For the most part they were harmless, but Malekith was never content to allow his mother free rein, and a message had to be sent reminding Morathi that the Witch King was aware of her ploys.

Malekith paced across the temple as the last of the hag queens pulled her lithe, blood-coated body from the great cauldron. He extended his will, letting Asuryan's flame burn from the cracks and gaps in his armour. The resemblance to the statue of Khaine was uncanny and it was this that had given Malekith inspiration.

'You know me as your king,' he intoned, ascending the steps to stand above the mighty cauldron of the Lord of Murder. He opened his arms, flame burning from his palms. 'Know me now also as the incarnate vessel of your lord and god, Khaine the Ruthless, the Bloody-Handed Messenger, Jaguar of the Night, the Manticore. In me has He invested His power in the mortal realm, so that He might lead you on the crusade of death.'

Hellebron had known this was to come and she hid her distaste well enough as she watched Malekith stepping down into the blood. The thick liquid roiled at the heat of his entry, bursting and splashing over the rim of the cauldron. Malekith crouched, allowing his head to sink beneath the surface, feeling the dark magic crawling across his armour. He latched onto the threads of energy and poured his own magic back along their channels.

The outside of the cauldron started to glow. The runes grew brighter and brighter until they blazed with ruddy energy, filling the temple with blood-red light. As Hellebron and the assembled Khainites watched, Malekith ascended from the blood, the life fluid blackened, caked across his armoured flesh. He turned his eyes on Hellebron and after a moment – a moment that signalled displeasure but obedience – she lowered to one knee and bowed her head, prompting the rest of the Khaine worshippers to do likewise.

'Send the word out across the world,' Hellebron intoned. Malekith emitted a little of his magical power, shattering the burned blood from his armour with a burst of fire. 'Celebrate and give thanks to the mighty Lord of Murder for delivering unto us his world-born son. We have been blessed and in His name we shall bare our blades in readiness for His will as voiced by His avatar. Hail Malekith, Eternal Khaine Incarnate.'

After Hellebron came two more from the blood cults: Tullaris, most infamous of the Executioners, and Satikha, Handmaiden of Shards, priestess of Eldrazor the god of blades. They each offered obeisance to what seemed to them the image of Malekith on his throne.

The last empty chair became the next subject of attention, until Lord Saesius of Karond Kar informed everybody that his sister had been slain during a northlander ambush en route to the capital.

'So now we must await the pleasure of our august majesty, as usual?' said Darkblade, sitting down. 'I wonder how long it will be before he graces us with his presence.'

Unseen by the Tyrant of Hag Graef, the Black Guard standing behind him took a pace closer, hands shifting grip on her halberd.

Malekith allowed his essence to burst forth, opening eyes like two pits of fire. Darkblade visibly flinched, hands grabbing the arms of his chair.

'Not long, my good friend Malus,' said Malekith, standing up to his full height, glaring down at the assembled council. 'Not long at all.'

NINE

A Salutary Example

To his credit, Darkblade calmed his squirming and offered no defence or apology. Malekith regarded the master of Hag Graef carefully, seeing something writhing in the dreadlord's heart, some daemonic power granted by illegal rite the Witch King suspected. There were whispers that the title Daemon's Bane was not mere affectation but also not entirely truthful.

Malekith looked away, assuring himself that Malus would receive his justified fate soon enough. Malekith's gaze swept over the others and finished upon Hellebron, who was staring with suspicion at Drusala, eyes narrowed like a cat's.

'Welcome back to Naggarond, chosen bride of Khaine,' Malekith said slowly, extending a hand of greeting to the leader of the Khainites. 'I offer my regrets that your temples have been so despoiled and your city ravaged.'

'Had your bitch mother played her part we would have seen the human cattle slaughtered at the walls.' Hellebron shuddered with excitement, eyes closing fully for a moment. She composed herself. 'No matter. The temples of Khaine have been anointed in battle. It is a dedication, not a desecration.'

Malekith accepted this with a nod and took a moment, one hand upon the hilt of his sword.

'Lord Vyrath Sor shall not be joining us,' Malekith's voice echoed across the chamber. 'He was slow to answer my summons and only arrived this morning. I reminded him of his obligations to the Circlet of Iron. The harpies should carry what's left of him back to his tower by sunset. It would pain me if the garrison of Nagrar were to think their master had fallen victim to some lesser fate.'

To emphasise his story, Malekith tossed an object onto the obsidian table. The gold chain clattered as it came to rest. Though caked in blood and shreds of flesh, there was no mistaking the sigil that had represented Vyrath Sor etched onto the chain's clasp.

Malekith stalked about the periphery of the chamber, drifting between the shadows like some prowling tiger. 'Do not mourn Vyrath Sor,' the king advised with mock sympathy. 'He decreed his own doom when he placed the defence of his miserable outpost before his duty to his master. The same doom any one of you might have earned by defying me.'

'Nagrar is lost, then?' the question was uttered by Venil Chillblade.

The Witch King made a deprecating wave of his hand.

'An inconsequence,' he declared. 'The garrison will fight to the last because they have no choice. They will die as druchii should, shedding their blood on behalf of their king. When the tower falls, the advance of the barbarians will falter. They will be some time plundering their conquest and slaughtering such captives as they take. It will take their warlords still more time to gather their animals back into a fighting horde.'

'But they will continue their advance, your highness?' The hesitant voice of Thar Draigoth, the great flesh-merchant, sounded more like a rodent's squeak than the words of Naggaroth's most infamous slaver. Like Venil, he had extensive holdings in Karond Kar. After seeing his interests in Clar Karond massacred by the triumphant invaders, he was doubly worried about protecting the rest of his property.

Malekith came around behind Lady Khyra's seat, one of his iron claws reaching down to stroke the shoulder to which her false arm was attached. The king glanced along the table, sweeping his gaze across each of his dreadlords.

'The Rhana Dandra is coming,' he announced. 'The End Times are upon us and the moment for action is nigh. You have all felt it, I am sure, and we have certainly all witnessed it as daemons and northlanders bayed at the gates of our cities. Ulthuan stands on a precipice. Usurpers and faint-hearts defend our ancient isle against a foe they cannot defeat. If our people – all of our people – are to survive the coming onslaught they will need strong leaders. Leaders only Naggaroth can provide.'

'The weakness of our cousins shall finally be their downfall,' said Lady Khyra. 'As soon as our city's defences have been repaired, we shall assemble the fleets and await your command.'

'Karond Kar suffered also,' added the dreadlord Eillhin, eyes flicking towards his rivals, 'but you can count upon our ships and warriors no less than any other city.'

'Once the northlanders have been driven back, all of Naggaroth will heed the call to arms,' said the male watch commander, whose name Malekith had not bothered to learn.

'You misunderstand my intent,' the Witch King told them, stilling their enthusiasm. 'The End Times are coming. The Realm of Chaos seeks to devour the world and the Chaos Wastes expand. The northlanders will pillage everything that has not been warped by the storm of magic descending upon us, and will squat in our fallen towers where they will be preyed upon by daemons sent by the masters they seek to serve.'

He stepped down from the throne dais and paced along the hall. All eyes followed him until he stopped upon the seal of

Aenarion set in gold and malachite in the floor. The sigil began to writhe, infused with the heat from Malekith's tread, seeming to come to life to light the Witch King with an auric glow.

'This blasted wilderness has never been our home. It was a refuge, nothing more, and it has become an anchor to our ambitions. It is time to cast free ourselves from its cold burden, and direct our fullest intention to the only home we have ever desired.'

'The defences of Ulthuan are considerable, even if our cousins are busy fighting daemons,' Ezresor said carefully. 'Lines of supply and retreat...'

'There will be no retreat.' Malekith's words echoed along the hall like tomb-slabs of mausoleums closing on the council. 'Naggaroth will die and any that remain or try to return will die also. Do not mistake necessity for vanity. We *must* reclaim Ulthuan or perish in the Rhana Dandra. Put all other thoughts from your minds. There is no failure on this expedition, only death or victory.'

This announcement was greeted with outbursts of disbelief and horror. The Black Guards stood ready and Kouran's eyes were fixed on Malekith waiting for the simplest of signals, but Malekith gave no indication of his displeasure. The Witch King saw his captain cast his gaze about the room, no doubt noting who protested the most, or did not, either perhaps a sign of a deeper plotting. Kouran turned his halberd in his hands, unnoticed by the others, until the blade pointed towards Ezresor, who was sneering and shaking his head at the posturing nobles.

Malekith would have killed any for such dissent only a year earlier, but his resources were dwindling rapidly and he needed these leaders of druchii society to support him. He allowed protests and veiled threats to wash over him, salving his pride with the knowledge that despite their haranguing every elf present would do exactly as Malekith commanded. Voicing a difference of opinion was one matter, openly disobeying the Witch King's orders another.

Hellebron's cackle cut through the uproar.

'Khaine's feast grows daily, and you think you can avoid the banquet?' Fingernails like daggers scratched the surface of the table. She turned her attention to the Witch King. 'All that is left is the bloodletting – what does it matter where the droplets fall?'

'The blood of the druchii belongs to me,' Malekith snarled. 'I and I alone have made you what you are. Mine is the will that has stripped all weakness from your hearts, mine is the vision that has poured strength into your bodies. All you think, all you dream, all that you are is as I have made it. The druchii are mine, formed from my vision, moulded by my cause. From the pathetic tatters of a vanquished realm I have built a great and terrible people.'

'But how does that help us save Naggaroth?' Malus asked, confidence obviously fuelled by the disapproval voiced by the others. Malekith cared nothing for their opinions, only for their uses.

'Ereth Khial take Naggaroth!' Malekith spat. 'Our treacherous kin are ripe for conquest! What would you do, spend the blood of your warriors to protect a land that you despise, a bleak desolation that has within it nothing but scorn and mockery? I tell you, I tell all of you, this will not be! We will not bleed our armies defending this abominable wilderness! If we are to fight, then we will fight a war that is worth fighting! We will fight to take the land that belongs to us! We will fight to claim the land that is our heritage and birthright! Naggaroth? Let it burn! Let it rot! Let it fall to daemons and beasts! It is Ulthuan we desire, it is Ulthuan that is the destiny of the druchii! Ulthuan and the crown of Aenarion! Ulthuan and the birthright of Malekith!'

The Witch King's eyes flared from the black depths of his helm. 'We will not waste our strength defending Naggaroth. We will instead gather every warrior in the realm, every knight and corsair, every beastmaster and shade. We will muster such a host as has never sailed against the shores of Ulthuan. Every black ark, every helldrake and galley, any ship worthy of the sea will assemble in the greatest armada the gods have ever seen. In the past, the druchii have faltered against the asur because always you restrained yourselves, you held something back. This time, such cowardice will not be permitted. You will throw the full strength of your realms against Ulthuan. Nothing will be held back, for there will be nothing to come back to. There will be only victory or death!'

There were nods of agreement, some more forced than others, but Malekith could see that the truth had lingered in their hearts for some time but was only now being acknowledged. The attacks of the northlanders had been bitter, but no more bitter for Malekith than the last six millennia of frustration and disappointment. Now his subjects could feel an iota of what he had felt for so long, trapped behind their walls, seeing all they had built brought to ruin by the failings and machinations of others.

'Naggaroth will never recover,' the Witch King continued, erasing all doubt from the minds of his councillors. He knew they would obey his command; they always did. He needed more. He needed them to believe in their cause with greater passion than ever before. For one time only, the entirety of the druchii had to be bound together by a common purpose: conquest or extinction. His voice rose to a shout. 'It is not the will of our people to slowly dwindle and die, cowering behind our walls. We are the bloodied blade that delivers fate's end. We are the hunters from whom no prey escapes. We are the victors of a thousand wars, the lords of countless lesser creatures, and we do not bow meekly to Morai-heg's decree. We are scions of Nagarythe, the people of Aenarion! We will reclaim our birthright or die!'

The dread lords and ladies sat in shocked silence at this decree, none daring to look at any other except their lord, who prowled around the table and stopped before his throne, standing between Drusala and Ezresor. Malekith looked at the sorceress and then the spymaster.

'Before you depart the Black Tower. Before you return to your cities to gather your warriors, a demonstration. A reminder of what must befall all who betray their king.'

Kouran rose to his feet and joined his master. From the darkness behind his Black Guards emerged Malekith's personal torturers bringing with them the wickedly barbed, hooked and pointed implements of their profession.

Kouran stood before the iron throne, the torturers flanking him at either side. The captain turned towards Drusala, then in a sudden whirl he fell upon Ezresor. The spymaster was caught utterly by surprise, the blade he had hidden in the sleeve of his robe pinned against his wrist as Kouran caught him, the point of *Crimson Death* a hair's breadth from the spymaster's throat. Ezresor was forced to his feet as the captain bent his arm behind his back.

Malekith seized hold of the struggling elf. His iron hand gripped Ezresor's gaunt face, forcing his mouth open.

'You were the eyes and ears of the Black Tower,' the king snarled. 'But what good are eyes and ears when the tongue will not relate what has been seen and heard?' The Witch King's iron talons reached inside Ezresor's mouth. A gargled cry escaped the spymaster as Malekith ripped the tongue free, blood sizzling on the Witch King's fingertips. He held the bloodied strip of flesh for all the Black Council to see, the organ charring rapidly. 'One of you bought Ezresor's tongue. Look well upon what you purchased.'

Dropping the gory talisman on the floor, the king stormed from the chamber, leaving Kouran to make an example to the others.

As the Witch King ordered, so it was to be.

Though Naggaroth was to be surrendered, it was not to be gifted to the northlanders and daemons. The slaves were slaughtered in their millions, their departing souls used to cast vile enchantments upon their bodies to bring plague upon those that came after. The earth itself was cursed so that no crop or grass or flower would grow again from the blood-soaked soil. The snows and the water courses were poisoned, and the subterranean rivers and seas of the Iron Mountains were spoiled. The sky was choked by a bank of black smoke from the burning cities and towers. Nothing was left as loot or comfort for the invaders.

Only Morathi remained at Ghrond, and the most demented of Khaine's acolytes fought endless war with Hellebron against the Bloodied Horde at Har Ganeth. All others of elven blood followed their lords to the coast and prepared not for an attack but for a migration, back to the land of their ancestors.

Because the fates have ever had a sense of drama, even at the hour of setting forth, as the sails of the corsairs' ships darkened the ocean and the great shadows of the black arks stretched across storm-tossed waves, so the last of the daemons attacking Ulthuan fell to the Sunfang, *Lacelothrai*, the blade of Prince Tyrion, and his brother Teclis banished their kind from the shores of the elven homeland at great cost to his own health and future. Tired were the defenders but they knew their enemies would think them weak and vulnerable. Muted were the celebrations as the dead were buried and the fortifications repaired.

Thus was set the stage for the opening scene of Ulthuan's last war.

PART TWO

TEN

The Battle of Eagle Gate

This was his land, his soil, and countless were the elven lives that had been sacrificed upon it. Malekith could almost feel the souls of millions of dead, lamenting their demise from the depths of the underworld in Mirai, who had shed their blood for the region the asur called the Shadowlands.

It was a disdainful name, dismissive of the great history that had been forged on the cold plains that had once been known as Nagarythe. This was the land of Aenarion, who had saved Ulthuan from the daemons, yet it was now regarded as a fell realm, spoken of in whispers. It was so typical of the elves of Ulthuan that they should dismiss so much of their heritage while lauding the weaker descendants of those that had created their civilisation.

More blood was watering the spiny plants and short grasses of the Nagarythe mountainsides as another column of druchii warriors marched up the valley towards the immense fortification known as Eagle Gate. No other elven keep or castle had ever rivalled the gates of the Annulii Mountains in size or imposition to attack. Each stretched across the valley it defended a score times the height of an elf, many walls deep, protected by batteries of bolt throwers, warded by the ancient enchantments of Saphery and garrisoned by thousands of Ulthuan militia.

Eagle Gate was perhaps the most impressive of all, protecting the approaches to Ellyrion on the Inner Sea. The walls were as white as the snow that topped the two peaks that flanked the awe-inspiring barrier. They had once been fashioned so well that not a crack or fingerhold would have been found on their smooth surface, but of late the relentless attacks of the druchii, and before that the assaults of the daemons, had defaced the ancient stone more than the proceeding millennia. The ramparts had suffered a battering by bolt throwers and sorcery, jagged in places like broken teeth, the slender battlements and arched revetments hastily replaced in parts by whitewashed wooden defences.

Of the eight curtain walls, only two remained whole. The outer walls had been breached in the recent daemon war and in place of enchanted stone the defence was held by resolute elves clad in white and gold. The colours of Tiranoc and Ellyrion and several of the other kingdoms rippled on the banners above the host. Here and there a few flags bore the red-and-green of Caledor, but only a few, belonging to warriors and knights that had come to the gate in defiance of Prince Imrik's wishes.

The bows of the defenders sang as clouds of arrows fell upon the advancing host, who were as yet out of range with their crossbows, unable to loose any retaliation that might drive the asur from the rampart. The snaking column of black that was the Naggarothi host seemed beset in a sea of foaming white as chariots and riders from Tiranoc to the south engaged them from the flank. From above, mages hurled purple fireballs into the ranks of attackers, setting fires in the flesh of the druchii, charring clothing and melting mail armour. Jagged blue lightning ripped into the silver-and-purple-clad warriors, turning living soldiers into drifting clouds of smoke and molten steel.

Beside Malekith Seraphon stirred, emitting a low growl that made the promontory rumble beneath the Witch King's feet. He patted her neck, her scales adequate protection against his burning palm.

'You hunger for the battle,' he said, sensing the bunch of her muscles as her instincts told her to hunt and rend. 'Not yet, faithful Seraphon. In time you shall be allowed to the banquet, but not yet. Their claws need a little more dulling, or we shall regret our haste.'

It was not the first attack Eagle Gate had weathered since the druchii had arrived, but Malekith was determined that it would not stand against him this time. He had given the honour, dubious though it was, to Malus Darkblade, but it was not to the warriors of Hag Graef nor the knights of the Tyrant that the Witch King truly entrusted victory. It was a simple fact that from the moment the immense druchii fleet had landed on the shores of Nagarythe and disgorged its hosts towards Ellyrion, the fate of Eagle Gate had been sealed, and the efforts of Darkblade and his regiments was simply a bloody teaser of the violence to come – a test of Malus's dedication to maintaining his veneer of loyalty to Malekith.

Malus was doomed to failure from the outset, and probably knew as much. He had saved his most precious troops, protecting them like a dwarf king hoards his gold, but the time had rapidly come when the first assaults had failed and the Tyrant was forced to commit his household troops: the knights of Burning Dark. He led them now on a desperate charge through the defenders, assisted by Drusala and her sorceresses.

No doubt the sight of Malekith standing beside Seraphon watching the proceedings did little to hearten the Tyrant. The Witch King was content to observe the lord of Hag Graef while he expended his forces, weakening his power with every failed attack, unable to defy his king. And the true beauty was that the attacks of Malus served Malekith's purpose in another fashion, drawing the eye of the enemy outwards to the Shadowlands, bringing in more of their reserves and forces from across the nearby kingdoms. Malus did not know that knights from Ellyrion had arrived, and dismounted they waited now amongst the bolstered ranks of the defenders. Flame-winged phoenixes drove away the harpies that had been scavenging the dead in the upper towers and then swooped upon the vanguard of Malus's latest assault threatening to scatter them as the early attacks had been thwarted. Every elf that died defending the gate was one less Malekith would face when he finally made his move, or one less to support Malus should he survive the encounter and make a claim for the crown.

Despite the forlorn situation, Malekith admired the knights and warriors bearing down upon the defenders. It was rare for him to contemplate such lowly subjects but he took a moment to acknowledge the unswerving dedication and bravery demonstrated by their sacrifice below. Many of them would die, of course, without knowing such regard existed, but the fortunate few that survived to see the dusk Malekith would reward for their endeavour, further undermining Malus's power. He was, after all, a magnanimous ruler when required. That which could not be coerced with dread was easily bought with gold and favour, and in the new world they would carve on these shores the druchii knew only a few would rise to the top of society and would happily betray each other for such position.

There was a great commotion at the front of the assault, but Malekith could not see clearly what passed. He saw an explosion of daemonic energy and the asur army was in disarray for a while. No doubt Malus had unleashed whatever power it was Malekith had sensed at the council. It mattered little; the assault was grinding to its inevitable stop.

The mountains rang then with deafening roars, followed by a tumult of cheering from the ramparts of the gate. A palpable aura of despair engulfed the druchii host pressing into the valley, from spearmen to knights, sorceresses to the beastmasters that drove Malus's two monstrous hydras into battle. Malekith turned to the south, knowing what it was that had caused such consternation so quickly, broken lips twisted into a smile.

Dragons.

There were dozens of the immense creatures, each ridden by one of the proud knights of Caledor. A rainbow of colours against the summer sky, a glittering chromatic display of raw strength. The surprise and delight of the defenders was all the greater for recent events. Imrik of Caledor had declined to help Tyrion against the daemon assault and had withdrawn his forces to the borders of his kingdom.

His aid had been unlooked for, but now it seemed the tide would be turned by Imrik's intervention.

Such relief and joy was untimely.

Malekith pulled himself up into Seraphon's saddle-throne and picked up the iron chains of her reins.

'Go,' he whispered. 'Go to your cousins.'

Shouts of encouragement from the druchii followed Malekith into the sky as those below thought he sought to take on the squadrons of Caledor single-handed. Jeers rang out from the defenders, mocking his arrogance.

The jeers faded and the praise of the druchii fell to silence as Malekith and Imrik guided their monstrous mounts towards each other, weapons bared. As he closed with the Caledorian prince, Malekith was surprised by just how alike he was to his ancestor whose name he had taken. It was impossible for the Witch King not to think back to a day of destiny, a battle fought six millennia before above the fields of Maledor to the north.

Sulekh's tail lashed, smashing into Athielle's horse, turning it to a pulp of blood and broken bones. The princess was flung through the air and landed heavily, left leg twisting beneath her. Malekith channelled dark magic, ready to unleash another blaze of fire to finish off the Ellyrian. A movement caught his attention, a swiftly approaching blot against the clouds. He looked up to see a massive red dragon plunging towards him, a golden-armoured figure on its back.

'Finally,' the Witch King said, all thoughts of Athielle forgotten. He raised his voice in challenge, his words a metallic roar that carried over the din of battle. 'Come to me, Imrik! Come to me!'

The companies of the White Lions and Phoenix Guard surged forward into the Naggarothi below while Malekith's black dragon leapt up to meet the Phoenix King head-on. Maedrethnir plunged down from the clouds uttering a roaring challenge. The shock of the dragons' impact almost threw Imrik from the saddle-throne, the two titanic beasts slamming into each other in a ferocious welter of claws and fangs. As a blast of fire from the red dragon splashed across Sulekh, Malekith laughed; even dragonfire was no threat to one that had survived the flames of Asuryan.

The two beasts parted and circled, gashes pouring blood from both. Imrik levelled his lance for the next pass, aiming for Malekith's chest. The Witch King spoke a single word, the True Name of Khaine, and the baneful sorcery of his shield was unleashed. The blood-red symbol on its surface bombarded Imrik with the cacophony of war and the taste of blood filled his mouth as Khaine's gift roused the Phoenix King's rage.

Malekith was almost upon his foe as he shook his head to clear away the effects of the dread rune. Just as the Witch King was about to strike, Imrik swung his lance as Maedrethnir rolled to the right, the weapon's shining tip scoring a wound across the flank of the black dragon as she passed by overhead.

The black dragon turned swiftly, almost catching Maedrethnir's tail in her jaw. The dragon dipped in the air to avoid the attack, exposing Imrik to Sulekh's raking claws. He turned and brought up his shield just in time, claws as hard as diamond ripping across its surface as protective energies blazed.

Gliding towards the ground, the two dragons closed again,

snarling and roaring. Fire sprang from Malekith's sword, surrounding Imrik with crackling intensity. The enchantments of his armour protected the Phoenix King from harm, the blue flames passing around him harmlessly. Maedrethnir grappled with the black dragon, their long necks swaying as each sought to sink fangs into the other. Claws raked back and forth, sending scales and blood spilling to the ground.

Bucking and twisting, the dragons descended, locked together by jaw and claw. Imrik let his lance fall from his grasp and pulled free Lathrain, *just as the Witch King lashed out with* Avanuir. *The two swords met with an explosion of lightning and blue fire. The shock threw back Imrik's arm and Malekith struck again, amazed when his foe managed a last-moment parry, turning aside Malekith's blade as it screamed towards the Phoenix King's head.*

The dragons gave no thought to their riders as they savaged each other. Imrik was tossed left and right as Maedrethnir struggled with his foe, wings flapping and tail whipping. Malekith clung to his golden reins with his shield hand, steam and smoke rising from his armour.

The gaze of the Phoenix King met the eyes of the Witch King. Malekith poured forth his scorn in the form of a blood-curse, his eyes locked to the pale gaze of the Caledorian usurper. The Sapherian charms hanging on Imrik's armour glowed as they warded away the Witch King's sorcery. Again Imrik turned aside a stroke from Avanuir *as the two dragons came close enough for Malekith to strike.*

The battle continued to rage around them. In their frenzy, the dragons trampled over friend and foe without distinction, Khainites and Ellyrians, White Lions and Naggarothi clawed and trampled by the two behemoths.

Imrik kept his focus on the Witch King, seeking an opening to strike. When the black dragon reeled back from an attack from Maedrethnir, the Phoenix King seized his opportunity. His sword cut down into the Witch King's shoulder, biting deep with a scream of tearing metal. Malekith felt the sorcery of his armour exploding from his wounded limb, snaking up the sword that bit into his flesh.

Maedrethnir gave a pained howl as the black dragon's claws found purchase around his neck. Jaw snapping, Imrik's mount seized hold of his enemy's wing, biting through bone and sinew until the black dragon released its grip in a spasm of pain. Blood was gushing from Maedrethnir's neck. The red dragon stumbled back leaving a stream of crimson on the rucked earth.

As the Witch King wrenched on the chain of the black dragon's reins, the beast lunged at Imrik. Her jaws closed around his arm, teeth cracking against the ensorcelled ithilmar. Lathrain *tumbled from his grasp. The straps of the Phoenix King's harness parted as the black dragon shook her head, dragging Imrik from the saddle-throne, casting him to the ground.*

Heaving in a gasping breath, Imrik pushed to his feet, seeking Lathrain. *He saw the glitter of metal in a tussock not far away and set towards it, hand outstretched.*

Malekith smashed Avanuir *into Imrik's back, launching him from the bloodied ground. The Phoenix King crashed down amidst the bodies of the slain Ellyrians, coming face-to-face with Finudel's dead visage.*

The black dragon struggled as Malekith tried to goad and steer her towards the fallen Phoenix King, eager to pursue Maedrethnir who had withdrawn, limping heavily, flanks scored with dozens of ragged gashes. The black dragon fared little better, her wings tattered, face and neck marked by claws and fangs.

The will of the Witch King prevailed and the dragon's head turned towards Imrik. Flapping ragged wings, Sulekh pounded forwards, jaws wide, dripping bloodied saliva.

Imrik looked up, fear written across his face as Sulekh's fangs reflected in the gems of his armour. Malekith laughed in triumph.

Victory had been so close that day. A single sword stroke away. By such margins had Malekith been thwarted on occasion, and history would have been so different but for the constant prickling of Morai-heg's twists of fate. Incompetence in the druchii ranks, infighting by the nobles and commanders, untimely storms, two Phoenix Kings committing suicide and the gods themselves had barred Malekith's path to ultimate victory.

Not today. Today there would be no intervention to spare Malekith's foes. He fixed this new Imrik with his dread gaze and lifted *Urithain*.

Cries of surprise and dismay sounded from the mountainsides as Imrik saluted with his lance and the two dragonriders turned towards Eagle Gate, the lord of Caledor following behind the Witch King of Naggaroth. In their wake came the gold and silver and red and blue scales of Caledorian mounts, but amongst them more ebon-hued beasts raised by the masters of Clar Karond and Karond Kar.

There was already fighting on the walls as Caledorian knights that had been part of the garrison revealed their true loyalty. Even as the dragons descended with claws and deadly breath the great portal of Eagle Gate's seventh wall was opening.

The druchii roar of glee was almost as thunderous as the cries of the dragons as Malekith's followers surged into the pass, intent on the doomed fortification.

ELEVEN

An Alliance of Necessity

'You have betrayed us all,' hissed Imrik as Teclis stepped aside to reveal his companion. Even though Malekith's avatar bore his original unmutilated form, his features were well known to the descendants of Caledor Dragontamer. 'You invite... that thing into the heart of my city?'

'Put down your weapon,' Malekith said calmly. He waved an incorporeal hand through one of the alabaster pillars that held up the domed roof of the private audience chamber. 'Even your ensorcelled blade will not harm this projection.'

Imrik pivoted, the point of his sword towards Teclis. 'This traitor is real enough for blood to be drawn.'

'Did you not receive my gift?' said Malekith, continuing to approach. 'I trust my ambassador was convincing in his entreaties.'

'The dragon eggs?' Imrik's sword arm wavered. 'I could not believe it was by your hand that they were returned.'

'This must be far harder for you than it is for me,' Malekith admitted in a conciliatory tone. 'I know that I have had many conflicts with your ancestors, starting with your namesake, the first Imrik *of Caledor, but I have never harboured any hatred for your king-dom or your people.'*

'So easily lies spill from your lips, kinslayer,' Imrik snarled. His attention moved back to Malekith, allowing Teclis to retreat sev-eral steps, content at the moment to allow the two elves to continue without interruption. 'You waged war upon Caledor as much as any other realm.'

'I resent the accusation,' said Malekith, genuinely offended by this claim. 'Never once did I send my armies into the mountains of the south. My agent, Hotek, was given explicit instructions never to cause direct injury to your forefathers or their realm.'

'You did not invade because you knew you would lose,' Imrik said boldly. He sheathed his sword and folded his arms, but Male-kith could already sense that the prince's indignation was now more by habit than deeply felt.

'I did not invade because I knew I would have to destroy Cal-edor to achieve victory.' Malekith's apparition shrugged. 'When I gain my rightful place as ruler of our people, the dragonlords will be the vanguard of my army. Only lesser kings would desire peasant woodsmen from Chrace as their personal guard when they could have the dragon princes of Caledor.'

Imrik's defiance wavered and his gaze slid to Teclis.

'You have told him of what we discussed before? Concerning the visitation of my ancestor?'

'I have not,' said Teclis. 'I wished Malekith to seek his own bar-gain with you, and that is why he is here.'

Imrik slumped into his chair, a gauntleted hand held to his fore-head for several moments. When he looked up his expression was pained, directed at the mage.

'There is no other way?'

Malekith answered before Teclis could reply. 'It takes a great leader to wage war, but it takes a greater leader still to forge peace, Imrik. None should claim to have greater grievance than I. Six thousand years I have borne the weight of my deeds without regret.' Malekith paused, suddenly aware of the emotion he was feeling. He had intended his words to be a salve to Imrik's pride but as the Witch King spoke, the truth of his claim choked his speech. 'Millions have died, but we have the chance to end that now. It is easy to cling to history, to be popular. It is far harder to be right.'

The thought that his heart's desire, his birthright, was so close to his grasp focused Malekith's thoughts, but it was with a surprisingly tired sword arm that he hewed his blade through the defenders of Eagle Gate while Seraphon gouged and slashed her way into their ranks.

Tower after tower tumbled under the assaults of the dragons while poisonous gas and dragonfire scoured the ramparts of life. Malekith's attacks were methodical, machine-like, and as he cut down a Tiranocii captain the Witch King wondered why he did not take more delight in the moment of victory.

He cast his gaze towards the dragon princes, where Imrik led the charge into a regiment of Ellyrians, though his lance seemed bereft of blood for the moment. Was the victory tainted by the Caledorians' betrayal? Did it somehow rob Malekith of the sense that it had been fought for and earned? Was it the deeper feeling that Imrik's alliance was driven by something other than loyalty, Malekith's unease fuelled by an inherent distrust of Teclis who had arranged the pact? Malekith had come too close to allow his future triumph to be built on such shallow foundations.

Or was it something even more fundamental that robbed the Witch King of joy at the very moment he overthrew the bulwark that had kept him at bay for so long? Perhaps a momentary acknowledgement that had he not bided his time a little longer, sought to woo the Caledorians and others more strongly, he might have legitimately succeeded Bel Shanaar?

But this Imrik was not the same as his forefather. He was

wrought of softer mettle, though he did not realise it. Caledor the First had never been prideful. Stubborn, taciturn and often ill-mannered, but ambition had never been a weakness to be exploited. The first Imrik had never wanted to rule. Already disenfranchised and distanced by the Phoenix King, ignored by Prince Tyrion, the current Caledorian ruler had been ripe for the turning.

He saw Imrik pause, his dragon alighting on the ruins of a gate tower less than a bowshot away. He was shouting directions to his warriors, calling off the attack as the defenders fled by the thousands along the pass to Ellyrion. Malus's forces were ill-placed for pursuit either into the mountains or towards Tiranoc, and the Caledorians bore up such knights and warriors of their own realm from the ruins of the gate, carrying them out of the path of the encroaching druchii.

Malekith hacked his way out of a press of defenders caught on a battlement, as content as Imrik to see his fellow elves escape. As much as he had wished them dead before the fortress had fallen, now Malekith viewed them as future subjects. When the Rhana Dandra engulfed the world he would need as many warriors as possible and the spear- and bow-armed militia of Ulthuan would make a fine first wave to absorb the venom of any Chaos attacks.

He directed Seraphon to land alongside the Caledorian prince, pulling tight on her chains before she lunged for the other dragon. Cowed, the black dragon hung her head and lapped at the puddles of blood on the wall.

Imrik turned in the saddle, his lance swinging towards Malekith's heart, but the Witch King kept his weapon lowered.

'Was that so difficult?' Malekith asked, waving *Urithain* towards the broken walls.

'The hardest thing I will ever do,' replied Imrik, the pain fresh in his eyes.

'I think not,' Malekith replied. 'Today is just the beginning. A battle, nothing more. Today was easy, a military objective to be achieved. Harder days will come.'

'How so?' said the Caledorian, shaking his head. 'What could be harder than slaying those I once called neighbour?'

'Meeting their families and asking them to follow you,' Malekith replied from experience.

As dusk fell Malekith waited in the uppermost chamber of one of the few towers that remained of Eagle Gate, and with him his new ally. Imrik was dressed in all his armour and finery, a resplendent figure of gold and rubies and jade surcoat, as bright and colourful as Malekith was dark and menacing, one the sunlight, the other the ember ready to spark into violent life. The expression of the Caledorian prince did not match his ensemble, sombre to the point of bitterness.

'Needless blood was shed today,' said the prince, pacing back and forth across the chamber. The room was sparsely furnished with desk, three chairs and a bookcase filled with tomes of watch rotations and the tower captain's journal. 'If I had made known my alliance with you before you attacked, the garrison would have surrendered if offered safe haven or retreat.'

'Perhaps,' said Malekith, 'but now your warriors have raised blade and lance against their kin, and the princes of Caledor have signed the pact with blood. The show of strength will also serve as an apt demonstration to the other kingdoms. Only by the strength of Caledor have I been thwarted before, and now that strength is mine to command.'

'*Mine* to command,' Imrik said sharply, stopping beside the desk. Malekith watched the prince's hand stray unconsciously to the hilt of his sword – the Witch King had allowed his ally to bear arms in his presence as a sign of trust and equality. The truth was that Imrik had nothing to gain and everything to lose if he tested himself against Malekith's battlecraft. 'We are your allies, not your subjects, Malekith.'

'Of course,' Malekith said softly, gesturing to the bottle of wine and two glasses set on the desk. 'I did not mean to imply otherwise.'

'Many a truth falls from slipped tongue,' said Imrik, regarding the Witch King with suspicion.

They stood in silence for a while longer, until Malekith realised that Imrik was not going to drink the wine.

'You think it poisoned?' Malekith said with a laugh. 'Tonight, so soon after sealing our common purpose?'

'History teaches that it is unwise to be a guest at your table,' said the prince. 'Bel Shanaar's shade would warn me to be cautious.'

'I would partake myself, but my... condition renders even the finest Cothique red a tasteless experience.'

'Why two glasses?'

'I am awaiting another guest.'

Silence descended again and Malekith moved to the window to look out over the two armies encamped in Eagle Pass. The druchii laughed harshly at their bonfires, singing victory songs as looted wine passed from lips to lips and bloodthirsty tales and exaggerated deeds of deadly prowess were swapped. Further towards the peaks the Caledorians camped in silence, the great shadows of their dragons dark against the rock, a few lanterns the only light to betray their presence.

Something caught Malekith's eye. It was a movement, or rather a lack of it, a space where there should have been something but was not. With mortal eyes he watched the patrols of the Naggarothi pacing around the limits of the camp, but with his magical sense, enhanced by the Circlet of Iron, he felt the twisting of the winds of magic, creating a swiftly-moving pocket, a void that passed between the sentries without notice.

The shadow that was not a shadow quickly negotiated the gates and ruins, coming to the foot of the tower unheralded. There was a flutter of shadow magic dispersing and a moment later a figure hooded and cloaked in grey appeared at the ruined door of the tower, stepping over the threshold before any other bore witness to the arrival.

'He is here,' said Malekith, turning back to Imrik.

The Caledorian prince looked towards the door, where a few moments later the cowled newcomer appeared. He threw back his hood to reveal an almost painfully thin face, gaunt to the point of wasted, eyes red-rimmed and bloodshot. A quivering hand removed a small phial from a pouch at his belt and the blue contents were quickly imbibed. The elf closed his eyes and breathed out a long sigh. When he opened his eyes again some colour and vigour had returned and his gaze was alert, flicking between Malekith and Imrik.

He cast the cloak over one of the chairs, revealing white robes beneath an outer mantle of twilight blue that seemed to contain pinpricks of star light that waxed and waned as the elf moved to the table and poured the wine into the two glasses. Magical sigils gleamed in the cloak of stars, dappling the floor with gold and red.

'Teclis,' said Imrik, instinctively taking the goblet of wine as it was handed to him by the mage. 'How? How are you here?'

'By great effort,' the High Loremaster replied. 'And I cannot remain long. I must be at my brother's camp by dusk two days hence.'

'He is so close at hand?' said Imrik, shocked. 'Two days' march from here?'

'Relax, Imrik, the steed of shadows bears me across Ulthuan faster than any mortal horse. Tyrion remains in Lothern,' the mage assured them. He took a long draught of wine and smiled. 'Events continue to pass as Lileath prophesied, and to each will come the allotted role. The gods will come again, in mortal form, and by their presence we will be delivered from Chaos and the Rhana Dandra.'

'The more you speak,' the Witch King said, 'the more I am convinced that you have taken council with my mother, who imagines that she is Hekarti reborn.'

'And perhaps she is,' Teclis replied. 'Perhaps she always was. Is it so hard to believe? We know Isha and Kurnous dwell in Athel Loren.'

'You hold that our gods walk amongst us?'

'Not all of them, but enough. The cycle of history has a momentum that overwhelms even kings. Willingly or not, we will repeat that cycle in mimicry of those who came before. What is the Rhana Dandra, if not the echo of our gods' last battle?'

'I am Nethu,' said Imrik, referring to the Keeper of the Last Door, Guardian of the Underworld, his whispered words spoken in sudden awareness of a hidden truth. 'I have opened a door that should have remained closed.'

'Say rather that you have opened the path to the flame,' Teclis corrected. 'But yes, the comparison is otherwise apt. Nethu's actions, though a betrayal, prevented disaster, and so have yours.'

Malekith considered this, alarmed by what he saw as Teclis's intent. He would no more be the vessel for a god than he would a daemon, and certainly not one whose mantle he had so casually assumed for purely political gain. When he spoke, his discontent was plain to hear. 'It is your contention, then, that I am to play the role of Khaine?'

'No, your path is not Khaine's. You have worn his persona as a cloak only when it has suited you.'

'Then whom?' the Witch King demanded, casting through the candidates in his mind: Malus, Hellebron, Tullaris? 'Who else is fit to bear the mantle of the Destroyer?'

'Khaine is not yet come. You know the stories – though he began the war of the gods, it was long before he showed his hand. At present he slumbers trifurcated, trapped in prisons of blood, soul and steel. Only when these three are one will he awaken. Your path lies elsewhere.'

Malekith's reply was forestalled by a screech from outside, the shriek of a harpy. He glanced at the window and saw the creature flash past, perhaps chasing a bat or night bird.

'There is only one god that can aid us,' Teclis said. 'Your father called upon him and laid down his life in supplication to protect his people.'

'Asuryan?' Malekith's laugh was like rusted blades on stone. 'The one that made me into this... this abomination?'

'The all-seeing king of the gods, patron of Aenarion,' Teclis continued quietly.

'My father would have better spent his time taking up the Widowmaker first than entreating the all-knowing, patronising Asuryan! If he had, perhaps he would not have seen his wife die.'

'And you would not exist,' Teclis replied with a sly chuckle. 'Is that what you really want? No. You must do as your father did. The other kings were frauds, you know this. Protected by the spells of their mages they lived, but you must die to be reborn.'

'Impossible!' Malekith's shout echoed long in the bare-walled chamber. The mention of stepping back into the flames caused a pain deep inside Malekith to flare into life. Teclis was right in one respect – death would be certain.

'No, it is the truth.' Teclis's voice was still calm. 'That is why almost all succumbed to madness. It was the price of that betrayal.'

'Leave, both of you!' Malekith snarled. 'Before I forget the services you have rendered, and let my Black Guard amuse themselves with your bones.'

Imrik looked as though he would argue but thought better of it, slamming his goblet on the table before departing with clenched fists and hunched shoulders. Teclis waited a while longer, eyeing Malekith carefully. They did not speak a further word but the look they shared conveyed a whole conversation – warning and counter-warning that they were both unleashing forces on the edge of comprehension and that the other would do well to remember the follies of the past.

Confident that his purpose was understood, Teclis wrapped himself about with his cloak and drew in the power of Ulgu to shield himself from perception, becoming one with the Wind of Shadow.

TWELVE

Servants to a Higher Cause

Eagle Pass made for a strange scene the following morning. Malekith had sent command to his minions that no hostile act was to be perpetrated against any son or daughter of Caledor and for the dark hours that decree had been obeyed, doubtless in no small part to Kouran's vigilance and the patrols of the Black Guard. Overnight the druchii and Caledorians had made their camps, the former amongst the ruins of the stronghold that had thwarted them so often, the latter on the higher slopes of the mountains. Dusk had swiftly laid a dark cloak over the aftermath of the day before, but as the dragons basked in the rising sun the full horror of what had occurred was laid bare.

Not a tower stood, and not a stretch of wall for more than thirty paces. The white stones were blackened, drifts of ash made of the bodies of the defenders piled high by the prevailing wind. Amongst the charred remnants were contorted, skin-sloughed remains of those that had succumbed to the breath of the black dragons. In other places the fortifications were coated with dried blood, splashed across the pale stones like the creation of some insane artist dedicated to Khaine's labours. Harpies, hydras and black dragons scavenged on the piles of corpses, gulping down the carrion feast as if there were not enough to last the day, though the piles of bodies were in places dozens deep.

Malekith had not slept – it was rare that his tormented dreams granted him any peace – and had paced the ruins trying to feel a sense of accomplishment. It had eluded him throughout the slaughter and it eluded him still as the magnitude of the carnage was revealed. He considered his words to Imrik the day before and realised that the Caledorian's experience was far different from his own. For Malekith, the choice to do what was right, what was needed, had been no less difficult, but the moment of action had been far less public.

It was the day before Bel Shanaar and Malekith were due to leave Tor Anroc for the council upon the Isle of Flame when the Phoenix King commanded the prince of Nagarythe to attend him in his throne room. Malekith walked quickly to the audience chamber, his instinct for intrigue curious as to what the Phoenix King had to say.

'I have been thinking deep upon your words,' Bel Shanaar proclaimed.

'I am pleased to hear that,' said Malekith. 'May I ask what the nature of your thoughts has been?'

'I will put your idea to the princes,' said Bel Shanaar. 'A single army drawn from all kingdoms will prosecute this war against the vile cults.'

'I am glad that you agree with my reasoning,' said Malekith, wondering why Bel Shanaar had brought him here to tell him what he already knew.

'I have also been giving much thought to who is best qualified to lead this army,' said Bel Shanaar, and Malekith's heart skipped a beat in anticipation.

'I would be honoured,' said the prince of Nagarythe.

Bel Shanaar opened his mouth to say something but then closed it again, a confused frown upon his brow.

'You misunderstand me,' the Phoenix King then said. 'I will nominate Imrik to be my chosen general.'

Malekith stood in stunned silence, left speechless by the Phoenix King's announcement.

'Imrik?' he said eventually.

'Why not?' said Bel Shanaar. 'He is a fine general, and Caledor is the most stable of all the realms at the current time. He is well-respected amongst the other princes. Yes, he will make a good choice.'

'And why do you tell me this?' snapped Malekith. 'Perhaps you seek to mock me!'

'Mock you?' said Bel Shanaar, taken aback. 'I am telling you this so that you will speak in favour of my decision. I know that you have much influence and your word will lend great weight to Imrik's authority.'

'You would raise up the grandson of Caledor over the son of Aenarion?' said Malekith. 'Have I not forged new kingdoms across the world at the head of armies? If not my bloodline, then my achievements must qualify me above all others.'

'I am sorry that you feel this way, Malekith,' said Bel Shanaar, unabashed. 'The council will endorse my choice, you would do well to align yourself with me.'

At this, Malekith's frayed temper snapped utterly.

'Align myself to you?' he snarled. 'The hunter does not align himself to his hound! The master does not align himself to his servant!'

'Choose your next words carefully, Malekith!' warned the Phoenix King. 'Remember who it is that you address!'

The Naggarothi prince mastered his anger, biting back further retorts.

'I trust that my protest has been recognised,' he said with effort. 'I urge you to reconsider your decision.'

'You are free to speak your mind at the council,' said Bel Shanaar.

'It is your right to argue against Imrik, and to put forward your-self as candidate. We shall let the princes decide.'

Malekith said nothing more, but bowed stiffly and left, silently seething.

In the corridor around the corner from Bel Shanaar's main chambers Palthrain stood with a tray upon which were stood a silver ewer and goblet, and a plate of cured meats and bread. Palthrain passed him the tray but Malekith's hands were shaking and the chamberlain quickly retrieved it.

Malekith took deep breaths, trying to calm himself as if summoning the power for a difficult spell. Ignoring the purposefully blank expression of Palthrain, the prince took the tray once more, now in control of his body.

'Are you sure this will work?' demanded Malekith. 'It must be final!'

'It is used in certain practices of the Khainites, to numb the senses,' Palthrain replied. 'In small doses it will render its victim incapable for several hours. With the amount I have put in the wine, it will be fatal. At first he will be paralysed. Then his breathing will become difficult as his lungs freeze, and then he will fall into a coma and pass away.'

'No pain?' said Malekith.

'Not that I am aware of, highness,' said Palthrain.

'What a pity,' said Malekith.

The Naggarothi prince walked down the passageway to Bel Shanaar's chambers, forcing himself to stride slowly so as not to garner attention. He knocked at the door and waited for Bel Shanaar's call for him to enter.

The Phoenix King was sitting at a writing desk, no doubt penning corrections to his speech for the council.

'Malekith?' he said, startled.

'Forgive the intrusion, your majesty,' said Malekith with a low bow. He stepped across the room and placed the tray on the desk.

'Why are you here?' asked Bel Shanaar. 'Where's Palthrain?'

'I apologise for waylaying him, majesty,' said Malekith. 'I wished to bring you your wine as a peace offering.'

'Peace offering?'

'I wholeheartedly wish to offer my apologies,' replied Malekith, pouring the poisoned wine into the goblet. 'I spoke out of misplaced anger earlier, and I caused great offence. My anger is not with you, though it might have seemed that way. I have endeavoured to earn your trust and to be a loyal subject, and it is my failings not yours that have led you to choose Imrik. I will be happy to support your choice.'

The prince passed the cup to Bel Shanaar, his face a mask of politeness. The Phoenix King frowned and for a moment Malekith feared that he suspected something. The Phoenix King took the goblet however, and placed it on the desk.

'Your apology is accepted,' said Bel Shanaar. 'I do trust you, my friend, but you have personal concerns that far outweigh any duty to me. I choose Imrik not just on ability, but on the fact that I would have you address the problems of your kingdom without distraction. I would have you direct your energies solely to restoring your rule, not pandering to the whims of other kingdoms.'

The goblet remained on the desk.

'Your consideration heartens me greatly,' said Malekith, keeping his eyes fixed firmly upon the Phoenix King lest he dart a betraying glance towards the wine.

'You will offer your support in the council?' Bel Shanaar asked, finally lifting the cup to his lips and taking a mouthful of the wine.

It was not enough for the poison to work and the prince silently willed Bel Shanaar to drink more.

'When the debate rages, none will argue harder than I,' said Malekith with a smile.

Bel Shanaar nodded and took another sip of wine.

'If that is all, then I wish you a fair evening and look forward to sailing with you in the morning,' said Bel Shanaar with a polite nod.

Malekith stood there watching for some sign of the poison's effect.

'What are you staring at?' asked the Phoenix King.

'Is the wine not to your satisfaction?' said the prince, taking a step closer.

'I am not thirsty,' said Bel Shanaar, placing the goblet back on the desk.

Malekith twisted and picked up the goblet and sniffed it.

'It is very fine wine, majesty,' he said.

'I am sure it is, Malekith,' said Bel Shanaar, pursing his lips. His voice became more insistent. 'However, I feel a little sleepy all of a sudden. I shall retire for the night and see you in the morning.'

Stifling a frustrated shout, Malekith lunged forwards and seized Bel Shanaar by the throat. The Phoenix King's eyes widened with terror as Malekith forced open Bel Shanaar's mouth and emptied in the contents of the goblet. The goblet tumbled from the prince's fingertips and spilt a cascade of red droplets over the white boards of the floor.

Clamping one hand over the Phoenix King's nose and mouth and dragging his head back by his hair, Malekith choked the king until he swallowed the deadly draught. He then released his grip and stepped back to watch his future unfold.

'What have you–' panted Bel Shanaar, clawing at his throat and chest.

Malekith lifted the parchment from the desk. As he had suspected, it was a draft of the Phoenix King's speech for the council. Thinking it better that no evidence of Bel Shanaar's support for Imrik was found, he crossed the room and tossed it into the fire burning in the grate. Turning, he saw that there was still life in Bel Shanaar's bulging eyes.

Malekith padded forwards until he was very close, and bent towards the dying elf's ear.

'You brought this upon yourself,' the prince hissed.

With a last gurgle, Bel Shanaar died, his face purple, his tongue lolling from his mouth. Malekith stood for a while, absent-mindedly looking at the contorted face, not quite believing that it was almost over.

'Well, I have to leave you now,' he said at last, affectionately patting the Phoenix King's head. 'I have a throne to claim.'

Kings and princes, all had thought to rob Malekith of his rightful inheritance and they all had been sent to the underworld of Mirai for their efforts. Malekith had some respect for Imrik for the simple fact that he had been able to break the cycle of history, realising that his future was beside the true Phoenix King, not against him. If only his forefathers had been so astute the carnage and waste of elven lives would have been avoided.

Malekith turned away from the evidence of the battle, wondering why he was so preoccupied with thoughts of death and the countless lives sacrificed in endless battle for possession of Ulthuan. It was a recent phenomenon, this train of thought, having grown in frequency in the couple of centuries since his defeat at Finuval Plain and his escape through the Realm of Chaos. Perhaps back then he had sensed the rising tide of Chaos that had engulfed the world and it had nagged at his thoughts.

It was strange also that while he did not regret a single druchii life lost in service to his claim, Malekith found it harder to contemplate the losses of the asur. His own folk were driven by greed and revenge, base desires that hung on the cloak of Malekith's quest for justice. In contrast, the asur's stubbornness had been a constant vexation to him, their blindness to his natural right and authority an affront, but all the same his hatred for their weak society and hand-wringing rulers had been tempered by respect for their tenacity in defending such a flawed civilisation.

A shadow passed over him and he looked up to see Imrik descending on his dragon. The prince left his monstrous steed on the broken ground between walls three and four and crossed the bloodied rubble with long strides.

'The dead should not be left to suffer such outrage,' the prince snapped, waving a hand towards the beasts devouring the corpse banquet.

'What would you have me do?' Malekith asked, knowing that it was too early in the alliance to simply dismiss the prince's squeamish concerns. 'Their souls are in Mirai now and the mortal remains behind make good fodder for my beasts.'

'Bury them, or at least make a pyre to mark their sacrifice.'

'An interesting idea,' replied Malekith, warming to the notion. 'The stones of Eagle Gate would make a fitting mausoleum and monument to those who died here. It is a shame that we do not have time to tarry to raise such an edifice. A pyre perhaps would serve better, and its pall would mask our advance from prying eyes.'

To make his point, Malekith gestured towards the cloudy skies, where the silhouettes of great eagles and the glitter of phoenix wings betrayed the avian allies of their foes. Imrik glanced up and shrugged.

'My dragons will teach them to be more circumspect.'

'Our dragons would be better employed securing the eastern end of the pass, until my vanguard arrives.'

Imrik considered this, not looking at Malekith, obviously caught between the logic of the Witch King's declaration and a desire to defy his will brought about by long centuries of stubborn defiance. No doubt the need to feel on an equal footing with his former foe also weighed on the Caledorian's thoughts. In the end Imrik's military sense prevailed and he nodded.

'The Ellyrians will desire to make a counter-attack. We shall dissuade them,' he said. 'Who is to lead your vanguard? It will be a risky position, for surely Tyrion will bring his whole force to bear upon our advance.'

'Riskier still considering I have no intention of following them along Eagle Pass.' Malekith laughed at Imrik's confusion. 'Your people are driven constantly by history, yet forever miss its lessons. I would no more march directly into confrontation with Tyrion than I would lay aside my shield in battle. I know that his bravery cannot be questioned and his sword arm is strong, but let us see whether this upstart who claims the blood of Aenarion can wield an army with the same skill as his blade.'

'You will march north, and attack Chrace?'

'*We* will, Imrik,' corrected Malekith.

Imrik said nothing, fingers toying with the hilt of his sword.

'Speak, or depart, but cease your vacillation,' said Malekith.

'When this is done, when we have won this war and you rule Ulthuan, what then?'

'Grief, strife and war,' Malekith answered plainly. 'I do not promise to end suffering, but under my leadership we will prevail against the adversity that is to come. I offer nothing but victory, Imrik, bear no misunderstanding in this matter. Should Tyrion be victorious, the elven race is doomed.'

'Perhaps it is simply the sealing of a doom that began long ago, and we should resist it no longer.'

'Feel free to end your own life if you desire,' said Malekith, turning away. 'Just leave me your dragons.'

THIRTEEN

The Tyrant Shamed

'My king.'

Kouran's quiet warning drew Malekith's attention away from the map he was studying with his generals. They stood just out of the shadow cast by the toppled fourth wall, marshalling the columns of druchii moving through the fortress while harpies nearby picked at the corpses buried in the rubble. The captain's gaze guided Malekith's eye to a figure standing beneath the arch of a gatehouse a short distance away.

Malus Darkblade was a forlorn figure, almost wraith-like in his pale nakedness. All that protected his dignity was the tattered remnant of a cloak, still smeared with the blood of the corpse it had been torn from. Around his neck hung his signature heavy talisman and in his hand he still bore the warpsword of Khaine, but save for these accoutrements his battlegear had disappeared.

He pushed himself away from the stone and tottered forwards a few steps, drawing the attention of the other druchii nearby. The whispers began a heartbeat later, subtle at first, but Naggarothi had never been known to hide their cruel humour and soon their taunts and jibes followed Darkblade across the ruin.

His bared flesh was marred with small cuts and bruises amongst older scars, and in places there were puncture wounds that looked as though his bones had split the skin, though he moved without any sign of physical pain. A particularly dramatic slash of lacerated flesh stretched from navel to throat, white in the morning light. Malus's eyes seemed darker and more sunken than usual, blood-shot and rimmed with the shadow of fatigue. Not all the blood was his; his skin was marked with bloody handprints and other smears.

Ignoring the sharp stones underfoot, Malus came directly towards Malekith. The Witch King eyed the warpsword in Darkblade's hand, the enchantment within the blade a blaze of colour in his magical sight. Numbered amongst the few weapons that could easily penetrate the armour of midnight, the warpsword was one of the reasons Malus had risen to the top of Hag Graef in a comparatively short time. Its true origins remained a mystery to Malekith, but knowing that Malus possessed such a weapon had sometimes been a source of some concern to the Witch King. He doubted whether Malus would ever dare test the magical sword against *Urithain*, but there was a crazed look in the Tyrant's eye as he approached and Kouran moved forward, *Crimson Death* at the ready.

Malus stopped about two dozen paces away. He seemed oblivious to the sneering remarks of the other elves at hand, gaze focused on Malekith. He swayed slightly, one eye twitching. The Witch King saw the Tyrant flexing his fingers on the grip of the warpsword and moved his hand to the hilt of *Urithain*.

'You are alive,' said Malekith, looking the haggard figure up and down. 'Mostly.'

A degree of focus returned to Malus's gaze and a frown creased his brow. He turned to glare at the other elves that were drifting closer to witness what transpired next, before concentrating on the Witch King.

'Mostly alive, yes, your majesty,' he said, bowing with a flourish.

He lowered to one knee, the point of the warpsword in the ground, head bowed against the hiltstone. 'My apologies, Lord Malekith, for my tardiness in reporting for my next commands. I was otherwise engaged during yesterday's triumph and could not share your victory.'

Malekith paced around Malus, who kept his eye on the Witch King for as long as possible until he was behind the Tyrant of Hag Graef. The king stopped behind Darkblade, noting the fresh cuts upon his back.

'Tell me, dear Malus, what matters of such import took your insightful counsel from my ears last night?'

Darkblade did not reply immediately, his head turning left and right in an effort to catch a glimpse of his tormentor. He sighed, long and languorous. 'Alas, our revered king, I was so caught up by Khaine's thirst that I pursued the enemy far beyond reasonable strategy and have only this dawn returned.'

'You were overwhelmed with bloodlust?' said Malekith, remaining behind Malus.

'That is true, your majesty.'

'And you pursued the enemy so vigorously that it took the night to return?'

'Apparently so, your majesty.'

'And which enemies did you pursue?'

'The traitors that held Eagle Gate, your majesty.'

'Be more specific, dear Malus. Which of the traitorous enemy did you pursue?'

'I believe they were Ellyrians, your majesty,' interjected Drusala, emerging from the crowd to Malekith's left. Malus stood up and faced the sorceress, quickly hiding a moment of confusion behind an indifferent mask.

'That would make sense,' said the Darkblade. 'They fled towards Ellyrion.'

'And so furious was your pursuit that you abandoned your cold one? Spite, isn't it?' asked the Witch King.

'In the melee before the gate was breached I was pulled from my saddle,' admitted Malus. 'I lost my mount and hope that one of my knights has recovered him and he awaits me in the camp of my household.'

'And your clothes and armour?'

Malus looked down at himself, as if realising his nudity for the first time. His gaze moved back to the Witch King and then to Drusala, and then around the gathered crowd who awaited his reply with unconcealed smirks and leering.

'Discarded, your majesty.' Malus looked at Malekith directly, daring him to gainsay a word of his testimony. Malekith had no idea what had happened and it was clear that only torture would loosen the Tyrant's lips.

'Discarded? In battle?'

'Forgive me, your majesty, for I was foolish and to heighten my battle prowess I imbibed some of the witch brew of Khaine before the fighting began. Just a mouthful, of course. Just enough to strengthen my sword arm for a long day of bloodletting. I did not realise how delayed its effects might be and in my Khaine-blessed rage to get at the Ellyrians I stripped off my armour which had been weighing me down, suffering as it had much damage during the fray so that many straps and buckles were broken and its efficacy much reduced.'

This was greeted with harsh laughter from much of the crowd, and shouts of derision. Malus rounded on the watchers with the warpsword raised. Kouran was about to take another step but Malekith gestured for him to remain where he was.

'You laugh, who allowed the enemies of our king to retreat without harassment?' Malus railed, spittle flying in his false indignity, eyes wide. 'You would let them rally and fight again, their resistance, their existence, an affront to our ruler? Smirk if you dare, those that were less than worthy.'

Malekith silenced the audience with a gesture and Malus's attention returned to him.

'You threw off your wargear so that you could pursue the enemy with more speed?' The Witch King shook his head, trying to decide if he was entertained or outraged by such an obvious lie.

'Yes, your majesty, it is just as you say. He fell to his knee once more, a fist clasped to his chest. 'I feel so ashamed, but there was nothing I could do to stop myself. I understand now why Hellebron and her bloody sisters wear so little.'

It took all of Malekith's will to quench the laugh that rose from his gut. He knew that he should have Kouran take off the treacherous dog's head there and then, but if lying was to be a capital crime under his rule he would have no subjects left. It was hard to see to what benefit Malus's current display was turned. There was no advantage to Malus being absent for the night – all of the most powerful druchii had been in camp with Malekith, so no collusion had been possible. There was a chance that he had conspired with agents of the asur, perhaps seeking to make a common foe of Malekith, but Malus was despised across Ulthuan almost as much as his king. Tyrion did not have the benefit of Imrik's flexible morality and Malekith had ensured there would be no politicking from the Phoenix King, Finubar.

'You vouch for this account?' he snapped, turning his wrath on Drusala. She met his infernal gaze without flinching, her face set in an expression of sincere attention. Her part in this worried Malekith more. She was Morathi's creature, no doubt, and if the queen was truly breaking bonds with Malekith the Tyrant of Hag Graef would make a well-positioned ally. Though the host of Hag Graef had been badly mauled in the three assaults upon Eagle Gate, if they were to combine with the army of Ghrond Malekith's resources would be outmatched, in the short term at least. 'How can you be so certain of friend Malus's movements?'

'He perhaps does not remember it, but he came to me last night, in a battle-fever, confessing what had happened and seeking my advice.' Malekith could not see Malus's face to see any reaction this stirred. Drusala approached, holding a bloodstained cloth in outstretched hands. 'He gave this to me, asking if I would present it on his behalf. Malus thought it terribly important, although I must confess my ignorance.'

She let the wind unfurl what she held, revealing a torn banner of light blue and white, with a prancing horse in gold thread stained with blood. The remains of a device of spread wings in silver could be seen beneath the grime.

'The banner of Eagle Gate,' said Kouran, stepping up to take the trophy from Drusala. He looked at Malus. 'The Ellyrians tried to escape with it?'

Malus tried not to look surprised, and failed miserably. He addressed his answer to Malekith. 'I have no reason to doubt the lady of Ghrond's account, your majesty, though my recollection of events before the sun rose this morning are... hazy.'

It was impossible to believe that they were telling the truth, but the threadbare nature of the story being woven by Drusala and Malus was enough for Malekith to believe it had not been prefabricated. They were extemporising, to what end Malekith did not know, but there was no sign of former conspiracy. Malekith was hardened to the fact that most of his subjects that did not hate him lusted after his position, and to consider every scheme a direct and immediate threat would have turned him into a paranoid lunatic many millennia ago. It also meant that the druchii were very adept at hiding their lies, so the obvious subterfuge confused him.

He gestured for Kouran to join him.

'What do you wish to do with these liars, my king?' asked the captain.

'You think their story lacks merit?'

'Barely a word they have spoken is truth,' Kouran answered with a shake of the head, 'but I can offer no proof to discount their version of events. Malus was pulled from Spite during the battle and then disappeared, that much I witnessed myself. He is not a coward, so I do not think he fled the fighting. What happened next, only Malus can tell us. Shall I summon your torturers?'

'I think not,' said Malekith. 'The day is too fraught to make any bold moves. Malus is always scheming about something, and I am sure Drusala has her own agenda, but it serves no purpose to create turbulence on the day after our greatest victory. I have allies now,' he waved a hand towards the dragons on the peaks, 'and should Imrik sense disquiet in my camp, the hint of division between my armies, I think he would reconsider which side he has taken.'

'We could slay them, my king, just to be sure,' suggested Kouran, running the fingers of his right hand along the flat of his halberd's blade. 'No mess, just a swift death.'

'Malus and Drusala both know that I need their warriors if I am to capitalise on the surprise of Imrik's turning and our victory here. I have a far better plan.'

'Friend Malus,' said Malekith, turning back to the Tyrant, motioning for him to stand. 'I must admonish you for your tardiness and appearance. It smacks of disrespect to turn up late to my council wearing nothing but an asur shroud.' Malus clenched his jaw and the tip of the warpsword in his hand rose a little, like the tail of a scorpion moving before the strike. 'Let the humiliation you have felt coming to kneel before me and my subjects be a lesson to keep good manner about you at all times. As for the reasons for your dishevelled look and late coming, I am impressed by your persistence. It is that sort of attitude that will be required to defeat the Ellyrians.'

'The Ellyrians, your majesty? What of them?'

'Fast, mounted, never staying in the same place. An elusive foe, but no match for one with your stubbornness, am I right?'

'No match at all, your majesty,' said Malus, taken aback. 'I will bring the Ellyrians to battle and crush them.'

'Very good, Malus,' said Malekith. 'I am sure you require to make preparations. Your army shall be the vanguard – have them take supplies for the march to Ellyrion and then lead them east.'

Malus said nothing for several heartbeats, eyes flicking between the king and Kouran, and then to the crowd, who were starting to disperse. His eyes narrowed and nostrils flared, but he simply accepted the command with a deep bow.

'And Malus,' said the Witch King as the seething Darkblade turned to leave, 'try to keep your armour on next time.'

FOURTEEN

Chracian War

Of the ten kingdoms, Malekith hated Chrace the most. In his mortal years he had found it a joyless, backward region ruled by peasant-princes and ignorance. When he had sought to claim Ulthuan's throne it had been Chracian hunters that had saved Imrik from Morathi's assassins – ever after honoured as the White Lions of the king's bodyguard – and it had been the Chracians that had stubbornly refused to bow to Malekith's rule despite every invasion and calamity he had set upon them. In short, the Chracians were far too stupid to realise when they were beaten, scrapping to the last breath for a mountainous wilderness that had nothing to recommend itself except for a certain savage beauty.

The rain rattled from Sulekh's scales and hissed into steam where it hit the Witch King's armour. Rivers cascaded down the mountain slopes, swelled to bursting from the spring deluge. The low clouds clung to the peaks like a shroud, swathing the pass in a thick haze. Malekith's army picked their way down a slope strewn with boulders and fallen trees, a winding column of black that disappeared into the grey mist.

Closing his eyes, the Witch King felt the bubbling winds of magic washing over the Annulii. With the circlet, he could see every slender strand, the smallest ebb and eddy of mystical energy. He searched for disturbances hidden to normal eyes, seeking the telltale swell and whirl of living things. Giant eagles nested in the heights of the peaks; mountain goats bounded up the slopes in large herds, gorging themselves on grass revealed by the recent thaw; a bear ambled from its cave seeking food; the trees were delicate slivers of life burrowing deep into the soil.

There was something else.

Further down the pass, Malekith detected the glow of fire, drawing the magic of flames to it. A camp. Several camps. Around them he spied the silvery flicker of elven spirits. He turned to the cluster of messengers who sat astride their black horses a short distance from Sulekh, their blinkered mounts trembling with fear.

'Warn the vanguard,' said Malekith. 'There are Chracians on the northern slope, where a bridge crosses a river. It may be an ambush.'

One of the riders nodded and headed off down the mountainside, his steed galloping hard, grateful to be heading away from the presence of the Witch King and his dragon.

It is almost an insult, thought Malekith. Did Caledor rate him so lowly that he thought the Witch King would be caught by such a simple trap? His armour creaking as Malekith turned his unnatural gaze back towards the east, where his army was still crossing the last shoulder of the mountain. It would be noon before they were all in the valley. It did not matter; he was in no hurry. He wanted his enemies to know where he was.

Malekith looked up, rain hammering into the mask of his helm. Droplets danced and spat on the hot armour. He tried to remember when he had last drunk water. He could not. The fires that burned inside him left him with a ravening thirst but he could not quench it. It was the same with food. Not a morsel had passed his lips since he had been sealed inside the armoured suit. Sorcery alone kept him alive, the magic sustained by the sacrifices bound within the plates of his artificial skin. It was sad in some ways, liberating in others. He could taste nothing but the ash of his own near destruction, but he could dimly recollect the sweetness of honey, the richness of wine.

Simple pleasures, taken from him by cowards and traitors. The jealous priests of Asuryan had cursed the flames so that they would not accept him. Yet their trickery had not succeeded. He had emerged from the flames with the blessing of the lord of gods. He would throw them into the fires they had tainted with their subterfuge and let them know what their god's judgement felt like.

The ground trembled. Malekith sensed it through a shift in the magical winds, a turbulence that flowed south along the vortex. His ravaged ears could hear little over the constant crackling of the flames, but the Witch King's magical sense was far more accurate. Boulders and logs tumbled down the slope from the camps by the bridge. He heard the screams of the warriors who had crossed over to attack the Chracians and felt their bodies crushed by the avalanche unleashed by the mountain-dwellers. The spirit of every dying elf flickered briefly, a pinprick of darkness that was swallowed up by the ever-shifting tides of magic.

There were more shouts and sounds of fighting. A column of march was no formation for battle and the vanguard had allowed itself to be surrounded, despite Malekith's warning. With a growl, he jerked Sulekh's iron reins and the monstrous beast launched herself from the rock, plunging down the valley in a swirl of cloud.

Nearing the bottom of the pass, Malekith saw several hundred Chracians fighting against his warriors. He saw the slew of debris blocking the bridge over which the vanguard had crossed, cutting off any reinforcement. Naggarothi warriors called for axes and bars to be brought forward so that the blockage could be cleared.

'Stand back!' Malekith roared as Sulekh landed on the near side of the river, clawed feet sinking into the soft mud of the bank.

He waited while the startled soldiers hurried back from the bridge. When they were clear of the crossing, the Witch King extended a hand, drawing in the threads of magic that invisibly wound down the valley, crushing them into pure energy with his force of will. He felt the icy touch of the circlet in his mind as he shaped the magic, a bolt of forking lightning leaping from his fist to smash into the boulders and hewn tree trunks. Stone and wood splinters exploded upwards, cutting arcs through the mist before drifting down on to the foaming water of the river.

'Is it safe?' one of the captains called out. The bridge had taken some of the blast, its stone wall collapsed for half its length on one side.

'That is not my concern,' said Malekith. 'Follow me!'

Sulekh leapt across the river and with a single flap of her vast wings carried Malekith up the far slope to where his embattled soldiers were encircled by axe- and spear-wielding Chracians. Some wore the prized white lion pelts for which their kingdom was famed, the furs heavy with moisture from the rain.

As soon as they saw Malekith approaching, the Chracians scattered, breaking off their attack to sprint back into the woods. Not all reached the safety of the eaves; Malekith unsheathed his sword, Avanuir, and launched a flurry of fiery blue bolts at the retreating warriors, slaying a handful with each detonation. The Witch King drew in more magic and with a shout unleashed it in a broad wave. Where it struck, the trees exploded into black flame, the fire quickly raging up the slope, engulfing even more of the Chracian hunters. Sap exploded and leaves turned to ash as the wave of fire continued along the mountainside, engulfing the tents and wagons of the Chracian camps.

Sustaining the magical fire took all of Malekith's concentration; as he weaved his metal-clad hand back and forth the fires spread further and further, the heat of the flames dissipating the mist as they engulfed the mountainside. The surge of dark energy flowing through him resonated with the runes of his armour, igniting dead nerve-endings, sending a shiver across the metal plates as if it were his skin.

With an effort, the Witch King cut off the flow of dark magic, pulling himself back from the brink of intoxication. The mystical flames guttered and died, revealing blackened stumps and bones littered across the mountain. The clatter of armour attracted his attention and he turned to see a squadron of knights galloping across the bridge.

'Captain, come to me,' Malekith said, beckoning to the elf who had been in charge of the vanguard.

The captain came forward, a bloodied sword in his hand, breastplate rent open from a Chracian axe. He dropped to one knee, eyes averted.

'My apologies, king,' said the soldier.

He knelt trembling, head bowed, as Malekith steered Sulekh to loom over him. The crest of the captain's helmet fluttered with each of the dragon's breaths, wisps of poisonous vapour coiling from her nostrils. The Witch King could feel the elf's fear dripping from his shuddering body.

'Do not fail me again,' said the Witch King. The captain looked up, surprised and delighted. 'Continue the march!'

The officer bowed and hurried away, anxious that his master might have a sudden change of heart. In truth, the captain had been ordered into the trap by Malekith and could not be blamed. His mother might dispense summary executions in such a situation, but her acts of spite were wasteful. The Witch King suffered no illusions about his opponents and knew he would need every soldier if he was to claim Ulthuan for his own.

Uncertainty keeps soldiers alert, Malekith told himself. He would not want to become predictable.

Half a dozen pairs of dead eyes stared at Malekith as he stepped out of his pavilion. The heads of the dreadlords were displayed on stakes around the entrance to the great marquee, each bearing the inverted rune of *senthoi* carved in their foreheads, a symbol of broken promises. The generals' remains served as an example to their successors that Malekith was in no mood for further setbacks, and certainly had no time for equivocation and excuses.

The druchii camp spread down the ridge below, and from his vantage point Malekith could see clear six leagues along the valley to the north. The forests of the snow-drenched slopes were known as the Whiteweald, a hunting ground of manticores and griffons, home to phoenixes and great eagles.

This had once been a wilderness jewel of Ulthuan, where princes and kings had hunted beasts and sojourned with their courts. Now it was a ravaged, twisted mockery of its former beauty. Even before the druchii had come Chrace had suffered dearly during the daemonic intrusion. Swathes of the forest had been warped by their presence, the ground itself ripped and buckled in abhorrence of their invasion. Mountaintops had tumbled and avalanches cut swathes through trees that had stood proudly for several thousand years.

The course of the daemonic attack could be charted by the warped, withered remains of the trees left in their wake: some were petrified, leaves of stone grey and lifeless; others had become ice structures, slowly melting as the season turned to summer, crystalline imitations of what had come before; whole mountainsides were desolate, nothing left but rotting stumps and a thick slurry of decaying mulch.

At first Malekith had been encouraged, finding Phoenix Gate barely held against him, and the advance across the Annulii had been swift. Trusting that his plan to draw the bulk of Tyrion's forces south with Darkblade's army had succeeded, the Witch King had readied his host to plunge down into the foothills and plains of Chrace, to sack Tor Achare and seize the coast where the crossing to the Blighted Isle was shortest.

From then nothing had quite played out as he had planned. The people of Chrace knew their lands as well as they knew their own families, and they used every part of it to their advantage.

The Chracians would not meet his force in pitched battle preferring, as they had done during previous wars, to wage a guerrilla campaign of ambushes and feint attacks. The mountains were dotted with concealed fortresses – outposts that could sustain a thousand warriors yet not be seen even if a scout passed within bowshot.

Even though the landscape had suffered much brutality in recent times, its ways and means were still a secret to be unlocked. The Whiteweald was no place for dragons to fight, the cover of the deep forests and caves more than enough sanctuary against the mightiest beasts of the sky. Whole Naggarothi regiments disappeared pursuing their foes into the wilds, but despite this the commanders who now adorned the rough trail leading to Malekith's pavilion had sent thousands to their doom in fruitless efforts to catch the elusive enemy.

Kouran approached, secretly alerted to his master's emergence by the Black Guard standing sentry around the pavilion. His face was stern as he saluted the king.

'My king, another three regiments were lost in the night,' the captain reported. He motioned to the right flank of the advance, on the other side of the steep valley. 'From the Ghrond host stationed to the north.'

'The north?' Malekith growled. 'You told me yesterday that our northern flank was secure. Not even a Chracian hunter would pass the picket, you claimed.'

Kouran answered with a silent bow of the head, admitting his mistake and accepting whatever chastisement Malekith was prepared to dispense. The Witch King glanced at the heads around him and knew that killing Kouran would almost certainly seal the fate of the expedition. With Morathi in Ghrond and the traitor Ezresor slain, Malekith relied almost wholly on the captain of the Black Guard to keep order and ensure the loyalty of his subjects.

'The blame is not yours,' said Malekith. 'There is more than the skill of peasant hunters at play here.'

He tilted his head back, closing his eyes to concentrate on his magical sense, allowing his consciousness to flow into the Iron Circlet. There was a jarring transition as part of his mind slipped into the Realm of Chaos and then back to the mortal world, for all intents and purposes detached from his physical form.

It was harder to maintain a sense of self in these mountains, where the howling winds of magic were funnelled into Ulthuan's vortex. The influx of daemonic energy and the expansion of the Chaos Wastes had turned the vortex into a wild maelstrom. In Naggarond it had been simplicity to move his thoughts from one part of the world to another, and even to project his avatar into far-flung locations. From the Annulii it was a trying task simply to maintain a coherent pattern of thoughts amidst the buffeting mystical storm.

Drawing on the depths of his will, Malekith moved his roaming eye from the camp, momentarily lifting away towards the clouds for an overview of his situation.

The black tents of the druchii cut across the valley about a third of the way from its heights, crossing the river at the base and up both sides. Reaper bolt throwers in wooden forts protected the outer reaches of the camp, but there were too many warriors for them all to stay within the watch of these guard posts. Several thousand tents spread east and south down the curving vale, until swallowed by the trees at the lower altitudes. The advance parties had done their best to cut trails through the forest, but every few leagues the vanguard regiments disappeared, slain by the Chracians. Their latest efforts were like pale scars in the canopy, gashes of brown and black against the snow.

Even so, progress should have been swifter, and now that he was suffused with the winds of magic Malekith could see why.

Against the flow of the vortex tendrils of magic drifted north from beyond the mountains, bringing mystical life to the trees and rocks of Chrace. Malekith knew this magic well, the energy of Avelorn, the power of the Everqueen.

He searched the valley for a sign of the asur's spiritual ruler but there was no pocket of earth power to betray her presence. Instead Malekith detected smaller pools of life magic, and he swooped down upon the largest of these magical concentrations.

The trees themselves quivered with the magic, alerted to the presence of the druchii, filled with vengeance for the axes and fire they brought with them. Treemen and dryads, spirits that normally did not stray far from the Gaen Vale, had come north to aid the Chracians. Other beings, elemental creatures of air and stone, had been roused to attack the Ghrondian forces, moved to battle by the presence of an elf enchantress.

Her spoor was mingled with that of the tree-kin, sharper than the musty magic of ancient centuries. Malekith found her, a handmaiden of Avelorn, marshalling regiments of the Everqueen's maiden guard not far to the east.

She was garbed in a flowing gown of deep green embroidered with blooms in reds and blues and purples, the lighter green of their leaves creating a swirl of lines and waves along the hem of the dress. Bangles of bronze set with topaz and opals and amber hung on the handmaiden's wrists and about her slender neck was a pendant of pure sapphire, neatly inscribed with the rune of *quyl-Isha*, signifying the tears of Isha, a symbol of mourning and sad defiance. Her hair was golden, heavily braided and pinned to leave a single plait hanging down each sharp cheek. Eyes that matched the colour of the sapphire regarded the dispersing maiden guard with affection and contentment.

The handmaiden emanated calm resolve, like the deep spring that feeds the well or the roots of the ancient trees. The grass at her feet stood straighter, the petals on the flowers close at hand gleamed brighter in her presence.

Malekith detested the enchantress immediately.

It was just this sort of moon-faced pining for the peaceful pre-history of his people that had made them weak. The world before the Coming of Chaos would never return and no amount of poetry and prayers to Isha would change that. Only strength of will and strength of arms had protected the elves since, no matter the protestations of the Everqueen and her ilk.

The presence of the handmaiden reminded Malekith that he would have to deal with the Everqueen before the matter was settled. His previous attempts to kidnap her had been thwarted by the same individual that now sought to oppose him: Tyrion. He had it on good authority that the prince was Alarielle's lover, and she would doubtless support her consort against Malekith's ambition. When Chrace was in his hands, a full scale invasion of Avelorn would follow, and this time he would not leave the destruction to a feckless host of daemons led by the vain and jealous N'Kari.

The female archers, several hundred of them, were following warriors cloaked with lion pelts along the hidden tracks of the woods, ready to spring their attacks on the advancing companies of Naggarothi. They broke into groups of a dozen or fewer warriors, able to move swiftly and unseen along the game trails and hidden paths.

More than that, the Witch King realised as the enchantress started binding the winds of magic to her will. The energy swirled, delving into the life-force of the forests. Roots burst from the ground and branches bowed down, forming an archway twice the height of an elf, broad enough for several to walk abreast. Fresh shoots erupted along the outline of the gateway, bright leaves and flowers catching the light of the early sun.

The interior of the gate shimmered with magic, an image of blurred brown and green that resolved into a vision of a forest glade. Malekith could see that beyond the gate lay a tunnel that wound its way through the vortex, leading to the south. By this means did the warriors of Chrace and Avelorn bypass the sentries and patrols.

'I've found you,' declared Malekith, manifesting a projection of his spirit in front of the enchantress.

The maiden guard reacted quickly, surrounding the apparition of the Witch King with a ring of golden spears and arrowheads. The handmaiden looked shocked, but her fear dissipated as she realised that Malekith was present in spirit only.

'Tell me your name,' said the Witch King, 'so that your kin can lament your passing in proper fashion.'

'I am Ystranna,' said the handmaiden. 'I am the right hand of Astarielle and by her command I will not let you pass.'

'You think to stop me with an army of vagabonds and hunters, earth-witch?' sneered Malekith. 'Or perhaps you hope that the blessings of Isha will be a match for my magic?'

'Strength eternal guards our lands, despoiler,' Ystranna replied, tilting her head to one side to regard Malekith with sapphire eyes. 'Have you not learned the lesson yet? Ulthuan does not want you as her king.'

'Ulthuan will be bound to my will just the same as every creature upon it,' Malekith said. He clenched a fist in front of Ystranna, fire leaking from the gaps in the gauntlet. 'You can tell Ulthuan that I will cut such wounds across her that she has never known and when I am finished she will never remember the days of green that once blessed her.'

The Witch King became aware of a nagging sensation, something relevant to his physical body. He looked at the maiden guard that surrounded him and waved them away with contempt.

'This is the elite of Avelorn? My Black Guard shall water the trees you love so much with your blood, and they shall fertilise the ground with your bones. If you desire peace, return now to your mistress and lay down your weapons. Only those that resist need fear my retribution.' None of the warrior-maidens moved. All regarded him with cold, unflinching stares. 'I thought not, but the warning has been given. Ystranna of Avelorn, you must bear full responsibility for what happens next.'

Malekith did not give her time to reply as he banished his projection and allowed his spirit to fly back to his mortal shell. Opening his eyes, he saw that Kouran had been joined by two elves dressed in the manner of the shades, and by a herald swathed in the cloak of a dark rider.

'A witch of Avelorn has bolstered the forces of the Chracians,' Malekith told his lieutenant. Blazing eyes regarded the scouts. 'You have fresh news of your own, I see.'

'An army from the west, my king,' reported Kouran. 'Less than a day's march away.'

'From Nagarythe,' Malekith said quietly. 'It seems that Alith Anar has decided he wants to play.'

'My king, our position has become vulnerable,' Kouran added quietly. 'If we press into Chrace the shadow warriors of Anar will attack the rear echelons.'

'And if we turn to face Anar the Chracians will do likewise.' Malekith turned his eye to the mountains in the west, where the sky was still purple, barely touched by the spreading dawn light. 'I presume that you bring me this news accompanied by a suggested strategy.'

'We should turn south and leave the forest to the tree-witch and her kin,' said Saidekh Winterclaw, whom Malekith had not recognised beneath the mask of blood dried on his face. His voice was husky and dry, never more than a whisper.

'A tempting thought,' said Kouran, nodding his agreement. 'There is little force in Ellyrion to stop a swift march. We would fall upon Tyrion's host unexpectedly. Perhaps we will even reach them before they have eliminated Darkblade's army, and the prince will be set upon from two directions, instead of us.'

'Tempting, but wrong,' said Malekith. 'We merely delay the entrapment. Anar's army can cross the mountains more swiftly than mine, and if not to bring battle then to speed warning to

Tyrion. Even should they remain solely in pursuit, I cannot afford to leave a sizeable force at the rear, gnawing away at my reserves, threatening to attack any day.'

Before the Sundering he had made the mistake of not cowing every kingdom completely before moving on, driven by unseemly haste. Though time was short – all time was short if Teclis was to be believed – Malekith would not fall prey to the same impulses that had beset him before. 'We will crush Chrace and seize the crossings to the Blighted Isle and with that route secured move into the weaker eastern kingdoms. The plan has not changed.'

The daemons had ravaged much of Chrace, but Malekith would see the remainder wiped out. No resistance would remain, and the death of the kingdom would serve as a warning to the others. The message would be learned – that this time Malekith would see Ulthuan accept him as its ruler or be totally destroyed. While his own armies were driven by the knowledge that there was no place for them to return, the princes of the ten kingdoms would come to realise that the only future left to them was at the mercy of the Witch King.

'But the threat that arises in the west, my king,' Kouran said to Malekith as the Witch King surveyed the mountain pass, knowing it was filled with traps and foes but there was no other way to get to his goal. 'The traitor warriors of Nagarythe have followed us along Phoenix Pass and will attack within the next day or two.'

'Let them,' said Malekith. 'If we turn to confront Anar he will disappear as surely as the shadows from which he takes his name. Archers in front and behind, and not an elf amongst them willing to stand and fight like a true warrior. I tell you, Alandrian, I will not be thwarted this time. Saidekh, gather together all of your clans – you are to lead the next attack. If the Chracians think their wild homeland has made them expert woodsmen and hill fighters, let them test their blades against the best of the Iron Mountains.'

'Their skin will make fine cloaks and we will gamble around the fires with their teeth,' said the shades' leader. 'Their hair we will weave into trinket bags for our children and their bones we shall leave as an offering to the Cytharai, whose wrath we will embody.'

'Just make sure their resistance is broken – what you do with them afterwards is no concern of mine.' Malekith looked at the dark rider, who had been summoned by Kouran to take messages to the army. 'Have Imrik and his dragons raze the lower slopes. Burn everything. If Ystranna and her allies wish to retreat from this valley, they must do so through dragonfire or across a charred desolation. She can risk the open ground or face the blades and missiles of Saidekh – the choice is hers.'

The rider turned towards his steed but was called back by Malekith.

'Ask Prince Imrik *nicely*,' the Witch King added. 'Be sure to say "please".'

FIFTEEN

The Battle of the Whiteweald

For the remainder of the day it was as Malekith commanded. In their hundreds the shades swept through the forest, a match for any Avelorn spearmaiden or Chracian hunter. Ahead of them, to the east, the dragon princes set about turning the forest to cinders. Dragonfire scoured the mountainside, slaying hundreds of beasts large and small but not a single elf corpse was found amongst the charred remains. Night fell but full darkness never came to the Whiteweald. A twilight cast by the burning forest lit the sky while smoke swathed the moons and stars.

To Malekith's growing anger, his foes would not show themselves. While his army stood guard in their camps, laughter and singing taunted the druchii and Caledorians. Arrows scythed from the darkness to slay sentries and patrols, but none dared go after the hidden archers while fey lights flickered between the trees and mysterious hisses and groans were carried on the wind.

Kouran arrived at Malekith's pavilion early the next morning, trailing muddy footprints across the hide rugs, blood on his armour from recent fighting. He bent to one knee before the

Witch King's throne, *Crimson Death* held out before him as an offering to Malekith.

'The fighting sounds close,' remarked the Witch King. 'It is as though I can hear the blades crashing and the arrows singing from here. Have the enemy finally decided to fight?'

'They have, my lord, but our forces fare poorly,' said Kouran, avoiding his master's eye. 'The initial attack came not from Anar's shadow warriors but out of the Whiteweald. Our eye had been drawn to the west too far, my king, and now the enemy have already slain the outer companies and are pressing towards the encampment.'

'The forces to the west moved in response and the traitor Naggarothi attack from Phoenix Pass?'

'Just as you say, my king. While the Karond Kar regiments broke camp the shadow army fell upon them. Three thousand are dead – the rest have formed a defensive encirclement and are surrounded.'

'A well-coordinated assault.' Malekith rose and strode past his underling, keen to see for himself the unfolding battle. 'Clearly Ystranna and Anar have been communicating in some fashion I have been unable to detect.'

Malekith stepped out into the dawn light. The sky overhead was still grey, the mountain clouds low despite the summer season. The distinct noise of battle rang through the valley, the clash of weapons, battle cries and screams of the dying and wounded. A constant whispering of bowstrings and arrows added a counterpoint to the more raucous sounds. Dragons roared and flames crackled as the Caledorians to the east responded to the Chracian and maiden guard offensive. Malekith could detect the hiss of hydras and snarl of cold ones.

There were other noises, of a more supernatural origin. The creak of trees and thrash of leaves magnified a hundredfold, accompanied by booming voices and the trilling of smaller forest spirits. The ground rumbled as animated boulders smashed through ranks of warriors, while the air carried a sibilant chorus from hundreds of wind sprites.

He smelt the smoke of dragonfire and the reek of cold ones, mingled with the aroma of sweat and fear. The pine resin scent of the forest was swamped by the iron tang of fresh blood, driving the army's manticores into a frenzy of frustrated bellowing as they strained at their chains.

'The ravens, my lord.' Kouran stopped a few paces from Malekith, cautious of the flames rippling across his armour. 'The shades caught several yesterday and learned that they were working for the Shadow King. We sent harpies to hunt them down but...'

Malekith turned his head to look down at Kouran. 'There are a lot of ravens in Chrace?'

Kouran nodded. 'Yes, my king.'

Malekith had to concede one point of admiration to his foes – when they committed to the attack they did not do so in half measures. It was as though the forest itself assaulted his army. More than a dozen treemen led the attack, crashing into the outer companies of druchii with fists pulping bodies and whip-crack branches severing limbs and necks. Behind them came smaller tree-kin and the dryad spirits, flooding around the treemen to despatch those trying to surround the ancient forest herders.

The Chracians formed one flank of the attack, driving a wedge into the darkshards and corsairs to the north-east, while the maiden guard formed a solid line to the north-west, their wall of glittering spears keeping knights and dark riders at bay while their bows took a toll of the same with relentless volleys of white-fletched arrows.

More archers rained arrows from a secondary line, targeting the druchii war machines and beast handlers. These were aided by several mages, including Ystranna. Malekith could detect the swirling winds of magic where the spellcasters summoned energy for their enchantments. Scything, razor-edged leaves swept out of the trees to slash through a regiment of shades that were trying to go around the flank of the asur force, while muddy behemoths rose up from the ground to wrestle with hydras and dragons. More traditional fireballs and magical lightning betrayed the presence of at least two Sapherian mages assisting the handmaiden of the Everqueen.

The western approaches were no less embattled. Overnight Alith Anar and his shadow warriors had stalked within striking distance and dawn had marked the start of the attack. The first volleys had cut down lookouts and patrol captains, silencing any alarm that might have been raised. The shadow warriors had stolen into the encampment and sliced the throats of hundreds of warriors in their sleep before the contingent from Karond Kar had finally been roused. Their leaders assassinated, enemy in their midst, the Ghrondians had retreated piecemeal to higher ground and were now being whittled down by deadly archery from an enemy hidden by surrounding gullies and boulders.

The Caledorians were slow to assemble, the princes fatigued by the previous day's labours scorching the lower slopes. The crackle of dragonfire was intermittent as some of the Caledorians sought to counter the awakened woodland bearing down on their camp while the horns of other princes summoned their steeds from their slumbering.

The speed and ferocity of the enemy attack was almost overwhelming. After endless days of chasing shadows, the druchii army had been taken unawares by the sudden change in strategy.

'What are your orders, my king?'

Malekith realised that his host was in danger of being overrun before it was fully mobilised. Kouran's question snapped Malekith from his contemplation.

'Give ground,' he said. 'Consolidate. Our line is too long, and we need to draw their archers out of the trees. Summon the tower captains of your regiment to stop it turning into a rout, and tell them that we must make an orderly withdrawal three hundred paces. Tell Imrik to form his dragons into two wings, one to act as a reserve to cover the withdrawal and counter any enemy break-throughs, the other to harass the shadow army to the west. The two asur forces must not be allowed to link up, despite the retreat.'

'As you wish, my king,' said the captain. 'And the mages?'

Malekith could see a pair of sorceresses supporting the Ghrond army, but they were ill-matched against the handmaiden and Sapherians. Drusala had, of her own volition, left with Malus Darkblade's army of Hag Graef, which left only one other option.

'Leave Ystranna and her cantrip-pedlars to me.'

Before Malekith could say anything else, another armoured figure approached, her helm dented, breastplate scored and scratched by spear blows. There was the broken shaft of an arrow jutting from her shoulder. She buried her axe into a tree stump as Kouran took a step towards her with *Crimson Death* raised, and approached unarmed. Her name was Aravenna, and she had been in charge of the Clar Karond host for only two days.

'Deepest regrets and apologies, your majesty,' she said, bowing before Malekith. 'We expected the Anar army to attack first. They were the better positioned for such an assault. I regret that we fell for the enemy ploy.'

'You believe it was a mistake to redeploy our forces to the west?' Malekith asked, turning his full attention on the newly promoted commander. She averted her eyes, shoulders slumping.

'In hindsight, that would seem the case.'

'The order for the redeployment came from me, Lady Aravenna.' Malekith's quiet words dripped with threat. 'Do you think I was outwitted by one of the Everqueen's soppy tree-lovers and a group of peasant hunters?'

'I...' Aravenna looked at Kouran, seeking support or perhaps a swift end. He gave her neither, replying to her plaintive stare with a casual shrug.

'Answer your king, Lady Aravenna,' said the captain. He flexed his fingers on *Crimson Death*. 'Swiftly and with brevity.'

'It was an impossible decision, your majesty,' the commander said, the words coming so quickly she was barely comprehensible. 'Nobody could know that the attack from the forest would come first, but to ignore the Anars would have been equally ill-considered, but given all that we know of the shadow warriors' hatred for us it would be reasonable to conclude they would seek the greater part of the bloodletting, and that a handmaiden of the Everqueen would be loathe to commit to battle.'

As Aravenna paused to take a breath, Malekith held up a hand to stop her.

'It hurts to know you have such a lack of faith in my abilities as your military commander,' said the king. Aravenna started to tremble, a reaction that clearly embarrassed her. A look of such self-disgust moved across her face that Malekith almost laughed.

'Return to your army and prepare for a counter-attack,' Malekith told her. 'The enemy are far more stupid than I had hoped.'

'Your majesty?' Aravenna clenched her jaw, conflicted, fighting back tears though she fought also to stop a smile of relief twisting her lips. 'I do not understand.'

'I deliberately weakened the eastern defence to bait the enemy into this bold venture. They have surrendered all of their natural and strategic advantages to face us in open battle, and now we will punish them for their lack of warcraft. I cannot imagine Ystranna ordered the attack, but some Chracian prince has made a fool of himself. Anar has been forced to move in support, though I believe he would have far rather preferred to kill us one at a time, never revealing himself. We must destroy them before they see the error of their assault.'

'As you command, your majesty.' Aravenna hesitated, her gaze lingering on the Witch King.

'You have a question?'

'How will we stop the enemy simply retreating back into the forests, your majesty? I do not wish to fail you again.'

'That is not your concern. Trust me in this matter as you failed to trust in my grander strategy.'

'Yes, your majesty. I have one other question.'

'You test my patience, but the thought of putting these wretches to the sword lightens my mood, so ask your question.'

'The Karond Kar army will likely be heavily mauled.' She shook her head, disbelieving, as she looked westwards. 'You knew this, your majesty? You sacrificed them to draw out the Chracians?'

'Your observation is correct, general. Be thankful that the host of Clar Karond was not in their place.'

Aravenna bowed again and hurried away, pulling her slender axe free as she departed. Malekith watched her run back down the slope to where her regiments were mustering behind the army of Karond Kar, which had taken the brunt of the Chracian assault as Malekith had planned.

'You spared her,' said Kouran, apparently so surprised by this fact he forgot to say 'my king'.

'She may not survive the battle, but if she does she will fight doubly hard to prove her loyalty, and from now on she will not question my orders. If I kill her I will simply have to repeat the lesson with another.'

Kouran accepted this wisdom with a thoughtful expression and a nod.

'The Chracians and the aesenar of the Shadowlands seem to be making quite a headway through my troops,' Malekith remarked, watching the lead elements of the two converging forces moving towards each other. 'Go now and convey my orders to the generals. I wouldn't want to accidently lose this battle when it promises such a sweet victory.'

When Kouran had departed he made his way up the ridge to where Seraphon had made her temporary lair. The other black dragons were already in the sky, duelling with great eagles, griffons and phoenixes, but Malekith's mount lay in the shade of a great outcrop, gaseous breath billowing down the slope.

'Come,' said the Witch King as Seraphon raised her head, opening her long mouth to reveal rows of wickedly serrated teeth. A draught of noxious air washed over Malekith, hot and wet. 'It is time that we educated these peons in the true art of war.'

The black dragon carried Malekith north, towards Ystranna and her maiden guard companies. It was her presence that was the greatest threat – without Ystranna the spirits of the forest would depart and the magic that bolstered the resolve of her followers would be broken.

As he scanned the forest below Malekith felt something glance from his armour. Turning in his saddle as he wheeled Seraphon to the left, an arrow ricocheted from his shoulder. Three great eagles rose up towards him, an elf prince atop the back of each, their bows levelled at the Witch King. Another flurry of arrows converged on him, sparking from the scales of his mount and deflecting from his breastplate. Malekith was about to turn away from his attackers, their missiles inconsequential, when something stinging lodged in his arm.

An arrowhead that glowed with golden energy had pierced his armour. Another mystical shaft sped past, leaving a welt across the side of his helm, a finger's breadth from his throat. He followed the flickering trail of magic back to one of the eagle-borne princes, who was fitting another enchanted arrow to his bow.

Flicking the chains with one hand, Malekith rolled Seraphon towards the impudent asur lordling. Even as the black dragon heeled around to face the eagle, the prince steered his mount higher, climbing over the great beast. More arrows skidded from Malekith's armour from the other two princes, a further distraction.

Leaving a wake of gold, another magical arrow sped towards Malekith as Seraphon laboured to turn after the far more agile great eagles, her tail lashing with rage. It struck the black dragon in the neck, parting scales with a spurt of thick blood. Seraphon snarled with pain, thrashing her head away from the impact, almost jarring the chains loose from Malekith's grasp.

'Enough,' rasped the Witch King, pointing *Urithain* at the offending prince. A bolt of black energy leapt from the tip, but the eagle had foreseen the attack and folded its wings, dropping beneath the blazing flash of magic. Malekith loosed another bolt and another, chasing the eagle down towards the forest, his prey twisting and turning. Pivoting on the immense bird's back, the asur prince shot another arrow, which tore through the skin of Seraphon's left wing, eliciting a further screech of pain.

Changing tactic, Malekith coiled the winds of magic to his will and focused on the prince's mind. A protective amulet about his neck started to glow, resisting the attack, but Malekith gritted his teeth and pushed harder. The amulet shattered, overloaded with dark magic. Reaching out across the gap between them Malekith let his hatred flow, filling the other elf's brain with shards of pure agony.

He saw the prince stiffen and cry out, his bow falling from flailing fingers as he toppled from the eagle's back. The bird stooped down to catch the falling elf but Malekith was ready and hurled another dark bolt that struck the eagle square on the spine, turning feathers to ash and flesh to dust. Crippled, the eagle spiralled down after its rider, the wail of the latter drowned out by the dying shriek of the former.

Shadow darkening the regiments below, Seraphon flattened her dive and ascended again. The other two eagles broke away, unable to harm the mighty black dragon and her immortal master.

More Chracians had joined the attack, charging from under the trees in lion-drawn chariots, driving deep into the flank of a spear regiment as they tried to fall back alongside a company of Black Guard. The white lions fell upon the druchii with claws and fangs, manes matted with splashed blood, while the chariot riders hewed to the left and right with long, slender-headed axes, cutting down those that eluded the wrath of the lions.

The attack threatened to turn the whole flank of the withdrawal, leaving Malekith no choice but to intervene. Seraphon's climb became another dive, claws outstretched as she crashed into the lead chariots like a thunderbolt, carving apart Chracians and druchii without discrimination. She seized a mighty lion in her jaws as Malekith swept down *Urithain* to behead the two chariot riders behind. Three bone-crunching bites and a huge gulp later and the lion was no more.

Traces and yokes whipped and cracked as the black dragon continued on her bloody rampage, sword-long talons dragging tatters of white lion hide and viscera. Malekith's sword crackled with dark power, blood fizzing from the infernal flame that burned along the blade. Another sweep cut a Chracian from groin to shoulder and a third sheared a lion in half across the midriff.

The impetus of their charge abated by the Witch King's attack, the lion chariots floundered and were soon beset by the Black Guard, who spilled around and over the chariots with halberds flashing, their hate-filled snarls and battle cries as ferocious as any mountain lion's. His task complete, Malekith steered Seraphon away, seeking the real enemy.

He arrowed the dragon towards the tree line, following the tendrils of forest magic to their source. In parts, the woods themselves had moved, encroaching upon the paths cut by the druchii the day before, following the lead of the treemen and their kind. The boughs of the moving forest were too close together for any mortal eye to penetrate, obscuring all sign of Ystranna. Malekith would have to hunt her down another way.

Seraphon seemed to feel his intent and strained at her chains to swoop down into the Avelorn contingent, her muscles bunching as she prepared for the dive. Malekith hauled back on the reins, dissuading her from the manoeuvre, eliciting a growl of frustration.

'I have a far more fitting fate in mind,' Malekith told the dragon. 'She thinks to rouse the spirit of Ulthuan against me? She will learn who is the true master of this isle.'

Sheathing *Urithain*, Malekith reached out his will into the forest below. The life magic pouring through the woods bucked at his approach, veering away from his presence in serpentine coils. Turning the extension of his self into a stiletto point, he struck out, pinning part of the retreating Ghyran with his mind. It writhed beneath his attention but could not escape, and slowly through the blade of the imaginary poniard Malekith poured forth his dark thoughts.

SIXTEEN

Ghyran, the Power of Life

Like ink spreading in water, the Witch King's magic started to pollute the stream of Ghyran brought forth by Ystranna. It was like forging against a river current, pushing against the resistance, but slowly, heartbeat by heartbeat, Malekith infected the magical current with his own will, corrupting it to his desire, perverting its nature.

The grass began to wither and the branches on the trees drooped as the life-force of the forest started leeching into Malekith's dark magic. The power that had sustained the greenery now fed his wrath, and the longer he suckled on its foul-tasting purity the stronger his own sorcery grew.

Suddenly there was a flash of golden sunlight, arrowing down through the canopy, enveloping Malekith's extension of will with an aura of warmth. He felt himself drawn out of his body, and blinked unreal eyes against the sudden light.

He stood in a quaint grotto, the sun overhead dappled by lustrous foliage swaying in a warm summer breeze. He could smell wild flowers on the banks of the dell – a sensation he had not enjoyed for several thousand years. His armour was no more, and he was clad in garlands of blooms and leaves, which coiled about him with a comforting embrace. A stream trickled through the grotto from a tinkling waterfall, fish of all colours darting to and fro beneath the surface.

'Why hate so much?' asked Ystranna. 'Hate has never created anything.'

She appeared part maiden and part light and part tree, her hair spilling like willow branches, her eyes wells of sunshine. Streamers of flowers grew from the ground at her feet and enveloped her nakedness with a gown of rainbow hues, shimmering like the sunlight on the waterfall.

'My hate created Naggaroth,' said Malekith.

'And what now of that creation? It has fallen, exposed as the pale imitation of life that it was. Something raised out of jealousy can never endure.'

'What do you hope to achieve here? To sway my mind away from destroying you and taking back that which rightfully belongs to me?' Malekith walked across the dell, feeling the soft turf beneath his bare feet, the grass between his toes. He closed his eyes, unable to avoid the memories stirred by the sensation. Memories of living flesh when he had thought he might love and be loved, fulfilled by duty and belonging.

'No, Malekith, I do not. This is not for you. Nature can be harsh as well as beautiful. I am here to kill you with kindness.'

Ystranna's expression changed. Her eyes became shards of ice and the garlands that wreathed Malekith revealed themselves to be the roots of the immense tree whose boughs spread over the dell, casting darkness across the Witch King. The roots tightened around his limbs and throat while thorns erupted from the tendrils, piercing his flesh, his splashing blood nurturing the ground to bring forth more bramble-like appendages.

The handmaiden stalked closer, her skin now like the bark of white trees, her fingers the clawing taproots that could prise open the foundations of castles and penetrate the walls of cities. Green and golden Ghyran continued to pulse through her body as she approached, hand outstretched.

'I think not,' said Malekith, letting free the bonds he had placed on his power to conceal it from Ystranna's awareness. Aqshy, fire magic, surged through him, burning away the grasping roots and branches in a moment, turning his avatar into a pillar of fire.

'You cannot harm me,' the handmaiden said, her scornful expression written in creased bark and cracked leaves. 'This is my realm and you are nothing but a projection of your will.'

The Witch King lunged at Ystranna's apparition and before she realised what was happening, insubstantial fingers closed on her throat. She gasped in shock as the fires of his projection died, leaving a shadow-figure in their place.

'Your realm?'

Ystranna looked around to see that the trees were withered, twisted things hunched over sickly-looking fungal growths. The ground had become a black mire, the river bubbling with the movement of fanged, slithering eels, the sun obscured by storm clouds.

'My will is strong indeed, Ystranna,' Malekith mocked. His blackened fingers become iron claws, digging into the flesh of Ystranna's neck, puncturing the blood vessels. His spite bubbled from the wounds like acid, flowing into her body to create a spider's web of blackening veins and arteries. 'Thank you so much for coming to me. You are the taproot, the motherstone, the source of the power and now you have opened it to me. You should have stayed hidden.'

Ystranna's flesh blistered and burned from within, pustules erupting to release clouds of spores that stung her eyes and choked her. She was immobile in Malekith's grasp, unable to put up the slightest resistance.

'Ulthuan will never be yours,' the handmaiden gasped. Ystranna's swollen veins started to pulse, splitting her bark-skin to allow sap-like fluid to run free, washing away Malekith's venom. Her form shrank, becoming a tangle of blossoming vines that fell from the Witch King's grasp. The blooms shattered like glass and where the shards landed, the decay of dark magic was dispelled, greenness and life returning to push back Malekith's curse.

Assuming his usual form, the Witch King stamped a flaming foot on the spreading patch of earth magic, leaving a cindered footprint. The patch continued to grow, running up the hunched boles of the trees leaving fresh shoots in its wake, cleansing the filth from the brook, changing pale, eyeless eels into gleaming fish once more.

'So crude, so clumsy,' Ystranna said, her voice coming to Malekith from all around, carried on the rustle of jade leaves and the trickle of fresh water, the creak of branches and swish of grass mocking him with subtle laughter. The words tore at his pride, so close to those barbed comments his own mother had made.

'Is that so?' he snarled in reply, striding up to the closest tree. He punched his fist through the bark and opened his fingers in the heartwood, letting his frustration loose as a flame that consumed the tree from within. Steam and smoke billowed from the wound as the core of the tree disappeared, leaving the mass of branches to collapse in a welter of splinters and cracking wood.

The sun broke through, a ray piercing the storm gloom to light Malekith with a pale glow, blinding him momentarily, forcing him back into the grotto.

'How can you defeat me when you cannot even find me,' taunted the handmaiden. As the Witch King recovered his sight he spied a faerie light bobbing in the shadows cast by the canopy, whirling left and right, up and down.

'You forget to whom you speak, child,' Malekith said as his body slewed into a new shape, armour dissipating like mist, his form becoming that of a giant panther with burning amber eyes, claws and fangs of iron. With a roar he pounced into the woods towards the light. The gleam dodged and fled, zigzagging between the trees, Malekith's claws tearing up the mulch as he chased it just a few steps behind, snarling and snapping.

The light cut sharply to the left behind the bole of a huge oak, and Malekith lost sight of it. He skidded to a stop, his gaze like a lantern beam as he passed it to and fro in the arboreal twilight. Suddenly he spied the hovering wisp of energy but before he could set off another appeared, a little further away. A third emerged from the leaves of a holly bush just a little way to his right. Within a dozen heartbeats there were scores of floating spheres, a tiny winged figure with the face of Ystranna in the heart of each.

Malekith looked past the glamour of the artificial world they had created to visualise their immaterial duel, seeing the raw winds of magic at work. Malekith was a knot of raw power, bloated and seething with unreleased energy. Dark magic required a focus, a fulcrum in the real world through which its power was harnessed. For the most powerful magic this was usually a sacrifice, to avoid the corruption of the mortal body of the sorcerer, but Malekith's immortal form placed him beyond such petty consideration.

In stark contrast, Ystranna's spirit was dispersed across the forest, absorbing Ghyran from everywhere. It was a structure of harmony and balance, kept alive by the interplay of energies themselves, taking from one area and giving to another. It was a creation of great intricacy, requiring intense concentration to maintain. There was no central point, no convergence for him to use to locate Ystranna. She was, as far as it mattered for the winds of magic, everywhere.

'Impressive,' he growled. 'But your parlour trick has run its course. I do not need to find you to defeat you.'

Malekith's panther body shuddered, black fur falling away, flesh becoming a thorn bush, his limbs extending and splitting into roots that delved deep into the earth. Down and down the Witch King pushed his avatar, striking out to find the roots of the trees, the rivulets of water that sustained them, deeper even than the Ghyran that Ystranna commanded. Spreading like an oil slick, Malekith's dark magic pooled beneath the forest, cutting it off from the swell of the winds of magic, forcing Ystranna to shift the balance of her counter-spell. Malekith probed and stretched, claw-like roots rasping at Ystranna's enchantment, seeking to tear through the harmonic web that made it possible.

He felt a stab of white fire as the other mages lent their support to the handmaiden, sensing that Malekith's plan might work. Their panic only strengthened his resolve and bolstered the dark magic coursing through his projection. Their fire guttered and died, leaving silver trails back into the minds of the Sapherians. Malekith's glee gave haste to his next attack. He pulsed dark magic into the thoughts of the mages and on the ground above they shrieked their horror as blood leaked from their eyes and bones split within their flesh.

'You should choose your allies more carefully,' Malekith gloated, feeling the pool of Ystranna's power dwindling with every moment.

The handmaiden was losing control of the Ghyran, unable to maintain the balance of power as Malekith's assault switched and veered from one place to the next, making inroads towards her.

All of a sudden Malekith felt the closeness of Ystranna, her magical presence within reach. He made a metaphysical grasp at her, ensnaring her will with his own. A moment later they both materialised back in the grotto, Malekith's fist inside Ystranna's chest, clutching her heart.

Feeding on the earth power the handmaiden commanded, Malekith's magical presence swelled, growing and growing to gigantic proportion, towering above the forest like a tornado of dark wind, crackling with lightning. Her projection crumbled into dust as she fled, cutting herself off from the winds of magic, but it was too late. Malekith laughed as her avatar slipped away, leaving a slender thread of green and golden sunlight in his hands, pulsing beneath armoured fingers. He had all the power he needed, Ghyran stripped of all its earth power to become raw magic. Swelled by this he became a bloated thundercloud of destruction that flowed between the trees and billowed into the air.

Atop Seraphon's back, Malekith opened his eyes. Much of the day had passed during his metaphysical battle; his forces below had been pushed steadily back and now formed a semi-circle around the encampment, hard pressed on three sides. Dusk was not far off, and defeat closer still.

With a grim smile, he unleashed his spell.

The ground shuddered, throwing asur and druchii alike from their feet, toppling trees and treemen. As the broken remnants of the forest swayed, the thunderous grinding grew even stronger until the Witch King's magic burst forth, fuelled by the strength of mountain roots, gushing directly from the vortex that whirled in the bedrock of Ulthuan. An immense chasm cracked open, swallowing hundreds of Ystranna's maiden guard in a tumble of boulders and broken trees.

Like a volcano erupting, the Ghyran-fuelled dark magic spewed into the sky, a black-tinged fog spreading out through the daemon-cursed trees, freezing every living thing it touched but bringing life to dead branches, filling petrified trees with vitality so that they lifted up limbs and roots and set upon the archers cowering beneath them with thorn-nailed hands.

Higher and higher swelled the sorcerous mass, touching the clouds that roiled overhead. Fire and lightning flickered in their depths and rain started to fall, droplets of flame that quickly became a burning hail and then a storm of flaming meteors that crushed elves and chariots, set fire to tree-kin and lions, obliterated shadow warriors and great eagles.

Malekith felt the burning in his heart first. The spell was channelling more and more power through his body, trying to break free of his control, the peripheral effect causing his already ravaged flesh to steam with fresh vigour, the fires that had crippled him burning behind his eyes and in his bones.

With a last snarl of hatred, Malekith let the spell end, collapsing exhausted in the saddle-throne. Seraphon continued to circle, keeping any potential attack at bay with blasts of gaseous breath and roars, while below the druchii surged out of their defensive line to charge the devastated Chracians and Avelorn maiden guard. To the west the aesenar slunk back towards Phoenix Pass, their retreat covered with hails of black arrows.

His vision dimming, Malekith directed Seraphon to the mountainside and dismounted, almost collapsing as his feet touched the magic-scoured rock. Hidden by the bulk of the black dragon, he knelt down, light-headed, limbs trembling.

Time passed but the Witch King could not mark how long. Eventually the crackle of ancient fires died in his ears and some measure of strength returned to his body. He opened iron-lidded eyes with some effort. It was dark but the clouds parted to reveal the Chaos moon in full ebb, the red orb glaring down like the eye of a wrathful god. The Witch King rose to his feet, flakes of ash drifting from his armour, and stepped past Seraphon to regard the battle below.

Total victory seemed certain. The spirits of the forest had gone, either destroyed by Malekith's spell or fled from the vengeful counter-attack of the Naggarothi. Malekith's army advanced in three prongs, while the Caledorians had flown eastward to the bottom of the valley in pursuit of the phoenixes and great eagles.

Malekith moved to pull himself up to Seraphon's saddle but stopped a pace away, sensing something changing in the winds of magic. He looked up, drawn to the Chaos moon, and it appeared as though its cratered surface were a skull glaring down at him.

Death. Death filled the air.

The winds of magic stilled, impossibly, as though the entire world had frozen. Malekith's breath steamed on air that had been hot a moment before. In the pass below both sides came to faltering stops as the embattled elves, always sensitive to magical change, felt the unnatural stillness. A cold terror filled the hearts of asur and Naggarothi together as they gazed up at the skull moon.

Malekith realised what was happening and he too felt a chilling dread. What if Teclis had been wrong? What if the Great Necromancer had awoken with all of his power?

SEVENTEEN

The Great Necromancer

'I suddenly feel... inadequate,' Malekith told his companion.

'Not even the Tower of Hoeth can rival it,' replied Teclis.

It had once been a mountain, standing on the edge of a massive crater caused by a meteoric impact during the Coming of Chaos. Centuries of labour had turned the peak into a fortress the like of which could not be found anywhere else in the world. Countless battlements and leagues of crenellations wound their way up the lower slopes, and as the mountain narrowed, jutting turrets by the hundred marked its flanks. Windows in the tens of thousands gleamed, lit from within by a pale witchlight. The summit was clad in permanent cloud, glowing fitfully with magical energy.

It was surrounded by rings of walls that made the great gates of the Annulii look like a fence between troublesome neighbours. In the depth of the crater stretched an inland sea, the waters murky, bubbling, tainted by the huge deposit of warpstone. The touch of that ancient meteorite was death and mutation to everything in the vicinity, leaving only the ghoulish descendants of cannibalistic humans to scavenge the mutant fish and loathsome slugs that survived in the tainted waters, when they did not feast on captives from rival tribes.

The warp-taint was so strong it pervaded everything, even the dry air, so that jutting stones had rictus faces. Plants resembled dangling bones and the only flowers that bloomed were black-headed roses with thorns like daggers. The wind hissed ghostly warnings on the edge of hearing that might have just been the fluttering of the thousands of tattered banners that decorated one of the shorelines, trophies taken during millennia of conquest and despotism. Arches of bone grew from the bare rock, an ossuary-avenue that led three leagues to the outermost gates of the fortress.

Nagashizzar, the most dread-inspiring fortress in the world.

Beneath the horrific castle toiled an endless army of the dead. Skeletal soldiers patrolled walls cracked and pitted by millennia of desert winds from the west. On the highest steeples and spires perched enormous dragons, ragged wings furled around half-skeletal bodies, drawn here from their dying fields on the Plain of Bones. Like monstrous gargoyles they appeared, hunched and malevolent, ready to drop down on any interloper, clouds of desiccating fume dribbling from dead lungs between cracked fangs.

Beneath the dark clouds swooped other dead things. The remains of enormous crows and buzzards, large enough to carry off a full grown elf, were themselves dwarfed by reanimated griffons and manticores that circled on endless watch beside horrific creations made from stitched body parts and bound together with necromantic magic.

The Wind of Death, Shyish, was ever-present, clinging to the rocks like fog, dribbling up through cracks and fissures in invisible steaming clouds. Wraiths haunted the deep caverns in the base of the mountains. On the higher flanks stood the cairns of wights, revenants of kings long dead sworn to the service of the Great Necromancer after whom the citadel was named.

Nagash.

Even thinking the name sent a thrill through Malekith, in equal measure jealousy and concern. There were few truly immortal beings in the world and Malekith was amongst them, but even he marvelled at the magical power that had once been at the command of the Great Necromancer. First in his Black Pyramid in Nehekhara to the south and later here, at Cripple Peak, his sorceries had blighted whole empires and laid low entire civilisations. Even the catastrophe of the Sundering unleashed by Malekith paled in comparison to such devastation.

In spirit form he and Teclis walked along a path of skulls that ran between two outer buttresses of grey rock. They passed into the shadow of Nagashizzar, the heat of the sun lost, and Malekith shuddered despite the fact that his avatar felt no mortal sensation. It was more than temperature that caused the reaction.

'You have never come here before?' Teclis asked. 'Never before been tempted to look on this grandest of evil works?'

'I had other matters to keep me occupied,' said Malekith, not willing to admit that he had dared not come here before, for reasons both of vanity and security. 'Besides, what purpose would it have served? There is nothing here except the mindless dead serving commands uttered three ages past.'

'Is that so?' Teclis made a gesture and the two of them disappeared, their spirits coalescing before an immense gatehouse, one of four that guarded the approaches to the citadel.

The gate itself was made of some black material that shone like burnished obsidian. Bone-coloured towers flanked it, each grander than the keep of Tor Achare, stouter than the forts of Karak Kadrin.

On the battlements above, motionless skeletons stood beside war machines of fused bone and sinew – bolt throwers loaded with the thigh bones of giants etched with dire runes and catapults whose phalangeal baskets held ensorcelled skulls that would burst into flame when launched.

Standing against the wall of each tower, to either side of the gate, were two rows of giant beings, made from the bones of dragons, *hippogryphs, nameless lizards of the southlands and other huge creatures, bound together by enchanted gold bands. The undying guardians held spears as tall as buildings and carried bows that could fire arrows capable of splintering trees.*

The pair stopped before the immense barrier and looked up, invisible even to the eyes of the undead.

'You mean to enter?' said Malekith. 'To what purpose?'

'To show you the truth,' Teclis replied. He looked at Malekith with an infuriating half-smile. Few patronised the Witch King, and no other lived long after.

'Not walls alone protect this place,' warned the Witch King. 'There are some powers that even I would not stir.'

'Did you think that the Great Necromancer would lie dormant for eternity?' Teclis stepped through the gate. Malekith, feeling ashamed that he hesitated, followed a moment after. Protective runes flared at the intrusion but Malekith was a strong enough sorcerer to bend aside the magical barriers set within the gate itself, emerging from the dark material to find Teclis waiting for him on a long road made from crushed bone.

'You mean to wake... him?' Malekith's projection flickered as he slid ahead of the mage to stand in his way. 'You tell me that the End Times come, that the Great Powers unite to bend their will to the enslavement of the world, and you seek to bring further ruin upon us?'

'The gods must return,' Teclis said, leaning on his staff, out of habit rather than tiredness. The top of the rod was cast in the shape of the moon goddess, his muse and mythical sponsor. 'The gates of Mirai must be opened, and there is only one that can wrest control of the underworld from Ereth Khial.'

Malekith almost said the name but thought better of it. Names had power and here in the Great Necromancer's fortress it was impossible to predict what attention the name of its creator might bring. 'You are mad. Even as the tide of Chaos comes in, you would raise up a cliff of the undead to crush us against.'

'Not so,' said Teclis, passing through Malekith's projection. Around them dead masons, withered to skin and bone, tapped with hammer and chisel at hieroglyph-covered walls, endlessly chronicling the turning of the world, day after day. The dead paid no heed to the wizards as they accelerated, becoming a blur of white and black until they reached the inner gates of Nagashizzar.

The presence of the warpstone was stronger here, making everything seem more tangible, a thickness to the air, of primordial, unrefined magic that invested every rock and bone. Sentinels crafted from the remains of trolls and ogres lined the corridor inside the gate, heads replaced with facsimiles of old Nehekharan gods, twice the height of Malekith, their scythe-like blades gleaming in the glow of green corpselight that suffused the innards of the fortress.

'The dead do not change. He that raised this citadel desires nothing but a world of the dead enslaved to his will.' Malekith noted that Teclis shared his caution regarding the name of the dread castle's architect. 'The powers of Chaos thrive on the changing ambitions of mortals, to provide the answers to questions only mortals ask. The dead have no need of rage and ambition, despair and charisma.'

'Two forces opposed,' muttered Malekith, seeing the clash in his mind's eye, the legions of the dead on one side, the daemon hordes of the Chaos Powers on the other. There was one problem with that scenario. 'And of those caught between? You choose to be a puppet of the Great Necromancer rather than the mutated spawn of Chaos?'

'We need a bulwark against Chaos. I have done what I can to prepare the humans, the dwarfs will do as they always have done and protect their own. In Lustria the great minds of the Old Ones' servants account nothing for our survival in their astromantic equations. This place holds our greatest chance of resisting the onslaught to come.'

They ascended, level after level as though they climbed through

Mirai itself, the caverns of the damned. The dead in their hundreds of thousands waited in endless ranks for the return of their creator or laboured in mines and forges to furnish wargear to an army three thousand years in the making.

'He will attempt the Great Ritual of Awakening,' Malekith said as they came upon the dread throne room, a cavernous hall at the height of the dead city. A hundred thousand tallows made of the fat of the living burned in sconces and candelabras across the titanic chamber.

In the flickering lights a platform of skulls heaped up at one end of the hall, becoming an immense throne of bones. It was empty, leaving Malekith disappointed and relieved in equal measure.

About the Great Necromancer's dais circled the only living things to be found in Nagashizzar, his disciples, necromancers brought here in fits of madness, chanting his praises as they made offering to the incarnation of undeath.

Malekith could sense the energy of Nagash pulsing like a shadow within the shadows, a constant murmuring on the edge of hearing.

'I have put in motion a series of events that will bring him back,' Teclis confessed. 'It is already too late to prevent his reincarnation.'

'I am prideful, but your arrogance puts mine to shame,' hissed Malekith. 'These are not forces we can control.'

'When you sought to shut down the vortex and bring about the tide of Chaos, did you think twice?' Teclis asked, suddenly as bitter as the Witch King. 'A deed so insane that even now we must deal with its consequences. It is not pride but desperation that pushes me to these extreme deeds.'

'My past actions do not alter the folly of your current plans. I will not allow this.'

The hall trembled, almost imperceptibly. The winds of magic that had been so sluggish started to swirl, eddying around the throne. The acolytes gave gasps of surprise and fear as the dark winds caused the skulls of the throne to begin chattering their teeth, the echoes of their chorus a hideous cacophony that filled the immense hall.

'Too late,' whispered Teclis.

The black furnace of Nagash's soul was growing in power. More brands on the wall burst into life – the blaze of a thousand torchlights brought fresh horror to the scene. Every surface of the chamber was covered in runes and hieroglyphs, which now danced in the flame light with a life of their own, melting and reforming to channel the winds of magic into the throne, the rumbling growing stronger with every passing heartbeat.

'All is in hand,' Teclis tried to assure Malekith. 'I have made sure that the Great Ritual of Awakening will not succeed, not in its entirety. Nagash will return, strong enough to thwart Chaos for a while yet not so strong that we will not be able to undo what has been done.'

Malekith thought he saw an apparition on the throne, wraithlike but terrifying, armoured and cowled, one hand replaced with a claw of metal clutching the arm of the chair, in the other dead grasp a staff of black iron wrought with Nehekharan sigils. The Great Necromancer raised his head, revealing a skull face, eyes blazing with warp-light. Though Malekith and Teclis were concealed by the greatest enchantments of stealth and darkness that they could weave, for an instant the Witch King was sure that the pale green light of those eyes fell upon him and saw him. There was no life there, no expression that could be read. The visitation lasted only a moment before disappearing.

A sudden blast of Shyish swept along the hall, the magic of death extinguishing every flame, hurling the acolytes to the floor. There was nothing else in the chamber, nothing physical at least, but Malekith sensed a pulsing in his head, as of a deep voice vibrating inside his mind. It was in a human language long dead outside these walls, but in his thoughts he recognised the concept behind the words.

I RETURN

Without thought or word between them, the spirits of Teclis and Malekith fled.

'Teclis, you are a fool,' snarled Malekith, aware of the tide of Shyish that was building in the Ulthuan vortex. Darkness swept over the pass as clouds of pure death magic swallowed the Chaos moon. Malekith pulled himself into the throne-saddle, iron skin fizzing with the energy of unlife. 'Your meddling will destroy us yet.'

He was too spent from his duelling with Ystranna and the opening of the great fissure to counter the rising tide of necromantic power. Likewise the handmaiden and her allies, if they sensed at all the catastrophe about to engulf them, were powerless to prevent the influx of Shyish.

Seraphon sensed something amiss too, snorting and whining with discontent that she had never displayed before. Malekith wrestled the chains of her reins, forcing her to launch into the skies, towards the roiling storm of undeath gathering above. The higher he climbed, the more awestruck Malekith was by the magnitude of the incantation being unleashed. The Circlet of Iron was like a crown of ice on his brow, as the Wind of Shyish blew across Ulthuan, across the whole world, shifted and congealed to a single purpose, bent to a single indomitable will.

Through the power of the Circlet of Iron Malekith's spirit soared, unexpectedly. Buoyed up by the swell of death magic, the Witch King felt his essence tugging at the bonds of flesh, unwillingly torn from the near-dead shell that had bound his spirit to the realm of the living for six millennia.

In that instant his senses were focused upon a single point, halfway across the world in tainted lands that sat overshadowed by the great mountains of the dwarfs. The region was awash with Shyish, spewing its revivifying energies across the whole of the world. Nagash had returned to the mortal world and now attempted to unleash the Great Awakening once more, as Malekith had feared.

The Witch King was caught on the outer edge of the impossibly powerful conjuration, and with all his willpower strained to maintain a grip on his armoured form, still sat astride Seraphon's throne-saddle far below. He focused his thoughts on the burning armoured figure of his body, turning his spirit against the raging current of the Great Necromancer's sorcery, diving back through the storm like a hawk caught in a tornado. Straining, pushing every iota of his last strength into the effort, Malekith seized hold of his body once more, hurling his essence back into the withered husk.

The pain of burning, the agony of Asuryan's curse, was the most welcome sensation he had ever felt. Tossed upon the brink of oblivion, almost drawn into the dark abyss of endless Mirai, Malekith cried tears of fire, so great was his joy at cheating death, so invigorating was the opportunity to claw another handhold in mortal existence. The pain was life, the agony proof that he could still achieve his ambitions.

Gasping and laughing, Malekith shuddered with ecstasy as around him the necromantic storm raged.

Nagash's curse of the Great Awakening, the most powerful spell ever unleashed, began with a single shaft of pale green lightning. Where the bolt touched the mountainside the body of a Chracian hunter twitched. Missing an arm, the dead warrior struggled to her feet, her blood staining the fur of her lion pelt cloak. Ghostlight shone from her eyes and with jerking steps she advanced towards the Naggarothi nearby, who stood transfixed by the storm above.

Another lightning strike hit the corpse of a Black Guard, coruscating across silver armour. He pushed himself to his feet, more viscera spilling from the axe wound in his gut, halberd levelled in dead hands.

'No,' murmured Malekith as the two dead things fell upon the Naggarothi, who cried out in horror moments before being cut down. 'No. Not like this. Not now.'

More lightning struck, again and again, increasing in frequency until the whole valley was ablaze with flashing energy.

A fog of undeath sprang up from the ground, reanimating all that it touched, shambling figures advancing within the green mist to beset the druchii companies that had stalled in their counter-attack.

Malekith watched as the eagle he had slain earlier flapped ragged wings, digging itself out from under a pile of broken branches. Its rider, the asur prince with the bow, emerged from the fog and mounted the great bird, and the two soared aloft, together in death as they had been in life.

Across the pass the Naggarothi counter-attack had advanced over thousands of dead and now the slain were returning, striking from behind their lines. Beset by the undead the regiments of druchii fractured, losing all coherence and strategy. Malekith bellowed out his rage, cursing Teclis's name, vowing to gut the meddling Sapherian when they next met, no matter the consequences.

All was not lost, despite Malekith's tirade. Even as the undead clawed and dragged down his warriors, so they also fell upon the asur. The Whiteweald had been a battleground for the past few days and before that the daemons had slaughtered thousands of Chracians. Now the Wind of Death breathed new vigour into rotting flesh and half-stripped bones. With sinews of magic driving them, the dead of the Whiteweald rose, falling on Chracian and maiden guard, aesenar and druchii without discrimination.

Malekith swooped low over the battlefield, searching for some presence of Ystranna. Though he had perverted the winds of magic to his needs, he had unfinished business with the handmaiden of Avelorn.

There was no sign of her, either mystical or physical, and Malekith bit back his frustration. She had escaped, no doubt with other commanders and mages. Her army was retreating, fighting through the dead of the Whiteweald, but protected from pursuit by the reanimated corpses of the recent battle.

The Witch King considered going after them, or commanding

TYRION,
THE DRAGON OF COTHIQUE

Although young, Tyrion has firmly established himself as the greatest hero of the age. He has led the armies of the asur in countless victories against their many enemies, and has gained the favour of the Everqueen Alarielle, amongst others. It is said that when Phoenix King Finubar finally passes from the world, Tyrion will be the natural successor to the throne of Ulthuan. And yet a darkness lurks at the prince's heart, for he is the heir of Aenarion, and something of the First King's madness lies within Tyrion. In battle, he is a merciless killer, and the wise fear what he may be capable of, should he emulate his ancestor and draw the Widowmaker, the cursed Sword of Khaine, from its resting place on the Blighted Isle. Others point to Tyrion's charm and wit and say that this could never be. And yet the shadow that lies upon the Dragon of Cothique never quite lifts...

THE LAST WAR OF THE ELVES

THE ISLES

BLIGHTED ISLE

Plain of Bones

Shrine of Khaine **4**

Rock of Galirian

Anlec

Blighted Woods

Shrine of Kurnous

The Amaranth Isles

Tor Dy

Desolation of Tethlis

Lion Fang Hills

Lion March

CHRACE

Elisia

Sundered Strand

NAGARYTHE

Dead Kings Peak

The Burned Glades

Tor Dranil

Tor Gard

Elyran Tarn

COTH

The Salvation Isles

Shadow March

ANNULII MOUNTAINS

Phoenix Gate

Everale Ridge

Oakheart's Pyre

Sky Forge

ANNULII **10** MOUNTAINS

Tor Inra **2**

Dragon Gate

Silverglen

Tor Saroir

Shadow Peak

Merokai

Unicorn Gate

Stone of Ellyrion

Mirror Woods

ELLYRION

Evershale

AVELORN

Shrine of Rememberance

The High Vale

Reaver's Mark

Tor Emyrath

Moonspire **1**

Isha's Circle **8**

River Vilu

Griffon Gate

Elrost Bay **3**

Everspring

Withelan

Tesselia

Night Wood

Whitefire Tor

Tor Finu

Eagle Gate **2**

Tor Elyr

Gaean Vale

Elarann Bay

Finuval Plain

Hawk Wing Pass

ANNULII MOUNTAINS

Shrine of Hoeth

Fallow Marsh

TRANOC

The Bleak Coast

SEA OF DUSK

THE INNER SEA

11

The Wheeled March

12 Isle of the Dead

The White Tower of Hoeth

Whitepeak

The Arcspan

Cold Drake Keep

SEA OF DREAMS

Port Elistor

6

Avethir

Shrine of Asuryan **5**

Circle of Night

Tower of the Winds

SAPHERY

Tor Sethai

Circle of Dawn

Angerrial

Darkstone Chasm

Stonesung Plateau

CALEDOR

Tower of Lysean

Summersong

Everwatch

The Bay of

Shrine of Addaioth

Shimmersung

Lothern **7**

EATAINE

The Dragon Spine

Shimmersward

Glittering Tower

Shrine of Lileath

Dragonette Cove

Caledor's Repose

Straits of Lothern

The Shifting Shrine of Loec

Vaul's Anvil

The Chaos Wastes

Naggaroth

Ulthuan

Eastern Steppes

The Old World

The Dark Lands

Araby

Tower of Stars

The Great Ocean

Southlands

Tower of the Sun

Tor Elithis

Lustria

Citadel of Dusk

Tor Elasor

Gates of Calith

Fortress of Dawn

Isle of [En]dless Chill

Rokhame

THE SHIFTING ISLES

[I]dar's Shrine

Mistnar

Tor Koruali

Tor Andar

Alin

Elendro Mere

The Dead Shale

Shrine of Mathlann

Farwatch Keep

Athel Tamarha

Isle of Aestuniae

Ruins of Sardenath

Tralinia

Wailing Fen

Shrouded Shore

[v]eli

[v]l

Drake Isles

1. Teclis and Tyrion lead a host to the Moonspire. Here, Teclis casts a purifying ritual that drives the daemons from Ulthuan altogether.

2. Malekith's final invasion of Ulthuan begins. Lokhir Fellheart makes diversionary attacks on the west coast. Malus Darkblade's hammer-blow then falls against Eagle Gate, supported by turncoat forces from Caledor.

3. By the time Tyrion realises that Malekith seeks the Widowmaker, Naggarothi forces have battled their way across Ellyrion and smashed through Phoenix Gate. Tyrion lands an army in southern Ellyrion, and meets the host of Malus Darkblade in battle on the plains of Reaver's Mark.

4. Tyrion's army catches up to Malekith on the shores of the Blighted Isle. The Witch King is already embattled against the crumbling armies of Yvresse and Nagarythe, who have given their all to defend the Shrine of Khaine. Malekith and Tyrion fight a desperate battle atop the shrine, and though he wounds Tyrion sorely, Malekith is defeated. In victory, Tyrion gives in to the curse of Aenarion and seizes the Widowmaker for himself, becoming the mortal incarnation of Khaine.

5. Tyrion establishes his court with Morathi in eastern Cothique. Meanwhile, Teclis brings Malekith to the Shrine of Asuryan in the Inner Sea. Here, Malekith walks into the Flame of Asuryan and becomes the true Phoenix King.

6. Prince Imrik makes steady gains for Malekith's cause, fighting his way through Eataine and Saphery, before pushing into southern Yvresse. Tyrion sallies forth and drives Imrik's armies back in disarray.

7. Korhil's forces push the foe back to Lothern. Korhil and Sea Lord Aislinn's forces are driven back by Malekith, now mantled as the vessel of Asuryan.

8. Korhil is recalled to Tyrion's side, where he joins an expedition into Avelorn to battle the army of Alarielle and Orion. Tyrion's attempt to seize the Everqueen by force fails, and his army is driven off. Alarielle returns to Athel Loren via the worldroots, there to rouse the Asrai to war.

9. Korhil steals the Widowmaker in a doomed attempt to restore his fallen liege to his senses, but is run to ground in the marshes north of Tor Alin. There, the Hag Sorceress defeats a Khainite army under Hellebron, captures Korhil, and reclaims the Widowmaker. The captain's fate for this perceived act of treachery is not kind...

10. Korhil's brave folly at least provides a distraction. Malekith leads a united army of dark, high and wood elves all the way to the passes of the Annulii Mountains.

11. Tyrion burns Avelorn to the ground. Reunited with the Widowmaker, he leads a frenzied campaign that drives Malekith's forces back to the White Tower of Hoeth.

12. Finally accepting that this war will prove a costly disaster no matter its outcome, Malekith agrees to Teclis's plans. The Phoenix King's host takes ship to the Isle of the Dead. There, Teclis begins an incantation intended to unmake the Great Vortex. He seeks to bind each of the winds of magic into a mortal champion, creating Incarnates with the power to resist both Tyrion's Khaine-lost horde and the Chaos Gods themselves. However, Tyrion's warhost has pursued their foes to the isle. A final, desperate battle ensues, for Ulthuan, for survival, and for the very soul of the elven race.

MALEKITH
THE WITCH KING OF NAGGAROTH

Malekith has been the undisputed lord of the dark elves of Naggaroth for six thousand years. Ruling with an iron fist, the Witch King keeps his followers in line with a combination of terror and ruthless unpredictability. The son of Aenarion and the sinister sorceress Morathi, Malekith sees himself as the true king of Ulthuan, and all who have worn the Phoenix Crown since his father as usurpers. In constant pain after being terribly burned by the Flame of Asuryan, Malekith is permanently encased in his armour, an eternal reminder of his continued failure to claim his birthright.

Of late, the Witch King has often been absent from his court, and it is whispered throughout Naggaroth that he has been gathering allies and making plans for another assault on the lands of the high elves – one which will seat him on the Phoenix Throne once and for all… or end his millennia-long reign.

Imrik to wipe out the Chracians, but the present threat of the undead curtailed the urge. Such had been the ferocity of the battle and the daemon invasion the undead outnumbered his host and the dragons were needed protecting what army he had remaining. It would avail him nothing to wipe out Ystranna's force only to have no army of his own to exploit the slaughter.

For most of the night he held the tide with *Urithain* and Seraphon, putting to the sword reconstituted manticores and hydras, slaying again dragons that had the day before been killed by war machine bolts and magic.

When his constitution had recovered sufficiently, in the greyness just before dawn Malekith tapped into the well of magic opened by his confrontation with Ystranna. He let the winds of magic spill forth from the fissure that broke the flank of the mountain, a wave of pure Ghyran washing away the taint of Shyish as one might cleanse infection from a wound, sending the last of the animated dead back to their graves.

All across the Whiteweald walking corpses collapsed, the light going from their eyes, undead grasps losing grip of weapons and shields. The druchii stumbled around in the aftermath, in no position to fight or pursue, their voices lifted in praise to their king and the gods and goddesses of the underworld.

Malekith could do no more and bid Seraphon to bear him back to his pavilion. Dismissing the dragon he issued one last command to the Black Guards that stood watch: he was not to be disturbed by anybody.

As soon as he passed out of their sight, Malekith slumped, overwhelmed by the exertions of the day. He staggered to his iron throne and collapsed into its embrace, weary in mind and body.

Sleep came, but brought with it a nightmare of death. Malekith's dream was filled with visions of Nagash's Great Ritual as the dead of the world burst forth from ancient graves and slid open the portal stones of their tombs.

In the Northern Wastes above the empire of the humans the corpses of thousands of dead marauders returned to life, breaking out of crude cairns to savage their former kinsmen. Chaos-cursed armies and knightly expeditions of battles long past fought again their wars of pillaging and retribution.

Across the realm of the dwarfs, runes and seals cast to prevent such magical incursion melted and burned, releasing tormented spirits that moaned and wailed through the chambers and halls of the mountain cities.

The gardens of Morr, the humans' guardian of the dead, were awash with the Great Necromancer's power, the rituals of the priests availing naught against the sorcery of the first Necromancer. The bodies of burghers and nobles clambered from ornate mausoleums while in the potters' fields beyond the walls of towns and cities generations of dead were revivified and fell upon the slumbering citizenry.

Eventually darkness came and Malekith dreamed no more.

EIGHTEEN

Fresh Plans

Though rested in mind and in body, Malekith awoke with a restlessness of spirit.

At first he could not fathom what disturbed him so. It was like an appointment he could not remember, or that he had misplaced some object and had forgotten that he should be looking for whatever was missing. He sat on the throne trying to work out what it was that vexed him, when suddenly he realised what it was.

There were only seven winds of magic.

The Wind of Death, Shyish, was gone. Not abated or dampened as he might expect following the immense raising of the dead by Nagash, but completely gone. Like a grin missing a tooth the winds blowing from the north were incomplete and it was this sensation that was so irritating to his psyche.

His smouldering form burned into fresh life as he bellowed for Kouran to attend him. With full wakening returned memory, and the recollection that Ystranna had escaped the trap she had unwittingly sprung.

'How long since the battle?' the Witch King demanded before Kouran could even offer a bow or salute.

'Three days, my king,' replied the captain. 'And two more nights. I despatched scouts by horse and foot and wing but there is no sign of the Chracians or the host from Avelorn.'

'Of course not,' snarled Malekith, standing. 'They have been bloodied and seek to bind their wounds. The mountains hold not only hunting lodges and peat-burners' huts. There are fortresses here, hidden, dug into the stone like dwarf-holes. The Chracians have gone to ground and wait for us to make our next move.'

'We shall not disappoint them, my king. The army is ready to march north at your word.'

'North?'

'To the coast, my king. Is it not your intent to seize the harbours and crossing to the Blighted Isle?'

This seemed presumptuous of Kouran, to explain strategy to the Witch King, but Malekith knew no insult was intended and let it pass.

'I would no more have that tree-witch dogging my heels than I would the Anars. We will scour Chrace until she and her army are destroyed.'

'My king, it could take a season to find them and they are ensconced within their hidden keeps, another season and more to break their defences.'

'I have three score of dragons!' Malekith roared, smashing a fist into the other hand, sending up a fountain of red sparks. 'Did you not see what happened at Eagle Gate? Have we not advanced further than on any campaign since I was first ejected from this isle? Ystranna cannot hide from me. I know her now, and many are the ways in which she can be hunted down.'

'If Tyrion grants us the leisure of such a pursuit, my king,' Kouran argued. Any other advisor would have uttered such sentiment with softer words, but Kouran showed no remorse for his indelicate tone. In fact Malekith could see nothing in the other elf's expression except earnest intent, so alien on the features of the druchii the Witch King barely recognised it.

'Tyrion.' Malekith spat the name. 'Tyrion? Let Tyrion come. Let this pretty prancing prince try his might against mine. He is nothing without...' Malekith stopped himself naming Tyrion's brother, not wishing to reveal his involvement with Teclis, even to Kouran. The alliance was best kept secret, a source of power hidden from his rivals, both in the asur camp and his own army. 'Without Imrik he wields a lesser force.'

'My king, you hunt rats with a hydra,' said the Black Guard captain. 'Ystranna's force is barely a fifth of ours. It is entirely her intent that we expend our limited days seeking her. It was only with a bait of ten thousand warriors that you were able to draw out her strike in the Whiteweald. She will not be tricked twice. Nor, I think, your own commanders. Alith and his aesenar have disappeared and Ystranna will not show herself again soon.'

'Until we turn our back on her,' Malekith said pointedly. It riled him that he had been so close to eliminating the handmaiden and her army, it felt like defeat to let her slip away unmolested. The dead rising had spoiled everything, ruining a perfectly executed strategy. 'The moment we head north the Chracians will be nipping at our heels, a company lost here, a war machine battery there. You would have us bleed from a thousand tiny bites.'

'We can spare a third of the army as rearguard, my king, and still have sufficient force to seize Tor Achare and the coastal towns.'

'A third? Which part of my army would you trust with such duties? The Ghrondians, who I am sure still answer to Drusala though she is absent? Perhaps the remnants from Karond Kar? They must be bursting with loyalty to my cause. There is not a contingent or commander that I can trust out of sight or further than my reach. I burned their cities to ensure they cannot retreat, but should they find welcome in the ranks of the asur...' Malekith held up his fist and slowly splayed his fingers. 'Your rearguard would melt quicker than ice in my grasp.'

'I would stand, my king.' Kouran said the words with pride, and Malekith did not doubt the captain. 'The Black Guard will hold the pass for you.'

'A worthy offer, Alandrian, but one I must decline. I have greater need of your eyes and your blades in my camp, lest those untrustworthy elements I speak of seek a more direct means of betraying me.'

'That leaves only one choice, my king, one part of the army that you can trust.'

Malekith thought about this for a moment. 'The Caledorians?'

'If Imrik gives his word he will keep it, my king.'

'If...' Malekith sat down again, settling his body to settle his thoughts. Kouran was right, of course, in principle. The death of Ystranna achieved nothing save to satisfy Malekith's desire for revenge. Her taunts still smarted and her continued existence was an insult.

But to slay her at the expense of the greater scheme was madness. His arguments against Kouran's course of action were revealed as thin excuses to allow the Witch King his vengeance. Malekith looked at the captain, who was waiting patiently for his master's next utterance.

'How do I deserve such loyalty, Kouran?' he asked.

The captain frowned, confused that the question had to be asked. 'You are my king.'

'Many others seek to be your king, or queen – what makes me so worthy that you cut them down at my word?'

'You are the true king of the elves, Malekith,' said Kouran, uttering his master's name for the first time since joining his service. 'You are the son of Aenarion, champion of the Daemon War, heir to the Phoenix Crown. It is your right by deed, merit and birth and I would give my life to see that ancient wrong reversed and your rightful position restored. As an elf I can think of no higher calling.'

Malekith received this testament in shocked silence. Not even his mother had ever spoken in such bald terms, and the words were like crystal water cooling his burning flesh. The simplicity of Kouran's assertion calmed Malekith's ire. He felt a moment of affinity with the captain, believing for the first time in his long life that there was perhaps one other who truly understood the nature of the pain that coursed through him – not the physical agony but the spiritual torment of rejection.

Pride was his greatest weakness. Malekith knew this, and it had perhaps been the undoing of his father but the affront that had been done to him, the insult to Aenarion's house, was so great that justice demanded an equally immense retribution.

But not yet. Kouran's short speech salved the wounded pride of the Witch King, clearing his thoughts.

'Go to Imrik,' he said. 'Bid him to pursue the Chracians and Ystranna to every corner of Chrace if necessary. I want her dead. We will march north, and with his dragons he will guard our advance.'

'As you say, my king,' said Kouran, showing no sign of jubilation or conceit.

'You really are unique amongst our kind,' Malekith said. 'Your dedication, your obedience and loyalty are like no other.'

'It is a lament that the Naggarothi do not value such traits as they once did,' said Kouran. 'I cleave to an older time, when Aenarion's word was his bond and his selfless sacrifice prevented the extinction of our kind.'

'Not just the Naggarothi,' said Malekith. 'All of elfdom. My father would have gladly fought beside you. If only you had been born in such distant times, and perhaps borne aloft his standard instead of that traitor Eoloran Anar, our history may have been very different.'

'I think not, my king,' Kouran confessed, 'though I take it as great praise. Khaine desired your father's wrath and the Great Powers feared him regardless of those he consorted with. Perhaps now we have the chance to restore what was broken.'

'We do, Kouran, we have that opportunity.'

Kouran saluted and left, leaving Malekith to plan the march north.

NINETEEN

A Hasty Council

The Witch King had studied the maps and reports from the scouts in great detail and was just about ready to call for his generals when he heard a commotion outside his pavilion. He heard one of his guards issuing a challenge and a sharp rebuke from Kouran – Malekith had expected Kouran to have been gone for the rest of the day and had left instruction that he was not to be disturbed, still weary from his recent efforts.

The argument grew louder and then ended suddenly with the sound of a sword swiftly drawn, a wet chopping noise and a dull thud.

Malekith turned to the door, half drawing *Urithain* as he did so, expecting treachery. The thought that even Kouran had, at the last, turned on him was almost as hurtful as the fires that raged in his body. The captain of the Black Guard strode into the chamber and stopped. Before the Witch King could say anything, another elf entered – Imrik, with blood-slicked blade bared.

'Were all your words as empty as your oaths of allegiance?' snarled Malekith, drawing his sword fully, squaring his stance to face-off against the two elves, the tip of *Urithain* moving from one to another.

'It is not as you fear, my king,' said Kouran. To prove himself, he tossed *Crimson Death* aside and held up his empty hands. 'There is no treachery.'

'Your guard threatened me first,' Imrik said, by way of explanation. He flicked the blood from his sword and sheathed it.

'I should think so too,' said Malekith, lowering *Urithain* a fraction. 'That is what guards are for when unwelcome visitors arrive.'

'He would not listen to my command,' said Kouran.

'*My* command had been explicit.' Malekith could see that there was no immediate threat and sheathed his blade. He sat down in his throne and beckoned the two elves to approach. 'Kouran, only one of my four guards saw fit to deny you entry. He has unfortunately lost his life for his dedication. The other three should fare no better for their disobedience.'

'I will attend to it presently, my king,' said Kouran, retrieving his weapon. 'There is a more pressing concern.'

Before Malekith could ask, the drape across the chamber entrance moved aside as Teclis entered, leaning heavily on his staff, looking even worse than he had at Eagle Gate. There was a dangerous look in the mage's eye nevertheless and he thrust his staff towards Malekith while with his other hand he made an arcane gesture and threw up a semi-transparent wall of gold that surrounded the mage and Witch King. Kouran slashed his halberd at the barrier and was rewarded by an explosion of sparks that threw him halfway across the throne chamber.

'I knew I could count on the treachery of one of you, at least,' snarled Malekith. His hand moved towards the hilt of his sword again, but stopped just short. A fight with Teclis would not be conducted with steel, no matter how ensorcelled. The Witch King started to summon the winds of magic to his will. 'Do you think me a fool?'

'The arch-traitor stands in accusation of me?' Teclis's rage was almost as great as Malekith's finest tirades. 'You have conspired and misled me since I first came to you in your dreams, and now you think that I have betrayed you? You are a gutless serpent, Malekith, and I curse the day I ever thought to trust you.'

'Perhaps it is your mistress, goddess Lileath, that has led you awry,' snapped Malekith. 'You come to my camp and threaten me, but it is I that is the traitor? How contrary.'

'Do not deny that you and your wretched mother have been trying to manipulate me from the outset.'

Malekith was stunned by the idea and was lost for words to utter any such denial. Instead he laughed, finding the accusation so ridiculous there was no other way to answer it.

'Even now she whispers into the ear of my brother, guiding him to his destruction.'

'You have taken leave of your senses, nephew. Morathi broods in Ghrond surrounded by thorns and northlanders. If she desires to whisper into the ear of any mortal it would be mine.'

Teclis hesitated, his anger wavering. 'She left Ghrond with you, in the guise of Drusala. You brought her to Ulthuan and then sent her with Malus to confront my brother, where she infiltrated his camp by means of another glamour.'

'Nonsense. You are getting confused in your fatigue. Drusala is one of my mother's chief sorceresses.'

'Drusala was Morathi.'

'I would see through such a guise in moments,' protested Malekith, but uncertainty gnawed at his confidence. 'Do you think I would not sense the soul of my mother?'

'And that is why I concluded that you must have been colluding with her,' said Teclis, but his tone was uncertain. He waved a hand and the shimmering barrier dissipated.

'No!' snapped Malekith as Kouran readied to launch himself at the mage. Imrik stood beside the captain looking confused. 'Something is wrong here. I will hear him speak.'

'Apologies, my king, but he lied to us,' said Kouran, glaring at Teclis with unconcealed homicidal intent.

'A lie of omission, perhaps,' admitted Teclis, never moving his eyes from the Witch King. 'I told you that my brother now marches north and that I needed to speak to your master. Both of these facts are still true.'

'Tyrion seeks battle,' said Malekith, pondering the import of this news.

'We need to prepare if Tyrion advances on our position,' said Imrik.

'What of Malus Darkblade and the vanguard?' asked the Witch King. 'Has he also turned against me?'

'Malus is dead,' said Teclis.

'Finally some good news,' Malekith exclaimed with a contemptuous laugh. 'I hope his demise was painful.'

'He was possessed by a daemon, which tore him apart from inside, before being slain by Tyrion.'

The elves thought about this in silence for several moments, even Malekith's bitter humour dissipated by the gruesome revelation.

'Settle this matter,' insisted Malekith. 'You swear that Drusala was my mother wrapped in a glamour?'

'I swear by Lileath,' said the mage. 'I recognised her immediately, as did my brother.'

'And I did not...'

'Sometimes the closest are the easiest to deceive,' said Teclis, pacing across the chamber to stop just short of Malekith. 'A riddle to resolve another day. Of import is that her deception has succeeded. My brother, in his vulnerable mental state, has fallen under her bewitchment. She has persuaded him that he must draw the Widowmaker.'

'The Sword of Khaine?' Malekith thought on this and then snorted with derision. 'Oh Morathi, you poor enamoured soul. You think that this princeling is Aenarion reborn.'

'I thought it odd that she relinquished him so easily before,' said Teclis.

'What are you two talking about?' demanded Imrik. 'You speak in half measures, and I would know everything we must face.'

Teclis looked at Malekith, intrigued. 'I did not realise you were aware of the event. You were, as I recall, indisposed.'

Malekith grimaced, remembering the time well.

'It is true that I was not of the mortal realm at that time, due to your efforts, nephew. You of all people should remember that we see much more when we have a different perspective and the Realm of Chaos gave me the greatest vantage point one might wish for.'

'What happened, my king?' asked Kouran.

'The Blighted Isle, one hundred and fifty years ago,' said Malekith. 'Always it seems our fates revolve around that little bloodied dark altar to the God of Murder.'

It was the blood magic that attracted his attention. It made ripples in the Realm of Chaos, drawing attention from across the spaceless abode of the Ancient Powers. The first drops quickly became a waterfall, channelled by a powerful mind into a torrent of energy that blazed across the immaterial skies like a beacon.

He had been drawn to it out of instinct, moving to its source with a shoal of other near-mindless entities to lap at the delicious sacrifice. More powerful creatures, servants of the Chaos Gods, followed swiftly, causing the lesser denizens to scatter, but he remained, the scent of the blood, the feel of it flowing through him and over reminding him of something he had once been.

As more blood was spilled on the altar of the elves' God of Murder further power thrashed through the Realm of Chaos, drawing a crimson scene upon the ever-changing world. He saw the rocks of an island – a place he had known – and two armies clashing. An altar of black stone was awash with blood, the basin-like temple around it filled with corpses of slaves and sorceresses. By the

altar itself stood a tall figure, hair thick with gore, wickedly jag-
ged sacrificial blade in hand, her naked form bathed in blood.

Looking upon the face, he remembered.

Morathi. His mother.

He was Malekith, king of the elves, and he had cast himself
into the Realm of the Gods to avoid death at the hands of the
mage, Teclis. He had no idea how long had passed in the mor-
tal world, but as he watched the scene unfolding in the pools of
blood around him he realised that something was amiss.

There was another with Morathi and at first Malekith was
stunned by recognition. It was his father, Aenarion, the defender
of Ulthuan and first of the Phoenix Kings. But the scene did not
resemble any act he remembered occurring before his self-imposed
banishment. His father had travelled alone to the Blighted Isle,
both to retrieve the Sword of Khaine and to replace it. Morathi
did not belong there.

With a shock Malekith understood. It was not Aenarion that
stood slack-eyed and entranced by the Hag Sorceress, but one of
his descendants, the Prince Tyrion. Malekith had no idea how
Morathi had come to capture the prince, or the Blighted Isle, but
it was obvious that her possession of these two at the same time
was not coincidence.

Becoming fully aware of himself and his sense of being, Malekith
was able to stretch forth his will into the Realm of Chaos around
him. The Circlet of Iron on his brow throbbed as it guided his
power, allowing him to move the image of the scene as he desired.
He saw that the asur army besieging the Shrine of Khaine was led
by Teclis, the twin of Tyrion, fighting desperately to free his brother.

Morathi's intent became clear. She was trying to use Tyrion as a
vessel for restoring Aenarion's soul to the mortal sphere. She was
bargaining in blood for Khaine to return the first Phoenix King,
to instil Aenarion's essence into the body of the prince.

In short, Morathi was trying to replace Malekith and put Tyrion
on the throne of Ulthuan.

He raged as he saw the ceremony reaching its crescendo, cursing his mother and urging Teclis and his host to greater efforts, impotently trapped in the immortal but immaterial world. Whether the ritual would succeed looked doubtful, but Malekith wanted his mother to fail, for throwing her son aside in favour of this gullible young prince, and for disturbing the eternal rest of his father.

Malekith's anger lent him strength, the same strength that had sustained him for thousands of years. He would not be usurped again!

Through an extension of pure will, Malekith reached into the mind of one of the Naggarothi looking on, one of the final line of defence against the asur counter-attack. The druchii's thoughts were filled with selfish desires and hatred of the approaching asur and it took only the smallest of influences for Malekith to subvert the elf's mind and turn it to his will.

With stolen body Malekith drew close to Morathi, stepping between the bodies of the dead, unnoticed as the Hag Sorceress shrieked her supplications and promises to Khaine. Drawing his blade, he thrust the sword between his mother's shoulder blades and tore it free as she fell. Another stroke cut the bonds around Tyrion, but the prince just blinked and looked dumbfounded, drugged or worse.

'Move, you cretinous dog,' Malekith snarled, slapping the prince across the cheek with the back of his hand. 'Wake up!'

Tyrion murmured and blinked again, as though rousing from a heavy sleep. Morathi was already pushing herself to her feet, the wound in her back sealing with magical energy.

'Go!' Malekith thrust the sword into Tyrion's hands as other druchii closed on him and the prince. 'Your brother approaches!'

Guided by instinct, Tyrion blocked a sword aimed at his throat and disembowelled the elf that had attacked him. Malekith threw his purloined body in front of a hail of repeater crossbow bolts, saving the prince as he charged the closing ring of Naggarothi. Blotting out the pain from his stolen flesh, the spirit of the Witch

King had one last glimpse of Tyrion cutting his way free and then his new body died, sending his essence wailing back to the Realm of Chaos.

Imrik listened to the end of the tale with a look of disbelief, while Kouran nodded silently, absorbing the import of what Malekith had said.

'I did not realise that you had intervened,' said Teclis, brow creased with a shallow frown. 'Rumour followed that an agent of Hellebron had freed my brother to confound Morathi.'

'A rumour I did not quash on my return,' said Malekith.

'Why did you not slay her when you returned, my king?' asked the Black Guard captain.

'My mother stood by me for five thousand years, and even when I sided with Bel Shanaar and took her into custody she never gave up on my destiny to become Phoenix King.' Malekith took a deep breath, his lungs burning and ragged while the pain of recollection swamped his thoughts. He shook his head to clear them. 'She thought I was dead, and sought another to fulfil her ambitions. I could not blame her.'

'The ritual guided you back from oblivion,' said Teclis, eyeing Malekith with wonder. 'When you disappeared into the Realm of Chaos I thought you lost forever, and wondered how it was that you managed to return.'

'It was the spark that reignited the flame of my spirit and gave me purpose again,' Malekith replied. His mood soured. 'Though it appears my leniency was misplaced and since that time she has been seeking to reunite with Tyrion again. I accused her of wasting away in Ghrond like a pining lover but her greater intent becomes clear. She did not warn of the northlander attack hoping that Naggaroth would be devastated, too weak to ever reclaim Ulthuan, and she would swoop upon Tyrion and usher him to the Phoenix Throne over the bodies of any that defied him.'

'That part of the plan has so far failed,' said Teclis, 'but the cycle of history turns again and this time we shall suffer for it if we do not act.'

'Why did you not dispel her bewitchment?' demanded Imrik. 'This matter would be simply resolved if you broke the hold Morathi has on Tyrion.'

'I cannot, for his heart is bound to her now by something stronger than magic.'

'Surely he cannot love her?' Imrik shook his head in disgust.

Teclis took a moment to drink one of his life-giving potions, gaining himself time to think. He looked directly at Malekith. 'What first drove your father to the Sword of Khaine and the embrace of your mother?'

'Grief,' Malekith replied without hesitation. 'His wife and children slain, or so he believed, he reached his darkest nadir and sought only vengeance for the ill that beset him and his people.'

'Tyrion's daughter is dead,' announced Teclis, looking away. Was it an expression of guilt? Malekith wondered. 'Princess Aliathra died trying to thwart the return of the Great Necromancer.'

'Aliathra was Finubar's child, the next Everqueen,' said Imrik, confused. 'Are you saying... ?'

'I knew it!' said the Witch King, earning himself looks of interest from the mage and Imrik together, but he did not care for their feelings. 'Well, I was almost certain, and now you confirm my suspicions. And here you are, nephew, at my camp, rather than at your brother's side doing your best to counter the machinations of my mother. Why might that be?'

Teclis did not answer.

'Answer Malekith's question, mage,' insisted Imrik. 'Your efforts would have been better spent curtailing the threat at source rather than bringing news of its unfolding to us.'

'Tyrion blames me for Aliathra's death. I was forced to flee.'

'Is that so?' crowed Malekith. 'An intrigue going amiss, nephew?'

Teclis said nothing but the Witch King saw his expression saddening even further, fingers tightening on his staff, jaw clenched.

'Or perhaps something worse,' Malekith continued, relentless, recognising the self-loathing behind Teclis's grief. His voice was filled with savage glee. 'You meant for her to die, did you not?'

The mage quivered with emotion, almost collapsing, but none of his companions made a move to assist him.

'Is this true?' demanded Imrik, while Kouran laughed with scorn.

'Enough!' snarled the mage, with such vehemence that Imrik and Kouran retreated a step. He glared at all three of them with eyes blazing with golden energy. 'She was my niece and I feel the loss no less for the fact that it was necessary.'

Malekith stepped down from his throne and loomed over the mage. 'You have always intended for Tyrion to draw the Widowmaker.'

Teclis nodded, defiant. 'By drawing again His sword, the curse of Khaine will be lifted from our line.'

'You would unleash the Godkiller on the world again?' Imrik's eyes narrowed dangerously. 'Just to rid your family of their curse?'

'We have no future while the curse remains,' said Teclis, dismissing Imrik's concerns with a wave of the hand. He slumped and looked earnestly first at Imrik and then Malekith. 'None of us. What better time for the Godslayer to be drawn than during the Rhana Dandra? I had planned to be beside my brother, to guide him through the turmoil so that he would be able to return the blade when the End Times were over and Chaos thwarted again.'

'You reckoned without the interference of my mother,' said Malekith, pacing away. 'It seems that your mistress's prophecies are not worth much, nephew.'

'It is too late to give up,' said Teclis. He hesitated before continuing. 'Nagash has returned and attempted to become the living embodiment of Shyish. As I promised, he was too weak and for the moment he has drawn the power to the land the humans call Sylvania. He seeks to regain his pyramid in Khemri and if he does so, perhaps he will also regain the means to take the Wind of Shyish into himself fully.'

'The embodiment?' Malekith had never thought such a thing possible. 'A physical avatar of a magical wind?'

'As I say,' said Teclis, looking uneasy at the mention of such a thing, as though he regretted having to bring it up. Malekith let his suspicions remain unspoken for the time being. 'Even now, across the ocean, the Great Necromancer's armies and the humans fight a great incursion from the northlands. The Chaos Gods have their attention focused on the realm of Sigmar and the endless legions of Nagash's lieutenants for the moment, but it will not linger there forever. Sooner or later the daemons will come again for Ulthuan and we must be united and ready. Lileath has shown me the way to victory and though my own plans follow a twisted path, the destination has not changed.'

'I did not say I had given up,' said Malekith, turning back to the others. 'We must seize the Blighted Isle first.'

'Do you intend to take up the Sword of Khaine, my king?' asked Kouran, who had observed the whole exchange without voicing any opinion. His expression betrayed no thought regarding whether he thought this a good or bad idea.

'It is not a gift, it is a trap,' said Malekith, remembering previous experience. 'One I have already avoided. It would be folly to put myself in such a position again on purpose.'

'You must, if it would prevent its power being controlled by Morathi,' insisted Teclis.

'How do we stop Tyrion if he wields the Widowmaker?' Imrik asked, aghast at the thought.

'I do not know,' admitted Teclis.

'That is why I plan to get there first,' Malekith said, avoiding the answer to the question. In this area he was beholden to the guidance of Teclis, and it irked the Witch King to trust the Sapherian, but he had no choice. This was a road he had chosen to follow, throwing in his fortune with the fate of others, and now he was required to follow its course to the end, bitter or otherwise. 'I suggest you impose upon your allies and cousins a sense of urgency.'

TWENTY

The Shadow of Khaine

The battle had descended into an anarchy of bloodletting and savagery as the violent shroud of Khaine fell upon all that participated in the fighting. The Blighted Isle was His domain and all blood shed on its shores belonged to Him, and all that lifted blade or bow offered up a prayer to His power. Manoeuvre and strategy, wheel and counter-wheel, lines of advance and echelons of attack had become meaningless as the druchii threw themselves at the small contingent of elves defending the Shrine of Khaine.

Kouran and his Black Guard were at the centre of the attack, the steel point of the spear thrust into the heart of the enemy, cleaving through archers and spearmen that fought beneath the colours of Yvresse, the banner of Naggarond flying proudly beside Malekith's lieutenant. The spears and arrows of Tor Yvresse's silverin guard met the tide of black-and-purple-clad Naggarothi dreadspears while the darkshards of the Witch King unleashed a continual storm of repeater crossbow bolts into the foe.

Overhead wheeled mages on pegasi and colourfully-blazoned

knights of Tor Gavel riding griffons, where black dragons duelled with flame-winged phoenixes and Sapherian loremasters aboard flying skycutters drawn by eagles and hippogriffs.

On the periphery of the battle stalked the aesenar, who had tailed Malekith's army through Chrace and made their own hidden crossing, led by the Shadow King. Many had been cut down by the advance of the Black Guard but the survivors sniped at regimental captains and slew the handlers of hydras and packs of war dogs, adding to the confusion and dread that reigned over Khaine's domain. They were not the only descendants of Nagarythe fighting in defence of the shrine, for the Revenants of Khaine held the grounds of the temple itself, ready to slay and be slain to prevent the Widowmaker being seized.

Not long ago it had started raining blood, crimson streaking down pale flesh and shining armour as a benediction of Khaine's pleasure at the slaughter. It hissed and spat from the armour of the Witch King as he tried his best to maintain some semblance of control over his bloodthirsty warriors.

Teclis stood not far away. As yet the mage had not committed to the fighting and was reserving his magical strength for some deed yet to come. The Sapherian felt the Witch King's gaze upon him and turned.

'Whatever happens, we must not let Tyrion take the Sword of Khaine.'

'My army bleeds to that end, nephew – what more do you ask?'

'Promise me that you will take up the Widowmaker instead, if that is what is needed.'

'What a strange life you have led. Does it shame you to think of the times you and your kin thwarted me in my attempts to rule, or are you simply filled with the warm glow of satisfaction from the realisation of my rightful claim? It must be so heartening that your life's work, your dedication, has led to this moment, when you would rather see me wielding the Widowmaker than your brother.'

Teclis said nothing more and simply glared at the Witch King.

'Worry not,' said Malekith, *Urithain* blazing to life in his grasp, 'your brother forfeited his hands the moment he started grasping for my crown. He will possess no fingers with which to claim the Godslayer.'

'That is not a promise,' Teclis replied, but the Witch King's thoughts had moved on, dismissing the mage.

Malekith's second wave of warriors were being torn apart by the griffons and their riders and with a gesture to the dozen black dragons that accompanied him, he took to the sky on Seraphon. As he rose higher, the crash of battle dimmed and the stench of blood lessened, and it reminded him of how different it had been the first time he had set foot upon this bare rock.

Malekith came to a wide, flat expanse near to the centre of the Blighted Isle. Here jagged black rocks veined with lines of red thrust up into the ruddy skies like a circle of columns. The ground within was as flat as glass and black as midnight. At the centre there stood a block of red-veined rock and something only partly visible shimmered above it. This was clearly the Shrine of Khaine, but as Malekith looked around he could see no sign of his father's resting place nor any remains of Indraugnir. They must have come here, for Aenarion had returned the Sword of Khaine to the very altar close to which Malekith now stood.

Even as his thoughts touched upon the Godslayer, there came to Malekith's ears a distant noise: a faint screaming. Now that it had attracted his attention, the prince looked at the Altar of Khaine more closely. As he did so, the sounds around him intensified. The screams of agony were joined by howls of horror. The ring of metal on metal, of fighting, echoed around the shrine. Malekith heard a thunderous heart beating, and thought he saw knives carving wounds upon flesh and limbs torn from bodies on the edge of his vision.

The red veins of the altar were not rock at all, but pulsed like arteries, blood flowing from the altar stone in spurting rivers of gore. He realised that the beating heart was his own, and it hammered in his chest like a swordsmith working at an anvil.

A keening sound, like a note sung by a sword's edge as it cuts the air, rang in Malekith's ears. It was not unpleasant, and he listened to it for a while, drawn by its siren call to take step after step closer to the altar. Finally, the prince of Nagarythe stood transfixed before that bloody shrine just as his father Aenarion had been.

The thing embedded in the rock shimmered before Malekith's eyes, a blur of axe and sword and spear. Finally a single image emerged, of a bulbous mace studded with gems. Malekith was confused, for this was no weapon, but rather reminded him of the ornamental sceptres often carried by other princes. It seemed very similar to the one borne by Bel Shanaar when he had visited the colonies.

It was then that the meaning came to Malekith. All of Ulthuan would be his weapon. Unlike his father, he needed neither sword nor spear to destroy his foes. He would have the armies of an entire nation in his grasp, and would wield them however he pleased. If he but took up Khaine's sceptre, there would be none that could oppose him. Like a vision, the future unfolded before Malekith.

He would return to Ulthuan and go to Tor Anroc, and there cast down the gates of the Phoenix King. He would offer up the body of Bel Shanaar to Khaine and become undisputed ruler of the elves. He would reign for eternity as the bloody right hand of the God of Murder. Death would stalk in his shadow as he brought ruination to the empire of the dwarfs, for such was the power of the elves that they need not share the world with any other creature. Beastmen were put to the sword by their thousands, and the carcasses of orcs and goblins spitted upon poles lined the roads of his empire for hundreds of miles.

Malekith laughed as he saw the rude villages of humans being put to the torch, their menfolk tossed onto pyres, their women with *their hearts ripped out, whole families with their heads dashed in upon the bloodied rocks. Like an unstoppable tide, the elves would conquer all that lay before them, until Malekith presided over an empire that covered the entire globe and the fumes of the sacrificial fires blotted out the sun. Malekith was carried forwards on a giant palanquin made from the bones of his vanquished enemies, a river of blood pouring out before him.*

'No!' cried Malekith, breaking his gaze from the sceptre and hurling himself face-first to the rocky ground.

He lay there for a long while, eyes screwed shut, his heart pounding, his breathing ragged and heavy. Slowly he calmed himself, and opened an eye. There seemed to be nothing amiss. There was no blood or fire. There was nothing but silent rock and the hiss of the wind.

The last rays of the day bathed the shrine in orange, and Malekith pushed himself to his feet and staggered from the circle, not daring to look back at the altar. Knowing that his father would not be found, Malekith gathered his senses as best he could and made for the boat, never once looking back.

TWENTY-ONE

The Battle of the Blighted Isle

The Blighted Isle was a battle-ravaged boneyard. For five millennia the druchii and asur had contested control of the island, neither willing to sacrifice their hold on the Widowmaker's resting place. Even before Nagash's spell the dead had never rested easily here, their spirits taken by Khaine, denied their eternal rest in Mirai. Now those dead were silent, the magical wind that had sustained them stilled by the return of the Great Necromancer. The bones of five thousand years lay knee-deep in places, the corpses of the last years' skirmishes still fresh on top of the charnel pile.

The white was splashed crimson with the blood of those now selling their lives for possession of the shrine, and great must have been Khaine's mirth at the carnage being wrought to deny his return to the world. Elves foundered through the bone-drifts, cracking bleached ribs underfoot while hydras and griffons snapped vertebrae and crushed skulls. Companies of spears crashed together, wading through mires of blood and rotting flesh, the scene made all the more grisly by the crimson storm that continued to pour from the black clouds overhead.

Desire and desperation found equal purpose in Malekith's heart and he fought with a fervour and strength he had not possessed for many an age. Not since the battles of his first war for Ulthuan had he known such spectacle and the pivot of history was swinging in his favour. If he prevailed this day all of Ulthuan would be his, as it should have been so many centuries before.

The knights of Tor Gavel could not match him. *Urithain* was a blur in his hand, cutting and slashing, severing griffon wings and princes' heads with equal abandon. Malekith trusted to the armour of midnight to protect him from harm. As his iron skin absorbed blows from the blessed steel of Yvressian princes so his spellshield devoured the bolts and flames of Sapherian enchantments. Seraphon shared her master's mood, claws and fangs leaving a tattered trail of bloody carcasses in their wake as they tore across the skies like a black thunderbolt. Behind them the other black dragons fell upon the archers and bolt throwers lining the boulder-strewn approaches to the Shrine of Khaine, cleaving bloody furrows in the ranks of the Yvressian militia.

While Malekith's blade cut flesh and bone, his magic consumed an equal number of foes with dark lightning and organ-charring flames. Armour melted as bolts of dark magic leapt from his fingertips and Yvressian knights shrieked their last breaths as his mind tore apart their innards and pulverised their bones. Pegasi fell from the skies like swatted insects, hearts stopped by a simple gesture from the Witch King, their riders' plunging death screams lost in the din of the armies clashing below.

Flying the colours of Lothern, a squadron of skycutters pulled by great eagles swept down into Malekith, the riders' spears glinting with magic. Seraphon turned into the descending skycutters, a barbed wing raking the guts from one of the eagles while her jaws snapped around the neck of another. Malekith was surrounded by a welter of claws and speartips that glanced shrieking from his armour, a flurry of feather and beaks blotting all view. *Urithain* split one of the attacking birds from eye to tail while a coruscating black flame incinerated the skycutter it had been pulling. The other skycutters fell away quickly, pursued by the vengeful Witch King, the roars of Seraphon hastening their retreat.

Malekith drew in the winds of magic, forming a storm of power around his upraised blade. It felt strange, the Wind of Shyish missing from the enchantment, but the vanished Wind of Death did nothing to lessen the raw power of his sorcery.

He sighted on the nearest of the Lothern chariots and unleashed the spell, but no sooner had the ball of fire left his hand than it fizzled into smoke, dispersing along the wind. Disgruntled, Malekith flung out a hand, willing bolts of power to leap across the sky towards his doomed victim. Sparks crackled across his fingertips but nothing more.

The Witch King felt the twisting of the winds of magic that had thwarted his sorcery. All thoughts of the griffons and skycutters forgotten, he steered Seraphon groundwards, seeking the elf that had thought to test their magic against his. Flying just out of bowshot above both armies, he found his prey upon a hillside to the west. The elf that confronted him was a young princess, and her features seemed familiar though he could not place them. More recognisable was the cage of magical energy that surrounded her, emanating from an amulet around her neck. As he descended on her, the Witch King thought he could hear dry, dead voices whispering on the winds, casting counter-spells against his sorcery, edged with the silvery-frost of Sapherian magecraft.

The Yvressian princess was so taken with her dispelling that she paid no heed to the black doom diving down upon her. Malekith saw her flinch, distracted, and at the same time he felt a pulsing on the winds of magic, a surge of grief that flowed from the princess's thoughts, a moment of severance. Her counter-spell scattered by this shock, the princess looked up to see Seraphon's plummeting form, her face a mask of terror.

Malekith laughed as he saw her pitiful attempts to reclaim the winds of magic from him. He snatched the whirling energy from her grasp, tearing it from her control as though plucking candied fruits from a child. He thought to obliterate her with magic for the affront of her resistance, but had not accounted for the speed of Seraphon's attack.

Two of the black dragon's claws punched into the princess like lances as Seraphon swept over the crest of the hill, lifting her from the ground. Flexing massive digits, the dragon pulled the maiden apart, separating her spine as innards spilled free. With a thunderous crack of wings flapping, downdraft knocking Yvressians to the ground, the dragon powered skywards again, flicking the two halves of the princess's corpse deftly into her mouth.

Malekith was about to order her to strike again, his eye drawn to a prince trying to rally a regiment of spearmen against a breakthrough by Kouran's Black Guard, when a chorus of horn blasts split the air. Ascending, Malekith looked to the east and saw the glitter of a new army arriving, marching beneath the colours of Lothern and Chrace. At their head, astride a pure-white steed greater than any normal horse, sat a figure in blazing gold armour, his sword lifted to the skies burning with amber flame.

'The so-called Dragon of Cothique,' shouted the Witch King. 'Welcome, Prince Tyrion, to your final battle.'

He was about to steer Seraphon towards the advancing column of Tyrion's host when he felt a shimmer on the winds of magic. It felt as though someone rode behind him on the saddle-throne and he heard the calm voice of Teclis.

'The Widowmaker, Malekith. Protect the shrine at all costs. I will meet you there.'

The mage's spirit was gone again in an instant, and Malekith considered ignoring his meddling advice. He would spit Tyrion on the point of *Urithain* and the battle would be over in moments, the Shrine of Khaine safe again. All of elvendom would know that their king had returned.

He was about to bring around Seraphon for the fateful attack when another thought struck him, as though from somewhere else. It was a moment of foreboding that sent a prickle of apprehension through his fire-ravaged body.

If he faced Tyrion he would die.

The thought suddenly seemed as solid as the world, as certain as the sun rising every dawn. Only the knowledge that he was meant to be king was as sure to Malekith for that heartbeat.

It was enough to give him pause for thought. Almost immediately Malekith suspected it was some trick of Teclis, an enchantment left in the Witch King's thoughts when the mage had contacted him. His anger started to rise again, but not so swiftly that it outpaced reason. Malekith's pride had often been his bane. He had seen this weakness in himself when he had been forced to flee Finuval Plain through the Realm of Chaos. His disembodied, timeless wandering had forced him to realise that often the greatest architect of his failure was his own arrogance. He had vowed never again to let ire be his guide, nor pride to steer his strategy.

This was the moment that such an oath had to be upheld. Morathi believed that Tyrion was Aenarion reborn. Regardless of the truth or not of such a claim, the prince was a naturally gifted warrior who had honed his skills in countless battles, and hardened the edge of his anger against the latest daemon incursion. Aenarion had triumphed with the Widowmaker and Tyrion had succeeded without, foregoing drawing the deadly blade of Khaine until Morathi's intervention.

There was no need for Malekith to confront his foe just yet. A whole army stood between Tyrion and his goal and if that proved insufficient, if the Dragon of Cothique was able to best thousands of warriors and a dozen Naggarothi captains and princes, Malekith would be on hand to finish the task. At the very end, if no other opportunity presented itself, he would draw the Widowmaker and kill Aenarion's heir, ending the curse by another means.

By such justification was Malekith able to quell the rage he felt at the insult shown him by Tyrion's opposition. When Tyrion was dead, when Malekith showed his eviscerated corpse to the pitiful weaklings that continued to oppose his claim to the Phoenix Throne, then Malekith would be satisfied and his pride sated.

He turned Seraphon and headed towards the Shrine of Khaine. A company of elves still guarded the megalith-circled temple, spears and bows at the ready. Armies could not match Seraphon and the Witch King together; a few hundred militia would be little more than a diversion.

Seraphon stooped, picking up speed as dragon and rider dropped towards the black stones of the shrine. A dozen heartbeats from crashing into the unforgiving rock the dragon snapped open her wings, turning the plunge into an effortless glide, jaw open, claws outstretched. Malekith leaned to his right with *Urithain* poised while the winds of magic churned at his command.

Something flashed past Malekith's left shoulder and his steed uttered a piercing cry of pain. The most majestic, powerful predator of the skies became a screeching mess of flying scales and blood, wing shredded by some missile from below. Malekith barely glimpsed a hooded, cloaked figure skulking in the shadows of the shrine – Alith Anar with moonbow in hand – before Seraphon's descent turned into a tumbling crash, ground and sky whirling together.

Dragon and rider ploughed across the bone-strewn hillside, spraying ivory-coloured shards in their wake. Malekith clung tightly to the dragon's chains, turning upside down over and over, his armour battering against uncaring rock every couple of heartbeats, ears ringing from the impacts on his helm. He lost his grip and fell under the rolling beast, only the armour of midnight stopping the last breath being crushed from his lungs.

They eventually came to a stop, sliding down a gore-slicked hillock some distance down the slope from the shrine. Dazed,

Malekith lay with Seraphon's bulk across his legs, staring up at the turbulent sky. He thought he heard his mother's voice, a single clear word that called out to him, but it was on the winds of magic that the voice came to him and he knew it to be a word of command.

He heard other voices, coming closer. The defenders of the shrine encircled the fallen monster and its rider, spears levelled, bowstrings taut as the ring of warriors tightened. Stars flashed across Malekith's vision, painfully bright.

Seraphon stirred, growling. Bone jutted awkwardly from her ragged wing and the jagged ground had torn wounds through the flesh and scales of her flank, but she heaved herself up, the broken remnants of the saddle-throne falling from her back. The asur backed away, suddenly uncertain of their oaths to protect the shrine unto death.

The dragon looked at him and Malekith saw hunger in her eyes. He saw himself reflected in the dark orbs, a twisted figure of metal and fire, and he knew he had not been a kind master. Hurting, lips rippling with the effort, the black dragon stood over Malekith, ropes of bloodied saliva drooling from her fangs.

With a bass whimper, the dragon dipped her good wing, dropping her flank so that Malekith could climb upon her bare back.

The Revenants attacked, loosing their arrows from the summit of the shrine while others charged down the slope with their spears gleaming. Seraphon swept out her good wing, blocking the storm of arrows falling through the sky, even as Malekith retrieved *Urithain* from amongst the broken bones. He hauled himself onto her back, spitting a curse that unleashed a hail of icy shards towards the shrine. A few heartbeats later dozens of archers fell, their bodies ripped asunder by the storm of magical splinters, skin turned to rags, flesh flensed from breaking bones.

Seraphon met the descending phalanx of spears head-on, crashing through the glistening points, jaws snapping. The Witch King leaned low to slash with his magical blade, splitting white-hafted spears and scale armour with broad sweeps. His gaze became death, shredding the minds of any that dared meet his fiery stare.

As Seraphon laboured up the hill towards the megaliths marking the perimeter of the shrine, Malekith cast his attention back to the battle. The druchii ranks had split. Elements from Ghrond were fighting against each other, while banners in the other contingents were splitting away, turning on their own kind.

Morathi.

Her single word had been a summons, calling those faithful to her to throw off the concealing veil of loyalty. The Black Guard remained steadfast at the centre of the attack, but the flanks were giving way as dreadspears turned on bolt thrower crews, bleakswords fought amongst themselves and sorceresses directed their spells against regiments of darkshards still following the Witch King.

Everything was collapsing into anarchy but there was no time to worry about the larger battle. The Witch King saw a white and gold blur carving its way through the disrupted line straight towards the Shrine of Khaine – Tyrion leading the charge. He had broken ahead of his army, leaving knights, white lions and militia to battle through in his wake. Above, Malekith spied a phoenix burning with a white fire cutting across the sky towards him. Alith Anar was already close at hand.

His enemies were growing in number and time was growing shorter.

Dragging her wounded wing like a ship that had lost a mast, Seraphon carried her lord up to the summit of the shrine-hill, leaving gouged and poisoned corpses in drifts behind her. At the moment they breached the crest, Malekith laid eyes upon the black rock of the altar.

Where the Godslayer had first appeared to him as a sceptre, a symbol that he could destroy the world with all of elvenkind as his weapon, now there rested a spear with a head of crimson lightning and a shaft of bone. It wailed to Malekith, begging him to take up his rightful gift from the God of Murder. Khaine had chosen him just as He had chosen Aenarion, and millennia of suffering had resulted from Malekith's denial of his birthright.

A last defender wearing the plume of a captain heaved himself clear of the dismembered remains of his warriors and stood before the Witch King and his monstrous steed, breaking Malekith's trance-like fascination. The other elf held his sword levelled at Seraphon's chest and there was blood trickling from a wound across his cheek, but the resolute defiance in his eyes stopped Malekith.

'I'm impressed,' said the Witch King. 'Your company died well. So will you.'

'I am Caradon, last of the Revenants of Khaine,' spat the elf, blood flying from broken lips. 'I curse thee, Malekith. I curse th–'

Urithain took off his head as Seraphon shouldered past a standing stone and Malekith leaned low on her back. The Witch King looked again at the altar and the spear that beckoned to him with subtle words of praise and promise.

A noise, barely audible amongst the cacophony of war and the patter of raining blood. A flutter, the faintest rustling of cloth. The sound of droplets pattering on metal.

Malekith acted without thought, *Urithain* spearing out as he turned towards the sound. The black-clad assassin twisted in mid-air as he leapt from the monolith, the Witch King's magical blade flashing just past his scalp. It was enough, the killing blow directed towards Malekith's neck missing its mark, though the blackened dagger tore through his iron-skinned shoulder, the enchanted blade splitting the armour of midnight as though it were a common mail coat.

TWENTY-TWO

Khaine's Promise

Malekith roared, lashing out with raw dark magic as the assassin tried to land on Seraphon's back. The instinctive spell smashed into the Khainite, hurling him into the piled bones at the shrine's edge. As the would-be killer rolled through the charnel debris, Malekith recognised his face. It was Shadowblade, most infamous of his calling since Urian Poisonblade, once Malekith's deadliest weapon and most effective defence against traitors. It seemed that Shadowblade's mistress, Hellebron, had decided to defy the Witch King, though to what ends he could not guess.

'Why is everyone trying to kill me?' bellowed Malekith, exasperated at another delay and distraction. 'Don't you know that I'm trying to save the world?'

The assassin staggered to his feet and with a flick of the wrist Malekith hurled another bolt of dark magic, smashing Shadowblade against a standing stone. As the Khainite stood up again, he shook his head and looked around as though waking up, an expression of confusion on his face. Startled by this reaction, Malekith held his next bolt for a moment. A moment too long.

The clatter of hooves and a flash of gold heralded the arrival of a foe even more dangerous than the stunned assassin. Malekith cast a glance towards Prince Tyrion as his steed forged up the slope of the shrine. He cast his spell even as he wheeled Seraphon to face the fresh danger, but Shadowblade was gone, the sorcerous blast turning a standing stone into a cloud of black splinters.

The Dragon of Cothique was a magnificent sight, clad in burnished plate and scale, his winged helm plumed with white feathers. He rode Malhandir, a steed as renowned as the prince, larger and swifter than any stallion of Ellyrion, as white as the snows of the Annulii.

In Tyrion's grasp flashed the Sunfang, *Lacelothrai*, a sword as long as Malekith's arm inscribed with runes that burned with the light and heat of the sun. The prince's armour was of pure ithilmar, forged on the Anvil of Vaul for Aenarion himself, reclaimed from the Blighted Isle after the first Phoenix King's disappearance.

Malekith gasped, for the vision that thundered up to the shrine was the image of his father, even the burning wrath that lit the Dragon of Cothique's eyes.

Their eyes locked and in that moment the separation of centuries disappeared, the bloodline that locked the destiny of both elves united again. No words passed their lips as they raised their swords, but nonetheless their thoughts spoke to each other.

'I see why they call you the Defender reborn, nephew.'

'And I know why they call you the Betrayer.'

'Give up! To draw the Sword of Khaine is to doom our people. My mother has bewitched you.'

'What do you care of our doom, architect of the Sundering? I will end your treacherous existence!'

'Do you not think I would have drawn the Widowmaker an age ago if I thought it would bring me victory? None that wield it can hope to survive its influence. Not even my father, and certainly not some spoiled prince of Cothique!'

'You shall see how strong flows the blood of Aenarion in my veins. And when I open them, how weakly in yours.'

Malhandir cleared the last of the slope with an almighty leap and Tyrion stretched out his sword arm, faster than any stroke Malekith had ever witnessed. The two warriors passed each other and Malekith wondered where the blow had struck, but he felt no fresh pain. The answer came when Seraphon arched back her head and let out a plaintive whine. Dark, thick blood bubbled from a glowing cut across her throat. Seraphon swept out her uninjured wing, barbs flexing, but Malhandir darted aside so that the blow caught only the crest of Tyrion's helm and tore it off, golden locks spilling free.

'Not nearly good enough.' Malekith swept down *Urithain* as Seraphon scrambled after the steed and prince, keeping her body low to bring the Witch King's crackling sword into range.

'You are correct.' Tyrion turned in the saddle and *Lacelothrai* was a golden shimmer meeting Malekith's sword with a flash of sparks and fire. 'You are not good enough, nor fast enough.'

The burning tip of the Sunfang looped around Malekith's guard and scored a deep wound across his breastplate, releasing a fountain of fire and blood, almost knocking him from the back of Seraphon. Sensing her master's injury, the black dragon heaved herself away while Malekith gritted his teeth against the pain of shattered ribs and cut flesh. The dagger still in his shoulder vexed his bones and muscles, making every movement an agony.

'You are fine with a blade,' admitted Malekith, drawing on the winds of magic. 'But without your brother, you cannot hope to defeat my sorcery.'

Seraphon attacked with wide jaws, forcing Malhandir back. Tyrion stared grimly at Malekith as the Witch King pointed *Urithain*, black flames burning along the sword's length. The fires became an inferno, rushing out to engulf the asur prince, but again his steed was too swift, circling around the Altar of

Khaine, the magical flames splashing harmlessly from bone and rock just behind rider and mount.

'I do not need my pathetic twin to fight fire.'

Tyrion raised the Sunfang, drawing on the enchantment placed on the blade by the loremasters of Hoeth centuries past. The blinding light of the noon sun exploded from the sword, carving into the black flames of Malekith's rage, the two spells meeting above Khaine's sacrificial stone. The Witch King drew in more power, blocking out the pain of his injuries, his resentment and rage further fuelled by a growing fear. Tyrion had never been so fast and determined before, and Malekith was already badly hurt and spent from a day of battle.

The thought returned that Tyrion would kill him.

The sudden dread of this thought surged through Malekith, but it did not cause him to falter, but steeled his will, the fear of failure falling on his rage like oil cast upon a fire. The black flame swept towards Tyrion even as the bolt from *Lacelothrai* waned, engulfing the prince.

Malhandir let out a piercing, chilling scream as the black fires fell upon his pure-white flank, while the runes of Aenarion's armour, forged as proof against even dragonfire, shone with magical power. But the regent of the Phoenix Throne had lost his helm. The black fire caught in his hair and scorched across his handsome face.

Despite the horrific injuries, Tyrion forced Malhandir towards Malekith, into the heart of the flame, driven by the battle-lust of Khaine. There were no taunts and threats between them now, only the silence of lethal purpose. With mane and tail burning, Malhandir leapt the altar, bringing Tyrion next to Malekith again. *Lacelothrai* crashed into Malekith's arm as he clumsily raised *Urithain* to fend off the blow, throwing him from the back of Seraphon.

His head swam as he landed heavily in a pile of shattering bones, *Urithain* almost jarred from his grasp. A cut ran the length of his forearm. It was a near-miracle that the limb had not been severed by Tyrion's blow.

Malhandir shuddered into a convulsing, burned heap beside the altar, but Tyrion did not pause, leaping effortlessly from the ash-stained saddle, *Lacelothrai* held at the ready. Seraphon made a last effort, the blood from her throat now a trickle, but even as she raised a claw to dash Tyrion against the altar her strength failed and she collapsed, chest heaving.

Malekith lay amongst the ruin and looked up at the golden figure striding towards him, the flicker of flames dying on his charred face, a shaft of sunlight gripped in his fist. How the daemons must have quailed at that vision, he thought, just as they had done when Aenarion took back Ulthuan. There seemed to be nothing that would stop the Dragon of Cothique, and he had not yet even taken up the Widowmaker.

It was not the first time Malekith had stood upon the threshold of Mirai's portal. He remembered well the blood-soaked day of Maledor Field.

Lacking any weapon, Malekith set about the servants of his tormentor with flaming fists, his iron hands punching through breastplates and ripping off limbs. Towering above the Phoenix Guard, he summoned dark magic, feeding off the escaping life-force of his foes, twisting it to his own ends.

He tried to draw the magic into himself, to heal the rents in his armour. The dark magic swerved and writhed, failing to take purchase in his body. Where the blades of the Phoenix Guard had marked him, tiny golden flames burned, keeping the dark magic at bay.

Dread filled Malekith's heart. Unable to heal his wounds, which streamed with rivulets of molten metal like blood, he realised he was about to die.

'Never!' he roared.

He drew himself up to his full height. The dark magic he had summoned to cure his wounds swirled around him, forming blades of blackened iron that slashed through the Phoenix Guard. With a final pulse of dark magic, he blasted the forest of magical swords into his foes, driving them back.

Leaking metal and fire and blood, Malekith turned and ran, leaving burned prints in the bloodied grass. He would not die yet, not here on this dismal moor, with the usurper looking on, laughing. The Witch King drew on the power of his circlet, reaching out into the winds of magic, grabbing all of the power he could. An oily black cloud formed around him, flickering with lightning, obscuring him from his pursuers. It spread further and further, a churning, living mass that snatched up the Phoenix Guard who came after him, twisting their bodies and snapping their bones.

He had fled then, and there were other times since when retreat had been the only recourse to avoid death. He felt no shame at this, for cowardice would have been to accept failure and to eke out his dwindling days in cold Naggaroth.

This time was different. Blood streaming from his many wounds, molten iron running with it, Malekith stood up, his left arm useless, *Urithain* in his right.

Malekith tried to draw in magical energy, to summon up an incantation that would shred Tyrion's flesh from his bones, would shatter those bones to splinters, would pulverise his organs and set a burning agony into his mind, but the fog of pain that invaded his thoughts was too thick. There was a more sinister sensation that had been spreading from the dagger in his shoulder.

Poison carried from the wound caused by Shadowblade.

The winds of magic swirled sluggishly so close to Khaine's altar and the Witch King found them slipping through his grasp. He could feel a fluttering on the winds of magic, a disturbance in Ulgu, the power of shadow, but he was too weary to make any sense of it.

The Sunfang flashed towards his throat and only at the last moment was Malekith able to raise *Urithain* to weakly deflect the blow. The enchanted blade exploded at the touch of Tyrion's sword, scattering shards of black metal. Pain seared up the Witch King's arm but it quickly dissipated, swamped by the numbness that was filling Malekith's whole being.

Malekith could do nothing as Tyrion's next blow, impossibly fast, crashed into the gorget protecting his throat. The impact staggered the Witch King, and he fell to his knees, a moment before his foe's armoured boot caught him in the face, breaking his cheek. His head crashed against the black Altar of Khaine and he slid to the bloodied ground, nearly all feeling lost in his limbs.

The Dragon of Cothique loomed over the Witch King. Tyrion's eyes were orbs of blood-red as he looked at the altar. In that moment Malekith and Tyrion were connected, and they too with Aenarion, who so long ago had set the Curse of Khaine upon his bloodline.

There was a sense of dislocation, of timelessness. Malekith looked on the fire-ravaged face of his distant nephew, but saw only the features of his father. The cycle came about, and all things that were ancient were renewed. Perhaps it was right that this happened. Perhaps he had fought against his real destiny for six thousand years. Together the Witch King and Ulthuan's regent witnessed the moment that had defined the existence of the elves for seven thousand years.

Even as Aenarion's thoughts touched upon the Godslayer, there came to his ears a distant noise: a faint screaming. The ring of metal on metal, of fighting, echoed around the shrine. Aenarion heard a thunderous heart beating, and thought he saw knives carving wounds upon flesh and limbs torn from bodies on the edge of his vision. The red veins of the altar were not rock at all, but pulsed like arteries, blood flowing from the stone in spurting rivers of gore. He realised that the beating heart was his own, and it hammered in his chest like a swordsmith working at an anvil.

Aenarion stood transfixed before that bloody shrine. The thing embedded in the rock danced and wavered before the Phoenix King's eyes, a blur of axe and sword and spear and bow and knife and strange weapons not known to the elves. Finally a single image emerged, of a long-bladed sword, cross guard curled into the rune of Khaine, its black blade etched with red symbols of death and blood.

Aenarion reached out... and stopped, his fingers a hair's breadth from the hilt of the sword. All became silent; not a movement stirred the air as the world and the gods held their breath.

Aenarion knew this would be his doom. All of the warnings came back to him, the words of Caledor merged with dire predictions of the daemons and the pleading of his dead wife. It all mattered nothing to him, for his spirit was empty and only the Sword of Khaine could fill the void within him.

As Tyrion switched the Sunfang to his left hand and reached out with his right, Malekith managed a sneer.

'At least my father paused a moment,' he snarled between bloody coughs. 'I turned away. You have no willpower.' Tyrion paid him no heed as he drew back, his prize in hand.

Widowmaker, Godslayer, Doom of Worlds, Spear of Vengeance, Deathshard, and Heavenblight. By many names it was called, by mortals and daemons and gods. But one name alone it truly held: Sword of Khaine, the Lord of Murder.

Tyrion admired the weapon with wide eyes. In his fist he held a warped mirror of the Sunfang. Where *Lacelothrai* was shard of sunlight, bright and golden, this new blade was as black as a starless night and as cold as the deepest abyss of space.

The storm clouds overhead roiled with cracks of thunder and shafts of blood-red lightning. Tyrion held up his new sword, lips curled in a manic grin. Malekith looked up helplessly, unable to move a muscle in retaliation.

'*Larhathrai*,' Tyrion whispered, naming the blade.
Icefang.

TWENTY-THREE

Brother against Brother

Something black and grey surged between the perimeter slabs of the shrine, a thick shadow bunching and releasing like the muscles of an immense horse. Slowing, the apparition did indeed become a half-formed image of a horse with midnight flanks and streamers of shadow for a mane. Teclis swung a leg and dismounted a few paces from Malekith and Tyrion.

'Brother, don't do this!' the mage shouted through the blood rain.

Tyrion gave no sign of heeding the words. He flexed his fingers around the Widowmaker's grip and swept the sword up. At once, the shadows about Malekith lengthened and the rain grew colder. Thunder cracked against the turbulent sky and dark laughter billowed in its wake. The ground shook; the skulls chattered and gibbered in sudden mirth and then fell eerily silent.

The shadow steed vanished, its magic undone by the Widowmaker's presence, and Malekith felt the winds of magic grow thin about him.

'I should be surprised to find you here,' the regent said at last, turning to face his brother, 'but little you do surprises me any longer.' His blackened lips cracked into a cruel smile as he prodded Malekith with his toe. 'Yet I find that I am pleased to see you. This... thing... is not yet slain, and I would like one witness to my triumph, even if it is a treacherous one.'

Thing thought Malekith? But he had not the strength to utter a contemptuous riposte.

'You cannot kill him,' Teclis said urgently. 'If you do, our people are doomed.'

Listen to your brother, Malekith willed, eyes drawn to the abysall blackness of *Larhathrai*. I am the saviour of our people. Pay attention!

'Our people will never falter while I am alive to lead them,' Tyrion laughed. 'Or at least, to lead those who prove worthy. The coming war will winnow out all others.'

Malekith managed a grimace, recalling similar words coming from his lips for these past thousands of years. Tyrion had been so noble, so exemplary of the finest traits of elvenkind only days earlier, now as bloodthirsty and cold as Malekith after six thousand years of hate-filled war. He looked at the fire-ravaged features of the Dragon of Cothique and could not help but make comparison to himself, ragged and burned by another flame. It made the Witch King remember, painfully, that like Tyrion he had once been lauded by the greatest of elvenkind as the epitome of elven nobility.

'Listen to yourself. These are not your words,' warned Teclis, staring at his brother but not moving. Malekith had to wonder if they had ever really been his, or put into his thoughts by another. 'This is our curse! This is the madness of Khaine!' As he spoke, Teclis's expression was desperate, betraying the doubt in his heart that his cautionary words would be heeded.

'There is no madness. The Dark Gods are rising.' Tyrion glanced at Malekith and the Witch King would have flinched except that fatigue and terror paralysed him in equal measure. There was unalloyed death in the prince's eyes. 'I see that now. Our folk are too soft to fight them as we are, but I will forge them into something better, something stronger.'

'And who has told you that? Morathi?' Teclis demanded, his voice raw with emotion. The words cut Malekith far more than Tyrion, who shrugged away his twin's concern. It was too much for Malekith to believe that six thousand years had been spent fighting for the ambitions of his mother, his whole existence a mocking puppetry of life as Tyrion's had now become. 'She's using you.'

'Is she now?' Tyrion asked amenably, but then his tone grew far darker. 'Then how very different in your dealings you are.' He raised the icefang high and Malekith's dread increased, though he had thought it impossible to be more afraid a moment ago. Seven thousand years, a whole civilisation wasted because he had been too weak to beat this upstart princeling. Worse, because he had been too scared to draw the Godslayer himself, or to kill his mother when given every justification and opportunity. 'It matters not. Today our ancient enemy dies, and a new sun rises.'

Larhathrai swept down.

Tyrion, dullard that he was, had been completely ignorant of the Hysh coalescing around Teclis. The power of light was heavy, but the archmage was well versed in tapping its deep roots, and to Malekith's eyes was becoming a twining column of white energy.

As the icefang began its descent Teclis let free streamers of Hysh that became ribbons of pure light that snared around Tyrion's arms, stopping the deathblow. Light magic twined about the prince's quivering limbs, growing brighter and thicker as Teclis released more of his accumulated Hysh.

If only Malekith could have moved even a finger or murmured a word of conjuration. As it was, he stared dumbly at the two brothers, watching the dark power of Khaine spilling from His bloodied altar, staining the purity of the Hysh that struggled up through the chattering skulls and clattering bones.

The enchantment broke with a crack as the blessings of Khaine poured into Tyrion. The edge of icefang gleamed blood-red as Tyrion turned on his brother. Hurriedly, Teclis threw together a shield of pure magical energy, thrashing together power from the seven remaining winds. The golden circle hovered in front of the mage for only a heartbeat before Tyrion swept through it, the hand clasping *Lacelothrai* knocking Teclis to the ground with one blow.

From his position propped against the altar, Malekith could see several things that the two brothers could not, intent as they were upon each other. The eddy of shadowy Ulgu power shimmered close to one of the standing stones at the edge of the shrine, and concealed behind the cloak of shadow crouched Alith Anar. Malekith saw a glint of silvery light as the Shadow King lifted the fabled moonbow and fitted a shaft to the slender string.

A white spark was also bright against the clouds above the shrine, growing larger. Malekith watched the gleam resolve into the shape of a stooping bird – a white-and-blue feathered frostheart phoenix. The ancient magical bird, its flames turned to ice by longevity, was ridden by a figure in white and ithilmar, bearing a blazon of Asuryan upon his armour. The Witch King knew from the reports of his agents that this must be Caradryan, the captain of the Phoenix Guard, silent warden of the Shrine of Asuryan.

There seemed to be no shortage of foes ready to kill Malekith. The moment of terror, of soul-destroying failure, had passed, and the Witch King found himself in a calm mood. He was not yet reconciled to his ending, but such were the horrific consequences of his death, the infernal pacts he had made that would now be paid, the lengths he had gone to in order that he would survive as long as he had, he could not comprehend it all and instead his thoughts retreated to a banal place of utter normal-ity. He idly wondered which of his closing enemies would finish him first, and hoped it was not Tyrion.

The frostheart phoenix swept low over the shrine and Caradryan slipped from its back, halberd in hand. He landed sure-footed amongst the detritus of bones, skidding to a stop between Teclis, Tyrion and Malekith. Past the Phoenix captain, Malekith spied Alith Anar moving position, his shot blocked by Caradryan's arrival.

Tyrion laughed without mirth.

'I am in no need of your aid, captain, though you might restrain my errant brother for me, if you wish to serve.'

Caradryan held his position. Malekith could not see his expres-sion but apparently Tyrion read something there, a look of defiance perhaps. Little comfort to the Witch King that he had seemingly acquired another ally, as he watched the Shadow King emerge from the gloom on the other side of the standing stone, moonbow rising once more.

Tyrion's eyes widened in sudden realisation.

'All about me are traitors now?' the regent demanded. 'Stand aside!'

Caradryan shook his head. Then, with an effort, he uttered the first word to pass his lips in decades.

'No.'

Tyrion laughed bitterly at Caradryan's refusal. He half turned away, then spun back, the Widowmaker hissing out to take the captain's head.

At that same moment, Alith Anar loosed his arrow, the shaft speeding true for Malekith's heart.

Suddenly there was nothing.

PART THREE

TWENTY-FOUR

Painful Memories

The impudent mage had natural flair and unparalleled concentration, but Malekith had been a master of sorcery for more than five thousand years and had learned at the hand of Morathi, the greatest sorceress in history. It was inevitable that the Witch King's spells would eventually break down the Sapherian's counter-incantations and shimmering protective barriers.

Malekith hardly paid any attention to the military situation. It mattered not that his champion, Urian Poisonblade, greatest blade-wielder of Naggaroth, had fallen to the sword of the asur's own hero. The armies of the Naggarothi were too numerous, too strong for the defenders of Ulthuan, and like the duel between Malekith and the mage of the White Tower it was simply a matter of time.

The last resistance of the asur would be crushed and Malekith would finally claim the Phoenix Throne, and ever after would be lauded the day he triumphed on Finuval Plain.

The winds of magic churned, telling their own tale of curse and counter-spell, enchantment and hex. Malekith's dark magic was *a tornado of energy, whirling, destructive, a storm of all eight winds forced together into an unstoppable mass.*

The Sapherian mage, the one whose wit and will had thwarted every advantage Malekith had gained on this long campaign, wielded a far subtler force. High magic was the careful distillation and blending of the opposing forces inherent in the winds of magic, like a smith smelting iron and charcoal for the perfect steel, or a chef perfecting a recipe with the smallest hint of spices and herbs.

As swordmasters crashed into the druchii spearwall and griffons tore at manticores overhead, Malekith hurled blast after blast of dark lightning at the emissary from Hoeth, trying to overcome his foe's defences with base fury. The Sapherian redoubled his efforts, ascending into the sky upon a pillar of magic to draw in the whirling winds of power gathered high above the battlefield.

From a magic-blasted hilltop Malekith summoned forth a storm of titanic proportion, torturing the air with dark energy until it gave vent to crashes of thunder and streaked the sky with blue and purple lightning. The mage manipulated Ghyran and Azyr, turning the tempest into tatters of cloud broken by golden rays of the sun.

Malekith cared nothing for the delay. Every elf that fell beneath blade and arrow that day fed the deathly Wind of Shyish, and from this pool of lethal energy he drew the greatest strength. The druchii could afford to lose two warriors for every asur slain and the elves of Ulthuan knew it to be true.

A sudden void in the winds disturbed Malekith's concentration. The Witch King was shocked by the rapid cessation of energy, an utter stillness in the winds of magic. Not since the likes of Caledor Dragontamer had he seen such a spell. A secret lost to history when Caledor had been swallowed by the vortex he had created.

The Sapherian soared over Malekith, clutching tight to his staff. It was as though the young, gaunt elf was listening to his magical rod, head tilted to one side in concentration. He then looked down at Malekith, and the image of the mage's face was etched forever in the Witch King's memories.

He saw nothing in the mage's eyes, none of the passion and life that ruled the minds of the asur. Instead the Sapherian looked down at Malekith with all the feeling of a shark, his gaze a predatory blank stare that the Witch King had only seen before from one individual – the eyes of his father before he had set out to return the Sword of Khaine, knowing he would not return. It was the look of a person that knew the world was about to end.

The winds of magic suddenly erupted into life once more, catching Malekith totally unawares, so entranced had he been by the mage's appearance. Only the first syllables of a counter-spell had left his ragged lips when the wave of high magic engulfed him.

At first it felt cool, like a waterfall in reverse, numbing him from foot to head, but then the heat followed. It grew from his heart, and with it brought back the memories of Asuryan's temple and the curse of the All-king.

Agony flared, as powerful now as it had been the first moment Malekith had set foot into the sacred fires. Renewed, invigorated, the fires burned, the dulling of six thousand years wiped away.

There was triumph, cruel victory, in the eyes of the mage as he glowered down at Malekith.

The pain was too much, the damage ravaging his body too brutal and all-consuming to bear. There was no spell or balm or talisman that could save him. In half a dozen heartbeats he would be dead, consumed as if he had stayed in the flame of Asuryan. There was only one way to escape and a moment to open the portal.

With a wordless shriek, Malekith ripped open the veil between worlds and hurled himself into the beyond, abandoning his mortal shell for survival in the Realm of Chaos.

Malekith awoke alone. The touch of Ghyran lay heavily upon his body, the Wind of Life mixed weightily, ironically, with the Wind of Metal, Chamon. He raised a hand but pain lanced into him, from his chest and gut, his shoulder and arm. The memory of what had happened at the end of his confrontation with Tyrion blurred with the disaster at Finuval Plain, but it seemed a wonder he was in one piece.

He opened iron-lidded eyes and saw the dulled gaze of Teclis looking down at him. The glow of the mage's desperate teleportation faded around them. There was white stone, walls and ceiling, and he assumed the hard floor beneath was the same. Something dark and bulky blocked out the light to the left – the barely-living Seraphon. Malekith glimpsed another figure on the edge of vision and recognised Caradryan.

'Rest,' said the mage, while Caradryan looked around, as amazed as Malekith to be alive.

Malekith could not argue. His wounds were many, the assassin's poison like acid in his body. Unconsciousness was welcome.

'Welcome back.' The voice was sudden, jerking Malekith's head around. In the corner sat a silver-armoured figure, his halberd held across his knees, helm laid on the white marble floor. Caradryan had spoken softly, but even his whisper seemed incredibly loud in this place, echoing from the beautifully crafted stone. 'Teclis's ministrations have had some effect, I see.'

'I thought your order was sworn to silence?'

'For their term of service,' said Caradryan, nodding. 'But my life was meant to have ended at the Blighted Isle.'

'It is written on the walls, is it not? The future of everything?'

'Not everything,' Caradryan confessed, 'but much that happens now has come before. You are one of the few people that witnessed the start as well as the end.'

'I am not sure how I am alive. Tyrion...?'

'Lives, unfortunately. Teclis tried his best to steer events along the path foretold by Lileath, but he was only partially successful.'

'Goddesses of fate can be terribly tricksome, I am told,' growled Malekith. 'I thought I was dead three-ways over.'

'Our companion's spell deflected Anar's arrow a fraction,'

Caradryan explained, standing up. 'It struck Tyrion in the chest, knocking him away from the altar though it did not pierce his armour. His blow fell wide of you, and in the next moment Teclis called upon Lileath to spare us and we were transported here.'

Light footsteps drew their attention to the archway, where Teclis appeared a moment later looking worried.

'You need to rest,' Caradryan said, pointing at the blood that oozed from Malekith's wounds, coating cracked armour plates. The Phoenix Guard captain left with the mage and Malekith fell back into a pain-wracked sleep.

In time Malekith, aided in part by the attention of Teclis, recovered sufficient strength to leave the shrine of Lileath where they had arrived. The mage had disappeared a few days earlier, and sent a ship to bear the Witch King and Caradryan to the Island of Flame, home to the Shrine of Asuryan. Seeing the huge temple brought back one of Malekith's oldest and bitterest memories.

The shrine itself was a high pyramid in form, built above the burning flame of the king of the gods. The flame danced and flickered at the heart of the temple, thrice the height of an elf, burning without noise or heat. Runes of gold were inlaid into the marble tiles of the floor around the central fire, and these blazed with a light that was not wholly reflected from the flame. Upon the white walls were hung braziers wrought in the shape of phoenixes with their wings furled and more magical fire burned within them, filling the temple with a golden glow.

All the princes of Ulthuan were there, resplendent in their cloaks and gowns, with high helms and tall crowns of silver and gold studded with gemstones from every colour of the rainbow. Only the Naggarothi stood out amongst this feast of colour, taciturn and sombre in their black and purple robes. Morathi stood with Malekith and his followers, the seeress eyeing proceedings with suspicion.

Astromancers were present too, seven of them, who had determined that this day was the most auspicious to crown the new Phoenix King. They wore robes of deep blues patterned with glistening diamonds in the constellations of the stars, linked by the finest lines of silver and platinum.

The astrologers stood next to the chanting priests of Asuryan, who weaved their prayers around Bel Shanaar so that he might pass through the flames unscathed. Behind the priests sat the oracles of Asuryan: three elven maidens of pale skin and blonde hair, garbed in raiment of silver that shimmered in the dazzling light.

Yvraine and her maiden guard had journeyed from Avelorn to join the ascension of her ceremonial husband. These warrior-women wore skirts of silvered scale edged with green cloth, and carried garlands of flowers in place of their spears and bows, for no weapon was allowed to pass the threshold of Asuryan's temple.

Bel Shanaar stood with the high priest before the flame, and about his shoulders was hung a cloak of white and black feathers, a newly woven symbol of his power and authority.

'As did Aenarion the Defender, so too shall I submit myself to the judgement of the greatest power,' Bel Shanaar solemnly intoned. 'My purity proven by this ordeal, I shall ascend to the throne of the Phoenix King, to rule wisely and justly in the name of the king of gods.'

'Your father needed no spells of protection,' muttered Morathi. 'This is a fraud, of no more legitimacy than the sham wedding to Yvraine.'

As the priests burned incense and made offerings to Asuryan, the oracles began to sing quietly, their verses almost identical but for a few words here and there, which rose into a joyful harmony as Bel Shanaar was ushered towards the flame of Asuryan. The Phoenix King-to-be turned and looked back towards the princes, with no sign of trepidation or exultation.

With a respectful nod Bel Shanaar faced towards the centre of the shrine and walked forwards, slowly ascending the shallow steps that led up to the dais over which the god's cleansing fires gleamed. All present then fell hushed in anticipation as Bel Shanaar stepped within the flame, which turned to a glaring white and forced the onlookers to cast their gazes away lest they be blinded by its intensity.

As their eyes grew accustomed to the bright burning of the flame, they could see the vague shape of Bel Shanaar within, arms upraised as he offered fealty to Asuryan. Then the Phoenix King turned slowly and stepped back out of the flames unharmed. There was a sighing of exhalation as the princes expressed their relief that all went well. The Naggarothi remained silent.

The entourage left, laughing and chattering, save for Malekith, who stayed for a long while gazing at the flame and pondering his fate. The sacred fire had returned to its shifting colours, now seeming dim after its dazzling eruption. To Malekith it seemed as if they had been diminished, tainted by the presence of Bel Shanaar.

Unaware of anything but that burning shrine, Malekith walked slowly forwards, his mind a swirl of conflicting emotions. If he but dared the flame and survived, without the spells of the priests to protect him, then surely it was the will of Asuryan that he succeed his father. Yet what if he was not strong enough? Would the burning of the flames devour him? What then would be left of his hopes and dreams for Nagarythe?

Without realisation Malekith stood directly before the fires, mesmerised by their shifting patterns. The urge to reach out gripped him and he was about to place his hand into the flame when he heard the footsteps of the priests re-entering the temple. Snatching his hand away, Malekith turned from the sacred fire and strode quickly from the shrine, ignoring the priests' inquiring glances.

There were to be many days feasting and celebration, but Malekith left as soon as the ceremony was complete, his duty having been fulfilled. He felt no urge to linger here, where his father had first thrown himself upon the mercy of the greatest god and been reborn as the saviour of his people. If Bel Shanaar wished to be

Phoenix King, then Malekith was satisfied to acquiesce. There were more than enough challenges ahead for him to overcome, Malekith knew, without inciting rivalry and discord. Content for the moment, he journeyed back to Anlec to take up his rule.

As he strode down the plank of their barque, every sinew, muscle, plate and rivet of his body screamed pain but Malekith ignored it, drawing on the immense willpower that had sustained him against such hurt for so long.

The sea surrounding the Shrine of Asuryan was thick with warships, but Teclis's spells had shrouded their arrival. The Dragon of Lothern blazoned upon every sail. Their crews pounded the ancient walls with every spell and siege engine at their command. These were Lord Aislinn's vessels, high admiral of the harbour city, the finest ships in Ulthuan. Another section of the shrine's outer walls collapsed into the sea under the bombardment.

The Shrine of Asuryan was not entirely defenceless. A chorus of screeches split the air as a flock of phoenixes winged across the water. Flames billowed in their wake and washed over a dragonship, timbers and sails catching light almost immediately. The fires spread hungrily, outstripping the crew's ability to quench them. Archers on neighbouring vessels loosed their volleys skyward, but the swirling phoenixes broke apart, reformed and dived against the next vessel in line.

Caradryan winced as the whine and crack of another volley struck the walls. Teclis hurried out from the depths of the temple, robes and cloak billowing around him.

'Well, this is glorious,' Malekith declared. The shrine shuddered, and he reached out to steady himself on a wall lining the road.

'It is insanity,' Teclis countered, his irritation palpable. Caradryan said nothing, though the worry on his face was plain enough.

'Come,' said the mage. 'We have no time to waste.'

Progress through the shrine was painfully slow, and every step was punctuated by the strike of an artillery bolt upon the walls, or the bellow of distant merwyrm. By the time Malekith and his companions had reached the entrance corridor's far end, the clamour of steel upon steel had joined the cacophony outside as Phoenix Guard vied with Aislinn's marines for control of the island beyond the temple walls. Malekith read in Teclis's concerned features a sorry conclusion – that the Island of the Flame would soon be overrun.

'Your plan seems to be failing, mage,' Malekith mocked as they passed through into the inner sanctum. Two-score Phoenix Guard marched past them and back through the closing gates.

'I had planned to bring you here at once,' Teclis reminded him, reliving the bitterness of that particular failure. 'But you would not be swayed, were determined to follow your pride. Who knows how many have died needlessly because of that hubris?'

The Sapherian took a deep breath. 'Now we shall both have to hope you are strong enough, despite your injuries. My brother has become Khaine, or something very like him. You know the legends. Only Asuryan can defeat Khaine – Asuryan, or his chosen vessel.'

'The flame rejected me once,' Malekith said. 'Why should it not do so again?'

'There was no rejection. You simply weren't strong enough. Asuryan always intended for you to succeed your father. Think on it. Why do you suppose every Phoenix King was shielded by mages in their passage through the fire? Even then, they all passed into madness of one kind or another. It was not just Aethis and Morvael – even those my people revere were consumed by the power or the guilt of a stolen throne.'

'And what proof have you of this?' Malekith demanded.

'Finubar told me,' he said. 'Why do you suppose he hardly fought you at the end? He, at least, was good-hearted, but the guilt ate away at him. That is why he so rarely led his people to war. He knew he was but the continuance of a subverted tradition. He was glad to die.'

Without warning, a new sound joined the battle outside: the deep, primal roar of dragons. Teclis gave a small smile. 'Imrik has come,' he said quietly. 'You owe him much, though I doubt you will ever accept that.'

'Even now, when you know I have no other choice, still you attempt to manipulate me,' said Malekith.

'It is my right to be Phoenix King,' growled Malekith. 'It is not yours to give, so I will gladly take it.'

'Traitor!' screamed Elodhir, leaping across the table in front of him, scattering goblets and plates. There was uproar as princes and priests shouted and shrieked.

Elodhir dashed across the shrine, and was halfway upon Malekith when Bathinair intercepted him, sending both of them tumbling down in a welter of robes and rugs. Elodhir punched the Yvressian prince, who reeled back. With a snarl, Bathinair reached into his robes and pulled out a curved blade, no longer than a finger, and slashed at Elodhir. Its blade caught the prince's throat and his lifeblood fountained across the exposed flagstones.

As Bathinair crouched panting over the body of Elodhir, figures appeared at the archway behind Malekith: black-armoured knights of Anlec. The priests and princes who had been running for the arch slipped and collided with each other in their haste to stop their flight. The knights had blood-slicked blades in their hands and advanced with sinister purpose.

At last they came to the chamber of the flame. At Caradryan's nod, the chamber's guards stepped aside and opened the heavy brass-bound doors. They, like the rest of the Phoenix Guard within the shrine, seemed to think nothing odd of the Witch King's presence. On the other side of the doors, a broad marble stair led upwards. The chamber was far grander than when

Malekith had last been here. At the top burned the flames of Asuryan.

They seemed dimmed to Malekith's eye, from what he remembered. Did that bode good or ill?

'Why do you think that Imrik fights for you?' Teclis asked as the doors slammed closed behind them. 'Why do you think that the Phoenix Guard have allowed you within these walls? Why was Caradryan ready to die for you? Imrik has learned the truth of things, and the Phoenix Guard have always known it.'

'Then why do so many of them march under Tyrion's banner?' Malekith demanded. Now that he was standing before the flame his uncertainties grew. Why after all this time were his dreams suddenly shared by so many others?

'They have fallen under Khaine's sway, like so many others. They knew that if they followed Tyrion, they would join his madness. But they knew also that it was their fate, and so went anyway.'

'A pathetic excuse.'

'No, it is an honourable sacrifice,' Teclis argued. 'To pledge yourself to the Phoenix Guard is to be haunted, every day, with the knowledge of how you will fail, no matter how flawless your service.' Teclis closed his eyes briefly. 'It is not a path I could have chosen. I need hope, and the Phoenix Guard know only certainty.'

'Weakness.' As he said the word Malekith felt blood bubbling up in his throat and he degenerated into a terrible, wracking cough. Bloody spittle oozed out through his helm's mouthpiece to drip to the floor. The Witch King stumbled, and would have fallen had Caradryan not moved to support him. Malekith pulled free. He took three staggering steps towards the flame, then stopped.

'If I pass into the fire,' he said without turning, 'my every striving has been a lie.'

Teclis waited for a moment before speaking, then chose his words carefully. 'Does that cause you to regret your deeds?' he asked.

'No,' said Malekith softly, without thought, but then his voice grew harder. 'No. I would do it all again.'

'Then nothing about you was ever a lie,' said Teclis, 'and by your words you prove yourself no better than those who stole the throne.' He sighed. 'But you are Asuryan's choice nonetheless. All that is left of our creator waits for you in the fire. If you can withstand the pain, there is perhaps a chance for us all.'

'And if I cannot?' Malekith asked.

'Then the last spark of Asuryan will fade, and those of our people who survive Tyrion's madness will be consumed by the Dark Gods.'

Malekith was serene; all trace of his earlier anger had disappeared. He walked slowly forward as his knights cut and hacked at the princes around him, his eyes never leaving the sacred flame in the centre of the chamber. Screams and howls echoed from the walls but the prince was oblivious to all but the fires.

Out of the melee, Haradrin ran towards Malekith, a captured sword raised above his head. With a contemptuous sneer, the prince of Nagarythe stepped aside from Haradrin's wild swing and thrust his own sword into Haradrin's gut. He stood there a moment, the princes staring deep into each other's eyes, until a trickle of blood spilled from Haradrin's lips and he collapsed to the floor.

Malekith let the sword fall from his fingers with the body rather than wrench it free, and continued his pacing towards the sacred fires.

'Asuryan will not accept you!' cried Mianderin, falling to his knees in front of Malekith, his hands clasped in pleading. 'You have spilt blood in his sacred temple! We have not cast the proper enchantments to protect you from the flames. You cannot do this!'

'So?' spat the prince. 'I am Aenarion's heir. I do not need your witchery to protect me.'

Mianderin snatched at Malekith's hand but the prince tore his fingers from the haruspex's grasp.

'*I no longer listen to the protestations of priests,*' *said Malekith and kicked Mianderin aside.*

His hands held out, palms upwards in supplication, Malekith walked forwards and stepped into the flames.

Prince, priest and knight alike were tossed around by a great heaving. Chairs were flung across the floor and tables toppled. Plaster cracked upon the walls and fell in large slabs from the ceiling. Wide cracks tore through the tiles underfoot and a rift three paces wide opened up along the eastern wall, sending up a choking spume of dust and rock.

The flame of Asuryan burned paler and paler, moving from a deep blue to a brilliant white. At its heart could be seen the silhouette of Malekith, his arms still outstretched.

With a thunderous clap, the holy flame blazed, filling the room with white light. Within, Malekith collapsed to his knees and grabbed at his face.

He was burning.

He flung back his head and screamed as the flames consumed him; his howl of anguish reverberated around the shrine, echoing and growing in volume with every passing moment. The withering figure silhouetted within the flames pushed himself slowly to his feet and hurled himself from their depths.

Malekith's smoking and charred body crashed to the ground, igniting a rug and sending ashen dust billowing. Blackened flesh fell away in lumps amidst cooling droplets of molten armour. He reached outwards with a hand, and then collapsed. His clothes had been burned away and his flesh eaten down to the bone in places. His face was a mask of black and red, his dark eyes lidless and staring. Steam rose from burst veins as the prince of Nagarythe shuddered and then fell still, laid to ruin by the judgement of Asuryan.

He looked at Teclis. There was concern on the face of the mage, and sympathy too, for it was plain which event plagued Malekith's thoughts at that moment.

'Courage,' said the mage. 'The courage of your convictions. See through that which you began so long ago, and do not be afraid.'

Malekith hesitated a moment longer and gazed levelly at the loremaster. Now that Tyrion had drawn the Widowmaker, what use did the mage have for Malekith in his schemes? Malekith's thoughts moved to Imrik. His forefather had been a usurper – perhaps it was the intent to replace Malekith again with the accursed line of the Dragontamer.

'If Lileath desired you dead your corpse would be an ornament for the Shrine of Khaine,' said Teclis, guessing Malekith's line of thought. 'I could easily have allowed my brother to kill you to seal his pact with the God of Murder. We need a Phoenix King, and you are Aenarion's heir.'

'What about the blessings of the priests? The enchantments of the mages?' If it had served the usurpers well enough, it would serve now. Every fibre of Malekith warned against stepping into the flames.

'You were right – one of Aenarion's true lineage needs no protective spells to survive the flame.' Teclis moved to lay a hand upon Malekith's arm as the king-to-be took a step towards the flame, and flinched back from the gesture at the last moment, feeling the heat that emanated from Malekith's armour. 'You must be ready. Asuryan demands sacrifice and your rebirth is not without pain.'

'Tell me of pain?' sneered Malekith. Fire flared between the plates of his armour. 'It was you that awoke the burning of Asuryan's curse at Finuval Plain, so tell me, Teclis, what you know of pain?'

Malekith remembered a battle long before Finuval Plain when the nature of Asuryan's touch had become clear to him, a time when rule of Ulthuan had been moments away from his grasp.

Sulekh's body slammed into Malekith, crushing him into the ground. Pinned by her massive weight, he heaved at her mass, trying to free himself, letting out a bellow of frustration. He dropped Avanuir to the ground so that he could use both hands to push at the massive corpse that lay on top of his legs and waist.

A prickle of sensation shuddered through Malekith: the touch of magic. He turned his head to the left seeking the source.

A wave of white fire poured towards him. It was beautiful, glittering like moonlight on the sea, flecked with gold and silver. He recognised the flames. He had stood within them to receive Asuryan's blessing. Now the lord of gods had come again to aid Malekith, as he had Aenarion.

With a surge of power, Malekith heaved free the body of Sulekh. He stood up and faced the oncoming fire, arms spread wide to receive Asuryan's blessing. The white flames crackled closer and closer, a chill wind against his red-hot armour. He closed his eyes as the fire engulfed him, waiting for the release from the agony that had been his companion for more than two decades.

Fresh pain seared through his chest and arms. Malekith gave a cry and opened his eyes.

It was not the flames of Asuryan that surrounded him, but the halberds of the Phoenix Guard. Each blade burned with the white fires of Asuryan, every blow they landed upon the Witch King igniting the flame that had been set within his flesh by the lord of gods.

The physical pain was as nothing compared to the pain of betrayal. As his iron flesh was rent and ripped by the swinging halberds of the Phoenix Guard Malekith realised he had not received Asuryan's blessing. His father had not endured the agony he had endured.

The Witch King's delusion fell away and he saw his punishment for what it was. Asuryan had shunned him, cursed him with everlasting torment. The shock of it brought Malekith to his knees as more blows rained down upon him, carving furrows in his black armour.

* * *

'You must endure,' Teclis insisted, ignoring Malekith's barbed words. 'You will be destroyed and renewed. When you last stepped into the flame you were almost destroyed, and if you had but remained for a few more moments the rebirth would have begun.'

Malekith looked down at the mage, head tilted to one side.

'I was not cursed?' He said the words quietly, slowly, trying to digest the importance of Teclis's message. 'Though I profaned Asuryan's temple with blood and sought dominion over my kin? Though I killed Bel Shanaar with my own hands, the Lord of the Cadai would have blessed me if I had endured for a few heartbeats longer? This... This pain... The wars... Six thousand years of grief, because...'

He could not bring himself to voice what he thought, but the mage knew exactly that which vexed him and spoke the concern out loud.

'Because you were weak, Malekith.'

Hundreds had died agonising deaths simply because they had thought such a sentiment and it shook the Witch King to hear it plainly spoken, but in that moment he felt no anger for Teclis, only a sensation he had not felt for more than six millennia: shame.

'Then let us be at it,' said Malekith and he stepped into the sacred fire of Asuryan.

TWENTY-FIVE

The Flame of Asuryan

He was burning, the scream wrenched from his throat fuelled by raw agony and despair. It was every moment of six thousand years relived, the pain of six thousand years welled up into one single instant coursing through his body.

The urge to flee, to throw himself clear, to escape again to the Realm of Chaos, was almost overwhelming. What did it matter if his people were destroyed – he would survive, he was the greatest of them, they existed to be sacrificed for his continued life.

But he denied the urge, listening instead to the beat of his heart rather than the fear of his mind. He remembered that he was Aenarion's son and held firm to the resolution that he would be reborn if he could but endure for a few heartbeats longer. Teclis had promised him as much, and if the mage sought to play him false it was better now to end his life knowing the truth than continue for another pain-wracked age beset by the doubt that he had been offered that which he desired the most and refused it.

It was not the physical pain that caused such torture. The mortal pain was only a memory of the spiritual pain. He had known in that moment he had stepped into the flames the first time that he was not worthy. The blood on his hands, metaphorical and literal, had been his guilt and he had carried it with him.

There had been no judgement laid upon him by Asuryan. The only punishment he suffered was self-inflicted.

In acknowledging that, he accepted his fate, remembering that his father had been willing to die for the protection of Ulthuan. To rule as Phoenix King one had to be raised up from the ashes of death. There was no other way.

As the fires consumed him, Malekith laughed.

The flames burned through him, touching every part of his body and spirit. There was no pain, no sensation at all. Malekith felt like a ghost, apart from the mortal world. He swore that a thousand voices were now chanting.

Malekith could see nothing but multicoloured fire. He was made of it. He lifted a hand in front of his face and saw nothing save the dancing flames.

Malekith wondered if he was dead.

His body felt as though it had wings, lifting him up, borne aloft by the flames like the phoenixes of the flamespyre. He closed his eyes but nothing changed; still the flames filled his vision. A gentle breeze washed over him, its touch smoothing away metal skin and charred flesh and broken bone, reducing him to delicate ash, all without the slightest hint of discomfort.

Sensation returned, the fire coalescing again into his form, creating body and limbs and head and fingers and every part of him from its essence. Opening his eyes, he turned and stepped out of the flames.

'I am ready.'

The priest nodded and signalled to his attendants. Each of them carried a piece of blackened metal, curved and rune-encrusted. Some were recognisable: breastplate, vambraces, gorget, gauntlets.

Others seemed utterly alien, strangely shaped, trailing sheets of black mail or fixed with awkwardly angled hinges.

The first piece was put into the furnace. The slaves were whipped to increase their labours at the bellows. Muttering prayers to Vaul, Hotek fanned the flames with magic, until they burned white-hot. Reaching his bare hand into the fires, he retrieved the piece of armour. Impervious to the heat, he carried it to Malekith, who watched the proceedings with the remains of his brow knotted in concentration.

'This will burn,' said Hotek.

Malekith's reply was a shrill laugh, tinged with madness.

'I can burn no more,' whispered the prince. 'Do it!'

An acolyte brought forward a smoking rivet in a pair of tongs. Hotek and his assistant crouched, the priest placing the hot piece of metal against Malekith's flesh with a hiss of vapour. Malekith giggled.

'Now,' said Hotek.

The acolyte pushed the rivet into place. With a few whispered words of enchantment, Hotek struck lightly with the Hammer of Vaul, tapping the hot rivet through its prepared hole and into the bone of Malekith.

The prince snarled with pain, and swayed for a moment. He wished he could close his eyes. Instead he set his mind aside, going to the place he had created for himself in the cold depths of his thoughts.

With a start, Malekith was dragged back to reality. Two bodies lay at his feet. His body burned with fresh fire, but it was no more than he had grown used to. Acolytes moved around him, painting blood from the sacrifices into the runes carved upon the pieces of armour put in place, following each curl and line with brushes made of elven hair.

His lower legs and feet were clad in the smoking black iron. He did not remember lifting his feet, but realised he must have done so. He could feel the rivets hammered into heel and toe and laughed at the thought of being shod like a warhorse.

There was chanting. His mother looked on silently, but her adepts' words swished around the chamber, verses overlapping, creating an arrhythmic harmony of magic. More rivets were driven into the scrawny flesh of his thighs, and links were riveted into place through the sides of his knees.

When next he perceived clearly what was happening, he was clad from foot to neck in the armour. Every part of him trembled. He could feel the energy of the spirit he had consumed slipping away.

'Too soon,' he muttered. 'I am falling.'

Morathi hurriedly beckoned to an adept, who sacrificed another captive and brought the blood to Malekith in a cup of ancient silver. Malekith took the cup and then stopped. He realised he had not held a thing for more than a decade. He examined the fingers of his new hand, each perfectly articulated. He recognised the dwarf-work that inspired the design and smiled to himself. Even now, his great adventures of the past were still bearing fruit.

The fires flared anew and Malekith was brought back to the present. A film of red covered his vision. His own blood, he realised.

He blinked.

The simple motion caused him immeasurable joy. The thinnest slivers of black metal had been fashioned into eyelids. Malekith blinked again, and then closed his eyes. He enjoyed the darkness and more time passed.

'It is done,' announced Hotek.

Malekith flexed his arms and bent his legs, trying out his new body. It felt like his own flesh, though the burning had not lessened. Half a dozen dead elves lay sprawled at his feet, throats slit, their blood anointed upon his forged form. He could feel their spirits sliding around him, trapped within the runes of the armour.

'Not finished,' he said. 'My crown.'

Hotek looked confused and turned to Morathi for explanation. She summoned an acolyte who brought forth a velvet cushion on which was placed a circlet of dull grey metal, spikes jutting at strange angles like a crown conceived by a lunatic.

Morathi reached a hand towards it, but Malekith grabbed her wrist. She howled in pain and tore free from his grip, backing away. There were burns on her flesh.

'You cannot touch it,' said Malekith. 'It is not yours, it is mine.'

He took up the Circlet of Iron. It felt icy cold to his touch. While Morathi fussed over her burned wrist, Malekith raised the strange crown to his head and placed it on his brow.

'Weld it,' said the prince. 'Make it a piece of the helm.'

Hotek did as he was bid, striking more rivets into Malekith's skull before securing the circlet in place with molten metal. Malekith reached up and tugged at the circlet, assuring himself that it could not be removed.

Satisfied, he closed his eyes again. He let his thoughts free from his body, tasting the dark magic seething around the dungeon chamber. He felt the inrushing of power and rode the wave of energy, spearing up through the roof of the chamber, passing through the many floors of his father's palace like a meteor called back to the stars. Anlec dwindled below him and he shifted from the plane of mortals into a realm of pure magic.

As at the first time he had worn the circlet, he looked at the Realm of Chaos, the domain of the Chaos Gods. On this occasion he had no fear. He materialised in his armoured form, burning white-hot, his presence blazing across the dominions of the Chaos Gods as a challenge.

Sentiences not of any mortal recognition stirred. Malekith felt their attention slowly drawn towards him.

'I am Malekith!' he declared. A flaming sword appeared in his hand. 'Son of Aenarion, the daemons' bane. Hear my name and know me, the rightful king of the elves!'

As a comet of power, he plunged back to his body. The runes of his armour exploded with dark flames as he re-entered his artificial form. He opened his metal eyelids, revealing orbs of black fire.

He looked down at the elves around him. They seemed small

and insignificant. His voice echoed strangely from the mask of his helm, filling the room.

'I have returned,' he declared. 'Pay homage to me.'

All present fell to their knees, instantly obedient to his words; save one, who fixed him with an expression of utter happiness.

'Hail Malekith!' cried Morathi, golden tears streaming down her face. 'Hail the Witch King of Ulthuan!'

The flame guttered and died behind Malekith, leaving the inner sanctum in darkness.

The ground trembled, and not from the bombardment, but from a movement deep below. With a loud snap, a crack appeared in the pyramidal roof, a shaft of light breaking through to illuminate the newly-blessed Phoenix King.

'Hail the Phoenix King,' Caradryan said, tone uncertain, lifting his halberd in salute. Malekith stopped, shocked by the similarity to Kouran, as though he were the light from which came the shadow that was the captain of the Black Guard.

Malekith noticed Caradryan's confused look and gazed down at himself, expecting to see pale skin, living muscle. Instead there was the same fractured and pitted metal, though the blood had stopped leaking from his wounds.

'You said I would be reborn!' bellowed Malekith rounding on Teclis. The mage back-stepped as the Phoenix King stalked towards him, one finger pointed in accusation. 'Look at me. Look at me!'

'In spirit,' the mage replied, stopping when he was beside Caradryan. 'Spiritually reborn.'

'This is a mockery,' growled Malekith, fighting the urge to fall to his knees and weep. He swayed, a hand across his face. 'Six thousand years encased in this prison...'

The temple bucked again, a sound like thunder reverberating from below. A chunk of masonry larger than Malekith fell from the roof to crash on the tiles close to the flame, shattering into white splinters. Another piece fell a moment later, just a few paces from the Phoenix King. The steps split, letting immense blocks of marble fall to the sanctum floor. Shards like immense icicles fell from the roof around the elves.

The sunlight flickered as the silhouettes of dragons passed over, their roars mingled with the shouts of clashing warriors and the crackle of flames.

'We should hurry,' said Teclis, another tremor causing him to flinch and stumble as he turned towards the doorway. 'Even if we escape the shrine, Aislinn's forces are all over the island by now.'

'Not that way,' said Caradryan, pointing across the inner shrine. 'There is another exit, known only to the Phoenix Guard.'

The former captain started across the sanctum at a run, Teclis on his heel. Malekith followed with a leisurely stride, ignoring the pieces of stone falling around him.

'Why do you tarry?' demanded Teclis, stopping to look back. 'The temple is about to collapse!'

'I do not think Asuryan invested me with his last power only to have me squashed by wayward masonry,' Malekith replied with a laugh. It was quite overwhelming, the mixture of elation and disappointment. He held out a hand and let his essence flow. The fire inside him burned white and he laughed again, delighted by this revelation. 'I have become the sacred flame.'

'I would prefer it that the flame was not extinguished quite so soon,' Teclis said, tapping his staff on the floor in impatient agitation.

'Do you not think I look magnificent?' Malekith said, stopping also, confounding the desires of the mage for a little more amusement. It was pleasing to see the Sapherian so uncertain for a change, after so much time dancing to the tune he called. A thought occurred to Malekith. 'You have not yet properly welcomed me back to the land of the living, nephew.'

'What?' Teclis shook his head and moved to continue his retreat.

'Teclis!' The Phoenix King's shout rebounded from the breaking walls, echoing in a strange way, its metallic intonation changing as it faded. The archmage stopped in his tracks, unable to ignore the call. Malekith pointed to the floor at his feet. 'Pay proper homage, nephew.'

'Now?'

'Now.'

Muttering, Teclis returned to Malekith, casting frightened glances about him as more masonry continued to crash down from above. The sound of shouts was close at hand, dulled only by the doors of the inner sanctum. Metal crashed against metal just outside.

'Hail the Phoenix King,' the mage said hurriedly, bowing his head.

'I am unconvinced by your display. Try harder, with more sincerity.'

Teclis glared at Malekith and the Phoenix King looked back, burning white eyes in the slit of his helm. Nodding, suddenly humbled, the mage dropped to one knee, his staff proffered before him.

'Praise Malekith, heir to Aenarion, rightful Phoenix King of Ulthuan.' Teclis looked up again, earnestness written across his features. 'Saviour of elvenkind. The Defender.'

The title cut through Malekith's cloud of self-satisfaction. He had been so obsessed with taking up his birthright it had never occurred to him what he would do as king. Now that his ascension had been achieved, he was unsure what to do next, but Teclis's tone made it clear what was expected.

'It is one thing to become Asuryan's incarnation, it is another to rule,' said the Phoenix King, gesturing for Teclis to stand. The thud of blades on the doors to the inner sanctum lent fresh urgency to Malekith's thoughts. 'Better that our foes do not learn yet of what has happened here. Caradryan, lead on!'

They followed the leader of the Phoenix Guard between two columns at the back of the shrine. Pausing at the wall, he ran his hand over the stone, his fingers tracing an intricate pattern while he whispered an incantation. He stepped back when he was done and the wall shimmered into a golden field, revealing a corridor beyond.

They stepped through and Caradryan restored the wall so that none would be able to follow. At the end of the passageway was a winding stair, which led further down into the island. Another corridor brought them out onto a broad loggia looking south across the Sea of Dreams. There were a handful of ships in view, but they were sailing west to the landing grounds.

Arranged along the balcony were a number of skycutters, their empty traces lying on the bare rock. Caradryan let out a shrill whistle and waited. It was not long before the flap of immense wings preceded the arrival of a mighty frostheart phoenix, the same one that had borne Caradryan into battle over the Blighted Isle.

'Ashtari,' said Caradryan, smoothing the feathers of the great bird's neck as it perched on the edge of the loggia. 'We have need to be far away and soon, and must not be seen.'

The phoenix stalked across to the nearest skycutter, claws leaving ice-rimed scratches in the floor. With Teclis's aid, Caradryan harnessed up the bird and all three elves stepped into the skycutter's platform. Caradryan spoke a word and the magic of the skycutter billowed into life, surrounding Malekith with a warm aura of Azyr.

'Go,' he commanded and Ashtari obeyed, leaping out over the waters, the skycutter lurching into motion behind.

They sped over the sea, the phoenix's wings almost touching the waves. A loud crack caused the elves to turn, in time to see the pyramid of Asuryan explode into brilliant white light. The temple collapsed in on itself, but the destruction did not end there. Cliffs fell into the sea and great fissures split the isle, letting the waters of the Sea of Dreams race in, washing away thousands of soldiers loyal to both sides.

Imrik's dragons whirled away as fire and water plumed into the sky. The ships of Aislinn's fleet put up their sails and turned away as the Island of the Flame sank. Some were too slow, the closest sucked into the maelstrom created by the island's demise, hulls shattered and masts split by the titanic whirl of water.

The wave created by this disaster raced after the fleeing Phoenix King, as high as a tower, a wall of dark destruction. Ashtari climbed higher, leaving a trail of ice in the spume of the tidal wave as it passed beneath them.

'Where shall we find sanctuary now?' Caradryan asked, sadness making his voice crack.

'Caledor,' said Malekith, pointing at the dragons streaming south-west. 'We shall wage the war from the land of the Dragontamer.'

TWENTY-SIX

The Longest Road

Over the past six thousand years Malekith had spent the equivalent of many lifetimes of lesser creatures dreaming of his moment of glory. When he had been young, his visions had been filled with adoring crowds and showered adulation. After the Sundering his thoughts had become bleaker, his coronation parade taking place along a road made from the skulls of his enemies, banners made from their skins flapping along the route. In recent times he had been content to have every prince of Ulthuan, hundreds of them, prostrate themselves before him, each in turn begging for forgiveness, giving thanks that their rightful king had finally been recognised.

It was something of a disappointment that his arrival in Caledor had more in common with the coming of a thief than the arrival of a triumphant king. What was perhaps surprising was that this clandestine approach was at his behest. They had escaped the Island of Flame unseen and it seemed to the Phoenix King the most sensible course of action to conceal not only his continued survival but his elevation to Asuryan's avatar. There would be a time to reveal his ascension, for maximum effect on morale and to dismay his foes, but it was not yet, not least because he wanted Imrik and Teclis to pave the way for the announcement, gauging the probable reactions of the other princes.

So it was under cover of darkness – Malekith swathed in a voluminous cloak, greeted by a handful of servants hand-picked by Imrik – that the Phoenix King arrived in Tor Caleda.

The city of the Dragon Princes sat high in the peaks of the southern Annulii; To the north, south and west the mountains and precipitous cliffs barred any approach save from the air; to the east a single pass held by many towers became an elevated road leading to the barbican of a mighty gatehouse.

Not much more than a high citadel with a broad curtain wall, it was the smallest of the elven capitals, a pale imitation of the former seat of power at Tor Caled. The ruins of Caledor Dragontamer's birthplace could be visited, several days north, petrified forever when the volcano on which it was built had erupted during the Sundering, burying city and elves alike in a torrent of fire and ash. Caledor had never been a populous realm and there had been little will to rebuild such a large settlement. The outpost at Tor Sarath had naturally grown to accommodate its new importance and taken the name Caleda in honour of the fallen city.

Now it was straining to contain the host of elves that wished to find refuge there. The causeway leading to the gate was thronged with crowds from dawn to dusk, pleading with the guards at the gate for entry. Prince and farmer alike, driven south by the fighting in Ellyrion, were all turned back by order of the newly arrived Phoenix King, though the order had been voiced by Imrik. There was too much risk that Tyrion's agents were concealed amongst the genuine refugees. What food and shelters could be provided were despatched, but it was little to help and the lords of the city were glad that it was summer – when the season of ice came the causeway would become a snow-covered graveyard if no other sanctuary was found for the dispossessed of Tiranoc and Ellyrion.

Malekith held his first court two days after coming to the city from the Island of Flame. The Phoenix King favoured only three elves to share counsel, even amongst those that knew of his arrival: Teclis, Imrik and Caradryan. All others were sent away with harsh words from their new ruler. Wine and food was left, along with a sturdy throne for the king fashioned by the city's foremost smithy, for no ordinary chair in the citadel could bear him.

'War.'

Malekith allowed the word to hang in the air, ringing from the crystal lanterns that hung from the vaulted ceiling. His councillors, standing around the throne, looked at each other, expressions grave.

'You told me that you wanted a guard of dragons when you became Phoenix King,' said Imrik. 'You have them. Lead us into the battle and we will see Tyrion defeated.'

'Not yet,' said Teclis. He gestured to the empty scabbard at Malekith's waist. '*Urithain* was destroyed. You have no blade, your majesty.'

'Have my sword if that is all you lack,' said Imrik. He moved to draw his blade but Malekith stopped him with an upraised hand.

'The Phoenix King does not ride to war with some hand-me-down heirloom of Caledor,' Malekith snapped. 'Tyrion already wears my father's armour and bears his sword – what further indignity do you wish to heap upon me?'

'What blade would be suitable?' asked Caradryan.

'I can answer that,' said Teclis. He had under his arm a wrapped bundle. Moving aside platters of meats, he made space on one of the tables to unroll his burden. Contained within were shards of bluish-black metal, which Malekith immediately recognised.

'The remnants of the Destroyer,' he said, reaching out his gauntleted fingers to touch one of the splinters. It was lifeless, all of the magic gone. 'How did you come by them?'

'They were brought with us when Lileath transported us from the Blighted Isle. I kept them, believing the goddess intended something to be done with them.'

'What can be done with a few broken pieces of sword?' said Imrik. 'Tyrion wields the Widowmaker, made by Vaul himself.'

'He calls it the icefang,' Malekith told them. 'I heard him name the blade as he drew it.'

'The name is irrelevant,' said Imrik. 'How does one fight a god-forged blade?'

Malekith looked at Teclis, guessing that the mage already had the answer. Teclis smiled and moved to a long, narrow chest he had brought with him.

'Do you remember, Imrik, the bargain you struck with our king to secure your alliance?' the mage asked as he started to unfasten the locks of the casket.

'All of the dragon eggs that were stolen, and the surviving weapons of Vaul forged in secrecy by Hotek for Malekith's army.'

'Indeed.' Teclis opened the chest and a magical blue glow coloured his face. He lifted out the box's contents, a heavy smith's hammer with a golden head emblazoned with a symbol of lightning bolts.

'The Hammer of Vaul,' whispered Imrik, eyes widening in amazement.

'Did you think I had thrown it away, or perhaps lost it?' said Malekith. He addressed Teclis. 'Now I understand why you insisted that it was included, in secret, with the artefacts Hotek created for me. Unfortunately, if you had told me your intent at the time I would have avoided today's embarrassment.'

'Embarrassment, your majesty?' Teclis frowned as Malekith stood up and plucked the Hammer of Vaul from his fingers. The Phoenix King swung the Smith God's divine instrument a few times, leaving a faint auric trail in the air as he walked down the hall. 'Your majesty, that is not a child's toy...'

'It's useless!' barked Malekith, spinning to face the others, the hammer pointed at Teclis. 'With Hotek gone there is nobody left that can wield it, you fool. Do you think that if I had been able to make armour and weapons with the Hammer of Vaul for the last four and a half thousand years I would have sent my troops into battle with iron spears and chainmail? I would have unleashed a legion ten thousand strong with blades that could cut the thickest armour and plate that resisted dragonrage!'

Malekith let the hammer drop from his grasp, cracking the dark stone floor where it fell at his feet.

'We have priests of Vaul...' suggested Imrik.

'So did I,' Malekith replied with a sigh, returning to his throne. 'Acolytes of Hotek himself.'

'They could not wield the power of the hammer?' said Teclis, picking up the artefact with a disappointed expression. 'They failed to forge anything?'

'In a manner of speaking,' replied the Phoenix King. 'They were deafened and crippled after one stroke. A few, after suitable prompting, tried a second, but they all died. Very grisly.'

'The world turns and Morai-heg reveals her intentions,' muttered Imrik, shaking his head.

'Speak clearly,' Malekith told him. 'What do you mean?'

The dragon prince looked at Teclis with an expression of disbelief and fear. 'Perhaps Lileath does guide your acts, in some fashion. I do not think I can tell you – I must show you.'

'Show us what?' demanded Malekith, losing his patience altogether.

'We must go to the Shrine of Vaul,' said Imrik. 'There is someone I think you need to see.'

A fine summer's evening greeted four mighty guests to Vaul's Anvil, greatest shrine to the crippled Smith God of the elves. Malekith flew upon Seraphon, who like the others had been saved by Lileath's translocation, and with him was Imrik on the back of Minaithnir, followed by Caradryan astride Ashtari the phoenix and, below, Teclis borne swiftly over the mountain tracks by his steed of shadow magic. The evening was settling fast when Malekith saw a bright fire in the distance. Situated at the very end of the Dragon Spine range, separated by a wide valley from the rest of the mountains, a solitary peak cast its shadow over the water's edge, shrouded with cloud and fume. To the northern slope the dragons turned, where steps were carved into the black rock, winding back and forth up the steep incline leading to a carved opening flanked by two gigantic pillars. Atop the columns were statues of bent-legged Vaul. On the left the god of craftsmen laboured over an anvil, a hammer of thunderbolts in his hand. On the right he was bound in chains, weeping over the Sword of Khaine he had forged.

Before these pillars landed the dragons. Their arrival did not go unnoticed, and acolytes garbed in heavy aprons and thick gloves came out of the shrine's opening to assist the dragon riders in dismounting. When they saw Malekith they recoiled in horror and some turned to flee.

'Stay!' Imrik commanded them. 'Behold your new Phoenix King!'

This caused some consternation, but Imrik was well known to the priests of Vaul and the presence of Caradryan and Teclis, both renowned for their loyalty to Ulthuan, mitigated their fears a little.

'It is strange that you should come to us on this day of all days, princes and king,' said one of the priests. He was older than the others, blinded eyes covered by a band of iron, though he moved without guidance.

'How so?' asked Malekith as they ascended the steps.

The priest hesitated before replying, and addressed his words to Imrik. Malekith ignored the insult for the moment, more eager to hear what the priest had to say than chastise his poor manners.

'The prisoner started ranting this morning, shouting to all that would listen that Vaul had forgiven him.'

'Prisoner?' Teclis said, and Malekith exchanged a look with the mage, unsettled by his surprise. If the herald of Lileath did not know what was occurring, was any of the Sapherian's plan truly god-sent?

'Take us to him immediately,' said Imrik, hastening through the arch into the ruddy chamber beyond.

They followed their guides down several levels cut into the rock of the mountain, and stopped beside a metal door at the end of a winding passageway. The door was barred by a dozen bolts, six to each side, and another thick metal spar across the width padlocked at both ends.

They said nothing as word was sent for the high priest to attend, and to bring the keys with him, but Malekith eyed the door suspiciously. He could feel waves of Chamon beating against the iron from the other side.

'Vaul's energy, the Wind of Metal,' Teclis said, slender fingers fidgeting on his staff. He narrowed his eyes towards Imrik. 'What have they got hidden in there?'

'He was found in the maze of tunnels beneath the shrine, many centuries ago. Lost, it seems, though how he came to enter them is a mystery,' explained one of the priests. 'We could see that he was blinded in the fashion of our order, but none recognised him. I think he must have been from the colonies.'

'Go on,' urged Teclis.

'He was mad, almost dead of thirst. He speaks little, but mutters the great incantations of Vaul. Much of what he says is nonsensical – even our most learned loresmiths can make nothing of it.'

The high priest, Fovendiel, arrived and set about unlocking and unbolting the door, visibly unnerved by the presence of Malekith. He turned before casting aside the final bolt, and looked directly at Malekith, his hand moving to within just a short distance from the king's chest.

'Dark work,' the priest said, fingers flinching from the heat of the armour of midnight. 'But a miracle, all the same. That we could once furnish such gifts to our allies. Our power is much diminished.'

'Open the door,' snapped Malekith, in no mood for reminiscing. Imrik's coyness angered him, as did the mystery of the prisoner.

Fovendiel did as he had been told, stepping aside to swing the door outwards.

The figure in the room was dressed in a plain robe of black, his white hair swept back by a worn band of black leather studded with ruddy bronze. His features were severe, with high cheek-bones and brow sharp. Most remarkable were his eyes, of pure white, just like those of the high priest.

He sat on a stool next to a plain bunk, surrounded by piles of tattered parchment covered with runes, writing and diagrams. Muttering, the elf was fixed upon the contents of a page on his lap.

'How long ago did you say he arrived?'

'That's the miracle,' said the high priest. 'He has been here for more than four thousand years. Some greater power sustains him.'

The prisoner looked up, blind gaze drawn straight to Malekith as the Phoenix King stepped across the threshold.

The burning would not stop. It raged in Malekith's mind long after his body was dead to the pain of the flames. Had his father felt like this? Is this what drove him to the Sword of Khaine, to escape the touch of Asuryan's blessing?

The thought calmed the prince of Nagarythe. As his father had endured, so would he. What was his torment but another chance to prove his superiority? When he next stood before the princes to declare his right to be Phoenix King none of them would argue. It would be plain for them to see the strength of his character. Who of them could deny that he had passed Asuryan's test? He smiled at the thought, cracked flesh creasing across the remains of his face.

Their resistance was fuelled by jealousy. The usurper, Bel Shanaar, had groomed Imrik like a prize stallion, though in truth he was nothing more than a plodding mule. The other princes had been blinded to the truth by the whispers of Bel Shanaar. When the evidence of Malekith's acceptance by Asuryan was presented, they would see through the falsehoods woven by the Caledorian and his supporters. Perhaps even Imrik would bend his knee, as Malekith had so graciously done at the foot of Bel Shanaar.

The curtain surrounding the bed stirred and Morathi bent over him. Malekith tried to rise to kiss her cheek but his body failed him. A spasm of pain along his spine trapped him beneath the covers, as though a great weight was laid upon him. His mouth twisted into a snarl of anguish.

'Be still, my beautiful son,' said Morathi, laying a hand on his brow. 'I have someone you should greet.'

An emaciated elf moved up beside Malekith's mother, face almost white, eyes pale and unseeing though they fixed upon the prince.

'Greetings, your majesty,' he said. 'I am Hotek.'

'Hotek?' Malekith whispered the name, knowing it was impossible that the ancient High Priest of Vaul could be in the same chamber, there and then. He glared at Imrik. 'This must be some kind of trick?'

'This is Hotek?' replied the prince, his surprise as genuine and as deep as Malekith's. He looked at the prisoner with wide eyes. 'How can that be possible?'

The old priest laughed, the lines on his face deepening, but there was no madness in the sound as Malekith had feared, only humour. Hotek stood up, setting aside his studies to appraise each of his visitors in turn with blind eyes. He sneered at Fovendiel and bowed his head to Imrik, and then stopped as his unseeing gaze fell upon Teclis.

'Another godhead,' said the priest, cracked lips twisting into a smile. 'I smell moonlight and mystery. Lileath has touched you, my friend.'

'More than that,' Teclis replied. He reached out a hand and laid it on Hotek's shoulder, but drew it back sharply when sparks erupted from the mage's fingertips. 'Vaul fills you with the Wind of Chamon.'

'I am his vessel,' Hotek said with a nod. 'I tried to tell these fools but the words would not come properly until now. It is as though a gag was lifted from my lips.' He looked at Malekith and moved splayed fingers towards the king's armour. 'May I?'

Malekith hesitated, but consented. The priest ran his hands over the armour of midnight, the cracks and welds, the scars and rivets, almost caressing the king, his fingers long since inured to the heat of furnaces and forge. When he was done there was a look of satisfaction on Hotek's face.

'It has lasted well,' said the priest, 'but alas my sense of time has become a little unfocused. I know that when I last set eyes on you, a thousand years had passed since the fall of Nagarythe. I came back here to reclaim the notes I had abandoned during my flight, and the rest is very hazy.'

'More than four millennia have passed since you left Naggaroth,' said Malekith.

'I see,' said Hotek, receiving this news with admirable calm. 'I see that my master's works take time. He came to me, Vaul, and said that I had despoiled his legacy, and that I had to make amends, on my behalf and his.'

'Is that so?' said Teclis. 'How are you to achieve this feat?'

'By forging the blade that can match the Widowmaker,' said Hotek. 'Vaul has gifted me his power and I can sense that you have brought me his hammer. There is something else I will need.'

Teclis was about to reply when Imrik stepped forward, standing between the priest and the other elves. He looked intently at Malekith.

'We cannot trust this traitor,' said the prince. 'He has betrayed Caledor before, to great detriment. What guarantee can he give that he will not do so again?'

'Because I am willing to pay the price for my previous ill-dealings. Always Vaul loved the mountains and dragons. Oh, I will need a dragon, if you can arrange it, while it occurs to me. Nothing smelts magical steel like dragonfire! Anyway, you will cripple me and chain me to the anvil, and my last deed will be to make the blade that can stand against the Sword of Khaine.'

'You seem very sure of this,' said Malekith, pushing Imrik aside to confront the priest. 'You served me before because you were promised the secrets of the dwarfs, to be wrested from their holds by our conquering armies. What do you want from me now?'

'All that is ancient history, my king,' said Hotek, dropping to one knee. 'You are Asuryan and I am Vaul, and you will need a blade fit for the king of kings. It will happen as I have seen.'

'You seem awfully quiet, nephew.' Malekith glared at Teclis. 'Your mistress did not reveal this to you?'

'No, but she did speak to you of this moment, did she not?' the archmage replied. 'Do you recall her third prophecy?'

'And comes forth the Crippled One's bane, the forgotten maker shall be found. On mercy's anvil shall hope be forged, and silence shall be unbound.'

Malekith hated this talk of gods and avatars, even though he had been through the flame of Asuryan and become one himself. The mythic tales were cycles, and he had no desire to repeat the war of the gods on the mortal plane, not at the dawn of the Rhana Dandra. But that was perhaps the whole point, to be mortal and to break the old cycles of treachery and death. He had been granted the opportunity to be the hub around which the spokes of the future might revolve.

'Very well,' he told Hotek. 'It will be as you say. Forge me a blade worthy of Asuryan.'

The Phoenix King stalked away, Imrik close on his heel while Teclis remained with the priests of Vaul.

'So you will ride to war when the sword is ready?' the prince asked. Malekith wondered why Imrik was so keen to see Malekith risking his life in battle, but it was not the moment to question his ally's motives. 'How long do you think it will take Hotek to make his weapon?'

'It took Vaul a year and a day to make the Sword of Khaine. Let us hope that Hotek is swifter.'

'Until then?'

'You must be the figurehead. Just as your ancestor stepped up to my challenge, you must be the visible opponent to Tyrion. The Dragon of Cothique is bewitched by Morathi and enamoured of Khaine, and there are those that will see the truth. He will become a warmonger, there is no other destiny for the chosen of Khaine. Your defection at Eagle Pass will be seen as a great moment of foresight – be sure to include Teclis in your accounts, the brother of Tyrion that has disowned him will lend further weight to your argument.'

'Very well, but it will take more than words to stop Tyrion. When do we fight?'

'When I sought to take this isle, I knew that my army could crush any force opposed to it, save for the dragons of Caledor. Your forefather knew that his dragons could defeat me but that they could not be everywhere at once. Neither he nor I was willing to place success or failure in a personal confrontation, and so our armies danced across the kingdoms like unwilling partners. As it was then, so it must be again. This is not a war one can win in a season, but it is a war that can be lost in a day. Give Tyrion no single enemy to destroy, but rouse up all opposition to him so that his forces must watch their backs, guard every town and garrison every fortress they take.'

'Any other lessons of grand strategy you wish to share?'

'Stay out of Nagarythe,' Malekith added, ignoring the prince's sarcasm, just as he ignored Imrik's continued refusal to call him king. Deference would come in time – all the Phoenix King required for the moment was obedience.

Malekith stopped and held a hand to halt Imrik. He stared at the prince, intent.

'Whatever happens, do not confront Tyrion directly. If you meet him in battle, you will die and all chance of victory will be lost.'

'And if I should happen to be on the same battlefield as he, you expect me to avoid him?'

'I expect you to run away, Imrik,' said Malekith, clenching his fist. 'Your pride is already spent – it has no value now. You are no good to me dead, and neither are your dragons. He wields the Godslayer, and you are not even a god.'

'What if he brings the war to Caledor? We would have nowhere left to retreat.'

'You had best make sure he does not come here, hadn't you? I suggest you start by taking Lothern.'

TWENTY-SEVEN

A Tale of Two Kings

As Malekith predicted, the opening stages of the war were characterised by caution. Imrik swiftly secured neighbouring Tiranoc, what little remained of the kingdom after the floods of the Sundering, and in a daring assault seized both eastern and western Eataine to lay siege to Lothern from both directions. The port capitulated quickly and within days black arks and Naggarothi corsair fleets were, for the first time in the long history of Ulthuan, passing through the harbour gates to bring war to the Sea of Dreams.

Aislinn, still smarting from the losses at the Island of Flame, was enraged by the fall of his home city and threw his flotillas at the druchii reavers with vicious abandon. The coast of the Inner Sea was littered with debris and corpses following these bloody naval conflicts but the Sea Lord came no closer to uniting with his ships trapped beyond Lothern in the Great Ocean and was eventually forced to take shelter in inlets and bays along the shore of Ellyrion.

This news pleased Malekith greatly, as did affairs at Vaul's Anvil. Hotek's work was progressing well; the shards of *Urithain* made fine material for his new sword. However, the priest was canny enough to avoid any promises regarding when the work would be complete, talking instead of cosmic convergences, spheres of power and opening portals.

The Phoenix King was not vexed by this, for his wounds at the hands of Tyrion, and the poison from Shadowblade's dagger, still left him weak and dizzy after any considerable exertion. Asuryan's rebirth had been more cosmetic than he had hoped. He would have died rather than admit to his allies that he was incapable of fighting, but the tale of waiting for Hotek's sword granted him valuable time to convalesce. It was of some concern to Imrik, but Teclis, who was likely not fooled at all by Malekith's talk of biding time and striking at the most opportune moment, revealed that his brother was similarly afflicted, leaving others to prosecute the war on his behalf.

Until, that was, summer started fading into autumn.

'And of the war in the east, Tyrion has withdrawn his forces from Yvresse's coast.' Teclis's sources, both mystical and physical, were the equal to the network Ezresor had once boasted, although those agents were now for the most part ranged against Malekith, reporting to Morathi instead. The age-long game of assassination and espionage continued; the pieces had simply changed sides. 'The daemon-haunted fogs make keeping any troops there costly, in casualties and morale.'

'Imrik moves on Saphery then? How fares the battle for your homeland?'

'My call for Imrik to be aided by the local militias has carried some weight. Imrik has agreed to respect the neutrality of the White Tower of Hoeth, and so far Tyrion does the same. I take it you concur with this approach?'

'If the loremasters and swordmasters of Hoeth wish to let us settle their differences without interference I commend them. There is little else in Saphery that can hope to resist dragonfire and lances. What else?'

'It seems my brother's convalescence has been concluded,' Teclis said quietly. He did not add 'faster than yours,' but Malekith inferred the comparison anyway. 'He marches for Tor Yvresse. I think he means to press Imrik to open battle.'

'Of course he does – we expected this,' said Malekith. Teclis's concern at this turn of events was itself a source of unease for the Phoenix King. 'Imrik's campaign in your brother's absence has gone well – we have made great gains in the time afforded us.'

'He claims the title of Phoenix King,' said Teclis. 'Tyrion no longer pretends to be regent, but names himself ruler of Ulthuan.'

Malekith considered this, his ire rising.

'And they follow him? The princes?'

'Some do, others say that he has not passed through the flame of Asuryan and cannot be king, but they are afraid to openly dispute his word.'

'Hypocrites!' howled Malekith. He crushed a wine ewer in his fist and hurled it the length of the hall, causing a spasm in his wounded shoulder. 'Worthless, baseless cretins! He bears the Widowmaker openly? He consorts with Morathi in front of them?'

'He does, your majesty,' admitted Teclis, stepping back as fire crackled and enveloped Malekith's raised fists. 'Is that important?'

'Usurpers!' shrieked Morathi, raising up her staff. Malekith leapt forwards and snatched the rod from her grip.

'No more!' the prince of Nagarythe cried out. 'I would not have the realm forged by my father torn asunder by this dispute.'

Malekith laid a comforting hand upon the cheek of his mother and when she was calmed, returned her staff to her. With a last venomous glare at Yvraine and Bel Shanaar, the seeress turned her back upon them and returned to the Naggarothi contingent to glower and sneer.

'I do not seek the throne of Ulthuan to become a tyrant,' said Malekith. 'It is to honour my father and see his legacy fulfilled that I would become Phoenix King. I do not claim this as a right

of birth, but surrender myself to the judgement of those here. If it is the decision of this council that Bel Shanaar should wed my half-sister and become king, I will not oppose it. I ask only that you consider my petition this one last time, for it is plain that we have allowed division and misconception to cloud our minds.'

The princes nodded in agreement at these well-spoken words, and gathered together under the eaves of the Avelorn trees. They talked for a long time, until dawn touched her red fingers upon the treetops and the morning mists drifted up from the fertile earth. Back and forth swayed the debate, for some were heartened by Malekith's gentle entreaty and believed that though he was his father's son, he had not wielded the Godslayer and so was not touched by its darkness. Others reminded the council of Imrik's prophecy that Aenarion's line was touched by Khaine, and argued that a child of Anlec could never be freed from its curse.

'We have made our decision,' Thyriol informed the Naggarothi. 'While Malekith is a fine prince, he is yet young and has much to learn about the world, as do we all. Now is a time for wisdom and guidance, not iron rule, and for these reasons we remain committed to the investiture of Bel Shanaar.'

Morathi gave a scream of derision, but Malekith held up a hand to silence her.

'The fate of Ulthuan is not for a single elf to decide, and I accede to the wisdom of this council,' Malekith declared. He crossed the glade and, to the amazement of all, bent to one knee before Bel Shanaar. 'Bel Shanaar shall succeed my father, though he cannot replace him, and with his wisdom we shall herald a new age for our people. May the gods grant our new king the strength to prosper and rule justly, and know that should ever his will falter or his resolve waver, Nagarythe stands ready.'

'They would not choose me because the darkness of Khaine lay upon me.' Malekith's laugh was shrill, rebounding from the vaulted walls in mocking echoes. 'A shadow of Khaine? A shadow? A hint? There were times, times of weakness, when my strength was withered and my ambition stunted, when I wondered if they had been right. I would think that the blood and mayhem was the curse of Khaine as Caledor foretold and the First Council had chosen wisely. Now the wisdom of elven princes is truly revealed. Pathetic! Had I taken the Sword of Khaine they would have quailed and begged for me to be king and we would have been doomed to slaughter ourselves into history and then extinction. Is that what they want? Do they really think this blood-hungry usurper will lead them to sanctuary?'

'They do not think,' Teclis said, his hands raised to calm Malekith. 'At least, they cannot think clearly. Their ancient enemy has invaded, swift on the heels of daemons that nearly destroyed their homes. Tyrion protected them then, and he bears the armour of Aenarion and his blood. The Widowmaker, it taints their thoughts, making them warmongers also, but it is fear rather than blood-thirst that drives them.'

'They shall all be slain, in turn,' Malekith declared, 'for their lack of loyalty.'

'They cannot be loyal to a king in hiding, your majesty,' Teclis said carefully. 'Is it your intent to make public your ascension?'

Malekith's first instinct, fuelled by indignation, was to declare that he would. His announcement would shake elvendom to its core, make known the fact that six thousand years of injustice had finally ended. The princes would see that he had been accepted by Asuryan and would flock to his banner as their ancestors should have done.

Teclis's calculating gaze punctured the illusion, reminding the Phoenix King of the wounds that still dogged him and the blade as-yet-unforged. To reveal himself as king now would make Malekith a target and Tyrion would come to Caledor with all speed.

'Better to let Imrik continue to goad the beast,' Malekith concluded, as though speaking the mage's thoughts for him. 'Like the bull bitten by too many flies, Tyrion will succumb to the rage and lash out. It is only a matter of time. His allies will be as mist in the growing sun when that happens.'

They concluded their conference swiftly, for the news that Tyrion now led the enemy army directly required careful counter. Teclis removed himself to consult with such authorities and agents as he could trust while Malekith was left to ponder the possible paths of his future.

Destiny demanded that he face Tyrion at some point. It was simply the way the godly cycles worked, and could not be avoided. He would not receive unexpected but pleasant news one day that a dragon had eaten his foe or a fireball had incinerated the pretender to his throne. Myths required more direct action.

Malekith was not sure at all that he would prevail, even with Asuryan's blade. The last time he had faced Tyrion, the Dragon of Cothique had wielded the Sunfang and fought alone. Next time he would have the Widowmaker and every sorcerous assistance Morathi could devise.

The Phoenix King regarded his options as though they were laid out on the table before him but he knew his perspective was skewed. He needed counsel, but Teclis had his own agenda and Kouran and Imrik were warriors whose advice was painfully confined to the military.

Requiring a fresh source of inspiration, Malekith spent some time preparing his audience room for a difficult ritual. Retainers came and went bringing candles and iron icons and other paraphernalia, laid out to their master's precise instructions. When he was done, Malekith sent his minions away, forbade any interruption and began his summoning.

Drawing on his dark magic, Malekith drew forth spirits he had trapped in the hinterlands between mortality and Mirai – the souls of his dead rivals conjured from the afterlife to serve him again as they had served in the Black Council of Naggarond.

They came as insubstantial spectres, their faces barely recognisable, but Malekith knew them all by name, deed and temperament. Lord Khaivan of Ghrond, founder of the city and one of Morathi's first lovers returned screaming to existence. Others followed soon after: Lyar Winterspear of Har Ganeth; Tyrios the Flayer; Kordrilian of Clar Karond. More than two dozen ghosts crowded into the circle of power created by the Witch King, hissing and moaning wordlessly.

'Speak,' commanded the Witch King. 'I would know your minds and the knowledge you bring from beyond the veil of death. Tell me how I might slay Prince Tyrion and defeat the wielder of the Widowmaker.'

Lord Shimmerghast, Dreadmarshal of Naggarond, floated closer. The first captain of the Black Guard regarded Malekith with hate-filled eyes, the skin of his ghost torn to tatters as it had been in life.

'No blade can match the Widowmaker. No warrior can defeat its wielder. You are doomed, Malekith. Doomed to join us in an eternity of perdition and pain!'

'How predictable,' said the king, dismissing the spectre with a wave of his hand. He glared at the other assembled spirits. 'You know, I could grant you the peace you desire, if you are willing to help. Do any of you have anything to say?'

'He that lays his hand upon the Widowmaker becomes Khaine's weapon,' wailed Lady Mystyr. Her face was veiled with black lace, hiding the bloody holes where her eyes had been gouged out by Malekith's torturers. 'Only the fire of Asuryan can defeat such a foe.'

'I know this already!' snapped Malekith. Mystyr screamed as he banished her soul back into the pale waters of undeath that flowed around the border of Mirai. 'I have taken the fire of Asuryan into myself and Hotek labours on a sword fitting for the king of kings. Surely there must be more than that?'

'You are bound by the cycle of life, the circle of myth,' said

Lothek Heartstealer. The former grand admiral of Klar Karond looked odd, his head lolling to one side on a broken neck, his floating torso missing legs and limbs. 'Time turns and Khaine will face Asuryan. Such is inevitable, King Malekith.'

With a frustrated shout, Malekith stood and swept his arm through the shimmering haze that encircled the ritual space, causing ripples of power to break apart the apparitions within.

'Useless!' he raved, snuffing the light from the candles with a surge of magic, sending braziers and talismans whirling across the chamber with a flicked hand. The surge of ire that filled the king made his head throb. 'As duplicitous and pointless in death as they were in life.'

Malekith cooled his anger, grasping his head in both hands, forcing the pain to subside, clearing his thoughts. There had to be another way. He was not prepared to gamble not only his life but the future of all elvenkind on the notion that the war of the gods would simply be repeated on the mortal plane. There was too much at stake to risk on the half-baked idea of mythical inevitability. He had been schooled and advised by the most devious minds in history and he would not relax until he found a weakness to exploit, an advantage to be gained.

He accepted the predictability of fighting Tyrion. The myths demanded a confrontation, but there was nothing in the legends that said Malekith could not try a few other plans first.

TWENTY-EIGHT

A King in Name Only

It chafed at Malekith to wait while others sealed their glories in battle and prosecuted his war, for he had always been an elf of determined action, following the example of his father. The knowledge that his enforced absence from the battlefield would bring him later victory was a salve to the frustration, but many a day and night he paced the halls and balconies of Imrik's citadel – the upper levels cleared of all but the most trustworthy souls lest word of Malekith's presence be discovered by Morathi.

He wondered at these times what happened further afield, not just in Saphery and Cothique but beyond the Great Ocean in the lands of Elthin Arvan and the jungles of Lustria. With Morathi gone, Ghrond would have been overrun for some time, the last bastion of the elves in Naggaroth save for the Hellebron-stalked ruins of Har Ganeth.

Sometimes he allowed his essence to fly over the waves to the lands of the humans, where living and dead fought against and beside each other, in a complex to and fro of alliance and treachery against the great beast of Chaos, the one called Archaon. He was the herald of the Rhana Dandra, that the barbarians called the Lord of the End Times, but the fate of the elves would not rest in his hands. The gods themselves contested for the fate of Ulthuan's children, not mere mortals.

Malekith was always careful to conceal himself on these excursions, unwilling to expose himself to detection by his mother. He could feel her sometimes scouring the winds of magic, seeking the telltale signs of his presence, and occasionally he was certain that she had found him. The magic of his armour, the force that she had poured into him to sustain him after his near death, were as distinctive as his seal. Yet however close she came, no matter how much he felt her lingering presence hovering over him as though she could set eyes upon him, he never felt that moment of connection that would reveal he had been discovered.

He brought up this matter with Teclis when the mage returned to Tor Caleda. They convened on a moonlit rampart at the summit of the fortress, the lights and sounds of the city far below while the odd footfall of a guard broke the still on the walls beneath them.

'You really do not understand that which you have hungered after for so long,' Teclis said, with a rare moment of genuine humour. 'Your majesty, you have become the Phoenix King and the fire of Asuryan burns within you. Morathi is no doubt confused, because she will see the fire but not recognise it.'

'Surely she would remember such a thing from her time with my father?'

'Her memories are splitting, her mind finally dissembling after so many years adrift on the tides of magic. She thinks Tyrion is your father reborn. Now that he has lifted the Sword of Khaine, has become the Lord of Murder, her self-deception is complete. She was young when Aenarion was Asuryan's chosen, and likely if she ever did witness him at that time the memory of it is quite obliterated by the towering force that was the blood-wreathed avenger he became. It was not your father she craved, it was the power of the Widowmaker.'

'My mother is more than just the power-hungry witch as she has been painted by the lies of the Phoenix Kings,' Malekith said. 'Of late a madness has consumed her, and her ambition has never been a secret, but I cannot doubt that she cared for me and loved my father.'

'It is nigh impossible for a son to think harshly of his mother,' Teclis replied. The moonlight made his pale flesh glow with silvery light as he turned away and looked east towards the Inner Sea. 'Family makes fools of us all at one time or another. I was blind for so long to Tyrion's weaknesses. He was lauded from Caledor to Chrace, and that works a terrible toll upon the mind. When you despatched your daemonic ally N'Kari to kill the Everqueen, and my brother saved her and became her consort, you initiated a turn of events that led us to this current point.'

'Your brother's amour and the Everqueen's poor choice of lovers is my fault?' Malekith gripped the rampart in metal fingers, clawing grooves in the stone. 'Is there any woe of the world for which you would not lay blame upon me?'

'You misunderstand, your majesty, or I do not explain myself well.' Teclis looked at the Phoenix King. 'All of the choices we have made have laid the path that brings us to the place we are in, here and now. When I came to you and offered to make pact with you, do you think it was easy for me? Lileath showed me the grief and death to come, and I could have ended it with a single blow of my sword. I could have slain Tyrion without effort, forestalling this war.'

'Your love of him stopped you?'

Teclis shook his head, saddened. 'No, my fear of the consequences did. Without Tyrion we would have failed against the daemons and you would be the lone survivor in Naggarond, fighting with your last breath against the very creatures of Chaos that you unleashed upon us so many times.'

Malekith wondered if he had ever really made a decision himself, or if they were all simply pawns of powers far beyond their comprehension, playing out petty games for the amusement of otherworldly entities. They fell silent, contemplating the past.

Turning, Malekith leapt up the stairs three at a time, chasing after his mother. Despite his haste, Morathi was already standing beside the balcony window by the time Malekith reached the top of the tower. She turned and smiled as he strode into the room, and held out an arm for him to hold. Sighing, the prince allowed his mother to lay her hand upon his and led her out onto the balcony. This time, the seeress-queen and prince of Nagarythe were greeted with rapturous cheers and applause. The streets were packed with elves in every direction, and windows and balconies were full as the people of Athel Toralien sought the best vantage point to see their mysterious, glamorous visitor.

'What are you doing here?' Malekith whispered as he waved to the adoring crowds.

'I have come to visit you, my wonderful son,' replied Morathi, not turning her smile from the masses below. 'A mother worries, you know that. Word came to me that you were heading off into the wilds for some ridiculous adventures, so I thought it best that I finally visit your new home before you left.'

'You will not dissuade me,' Malekith warned her. 'I am ready to leave within days.'

'Dissuade you?' said Morathi with a faint laugh. 'Why would I not want you to go? Was it not me that stood upon the quayside when you left Nagarythe, and told you to earn glory and renown for yourself and your people? Have you not done so, and have I not looked upon all that you have achieved with great love and pride?'

'Forgive my misunderstanding,' said Malekith. 'If you are here to lend your support, then I am very grateful.'

Morathi did not reply straightaway, but instead indicated discreetly that they should retire inside. With a final wave and a grin, Malekith stepped off the balcony and his mother followed. Closing the window, Malekith rounded on his mother.

'So why is it that you are here?' he asked, not with accusation but with genuine curiosity.

'It is not my support that you need, at least not in any physical way,' Morathi replied.

Seeing his mother wave a hand towards the bottle upon the desk, Malekith took a clean glass from one of the many cabinets in the room and poured wine for Morathi. She took it with a nod, had a sip and then continued.

'You have been away from Ulthuan for too long. I was of a mind to persuade you to return rather than go gallivanting across the Wastes, but then I realised that such a course of action would be a fool's errand and only earn me your enmity, perhaps even your disdain.'

'You are right, I will not return to Ulthuan,' said Malekith. 'Why do you think it is so important that I do so now?'

'Not now, but soon,' Morathi said. 'I sense that Bel Shanaar's rule is fading. His usurpation of your relationship with the dwarfs was an attempt to bolster his flagging fortunes. Now that the colonies are well established, all of the kingdoms enjoy the comfort and wealth that the realms overseas bring to us, Tiranoc no less so, nor more so than any others. Nagarythe's most adventurous spirits have departed the shores of the isle, for new generations look to the likes of you to emulate, not to the staid and overly sincere Bel Shanaar. In comfort there is frailty, for a sword must be forged in the burning fires before it can rest in its scabbard. There is no more fire in Ulthuan. Even as her empire continues to grow, Ulthuan herself is diminishing.'

'If Ulthuan has become lessened, then it is the fault of the princes who rule there,' said Malekith, pouring himself some wine.

'That is my point,' snapped Morathi. 'There is none capable of succeeding Bel Shanaar – his court is as weak as he is. Your achievements here have been rightly lauded, but your success has been copied and appropriated and demeaned by others. If only you had returned to us before Bel Shanaar accorded himself and his rule with *the dwarfs and stole your victory. It is time to create a new legend for yourself, and return in triumph to reclaim what is rightfully yours.'*

'What would you say if I told you that I wish never to return to Ulthuan?' said Malekith. 'What if I have decided that my life is out here, away from the coddling embrace of Ulthuan?'

'Then I would curse you for a fool and cast you out of my life,' said Morathi. 'But that is not really how you think. You do not like Ulthuan, and I cannot blame you. She is like a maiden that you love, gripped tightly within the arms of a less-deserving amour. But, just as you turn away from that sight, within your heart still lingers that love for the maiden, no matter what she does.'

'You are right, of course,' admitted Malekith. 'She is like to me as a lover who has spurned my attentions many times, and yet her gaze lingers upon me always, tempting me with the notion that one day she will accept my advances. However, if what you say is true, then perhaps it is too late for me. The beauty of youth has faded and Ulthuan perhaps is on the decline into infirmity and then a swift passing away. Perhaps it is better this way – that we break our ties to that small isle, and reach out to the wider world.'

Morathi strode across the room, her face a mask of fury, and slapped Malekith across the cheek. In instinct he raised his hand to reply in kind, but Morathi was as quick as a serpent and snatched his wrist in her fingers, her long and sharpened nails digging so deep into the flesh that blood trickled across her hand.

'How dare you!' the seeress hissed. 'Your father gave his life for Ulthuan, and it took his death to save her! I thought I had raised you better than this. I thought that you had not become one of those prancing, preening fools that pass as princes in Bel Shanaar's court. How dare you condemn Ulthuan to death by indifference! Your father laid down his life to protect our isle – who are you to do differently?'

Malekith snatched away his wrist with a snarl and made to turn, but Morathi was relentless and grabbed his arm and spun him around to face her.

'You dare to turn your back on me, just as you turn your back on your homeland!' she snarled. 'Perhaps the First Council was right not to choose you, not because of a darkness upon you, but because you are weak and undeserving.'

'What more could I do?' demanded Malekith. 'I have conquered new lands in the name of Nagarythe, and brokered the greatest alliance our people will ever see. What more can I give to Ulthuan?'

'Yourself,' said Morathi. 'When Aenarion died, he left Ulthuan a legacy, and you are part of it. To rule is also to serve – Aenarion understood that. He served Khaine, for there was no other master worthy of his fealty. You must be prepared to serve a high purpose, a great power.'

Morathi paused and took a deep breath, calming herself. When she continued her voice was low but insistent.

'Serve Ulthuan and you will be Phoenix King. Protect her from enemies outside and within and she will embrace you in return. Go into the north and learn of the race of men. Head into the chilling Wastes and confront the dark powers that hunger over our world. Then return to Ulthuan and take up your place as ruler, to shield us against their unnatural thirst. I fear that only you can protect us against the dangers I have foreseen. I see fire and bloodshed sweeping Ulthuan again. The colonies will burn and all that we hold dear will be cast upon the rocks and be for naught.'

'What have you seen, when will this happen?' asked Malekith.

'You know that there is no future that is certain,' replied Morathi. 'I have simply cast my gaze ahead along the path of my life, and I see death. War will come again and the Naggarothi will be called upon as they were by your father. I warned the First Council that it would be so, but they did not listen. You must learn what you can of Chaos, and of humans, for our future is entwined with both. When you are master of your fate, then return to us and take what has been kept from you for so long. Let Anlec be a beacon of hope again.'

Malekith saw desire and fear in equal measure in the face of his mother and his love for her stirred him. He laid an arm about her shoulders and pulled her close to him. She quivered, though whether from anxiety or excitement he could not tell.

'It shall be as you say,' said Malekith. 'I shall go into the north and seek whatever destiny awaits me there. I will return to Ulthuan, and I will guard her against whatever comes to pass.'

'I have given myself to Ulthuan,' he whispered.

'What was that?' Teclis had been lost in a reverie of his own, or perhaps trying to discern the unwinding paths of the future guided by the whispers of his goddess.

Malekith straightened and flexed metal-bound limbs. He felt neither heat nor cold, but could tell that this year the season of ice would come swiftly. It would make no difference – the fighting was moving south towards Lothern and the campaign would continue through the winter while the north of the isle was gripped by blizzards.

'I stepped through the flames, and gave myself to Ulthuan,' Malekith replied more volubly. 'I stayed in the fires and received Asuryan's blessing. My mother told me long ago, before I travelled into the Northern Wastes, that I had to accept her and be accepted to rule the island. I had forgotten that these past six thousand years. Ystranna said something similar. I could never take Ulthuan by conquest.'

'A wayward step has been corrected, your majesty,' said Teclis, 'but the journey has only just begun.'

'There is something that plagues my thoughts in recent times,' Malekith admitted. 'I try to wrangle meaning from it over and over, but it makes no sense to me. If I was the chosen of Asuryan, if it was my destiny to become Phoenix King, why did the First Council reject me? Why has it taken so long?'

'The wiles of Chaos, your majesty. The designs of the Great Powers spool across countless lives of mortals before they are fully woven. In your case, the Prince of Pleasure sowed the seed of lust and power in the heart of your mother when she was captured by His creatures. Thus was the course of history changed. It was not the darkness in you that the First Council feared, it was the taint of Chaos in Morathi, though they did not realise that. Rather than see a reign of Phoenix Kings from Aenarion unbroken to the present day over an unbroken civilisation, the Chaos Gods divided the elves and created war and strife, feeding deep on the dreams and nightmares of a broken people. Now we have one opportunity to unite again and survive, or else we will perish.'

'From that moment, we were doomed to millennia of war?' Malekith took a deep breath and exhaled slowly, the heat of it billowing like dragonfume in the cool night air. It was hard to still the anger that burned inside, stoked by the mage's revelations. 'My acquiescence to the council, my attempts to bring favour back to the house of Aenarion, were for nothing?'

'All were worthy attempts, your majesty,' Teclis assured him, turning with his staff clasped in both hands. 'Had you slain your mother on that fateful day in Anlec, had you refused her offer to give you control of the Cults of Pleasure so that you would manipulate your way to power, your claim would have remained untainted and Bel Shanaar would have named you successor in time. A little faith, for a little longer, is all that was required.'

'No!' Splinters and sparks showered from the battlement as Malekith's fist struck the dark stone. 'No! The other princes had already rejected me. Imrik was their favourite.'

'Your mother's words,' Teclis snapped, his stare unflinching. 'Her lies in your head. That was the moment the Chaos Powers won. Not when you slaughtered the princes in the shrine, nor when you murdered Bel Shanaar. Those were simply the consecrations of your betrayal.'

'But... I spared her out of love.'

'And that love was greater than the love of Ulthuan and her

people,' Teclis continued. 'You chose the wrong mother, Malekith, and we all had to pay the price.'

Malekith sagged, leaning against the battlement. 'Go,' he whispered. 'I tire of this conversation.'

'As you wish, your majesty,' said Teclis. 'On the morrow I depart for the fields of Cothique where my brother makes great gains. We must hold council before then.'

'Leave, meddling loremaster,' Malekith growled. 'Spare me more of your twisted words.'

Malekith listened to the footfalls of the mage until they were gone. The rage was too much to contain and with a snarl he ripped free a block of stone and incinerated it in his grasp, hurling the broken, burned fragments over the parapet.

He hated Teclis. More self-righteous than any other mage, so convinced of his own superiority and correctness.

He hated even more that Teclis was right.

The Phoenix King's brooding presence spread to other parts of the citadel, his sour mood infecting the spirit of the guards and servants and beyond to the streets of Tor Caleda. There were whispers and dark rumours of what lay in the upper reaches of the keep, some as outlandish as to suggest Imrik had summoned forth a daemon, others more unsettling but closer to the truth – that the prince had sealed a pact with a dark spirit from the past.

Malekith's self-imposed imprisonment started to take its toll on his temper. Daily he sent missives to Hotek demanding news on the priest-smith's work. Daily the replies returned that Hotek's labours continued without pause.

The risk of magical discovery stopped the Phoenix King from transporting his spirit beyond the castle, forcing him to rely upon conventional and far slower means of news. In concert with this, Teclis came only rarely to report the progress of the war, and spoke in equivocating terms, but it was plain that Tyrion's direct intercession had rolled back Imrik's forces to the borders of Eataine and the coast of the Inner Sea. Though supported by the mighty fleet of Naggaroth, the dragon princes were suffering setback after setback.

One evening there was commotion in the lower levels of the citadel, rousing Malekith from a days-long fugue of depression. Panicked shouts brought the Phoenix King to full awareness, and calls for aid carried him out of the halls he usually haunted and into the main part of the keep.

His appearance caused terror and consternation, and only by the intervention of Caradryan was a band of Caledorians prevented from attacking their king. Malekith demanded to know the reason for the tumult and he was led to a stately hall close to the citadel gate.

Within was a bustle of courtiers and servants. At the centre of the chamber a tall figure in bloodstained armour stood over another in gilded plate. There was blood on the floor and apothecaries and mages shouldered and fussed at each other, competing in their attempts to attend the wounded knight.

'Let me see,' Malekith growled.

The crowd parted at once, save for a female mage who knelt beside the forlorn figure, channelling waves of rejuvenating Ghyran into the injured warrior's body. The knight flailed a crimson-covered hand at the sound of Malekith's voice, beckoning him closer. He turned his head, revealing the features of Imrik, ashen-faced and drawn.

'What happened?' the Phoenix King demanded, striding along the hall. He directed the question at the other Caledorian prince, whom he recognised as Marendri, an older cousin of Imrik.

'The usurper came upon us at the shores of Lake Calliana, in Saphery,' Marendri explained, his gaze moving quickly between his prince and his king, brow furrowed. 'He must have marched day and night for five days or more. Possessed he was, falling upon a host five times the size of his own with just a vanguard and the griffon-knights. Tyrion led the attack, killing dozens, driving into the heart of the army before we could reform.'

'Imrik attacked, didn't he?' Malekith said grimly. 'He ignored my orders and confronted Tyrion.'

'He saw no other way to save the battle,' Marendri admitted. 'He did not seek prolonged engagement, but thought that if he could but drive Tyrion back for even a few moments, our knights and spears would reset and be better prepared.'

Malekith looked at Imrik and saw that his dragonplate armour was cut from left shoulder to the centre of his breastplate. The female mage was trying her best while others were unbuckling pieces of bloodied armour and cutting away the padded jerkin beneath to see the wound more clearly.

'He struck a fine blow,' Marendri said earnestly, kneeling to lay a hand on his prince's leg. 'It pierced Tyrion's breastplate, I swear. Any other warrior would have been slain.'

'Tyrion is no ordinary warrior, not even before he took up the Widowmaker.'

'It was terrible, like a slash of midnight. It shattered Imrik's shield like glass...' Marendri started to weep, a display that made Malekith's lip curl in disgust. 'Neremain, Astalorion and Find-ellion were on the usurper in moments, while I snatched Imrik away to safety. They died, as did three fine dragons.'

Malekith baulked at this thought – that even after being wounded Tyrion had single-handedly killed three dragon princes and their steeds. If Imrik died Malekith would have to lead the army himself. He looked at Imrik, seeing only the barest hints of life remaining despite the healer's efforts.

'Your life magic will not avail here,' Malekith declared, waving the maiden aside. 'He has been marked by a far darker power. One that must be matched tooth for tooth and claw for claw.'

A nimbus of dark magic coalesced around Malekith's out-stretched hands, forming a pulsing cloud of purple and black. The attending nurses and apothecaries scattered at the display of sorcery, some running wailing for the doors, others whisper-ing mantras of protection against evil.

'Settle yourselves,' snarled the Phoenix King. 'A little sorcery like this is child's play.'

'You seek to bring him back from the dead?' The female mage was aghast.

'You have a crude view of life and death,' Malekith told her. He unleashed the dark magic into Imrik, sending it rippling through every part of his body. The prince convulsed, armour clattering on the bloodied tiles, his life fluid spilling from the gash in his armour, head arched back in a silent scream.

Malekith knelt beside the broken prince and poured on more energy, willing severed arteries and veins shut, forcing blood to clot and muscles to knit.

'You're killing him!' screamed the mage. Marendri intercepted her as she lunged towards the Phoenix King, fireballs glowing in her hands. Malekith darted a look in her direction and she shrunk back as if struck, her spell steaming away under his burning stare.

'He is nearer dead than alive. What the life-giving forces of Ghyran cannot mend, sorcery can reanimate. How do you think I stand here, seven thousand years after my birth, through all of the trials this mortal form has faced?'

So he spoke, and so it was seen in the body of Imrik. Dead tissue came back to life, flooded with freshly pumped blood from a jolted heart, colour returning to the skin. Imrik opened his eyes with a pained gasp, his gaze roving madly around the room for a few moments before it settled on Marendri. Familiarity brought calm. The prince panted as he sat up, his gaze moving to Malekith.

'I couldn't run,' the prince croaked.

'You were weak,' Malekith replied, standing up. 'I still need you. Be stronger next time.'

The Phoenix King turned and marched from the hall, his mood at its blackest for a long time.

TWENTY-NINE

The Bringer of Silence

The day finally arrived, on the cusp of the season of ice, when Fovendiel arrived from Vaul's Anvil, accompanied by a procession of lesser priests, carrying a rune-etched casket of white wood. Teclis had arrived the night before, bidden, he claimed, to attend the Phoenix King by Lileath – the reason becoming clear when news of Fovendiel's arrival came to them.

The High Priest of Vaul was admitted to audience with the Phoenix King, but Malekith was in a poor mood and sent away his entourage of smith-priests with thinly-veiled threats, leaving himself with the high priest and Teclis.

'Does it have a name?' Malekith asked, as Fovendiel worked the clasps of the casket.

'*Asuryath,*' Teclis answered before the high priest could speak. The bringer of silence. 'Asuryan's sword is named *Asuryath*.'

'Give it to me,' rasped Malekith, snatching the box from Fovendiel.

He wrenched open the lid with clawed fingers, breaking the intricate bronze clasps and hinges, to reveal a shard of purest white. To the elves white was the colour of death, purity and silence, the three being indivisible. Thus was Asuryan the true guardian of their spirits, despite Ereth Khial's rulership of Mirai. His was the last word, His flame was the purifier and His colour – or lack of it – was the blank sheet upon which new futures were written by Morai-heg and the other goddesses of fate.

'*Asuryath...*' Malekith breathed the word, tasting it, savouring it as his fingers closed around the hilt of the bringer of silence. He lifted the sword clear, its blade bursting into pale flame in his grasp. The weapon felt as light as air in his grasp, effortless to swing and thrust and parry. Carving sigils of flame around him, Malekith wove the tip of *Asuryath* in a complex series of feints, attacks and killing blows, artfully spelling out his own name with wisps of fire as he did so. He laughed, holding up the sword. 'Hotek is indeed Vaul reborn. This is the blade to match the Widowmaker. Send him my deepest compliments and break his shackles. Tell him he is free to roam wherever he wishes.'

'Hotek is dead, your majesty,' said Fovendiel, head bowed. 'We found him this morning, this blade sheathed in his chest, his hands about the hilt.'

'He killed himself with it?' Teclis recoiled from the blade, looking at it as though it were a serpent about to strike.

'He anointed it,' Malekith said, shaking his head in disbelief, new-found appreciation for Hotek's dedication rising. 'Vaul gave his own blood for the last tempering of the blade, and he will forge no more weapons for the gods.'

'This is timely,' Teclis announced, recovering his composure. 'Tyrion's army marches for Lothern.'

'Leave us,' Malekith told Fovendiel, not wishing to discuss his mind in front of the priest. He could barely bring himself to confide in Teclis, but there was no alternative. When the high priest had said his farewell and departed, the Phoenix King confronted Teclis. 'Is it enough? Can I beat your brother with this sword?'

'You fear to face him, even with *Asuryath*?'

'I would expect you to be the last to throw accusations of cowardice,' Malekith replied. There was a white-enamelled scabbard decorated with rubies like drops of blood in the casket. Malekith sheathed his sword. 'You know that if I perish all will be lost – I must weigh every risk. I will face Tyrion when I must.'

'It was a genuine question, not an accusation,' Teclis said. 'I cannot give you an answer. We shall only know if you are ready when the time comes. Fortunately, that time is not yet here. I am certain that Tyrion has left his army. He has gone north with Morathi, seemingly content after besting Imrik, and has left the prosecution of the war to Korhil.'

'The name is unfamiliar to me,' admitted the Phoenix King.

'The captain of the White Lions. Stubborn, strong, courageous. He is a competent strategist, far more patient than my brother. He musters for a final assault on Lothern and must be stopped.'

'Must?' Malekith hung *Asuryath* on his armour, tying the silver hangers to his belt. It felt as natural as the Destroyer had done ever since he had lost *Avanuir* at Maledor. 'That sounds like instruction, nephew.'

'No, your majesty, simply a statement of strategic imperative. If Lothern falls Lord Aislinn will reunite his fleet and sweep away our ships in the Sea of Dreams. From Lothern they can attack Caledor directly. If we do not stop their advance at Lothern, Tor Caleda will be besieged before midwinter.'

'The geography lesson is appreciated,' Malekith growled. 'Your assessment is pessimistic. The defences of Lothern are strong and our fleet outmatches any seaborne-attack Aislinn can muster. Why must I intervene now?'

'The warriors of Lothern will not fight for long for a cause that is, at best, nebulous to them. It is only the presence of the Caledorians that stiffens their resolve for the moment, and only Imrik that led the Caledorians. However, unless you wish to see a reversal of the events at Eagle Gate, the people of Eataine need a focus for their loyalty. The time has come to reveal to them and all of Ulthuan that they have a Phoenix King, and it is not Tyrion.'

Malekith accepted this appraisal without comment, and after some time Teclis interpreted his silence as dismissal and left the Phoenix King to ponder his decision.

The king had been quick to quash any thought of cowardice, but alone in that hall he was free to admit to himself a very physical, mortal fear. He could hide it behind talk of surviving to lead his people, and justify his continued absence from the battlefield as sound strategy, but the truth was that he was afraid to test himself against Tyrion again. He had barely survived the last encounter and, *Asuryath* or not, he was in no hurry to repeat the experience.

Tyrion was every bit the swordmaster that Aenarion had been and now he wielded the Sword of Khaine. There was no deadlier fighter in the world.

It did not matter that Tyrion was not at Lothern in person. Malekith could break the siege, he was sure of it, but the moment he revealed himself the future would be set, the wheel would turn along the rut that led to the fight between Asuryan and Khaine, Malekith and Tyrion. Was there any more that he could do to prepare himself for that confrontation?

THIRTY

The Battle of Lothern

The war was within view of Lothern's walls. To the east the fields burned and the skies darkened with smoke. To the north the flotsam of sea battles, timbers and corpses, washed towards the city on lapping waves. The wind carried the clamour of battle, the crash of weapons, the curses and war cries, distant yet all-consuming.

The corpses of dragons mouldered on the hillside meadows, iron-hard scales pierced by hundreds of arrows and the bolts of war engines. Griffon bodies lay beside the feathered remains of phoenixes and harpies, figures cloaked in lion pelts and sea dragon hide, casualties of Ulthuan and Naggaroth combined, slashed and stabbed, decapitated and burned.

The air danced with Azyr lightning and Hysh thunderbolts. Sorcery and high magic whirled in multicoloured thunderheads and opened chasms lined with jagged boulder-fangs. Trees enervated by Ghyran magic uprooted themselves and hurled their branches at any creature encroaching on their woodlands, while walls of fire incinerated farms and hostelries, fed by growing waves of Aqshy. Bear, lion and panther followed the call of Ghur, and unseen lurking things crept in the shadows of Ulgu. Ancient spirits wailed their laments, their chill weapons freezing the hearts of those that came near their mausoleums, and the lodestones that powered the vortex crackled and fizzed with discharging magic, unable to beat the huge influx of magic pouring from the Northern Wastes.

The archers and spear-wielding militia on the walls of Eataine's capital tightened their grips and looked east, seeing the first ranks of the retreating columns marching into view. The dragons appeared overhead, manticores amongst them, duelling with skycutters and great eagles.

The banners of Caledor and Eataine fluttered at the head of the returning army, but there were other standards too – grisly icons of the Cytharai, dire runes carved into steel and bone, wound about with thorny branches and hung with entrails. These were the marks of the druchii, vicious and depraved, but made uneasy allies by some means by which a great many within the city were unsure. Their princes vowed for the alliance and they fought for the princes, but it was unsettling to see the black-and-purple-clad legions of Naggarothi bearing down upon the landside gates.

And the enemy were almost on the heels of the returning host, many thousands of knights on horseback, the chariots of Tiranoc rumbling through the fields and along the white-paved roads. The banner of Cothique flew high above many of the advancing regiments, along with those of Yvresse and Chrace. White Lions and Phoenix Guard, once symbols of Ulthuan's unyielding defence, now threatened to sack Lothern.

Across the Inner Sea came Aislinn and his fleet, and this caused even greater consternation. Born of Eataine, the Sea Lord now seemed content to see his own city ruined rather than held by another. Magical bolts flew from the decks of his ships to crash against the stones of the sea walls, while seaguard loyal to Aislinn unleashed volleys of arrows against former companions that remained true to the defence of their city.

No order was given for the gates to open, and none demanded. The Caledorian dragons turned and formed a rearguard, passing across the lead elements of the following host with fire and claw, driving back the enemy for a short while, until press of numbers and threat of being overwhelmed caused them to fall back. The task was complete, however, and the army that now fell under the command of the Naggarothi corsair Lokhir Fellheart formed for the final battle for Eataine, perhaps even the last meaningful battle for Ulthuan.

Flying at speed across the city, Malekith sensed the changing tide of war as a prickling on the skin. He had not felt as invigorated as he did now since the Battle of Maledor, when first his plans to rule Ulthuan had been crushed. More than that, it was at Maledor that he had come to believe Asuryan had rejected him, and it had been that revelation that had soured his ambition for the following millennia. Now that he had been accepted again by the king of the heavens, Malekith felt enlivened, dedicated to his cause by a fresh enthusiasm that could sustain him for another six thousand years of war.

His laugh was carefree, and something of his old flair for exhibition filled him. Beneath him Seraphon sensed his mood and let out a roar. Just as she had been raised from a captured egg by his hand, she had been restored to full health by his dedication and sorcerous attendance.

Malekith drew *Asuryath* and laughed again, buoyed by the flame of Asuryan that burned from the blade. The sword left a trail of silver and white across the grey skies, and bathed both black dragon and rider in a pale halo.

The Phoenix King realised just what it was that he felt, and he marvelled that he had missed it for so long.

Righteousness.

It had been stripped from him that day on the field of Maledor, tainting his ambition, perhaps fuelling an inner doubt ever since. Now he knew that he fought not only for himself but for Ulthuan and for the elves.

For an instant, a fleeting heartbeat, he was wholly at peace with himself.

He swooped down upon the oncoming army like a comet, a dozen black dragons in his wake. At his arrival Lokhir Fellheart signalled the counter-attack and trumpets blared across Lothern, ordering the gates open and the companies within to spill forth. On the western horizon the looming shapes of massive black arks, each a castle brimming with warriors and war machines, closed on the fleet of Lord Aislinn. Fellheart's own black ark, the *Tower of Blessed Dread*, led the seaborne charge, bearing directly for the gates of Lothern.

The clarions of the attacking army quickly changed from calling the advance to sounding the retreat. On the Sea of Dreams Aislinn's fleet quickly hauled about and set to the east, fleeing for the shallower waters of the Sapherian coast. Imrik, though not fully recovered, had insisted on accompanying the Phoenix King and he joined his dragons in pursuit of the breaking ships while Malekith's black drakes savaged the fleeing elements of the land-bound host.

After the initial exhilaration of the charge, three dozen foes cut effortlessly apart by *Asuryath*, as many again torn to shreds by Seraphon, Malekith's mood deflated. He broke off his attack, uncharacteristically bored by the mindless butchery. The battle had been won at the moment of his arrival, that much was clear, and it seemed pointless to slaughter his new subjects to settle the point.

It was then that he did something entirely against his normal judgement. He signalled his forces to stand fast, ordering them to marshal the thousands that had surrendered. This allowed Korhil and the rest of Tyrion's force to flee eastward. Imrik responded after a time, returning from his pursuit to find the Phoenix King atop Seraphon in the shadow of the eastern wall watching the captives filing back into the city.

'We had them!' barked Imrik, stowing his lance behind his saddle-throne. 'We could have crushed them, destroyed all resistance in one attack. What madness in Asuryan's name has taken your senses?'

'Asuryan's name indeed,' Malekith snapped back. He waved a hand to encompass the rainbow of kingdom colours flying above the returning army, and the darker icons of the druchii amongst them. 'These are my people now, Prince Imrik. I have killed more than you can ever count, and a thousand-thousand times that number are dead because of my commands. But I am not their enemy, I am their king. I have shown mercy today. I have shown those that follow Tyrion that there is an alternative.'

'It will take more than a few spared lives to change six thousand years of history, Malekith,' said Imrik, but his protest was spoken softly, a touch of admiration in his voice. 'But I suppose today is as good a day as any to start making amends.'

'Amends?' Malekith sneered. 'I do not seek their forgiveness, only their compliance. Let the survivors take back the word that I can be merciful. Those that choose to face me again will learn that I can still be merciless.'

Teclis had been amongst the army retreating to Lothern, and sought out Malekith soon after, finding him in council with Imrik discussing the next moves in the war. King and prince were in disagreement, with Malekith keen to consolidate the victory in Eataine and Imrik pressing to move the army after Korhil, pushing back into Saphery and Yvresse.

'We cannot win this war by battles alone,' Malekith told them. 'Tyrion will not give up his claim while he lives, and will spend the lives of his followers to the last elf in prosecuting that claim.'

'As will you?' said Imrik.

Malekith answered with a silent stare.

'Or the war ends with your death or Tyrion's?' the prince continued.

'Be sure to know that you will not outlive me, son of Caledor,' Malekith replied abruptly. 'And your people will die screaming soon after.'

'The king has it right, Prince Imrik,' Teclis intervened before Imrik could retaliate. 'We must win Ulthuan to our cause and rob my brother of forces, so that when the confrontation that must happen occurs he is entirely outmatched. We must begin here, with a proper triumph, so that the citizens of Lothern can see who their saviour is and spread the word to the other kingdoms.'

'I have seen the manner of reaction my presence provokes, in Tor Caleda,' Malekith said sourly, flames rippling from his body to demonstrate his meaning. 'My name is poison on the tongues of the asur, my image a vision of hate and dread.'

'The first will be nullified by your title, King Malekith, the second...' Teclis appraised Malekith for a while and then started an incantation. The Phoenix King felt the seven winds of magic binding around him, guided by the power of light, Hysh. He felt no physical change, but saw Imrik's eyes widening in surprise.

'A glamour?' the king said, holding up his hand. He saw only dark, scarred metal and turned to Imrik. 'What do you see?'

'You, your majesty,' the prince replied, his tongue faltering over the words. 'The image of a king, the line of Aenarion, in golden plate.'

Malekith straightened to his full height, impressed by Imrik's reaction.

'Then let us share our triumph with the people of Lothern,' the king declared. 'Let them see the magnificence of Aenarion born again, and be glad in their hearts that the true Phoenix King walks amongst them.'

And with these words, Malekith set off for the city.

THIRTY-ONE

A Heavy Crown

Malekith's will held sway after the victory at Lothern, and his army spent the early winter restocking supplies and garrisoning towns and castles that had been abandoned by Korhil's swift retreat northwards. He expected a counter-attack, either along the coast or across the sea, but none came. Concerned that his own forces, many of them corsairs of the fleet, would grow increasingly unruly if left to grow idle, he despatched several columns into Saphery and Yvresse, hoping to prompt a response from his foes.

It was not only Malekith's armies that coped poorly with idleness. The king himself, now that he had revealed himself to friend and foe, was the centre of much attention. Princes of Yvresse and Eataine were keen to make audience, and under Teclis's urging the king granted such meetings to foster fresh alliance and reveal Tyrion's falsehoods. These affairs were tedious in the extreme, a succession of pontificating nobles that seemed to think they had the secret to winning the war, who deemed their opinions of any interest to Malekith at all.

Painfully aware that he could not simply have them killed out of hand – this was not the Black Council of Naggarond – Malekith tried his best to endure their bird-like twitterings and ill-informed grasps at politics and military strategy, but all too often his shortness of temper betrayed him and the emissaries left with stinging insults in their ears, if not bellowed threats following them out of the Sapphire Palace of Lothern, where Finubar had once ruled.

'You cost us valuable friends,' Imrik complained to the king a dozen days after Lothern had been saved. 'Teclis has given you the appearance of a true king, but you have none of the nobility.'

'You would talk to me of nobility?' asked Malekith softly, wondering just how much longer he would require Imrik's support. He longed for the day when the dragons answered to Malekith directly, and he could dispense with the swaggering, overblown descendant of the Dragontamer. 'These princes try to tell me how to wage war, and seek to advise me on how best to rule my people. They are dolts and dullards, and it is a wonder that with such cretinous commanders your armies ever held against mine.'

'A history it is best not to bring up with them,' Teclis said smoothly, having entered unheard and unseen through one of the side doors of the great audience hall of the Phoenix King. He looked weary again, the flush of energy that had filled him following the defeat of Korhil now vanished. 'I have spent the better part of the last two days salving the wounds your harsh words have caused, your majesty. Prince Imrik is correct, you must try to resist these intemperate moods.'

'Moods?' Malekith said the word slowly, with menace. 'Lackwits try to surround me with their idiocy and I am prey to moods? The whole of the Naggarothi people were dedicated to my every word, they lived and died by my will and whim. They recognised my leadership and knew when to offer their opinions and when to listen. Perhaps I should make a few more obvious examples, so that these pretentious princes understand the nature of my kingship?'

It was in this state of mind that Malekith later received word that one of his corsair captains, Drane Brackblood, had led an attack on an outpost at Allardin, slaughtering all within and looting as was the nature of the black ark crews. Such violence against Malekith's new allies was wholly unacceptable and the Phoenix King feared that unless he sent a strong message to the other druchii tensions between them and the asur would split apart the fragile alliance he had forged.

Turning in these troubled times to his most trusted companion, he despatched Kouran, who for some time had been working with the Caledorian princes integrating the armies of Naggarond and Caledor. The captain of the Black Guard's orders were clear and would be carried out without hesitation – Brackblood and all of her officers, and any that took part in the killing at Allardin, were to be summarily killed.

Five days later Kouran returned to Malekith with the news that the deed had been done. The bodies of the dead were displayed from the battlements of Brackblood's black ark *Shadow Tide* in the harbour of Lothern and Malekith delivered a speech to his court in which he told his allies that the perpetrators of the attack at Allardin had been apprehended and executed, and he told those from the druchii contingent that any violence against the asur when not in open battle would be punished in the same manner.

The show of strength had the opposite effect to that which Malekith had desired. Amongst his own ranks there were desertions as companies and commanders decided that Malekith no longer represented their best interests, hoping to find better understanding amongst those that had followed Morathi to Tyrion's side. From the asur princes came an outcry against the king's brutal actions, complaints about the tyranny of Naggaroth being brought to the homes of Ulthuan.

The following night fighting broke out in the Sapphire Palace. The battle was swift and one-sided and when it was concluded

Malekith was visited by Kouran and Caradryan, whose body-guard forces had combined to form the Shadowfire Guard, one sinister figure in black the other a bright hero in white, as though a telling embodiment of the Phoenix King's own duality.

'Prince Torhaeron rallied a company of the White Lions still in Lothern, your majesty,' reported Caradryan. 'They served once as Finubar's bodyguard and were on their way to kill you.'

'This Torhaeron, where is he now?'

'Caradryan took his head, my king,' Kouran replied, with a hint of grudging admiration in his voice. 'The others all fought to the death too. There were no survivors.'

'We can expect there to be other attempts on your life, your majesty,' the former Phoenix Guard captain told him. 'We have organised a standing guard of two hundred warriors that will attend to your security at all times.'

'One hundred of mine and one hundred of his, my king,' added Kouran, 'regularly rotated from the rest of the companies.'

'You think this was a serious threat to my life?' Malekith growled.

'Perhaps not this time, but the danger will grow when Morathi learns that you have taken up the Phoenix Crown, your majesty,' Caradryan said, his expression stern.

'I do not need two hundred shadows dogging my footsteps, getting in the way.'

'We are resolute on the matter, my king,' Kouran added, literally standing shoulder to shoulder with Caradryan. 'Shadowblade tried to kill you on the Blighted Isle, and his whereabouts have been unknown since. There are too many people that want you dead, my king – we will not be refused on this.'

Malekith was stunned by the insolence, even as he was unsettled by the accord between the two captains. They could not have been more dissimilar in temperament and ambition but they now presented a united front.

'You are right, there will be others,' the king snapped. 'You can have your guard of two hundred warriors, but I want a thousand more out there in the city, in the towns, scouring for signs of rebellion before they take root. Cut out any disease, eliminate potential threats before they become a problem.'

'Yes, my king,' said Kouran. Caradryan seemed uncertain, but said nothing in protest.

When they had gone, Malekith walked through the palace, coming to the high tower that rose needle-like over the east wing. Finubar's Point it was called, raised by the previous Phoenix King, where he would retire and think. At the summit was a crystal-domed observatory, for Finubar had been known as the Seafarer and even after his voyages had ended he had spent many days looking out at the stars, charting their course across the heavens, gazing towards distant horizons only he could see.

The doors had been broken in, the enchanted planks split apart by many heavy axe blows. Malekith stopped at the threshold, disturbed by the last words Finubar had said to him.

The starlight beyond the dome was reflected in the still scrying pool on the raised dais at the centre of the room, like a sheet of inky blackness dotted with tiny diamonds. A ripple disturbed the water, which in turn disturbed the watcher, for Finubar had not moved for many hours and there was no breeze to cause such a thing.

The Phoenix King straightened in shock as he saw a face at his shoulder reflected in the settling water. He spun, the punch passing through the apparition of a dark-haired, lean-faced elf.

'So it's true what they say,' Malekith's spirit said lightly, stepping through the scrying pool. He stopped at the centre and turned, one finger tracing a line in the water though the rest of his projection was as insubstantial as thought. 'Sailors, always ready with their fists!'

Finubar stepped back, eyes narrowing, a glance directed towards the door.

'The wards... They are not broken. How did you pass them?' The Seafarer stopped his retreat as his legs met the edge of a

cabinet by the wall. 'The loremasters assured me the barrier was inviolable.'

'Magic can be a tricky thing, my friend,' said Malekith. 'But you are right, my mother and I tried for many years to breach the warding spells on this tower without success. Trickery, brute strength, nothing we tried worked. A shame we didn't have an earlier opportunity to exploit treachery.'

'A traitor.' Finubar had recovered some of his composure, comporting himself again as ruler of the elves. 'A traitor amongst the loremasters of Hoeth? Who could gain by such a thing?'

'Not quite a loremaster, not really.'

'Teclis?'

'I'll grant you this, you are one of the cleverer Phoenix Kings I have killed.'

'So, you intend to kill me. It will not help – my death will bring you no closer to the Phoenix Throne.'

'Actually, it will. Or so I have been told, from a reliable source.'

Malekith strode out of the pool and looked up at the stars, marvelling at the way the rays of light seemed to pass through his not-quite corporeal body.

'Teclis again? It was a moment of weakness, assisted by wine, the night I confessed to feeling guilt at our deception.'

'Deception? Confession?' Malekith smiled, or at least the representation of him did. 'Please continue.'

'You know of what I speak. The coronation to become Phoenix King, it is a sham. I no more passed through the flames of the king of kings than you did.'

'I knew it!' Malekith snapped his fingers, his smile broadening to a grin. 'There had to be something that made Teclis seek me out. He thinks the Rhana Dandra is coming, you know? He needs the true heir to Aenarion to sit on the Phoenix Throne, to save elvenkind.'

'His brother T–'

'Tyrion is useless, a vacant slave to his lusts for the Everqueen, cursed by the taint of Khaine as pronounced by Caledor Dragon-tamer. Have you not been paying attention? He even has a child from his rutting, a dirty secret to keep from the court.'

'Alarielle has borne only my child, Aliathra.'

'Save your lies – you know that she is not yours. What a noble spirit Tyrion must be. To cuckold the Phoenix King and sire the next Everqueen? That must be why you never named him as successor, but always spoke well of Imrik though the prince of Caledor despises you for the most part.' Malekith was guessing much of this, but he enjoyed the look of pain that twisted Finubar's face as each accusation was made and took it as further proof. 'It gnaws at your heart, doesn't it? To think that the Dragon of Cothique is lauded so highly when in truth he is nothing more than an adolescent, getting into fights and bedding your wife. Even you, noblest and most worthy of all the princes, even you cannot swallow that shame and accept that failure in your heart.'

'Many times has the marriage and consummation between the Phoenix King and Everqueen been purely... ceremonial.'

'More sham, more guilt?'

Finubar bowed his head, averting his gaze. He mumbled something that Malekith did not quite hear.

'Was that an apology or a prayer?' said the Witch King. 'Neither will be heard.'

'You cannot harm me here,' Finubar announced, suddenly emboldened. He waved a hand back and forth between Malekith's left and right shoulder and then up through his face. 'You could not transmaterialise yourself within these walls, even with Teclis's assistance. He has opened a window for you, nothing more. In fact, I would think that Teclis does not want me dead, not yet. He is right, I have seen in the heavens that the Rhana Dandra is upon us. The gods of the stars fall back to the world and the gate in the north opens. The daemons will be upon Ulthuan in a matter of days and Teclis knows that our people need my leadership.'

'I cannot say for sure what Teclis intended, but rest assured I have not hidden my motives.' Malekith's apparition started to make signs in the air, weaving jagged rune-shapes with the tip of a finger. 'Well, not for this night. I will, however, dispense with his alliance as soon as it becomes unnecessary. Once he has handed me Ulthuan's keys, he will find me a less pleasant companion. You are correct in your assertion that I cannot lay physical hands upon you, much to my pity. There are other ways in which I can extend my reach.'

'What are you doing?' Finubar demanded, moving towards the door. Malekith's apparition stalked after him, whispering an enchantment. With his words the floating incantation formed a circle that started to revolve around the scrying pool.

'Dangerous things, windows,' said Malekith, coming between the Seafarer and the door. He pointed back to the pool whose waters were colouring with blood. 'The sisters of Ghrond have learned such lessons in very hard circumstances. Sometimes other things look back through the windows. Also, some windows can be opened, you see.'

'What have you done?' Finubar's voice was choked as he dashed to the side of the raised pool and stared into the depths of his scrying-water.

'Just a little portal,' said Malekith. 'It won't last long enough to threaten Lothern.'

'A portal to where?'

'See for yourself.'

Finubar leaned over the edge of the pool. A hand with red skin and black claws shot out of the blood-coloured water and seized the Phoenix King by the throat. The waters boiled and a horned head emerged slowly, white-eyed, fanged mouth open in an ecstatic grin.

'I cannot, as you said, transubstantiate my body within these walls, but daemons rarely have such problems.'

'They'll never accept you!' Finubar pulled himself free from the grasp of the emerging daemon, tearing bloody welts from across his throat. *'Ulthuan will drown in blood before you are hailed as the Phoenix King!'*

Malekith said nothing as the bloodletter of Khorne leapt from the waters, hands seizing hold of Finubar while a forked tongue ran across its razor-sharp teeth. The daemon turned a hungry look on Malekith and the Witch King wondered if it would be able to follow him through the breach Teclis had made in the wards.

It was probably better to be safer than sorry, and Malekith ended the spell, pulling his spirit back to the Black Tower in Naggarond.

Malekith did not step through the broken door, but remained there in thought. After a while he turned and beckoned to one of the guards close at hand. The elf was Eataine-born, and approached with caution, her shield and spear trembling. Malekith thought it fear and then remembered Teclis's glamour. It was not dread that unsettled the guard, it was awe.

It felt good, and was proof that Finubar would be wrong.

'Send word to my seneschal, Kouran. This door is to be barred again. Understood?'

'Yes.' The elf nodded and then remembered whom she addressed. 'Your majesty.'

With a flick of the hand the Phoenix King dismissed her from his presence and thoughts equally, and turned his mind to more difficult matters. Recalling the conversation with Finubar had reminded him of another thorny obstacle to be overcome if he was to legitimately become Phoenix King – marriage to the Everqueen. While Alarielle was not his half-sister, there could still be other objections, not least by the Everqueen herself.

THIRTY-TWO

The Everqueen

It transpired that Tyrion had encountered similar issues in securing the Everqueen's endorsement. News from the north was of a great battle under the eaves of the Avelorn Forest, and it seemed that Prince Tyrion desired to take by war that which had once freely been given by the Everqueen. Details were sparse, for not only Morathi's conjurations prevented scrying, but Alarielle's presence also confounded attempts at magical observation.

As had become his habit, Teclis arrived at nightfall following word of Tyrion's attack reaching Malekith's ears. The mage travelled far and fast upon his shadow steed, but the magic was costly. The Phoenix King had noticed the disturbances in the winds of magic growing greater, filling the vortex of Ulthuan with unprecedented power but making spells of any subtlety and nuance all but impossible.

'The King in the Woods fights alongside Alarielle,' said the breathless mage as he was admitted to Malekith's great hall. Imrik, Caradryan and Kouran were hard on Teclis's heels, having been alerted to the mage's imminent arrival by the many spies, both physical and not, surveying the Sapphire Palace and city of Lothern. 'Your majesty, the host of Athel Loren has come to the Everqueen's aid.'

'How is that possible?' asked Caradryan. 'An ocean and continent separate the two.'

'The more pertinent question would be why,' said Malekith. 'Our forest-bound cousins have never seemed interested in our continuing struggle for the isle of their ancestors. What brings Orion and Ariel to these shores now?'

'Something of that might be answered by knowing that it is Orion alone that has come, your majesty,' said Teclis. 'Of the avatar of Isha, nothing has been seen. Avelorn and Athel Loren, though divided, have always been bound together in ways that we cannot fathom. The spirits of the Everqueen and immortal Ariel connect in a fashion, both stemming from the power of Isha. With the gods returning to the world, that ancient conjunction is perhaps showing itself in new ways.'

'What if Tyrion wins, my king?' Kouran asked, always of a practical mind. 'If the pretender seizes control of Avelorn, his coup is all but complete. None know what happened in the Shrine of Asuryan and with the Island of Flames swallowed by the sea it is your word alone that claims Asuryan's blessing.'

'And my presence,' snapped Malekith. 'Does not the fire of the All-king run through me? Does not his blessing emanate from my being?'

'No disrespect was intended, my king, but trickery has been used before and your opponents will dismiss such things as an artifice of the Sapherian.'

'Should we send our forces to aid Alarielle?' said Imrik. 'It will take some time to arrange passage on ships but the dragons could be there in a matter of days.'

'Just in time to see the forests burning and hear Morathi's laughs of triumph,' said Malekith. 'She has always hated the

Everqueen, and will stop at nothing to see her dispossessed, the power of Avelorn broken.'

'*Chosen by whom?' asked Morathi contemptuously.*

'*By the princes and the Everqueen,' Bel Shanaar replied, standing to one side of the holy tree of Isha.*

'*Astarielle was slain,' Morathi said. 'The reign of the Everqueen is no more.'*

'*She lives on,' said a ghostly, feminine voice that drifted around the glade.*

'*Astarielle was slain by the daemons,' Morathi insisted, casting her gaze about to spy from whence the voice had come, her eyes narrowed with suspicion.*

The leaves on all of the trees began to quiver, filling the glade with a gentle susurrus as if a wind whispered through the treetops, though the air was still. The long grass of the glade began to sway in the same invisible breeze, bending towards the Aein Yshain at its centre. The glow of the sacred tree grew stronger, bathing the council in a golden light dappled with sky blues and verdant greens.

In the shimmering brightness, a silhouette of greater light appeared upon the knotted trunk, resolving itself into the form of a young elf maiden. Morathi gasped, for at first it seemed as if Astarielle indeed still lived.

The maiden's golden hair hung to her waist in long plaited tresses woven with flowers of every colour, and she wore the green robes of the Everqueen. Her face was delicate, even by elven standards, and her eyes the startling blue of the clearest summer skies. As the light dimmed, the elf's features became clearer and Morathi saw that this newcomer was not Astarielle. There was a likeness, of that Morathi was aware, but she relaxed as she scrutinised the girl.

'*You are not Astarielle,' Morathi declared confidently. 'You are an impostor!'*

'*Not Astarielle, you are right,' replied the maiden, her voice soft* yet carrying easily to the furthest reaches of the glade. 'I am not an impostor, either. I am Yvraine, daughter of Aenarion and Astarielle.'

'More trickery!' shrieked Morathi, rounding on the princes with such an expression of anger that many flinched from her ire. 'Yvraine is also dead! You conspire to keep my son from his rightful inheritance.'

'She is Yvraine,' said Oakheart, his voice a melodic noise like the sighing of a light wind through branches. 'Though Astarielle remained to protect Avelorn against the daemons, she bid us take her children to safety. To the Gaen Vale I carried them, where no other elf has trod. There my kin and I fought the daemons and kept Yvraine and Morelion safe those many years.'

At this there were gasps from the Naggarothi, none louder than the exclamation of Malekith.

'Then my half-brother also still lives?' the prince demanded. 'Aenarion's first son is alive?'

'Calm yourself, Malekith,' said Thyriol. 'Morelion has taken ship and sailed from Ulthuan. He is a child of Avelorn, as is Yvraine, and he seeks no claim to the rule of Nagarythe. He is blessed of Isha, not a scion of Khaine, and seeks neither dominion nor fealty.'

'You kept this from Aenarion?' Morathi's tone was full of incredulity. 'You allowed him to believe his children were dead, and raised them separated from their father? You have hidden them from–'

'I am the beloved of Isha,' said Yvraine, her voice stern, silencing Morathi. 'In me is reborn the spirit of the Everqueen. Anlec is a place of blood and rage. It could not be my home, I could not live amongst the taint of Khaine, and so Oakheart and his kind raised me in the manner and place fitting for my station.'

'I see now your conspiracy,' said Morathi, stalking across the glade to confront the princes. 'In secrecy you have muttered and whispered, and kept the Naggarothi from your counsels. You seek to supplant the line of Aenarion with one of your own, and wrest the power of Ulthuan from Nagarythe.'

'There is no power to wrest, no line to break,' replied Thyriol. 'Only in pain and death does Nagarythe prevail. We sent messengers to Anlec and you turned them away. We sought to include you in our deliberations, but you would send no embassy. We gave you every right and opportunity to make the claim for your son and you chose to tread your own path. There is no conspiracy.'

'I am the widow of Aenarion, the queen of Ulthuan,' Morathi snarled. 'When the daemons preyed upon your people, did Aenarion and his lieutenants stand by and discuss matters in council? When Caledor began his spell, did he debate its merits with the peons? To rule is to wield the right to decide for all.'

'You are queen no longer, Morathi,' said Yvraine, ghosting softly across the glade, her steps as light as settling snowflakes. 'The Everqueen has returned and I shall rule with Bel Shanaar, just as Aenarion reigned with my mother.'

'You will wed Bel Shanaar?' asked Morathi, turning on Yvraine.

'As Aenarion wed my mother, so the Everqueen will marry the Phoenix King, and ever shall it be down all of the ages,' Yvraine declared. 'I cannot marry Malekith, my half-brother, no matter what his entitlement or qualities to succeed his father.'

The debate continued long into the night, but it was Malekith's decree that any force sent to bolster the defence of Avelorn would be wasted. While Tyrion's focus was on the Everqueen it made sense to gain ground in the southern and eastern kingdoms, and perhaps to even take Ellyrion so that Tyrion would have foes to the east and west of his position.

As dawn lit the night sky, clear clarions were heard to the east. Suspecting attack, the defenders of Lothern rushed to their posts, while Malekith and his princes alighted on their dragons and took to the skies. What they saw to the east was almost like illusion, a semi-real phantasm of the dawn light.

An army marched to Lothern, but not of Tyrion or his commanders. Maidens with bows and spears led the way, and on a unicorn in their midst came Alarielle herself, flanked by companies of leaf-cloaked archers and stag riders. A morning mist followed them, creating an otherworldly air as though the army marched not on the ground but through it, passing hedge and thicket without impediment. As the sun rose higher the apparitions took more shape, their gonfalons and banners snapping in the breeze, their regiments marked out in summer and autumnal colours, greens and browns and deepest reds.

Malekith and Imrik sped back to the Sapphire Palace to make ready for a proper welcome to the Everqueen while the other dragons flew escort to the eagles and drakes that accompanied the combined army of Avelorn and Athel Loren.

The gates were opened for the Everqueen and, followed by her handmaidens, she entered the city along streets that were littered with hastily-procured leaves and petals, while choirs of children sang hymns in praise of Isha. Only once before had Alarielle come to Lothern, to publicly wed Finubar when he had been chosen as Phoenix King, and there was rampant rumour in the city regarding this unheralded arrival.

Malekith, who had no experience of how these matters were handled on Ulthuan, allowed himself to be guided by Teclis's counsel. In the wide plaza before the Sapphire Palace a stage was quickly raised and bedecked with garlands of such flowers and plants that could be found in the palace and the gardens of the local nobles, while word was sent to those same ranking elves to attend a feast that afternoon.

Alarielle's procession through the city was stately, and for Malekith thankfully slow, so that by the time the Everqueen and her entourage arrived at the Sapphire Palace the inner plazas of the city were thronged with princes and nobility ready to cheer her in welcome.

Following Teclis's advice Malekith had left his immense iron throne in the audience chamber, and instead two ornately carved chairs, equal in size, were placed at the centre of the stage.

Standing to one side of these, the Phoenix King, his glamour-image resplendent in dragon armour and swirling scarlet cloak, waited for Alarielle to complete her parade.

'Bow, your majesty,' whispered Teclis, as Alarielle mounted the steps to Malekith's left.

'What?' snapped the king. 'Why?'

'She is the Everqueen, greater than the Phoenix King, and you seek her commendation,' Teclis said hurriedly. 'Your majesty.'

Malekith almost refused, thinking it beneath him. Alarielle was no more a great queen of the elves than any of the fake kings she and her foremothers had endorsed in his place over the centuries. However, when he saw the light of Ghyran that shone from the Everqueen, highlighting a beauty that was ethereal and entrancing, he allowed his old charm to surface and did not bow, but sank to one knee.

Surprised, the Everqueen stopped a few paces away while her handmaidens and grim-faced guard lined the square. Malekith had already placed warriors from the Shadowfire Guard on all the roofs and surrounding buildings lest an agent of Tyrion try to assassinate the Everqueen, but Alarielle was used to seeing to her own fortunes.

'Welcome to Lothern,' said the Phoenix King, standing up to offer his hand.

Alarielle looked at it, and Malekith realised that the glamour had no effect on her. She saw the truth of what he was, a haggard half-corpse in blackened armour. He left the hand out and tried to smile, though his helm hid his withered lips.

Alarielle took the hand without comment and stepped beside the Phoenix King, turning her radiant smile on the crowd. Their cheers shook the buildings as she nodded regally, her gaze passing over everyone in her audience, seeming to touch all present with a glance of wry humour or earnest intent as their expectations warranted.

Releasing her grip, Alarielle moved to the front of the stage and held out her hands for quiet. A break in the clouds bathed her in golden sunlight and a still descended, so that not even the birds nesting in the eaves made any sound. Her voice when she spoke was as clear as running water, calm but strong, carrying on the wind easily.

'Great are the tribulations that have troubled our lands of late, and the turmoil to come is greater still. Yet in adversity can also be union, and so it is that with profound pleasure I can tell you that the houses of Avelorn and Athel Loren have been united once again. Those that were estranged are now as one.'

She gestured to the wood elves that had followed her into the square, and there was a ripple of polite applause for them. Alarielle straightened, her hands resting lightly on her girdle, and took a deep breath. Malekith could sense her nervousness now, though she did not look back at him, and knew what troubled her thoughts.

'And of other unions I must speak. Divided are the kingdoms of Ulthuan, and divided are the loyalties of their princes. This must end, and so I have sent my maiden guard to roam wide across Ulthuan bearing the declaration I speak to you today.' She then turned a little and beckoned to Malekith, who dutifully stepped forward. 'As is the right and proper tradition, Malekith of Nagarythe, prince of Ulthuan, heir to Aenarion the Defender, has entered the sacred fires of Asuryan and been reborn. When his prosecution of the current war has successfully driven out the dark forces that would see us plunged into a nightmare of blood and eternal night, we shall be united in marriage, Phoenix King and Everqueen as ever it has been since the time of Aenarion.'

More rapturous cheers and claps thundered across the plaza. Someone started to chant Malekith's name, and the shout was taken up by others. To hear voices raised in praise of him in such a fashion was something he had not experienced for a long lifetime. Spears and halberds were raised, swords clashed against shields, adding to the tumult of adulation. Yet for all the noise of his supporters there were many in the plaza that did not join the celebration. He saw elves slinking away through the streets and alleys with backwards glances, concern and distaste on their faces. Kouran had noticed them too, it seemed, for almost imperceptibly groups of former Black Guard broke from the crowd and followed these dissidents.

When the clamour had died down, Malekith and Alarielle walked together back to the Sapphire Palace, but once concealed within the gates the Everqueen took her leave of the Phoenix King and retired with her handmaidens to the south halls. Malekith returned to his chambers to assimilate the day's events and before long the guards called out the arrival of Teclis and Imrik.

Malekith sent for refreshments for his advisors and sat silent in his throne while they debated the course of events that had led to Alarielle's arrival. Orion was dead, all reports claimed, slain by Tyrion but not before the King in the Woods, the incarnation of Kurnous the Hunter, had gravely wounded the prince with his spear. Many other heroes of Avelorn and Athel Loren had died in the forests of Withelan, but a great toll had also been taken of Tyrion's forces. Morathi's attempt to claim the power of the Everqueen had again been thwarted though Avelorn itself was now abandoned.

'Alarielle remains uncertain,' Malekith declared. 'Why else would she pronounce that the war will end before we are wed? It is a soft proclamation, one that our rivals will seize upon as proof that Alarielle only backs me out of coercion.'

'Her words are more significant even than that, your majesty,' said Teclis. 'She talked of reuniting Ulthuan with Athel Loren. All three of our split kindreds are again becoming one. Druchii, asur and asrai, all of them returned to Ulthuan now, under your rule.'

'It is inevitable, is it not?' Malekith tapped his fingers on the arm of the throne. 'I am Asuryan reborn, Aenarion's heir, the king of kings. Not for me the false throne of Ulthuan. When I prevail I shall be ruler of all the elves.'

'A war still lies between us and that eventuality,' said Imrik. 'The endorsement of the Everqueen stands in our favour and her troops are well-received, but the greater part of Ulthuan is still loyal to Tyrion. While he is wounded we would do well to strike fast and make what ground we can, spreading the word of Alarielle's blessing.'

'Summon the princes and generals to council tonight,' commanded Malekith. 'Come dawn the last war for Ulthuan will begin.'

The next morning the combined army of Malekith and Alarielle marched forth from Lothern, the Phoenix King and Everqueen at its head, one a figure of dark majesty, the other the embodiment of life and light. The banners of Ulthuan, Naggaroth and Athel Loren streamed behind them and the host that followed numbered tens of thousands.

The war that followed was a terrible time, fought as bitterly and savagely as when Malekith had first attempted to seize the Phoenix Throne. Wherever Tyrion rode the Shadow of Khaine followed, filling elves with a bloodlust and desire for battle that brought them flocking to his banner. To counter this Malekith and the Everqueen seemed to be everywhere, calling on the elves of Ulthuan to swear allegiance to the new Phoenix King.

Malekith's army had one great advantage over Tyrion's, and that was Alarielle's mastery of the World Roots. These ancient magical paths were the means by which the warriors of Athel Loren had come to Avelorn, and they allowed bodies of troops to move from kingdom to kingdom, across the mountains and Inner Sea, undetected and unopposed.

It was well that the Phoenix King's host had such advantage. Though victories and defeats seemed in equal measure between the two sides, always it seemed that Tyrion's army was swelled by every conflict and Malekith's diminished.

Too many are the tales to be told of that bloody affair, of armies routed and scores of dragons duelling in the skies. Morai-heg laid many a twist and turn on fate's path over the coming seasons, so that the battle for Ulthuan was marked as much by treachery and rebellion as it was valour and sacrifice.

Most notable of these events was when Korhil, who had led Tyrion's army to the walls of Lothern, broke free of Tyrion's grip and Morathi's enchantments. In a daring episode, the captain of the White Lions took the Widowmaker and attempted to bring it to Malekith's camp.

Morathi's hunters scoured the wilds for Korhil and the stolen Sword of Khaine but in a twist that would have made Morai-heg cackle with joy, they were set upon by rival Khainites under the command of Hellebron. The hag queen had finally abandoned Har Ganeth, and having learned that her favoured assassin Shadowblade had been ensorcelled by Morathi when he attacked Malekith, sought to avenge herself on the Hag Sorceress and her consort. Long was the rivalry between Har Ganeth and Ghrond and now that enmity was given full freedom. Cothique and Yvresse were awash with blood as the two sects of devotees to the Lord of Murder tried to outdo each other in their dedication and bloody sacrifice, but it availed Korhil nought, for he was captured and the Widowmaker returned to Tyrion. For his bravery the Lionmane was beheaded with his own axe.

The fighting moved to the mountains of Saphery, where the vortex of magic swirled strong and beasts of all size and manner were brought to the battles by both sides – manticores and chimeras, griffons and hydras. While spell and counter-spell lashed across the peaks the roars and bellows of the beastmasters' charges heralded a deadly confrontation of fangs and claws, scorpion-stings and petrifying stares. The skies were split by thunderbolts and the earth trembled with the summoning of elementals.

The threat of assassination and treachery was rife. Though the direct attempts on Malekith or Alarielle were few, greater were the desertions and small coups. Garrisons would hail for Tyrion and ambush supply caravans destined for the armies, while ship's captains and town elders would transport and hide the agents of Morathi, conveying the spies into the heart of Malekith's holdings in return for promised riches and power when Tyrion was victorious.

Word often reached Malekith's ear of a prince's wavering loyalty or of seditious words spread through the companies of a particular general. Having learned from the fiasco of Brackblood's execution Malekith did not act overtly against these naysayers and faint-hearts, but sent them to the areas where the fighting was hardest, allowing Tyrion's warriors to cull the dissenters.

And throughout the war Malekith and Tyrion avoided matching each other blade to blade. Both knew that they were evenly matched. Malekith had fresh experience and his pride still smarted from his last confrontation with the Dragon of Cothique, while Tyrion was wary of Malekith's new-found power and reforged blade, reminded that in the old myths Khaine was laid low by Asuryan's wrath.

Even when by miscalculation or poor fortune the two found themselves on the same battlefield they would be circumspect in their fighting, such clashes becoming brief skirmishes before both sides withdrew.

At Tor Ellian Malekith's army faced a disastrous defeat and only the arrival of warriors and spirits from Athel Loren along the World Roots allowed the Phoenix King's forces to disengage in any semblance of order. Alarielle herself had almost been slain and the elves from beyond the Great Ocean vowed that they would never leave her side.

Tor Ellian signalled a shift in fortunes for Malekith. No matter what he tried, still Tyrion's forces prevailed more than they lost. Engulfed by the Shadow of Khaine they would fight to the last, selling their deaths dearly while Malekith's warriors were forced to retreat again and again to fight another day. With each encounter the Shadow of Khaine spread to more soldiers and princes once loyal to Malekith, sapping the strength of his hosts even more.

THIRTY-THREE

A New Ending

His desperation growing, Malekith sent Teclis across Ulthuan, demanding of the princes not yet committed to show themselves loyal to the Phoenix Throne, in battle. A great many of the nobles finally sent forth their households, but as many that declared for Malekith were matched by the number that moved to the camp of Tyrion, and an equal number refused to pick between two equally bloodthirsty tyrants.

No matter how bloody a pursuit became, nor if an army was outmanoeuvred and on the brink of destruction, there was one kingdom of Ulthuan that neither side violated. Nagarythe, a fog-shrouded desolation, was home to the Shadow King and his aesenar and neither side dared the borders of Aenarion's ancient realm for fear of rousing the wrath of Alith Anar. Now Malekith risked the Shadow King's neutrality and despatched Teclis to seek audience with the self-appointed ruler of Nagarythe.

It was with some trepidation that Malekith awaited his emissary's return. In the guise of a flock of crows Teclis came back to the camp of the Phoenix King as the army was camped on the shore of the Inner Sea close to the border between Eataine and Saphery. Malekith knew immediately from Teclis's expression that his advances had been rebuffed.

'The ranks of the aesenar swell, as they did when the Anars first raised their banner in opposition to Morathi before the Sundering, your majesty,' said the mage. 'Tens of thousands of refugees from across the kingdoms have sought sanctuary under his banner, turned aside from the other kingdoms.'

'A force that could swing the war yet he sits on his hands like a coward,' snarled Malekith. 'Does he not know that Tyrion and Morathi will slaughter them all once they have secured Ulthuan?'

'He does not care, I think,' admitted Teclis. 'He is a bitter spirit, and your treachery still burns cold in his heart.'

'My treachery?' The king's protest was like iron scraping on stone. 'The Anars swore their oaths to me, delivered Anlec to me, and then they turned on me. He owes me an army!'

'Nevertheless, there will be no army from Nagarythe, your majesty,' said Teclis. The two of them walked to Malekith's pavilion and stopped under the shade of the great awning over the entrance. Servants brought Teclis wine but he waved them away and instead imbibed one of his constitution restoratives.

'We are being beaten, nephew,' Malekith said quietly. 'The time fast approaches when I must risk all or we shall lose by degrees everything we have until there is no army left to fight with.'

'Personal combat?' Teclis flexed his fingers as though they were stiff and rolled his shoulders with a pained expression. As much as anyone the war had taken its toll on him. 'Do you think you can win?'

'I think the first problem is drawing Tyrion into a fight he cannot avoid,' said Malekith. 'His army grows stronger every day, and with each the reasons to match his blade against mine lessen. I have misjudged this war. The Shadow of Khaine lies too deeply over our people, and loyalty to the Phoenix Throne is scarce.'

'What do you suggest, your majesty?'

'Do not be coy, nephew.' Malekith stepped inside the pavilion and Teclis followed. He did not speak again until they were alone in his audience chamber. 'You have always harboured a grander plan for the conclusion of this effort, have you not? Do not seek to dissemble any longer – the time is upon us for frank discussion.'

'You speak of the vortex, your majesty.' The mage did not look at the Phoenix King but busied himself at a platter of meats and breads on a side table. 'An attempt to harness the winds of magic to end forever the threat of Chaos and the daemons.'

'I knew it would be grandiose, nephew, but I never quite thought you could have such a high ambition! Ultimate victory over Chaos? Peace and love in our times? Wolf and lion living in harmony? I am surprised you waited this long before making your confession.'

Teclis turned but before he could speak Malekith stopped him with a raised hand.

'You are aware that I have some personal experience in this matter, yes?' said the Phoenix King. 'Interfering with the vortex, I learned at great cost, can have severe consequences.'

The throne room at the heart of Aenarion's palace was shrouded in darkness. The only light came from the glow of the Witch King's armour, casting flickering shadows from the twelve figures that stood before him.

The humiliation hurt more than his wounds, though they were grievous; the blows of the Phoenix Guard had reignited the fire of Asuryan that had been set in his flesh. Malekith did not retreat from the pain as he had done before. He embraced it. He nurtured it. The agony in his body fuelled the rage in his spirit.

'I will not be denied,' Malekith growled.

'We are defeated, master,' said Urathion, the sorcerer-lord who ruled over the citadel of Ullar. 'There are barely enough troops to

defend the walls and the army of the accursed Anars will surely come soon.'

'Silence!' Malekith's shout reverberated around the hall, echoing from the distant walls. 'There will be no surrender.'

'How can we resist with our armies scattered?' asked Illeanith. The sorceress, daughter of Thyriol, asked the question in a whisper, voice full of fear. 'It will take too long to withdraw our garrisons to the city.'

'We will have a new army, one that Imrik and his fawning minions will never defeat,' said Malekith.

The Witch King stood up, armoured feet ringing on the stone floor as he took several steps closer to the ring of wizards. He held out a smoking hand and cut the air with a finger. A line appeared, bulging with energy; a torrent of formless colour and noise screamed from the tear in reality. The line widened to a gap, pulled apart by clawed hands to reveal leering daemonic faces. A scaled arm reached through.

The rift into the Realm of Chaos wavered. The arm withdrew as the rent sealed itself, disappearing with the sound of tearing metal. It had lasted a few moments, but left no trace of its existence.

'Daemons?' said Urathion.

'An endless army to command,' said Morathi, stepping into the circle, her skull staff in hand. 'Immortal and impervious. What better host to serve the lord of Nagarythe?'

'It would take all of our power to summon a handful of daemons,' said Drutheira, once an acolyte of Morathi, now a fully accomplished sorceress. Her dark hair was twisted with silver and her pale skin painted with runes. 'There are yet the artifices of Vaul that can destroy a daemon's form, enough weapons to defeat any host that we might conjure.'

'We do not have to summon them,' said Malekith. 'We need only to break the bars that keep them imprisoned in the Realm of Chaos.'

There was silence as the cabal considered what this meant. It was Urathion that broke the quiet.

'You mean Caledor's vortex?' said the sorcerer.

'It cannot be done,' said Drutheira. 'The vortex is powered by the lodestones of Ulthuan. We would have to destroy them, and most are in the lands of our enemies.'

'It can be done,' said Morathi. 'Not by destroying the lodestones, but by overloading them.'

'A sacrifice,' said Malekith. 'Together we will create a surge of dark magic, enough to disrupt the harmony of the vortex. Its own power will do the rest, dragging that blast of energy into its heart.'

'Is this wise?' asked Urathion. 'Without the vortex, the Realm of Chaos will be set free upon the winds of magic. Not even together can we control that power.'

'It does not need to be controlled, simply directed,' said Malekith. He raised a smouldering finger to the circlet set into his helm. 'With that power turned to our ends, I have the means to focus its energies. Our enemies will be swept aside by a tide of daemons. Only those favoured by me shall survive. I will have both victory and vengeance in one stroke.'

The cabal looked at each other. Some seemed eager, others more concerned.

'What other choice do we have?' asked Auderion, dragging black-nailed fingers through his white hair. His gaze flickered nervously from one member of the cabal to another, never stopping. 'We cannot hold out forever, and our lives will be forfeit.'

'Our spirits are already forfeit,' whispered Illeanith. 'Bargains we have made and promises of blood have not been kept. I will not go easily to that fate.'

'Imagine their terror,' said Drutheira. 'Imagine the horror unleashed upon those that scorned us, abandoned us. We will rid the world of the Dragontamer's legacy, reverse the mistake he made and erase the insult upon Aenarion's legend.'

Some of the cabal remained silent, not daring to speak though their unease was as palpable as the heat from Malekith's armour. Worried eyes glittered in the gloom.

Urathion bowed his head to Malekith.

'Forgive my objections, master,' he said, dropping to one knee. 'What must we do?'

'Return to your castles and gather such acolytes and slaves as you still possess. Morathi will furnish you with the details of the ritual you must undertake. At the appointed hour, midnight ten days from now, we will begin. The blood of our sacrifices will draw the dark magic and our incantations shall send it as a storm into the vortex.'

'What of the Sapherians?' said Illeanith. 'My father and his mages will try to stop us.'

'How can they?' said Morathi. 'By the time they know what is happening, it will be too late for them to intervene.'

'Even if they do, they do not have the power to stop us,' said Malekith. 'The vortex was wrought by Caledor Dragontamer at the height of his strength. Not even your father can contest such a spell.'

There were no further questions or objections. The sorcerers and sorceresses bowed and departed, leaving Malekith alone with Morathi.

'If you are wrong?' said Morathi. 'If we cannot harness the vortex?'

'The daemons will rampage across the world and all will be destroyed,' said Malekith.

'And you are sure you wish to risk such an end?' said Morathi.

'Risk it?' Malekith replied with a harsh laugh. 'I embrace it! If Ulthuan will not be mine, then none will rule. I would rather our people perished than see them laid low by the hand of another. Better it is to see the world torn asunder than suffer this eternal torment.'

'I would not seek to break the vortex, but to channel it away from the lodestones into fresh vessels,' Teclis explained, his expression thoughtful. 'The stasis upon the Isle of the Dead is already weakening. The Dragontamer has sent his spirit to Imrik and has passed on his wisdom to me. In this time when the Realm of Chaos expands the vortex is not powerful enough. Only a living, immortal host can contain the power unleashed.'

'What happened with Nagash and the Wind of Shyish...? The Great Necromancer has become the embodiment of death magic. You would do this with the other seven winds?'

'The return of the gods is not a metaphor, Malekith, it is a necessity. Lileath has shown me how it can be done.'

'And these other avatars, who would they be? You have chosen them already?'

'You would be one, your majesty. Think on what you have achieved wrapped as you are in a shell of sorcery, as bound to your armour as a fish is to the ocean. Now imagine being freed, becoming an incarnation of magic, a source of power that would never wane.'

Malekith imagined it, and the thought was pleasing.

'Alarielle, obviously, yourself, Imrik – who else is on your list?'

'For the moment it does not matter, your majesty. Much can happen between now and the moment the vortex is released. The winds will find their way to the most suitable vessels – we need only unshackle them from the lodestones and help them on their way.'

'That might cause some problems,' Malekith said with an affected wave of the hand. 'You weren't there so I forgive you forgetting, but the last time I tried to "unshackle" the vortex, I sank two kingdoms beneath a wave.'

Teclis grew solemn and he did not speak for some time. When he did his voice was quiet.

'Ulthuan will not survive,' he admitted softly, meeting Malekith's gaze. 'Without the vortex our island will sink beneath the waves entirely. For seven millennia the winds of magic have eaten at the bedrock of Ulthuan and now there is nothing but the magic to keep us afloat. When it is gone, Ulthuan will drown.'

It was Malekith's turn to remain silent for a considerable period, shocked by what Teclis was proposing. Talk of the vortex brought back an ancient, conflicted memory.

The hall was awash with blood. It moved with its own sluggish life, hissing and sizzling at Malekith's feet, lapping over the twisted bodies of his victims. Morathi chanted, staff held above her head, an incantation calling upon all of the daemons and powers with which she had made pacts during her long life. The air seethed with dark energy, flowing from walls to ceiling, making the symbols and runes painted in blood on the stone glow with ruddy power.

Through the circlet, the Witch King could feel the rising tide of dark magic across Nagarythe. In castles and towers across the barren kingdom his followers despatched their sacrifices and used their deaths to draw on the winds of magic, the mystical forces congealing together under the sorcerous influence of the Naggarothi.

Morathi's incantation was reaching its crescendo. Her voice was a wail, her body shuddering, the coils of dark magic thickening and strengthening as they whirled around the throne room.

Reaching out his hands, Malekith felt the slick touch of the magic on his iron skin. The circlet gleamed on his brow and filled his mind with ice as the Witch King grasped and manipulated the formless energy with his will, shaping it, turning its convoluted waves into a rhythmically pulsing cloud.

'Now!' screamed Morathi, her staff blazing.

Malekith flung the dark magic up, spearing its energies through the palace of Aenarion. He could feel the other columns of power erupting across his kingdom, pillars of pure magical energy roaring up into the heavens.

Malekith strode to an iron balcony adjoining the chamber, Morathi hurrying after him. He turned his flaming gaze to the east and saw the ravening energies gathering across the mountaintops.

'It is done,' said Morathi.

She pointed high into the heavens, to the north. Lights burned in the sky, silhouetting the horizon with a rainbow of colours that were constantly shifting. The magical aurora flickered, spitting bolts of energy to the ground and up towards the disappearing stars.

Malekith could see through the anarchy of shape and colour: towering spires of crystal and rivers of blood; cliffs with screaming skull-like faces and forests of waving tentacles; castles of bronze and a huge dilapidated mansion; plains covered with splintered bones and white beaches rippled by purple waters; clouds of flies and miniature suns that glared with cyclopean eyes.

And he heard the roaring and the howls, the screaming and the growls. Marching and slithering, swooping and leaping, a host of daemons poured forth.

'The Realm of Chaos opens,' he rasped, feeling triumphant. 'My legions awake!'

'No!' screamed Morathi.

Malekith felt it too, a presence he had not known for more than a thousand years. The Dragontamer had returned. The Witch King did not know how, but he would not be defeated so easily. He poured out all of his scorn and hatred, looking to wrench control of the vortex from the elf who had betrayed his father. Morathi sensed what he was doing and added her own sorcery, seeking to overcome the Dragontamer's spell.

The two waves of magic clashed within the vortex, detonating with a blaze of multicoloured light that swept away the storm, converting both high and dark magic into a huge detonation. Malekith felt it as a shockwave that pulsed across Ulthuan, flattening trees and toppling towers. He sensed the mountains lurching as the vortex spun again.

He felt something else too, like the world was tipping on its axis. The magic unleashed rocked Ulthuan, ripping earth and sky with its power. A crack appeared in the city wall of Anlec as a huge fissure opened up in the ground to the north. Roofs collapsed and walls toppled as Anlec convulsed. Everywhere across Nagarythe

the dark magic earthed itself, mighty spires of rock erupting from the ground while huge pits and crevasses dropped down.

'What is that noise?' said Morathi, looking to the north.

Malekith turned, gripping the rail of the balcony tight as the palace swayed on its foundations, turrets and towers crashing down onto the buildings below in a flurry of broken stone and tiles.

To the north was a wall of white. It looked like fog at first, a bank of cloud swiftly approaching from the north-west. It brought an odd hissing, which deepened as the cloud came closer.

Malekith felt a moment of dread as he realised it was not a cloud that approached, but a wall of water. As though the ocean had heaved up itself in protest, a tidal wave stretched across the horizon, shining in the moonlight, as high as the tallest tower of Anlec.

'No,' said the Phoenix King. 'I forbid it. I stand at the moment of achieving my dreams and you would throw it all away on the vacuous whim of a goddess. I will hunt down Tyrion and slay him and Ulthuan will rejoice and forever praise my name.'

'As you command, your majesty,' Teclis said with a bow. As the mage left Malekith knew well that his nephew could not be trusted and considered whether this was the time he had finally outlived his usefulness. For the moment the Phoenix King's alliance was too fragile, the battle in Saphery still finely balanced. Soon, though, Malekith thought, Teclis would no longer be required and his insane scheme to destroy the Dragontamer's vortex would prove a useful story to cover his removal.

Despite every effort on the part of Malekith, Tyrion flatly refused to meet his rival in battle. Every passing day brought fresh news of the pretender's host growing or some defeat of Malekith's forces, yet the Phoenix King would not countenance Teclis's plan.

Matters were brought to a head as the Phoenix King gave the order to break camp not far from the Tower of Hoeth, at least a dozen leagues from the closest of Tyrion's armies. At first light

Imrik called upon the king and asked that he summon Teclis and Alarielle to hear what the prince had to say. Imrik was a picture of agitation, pacing the rugs back and forth as he waited for the Everqueen and mage to arrive. Malekith studied him closely, wondering what might have brought about such a disturbed disposition.

Eventually the others joined Imrik and Malekith and the prince was free to speak his news.

'The Shadow of Khaine is growing,' said the prince, fists balled in front of him. 'For a time now there have been missing sentries, bodies found slain in their sleep. We thought it was assassins employed by Morathi but I have now seen the truth for myself.'

The prince shuddered and poured himself water. He downed the goblet and waited a second before continuing, haunted eyes moving from one companion to the next.

'Marendri, my own cousin, who swore allegiance to you at Eagle Gate, has broken faith with us and attempted to desert last night.' Imrik shook his head. 'A more loyal warrior you would not have found in all of my kingdom, as close to me as fabled Thyrinor was to Caledor the First. He slit the throats of his brothers, all three, and only a chance encounter with the sentries revealed his crime. His tent was next to mine! My own kin, close at hand for counsel and comfort, poised to drive the dagger deepest into our heart. I heard the fighting and confronted him. A wild beast I saw, with blood-red eyes and foaming mouth. He spoke in curses of blood and I ended him quickly, mercifully so.'

Shuddering, Imrik turned away, the goblet falling from his trembling grasp. Alarielle addressed Malekith while Teclis moved to comfort the dragon prince.

'We have striven in every way we can, but we cannot fight this. Khaine feeds on death and war – we must seek an end to this slow execution.'

'You have spoken to Teclis?' Malekith asked. He did not wait for answer – it was clear the mage had colluded with the Everqueen despite Malekith's orders. 'It is madness, for which I was damned for a seeming eternity.'

'What would you give for victory?' asked Alarielle, stepping closer. She laid a hand on Malekith's, her touch warm yet also cooling the fires inside the Phoenix King. 'Would you give your life?'

Malekith considered this and nodded. 'I stepped into the flame of Asuryan and did not know if I would survive.'

'Would you see countless dead on the battlefields of Ulthuan?'

'You know my legacy as well as any. Countless already are the lives I have expended in my quest to rule.'

'Would you be willing to lose everything? Would you give up your claim to save our people?'

Malekith found no ready answer to this question. He withdrew his hand from Alarielle's grasp and stood up, turning his back on her.

'I would see no other as Phoenix King while I live.'

'Yet if you continue to face Tyrion as you do, you will lose the war and Tyrion will prevail. What you once condoned out of spite, you will not do now for justice?'

'Justice? Where was justice these last six thousand years?' Malekith whirled around and glared at the Everqueen. Unknowingly reliving the act of rage that had propelled his father to the Sword of Khaine, the Phoenix King snatched up his throne and heaved it over his head. With a wordless shout, he dashed it to the ground, smashing it into pieces. 'No more!' he roared. 'This is a price too heavy for me to pay!'

Fire burst from his armour as he staggered away, fending off Alarielle's attention with an outstretched hand. Malekith's gaze next fell upon the banner of Nagarythe in its stand behind where the throne had been, woven with silver thread and inlaid with pearls and diamonds. He grabbed the haft of the banner and lifted it clear, ready to snap it across his knee.

'Your majesty!' Teclis's stern words cut through the anger that threatened to swallow Malekith, water splashed on embers. 'We will not fail.'

'If we do,' croaked the Phoenix King, 'none will survive to know it.'

There was a long silence and none of the elves would look at each other.

'Do we proceed with Teclis's plan to unfurl the winds of magic and anchor them in mortal form?' Alarielle asked. 'We must be unanimous.'

'Better to die in glory than live enslaved,' said Imrik, his sorrow now replaced with a vengeful expression. The words might have come from Malekith himself in another time.

The Phoenix King replaced the banner of Nagarythe, the flames of his body dimming.

'When Ulthuan sinks, what becomes of our people?' he asked, voice barely more than a whisper.

'They become free,' said Teclis. 'Free from the touch of Chaos, free from the Shadow of Khaine, free to live out their lives in sanctuary. Lileath has shown me this.'

'Athel Loren will welcome us,' said Alarielle. 'It always has.'

'Make your preparations, nephew,' Malekith said, his voice gaining confidence as he acknowledged the inevitability of the decision. 'The gods demand a battle the like of which they have not seen for many ages. Rule of the elves is not high enough stakes for such a cataclysm, so let us again fight for the future of the world!'

THIRTY-FOUR

The Final Battle

On the Isle of the Dead was the fate of the world to be decided, at the very heart of the vortex raised by Caledor Dragontamer. Astride Seraphon, Malekith held the centre of the line, surrounded by warriors from ten kingdoms and further afield, all drawn together in his cause.

The air crackled with the whirl of magic, condensed into its rawest form by the eight lodestones that formed a circle at the very centre of the isle. A loremaster stood at each sparkling stone, though the monolith for the Wind of Shyish was dull and lifeless, its power stolen by Nagash.

Teclis sat atop his shadow steed to Malekith's right, sword in hand, expression pensive. To the left Alarielle and her asrai followers guarded the approach to the inner stones, bows at the ready.

'Protect the loremasters – that is all that matters,' Teclis shouted up to the Phoenix King. 'Do not let Tyrion's forces break through. It is as when the vortex was made and Aenarion fought as the shield of the Dragontamer.'

'I know the strategy, nephew, and have no need of another of your history lessons,' Malekith replied. He felt calm, committed now to a course of action from which there could only be two simple outcomes. He would be victorious or he would be dead. It was strangely reassuring to have such clarity of purpose. 'Just mind your own deeds, and I will see to mine.'

The Phoenix King drew *Asuryath* and a great cheer rose up from his assembled army as the splinter of light shone against the multicoloured sky.

'I was expecting more of them,' the king commented, as Tyrion's army approached. It seemed if anything that the Dragon of Cothique was slightly outnumbered. Blood-frenzied hags and vicious corsairs led the attack while companies of bows filled the air with barbed shafts and phalanxes of spears moved to the flanks. Malekith's force arrayed in deep ranks to await the assault, their banners flying colours from all of the kingdoms of Ulthuan.

Tyrion himself could be seen at the centre of the line, a golden figure amongst red and black. He raised the Sword of Khaine and a hush fell across the island, the sight of the Widowmaker causing even the bravest heart to flutter for a moment. Malekith felt the vortex churning around Tyrion. At first he thought it was the sorcery of Morathi, but he sensed his mother's presence elsewhere. It was tempting to seek her out, to rend her limb from limb for her betrayal, but the cautioning words of Teclis held Malekith to his task. If she survived the battle vengeance would come later.

Whatever enchantment was being wrought by Tyrion, its energy flowed over the Isle of the Dead and into the sea, causing the waves to boil, washing deep spume upon the shores. There was movement in the waves, figures approaching from the waters.

Lurching and staggering, the dead of the seas answered the summons of Khaine. Bidden to the Isle of the Dead, the restless corpses of thousands forged out of the sea, some less than a day in their watery graves, others seaweed-clad skeletons who had fallen in millennia past.

Dismay flowed through Malekith's army as these unearthly reinforcements followed after Tyrion's host, their ghastly moaning and groans a bass background to the shriller war cries and wails of the Khainites.

'No retreat!' Malekith bellowed, brandishing his blade again.

There was little strategy and Malekith charged into the heart of the enemy with his black dragon, cutting to the left and right with Asuryan's holy blade, leaving corpses wreathed in white fire behind him.

He knew little enough of the unbinding ceremony, but could feel the vortex loosening around him. He tried to concentrate on the foes in front and behind, urging Seraphon deeper into the fray to slick her claws and fangs with the blood of the enemy.

Time lost meaning. Around Malekith the battle raged, physical and magical, and the skies whirled with skycutters and griffons, mages on shining platforms and roaring manticores. He paid little heed to anything else and cut down hydras and elves, charioteers and cold ones with equal cold ferocity.

He was dimly aware of bright fire and screams when Imrik's last surviving dragons charged the flank of Tyrion's army, slaying with dragonfire and claw. The stench of saltwater and decay washed over him and he saw that the dead of the seas had reached the battle line. Some fought with their weapons, broken shields and rusted swords, others had clawed hands and wide maws filled with needle-like fangs like some deepwater fish.

He hewed down reanimated corpses to the left and right, though around him his followers were unsettled by the assault of the dead and began to give ground. Not wishing to become isolated, the Phoenix King was forced to back away, and in the break this granted him he saw why the dead had caused so much consternation.

At their head marched five figures, resurrected from their

tombs upon the Isle of the Dead. In regal cloaks and armour, with swords and shields and necklaces and bangles about their mouldering bones, five dire warriors led the charge of the undead.

The Phoenix Kings of ages past.

Five alone of the ten, whose bodies had been interred in the mausoleums upon the water's edge. Finubar was there, though less than three years dead his body rendered to gleaming bones by the magic of the vortex. After him came others, glowing with fey light, eyeless sockets gleaming with magic. Confronted by the kings of times past the host of Malekith drew back, bending before the advance of the undead like the bow wave of a ship.

Malekith saw that Tyrion's forces were gathering again for a fresh attack in the wake of the undead advance. Knights and griffon riders were set ready to charge, while Tiranocii chariots mustered to force any breakthrough.

Looking on Finubar's skeletal features Malekith was filled with a loathing born not of horror but anger. Arrayed before him were five of his worst foes, who had thwarted him in life and now their bones were beholden to a brain-addled slave of Khaine. Their weakness sickened Malekith and he rose up in Seraphon's throne-saddle in disgust.

The vortex was like an unchained beast around him, bucking at the lodestones to tug free, smashing into the ground and whirling into the air in a storm of sparks and clouds. His simplest thought caused ripples to eddy out into the maelstrom. Shaped by his hatred of the dead kings pressing towards him, the vortex responded, gathering in his body, fizzing along fingers and limbs.

Infused with magical power, Malekith burst into flame, his armour burning white, *Asuryath* like a lick of fire in his hand. And in that moment Malekith understood his destiny and accepted who he was.

Asuryan reborn.

Malekith's laughter echoed across the battlefield.

'Kings of Ulthuan!' the Phoenix King spat the words as a curse. 'You are usurpers and thieves. You owe me a debt. In my name, and in that of my father, I call upon you to repay it now!'

The magic was too much to control and Malekith had to give vent to his righteous wrath. He thrust *Asuryath* towards the oncoming host of the dead and white fire sprang from the blade to create a ball of blazing destruction. The bones of the dead kings shattered at the impact of his magical missile, scattered to the winds as ash. As it screamed through the ranks of the undead the fire took on a shape, becoming the image of an elf.

Of Finubar, as he had been in life.

Though the fire burned out quickly, leaving a ring of charred corpses on the ground where it had stopped, the gleaming figure of Finubar remained where the bolt had exploded, glowing with white light. Drawing an ethereal blade, the shade of Finubar charged into the foe.

'Spirits of the fallen kings, answer me now!'

Malekith hurled another fireball, which coalesced into the image of Bel-Hathor. From his fiery birth the Phoenix King known as the Sage strode forth unleashing blasts of power from his fingertips, eyes ablaze with magical energy. Eight more times Malekith cast the incantation and eight more times the spirits of the Phoenix Kings past answered his summons, appearing in coronas of white fire, reborn by the power of Asuryan, the Phoenix of the Gods.

All came that were bidden, whether warrior like Tethlis and Caledor and his son, or magic-weaver like Caradryel the Peacemaker and Bel-Korhadris the Scholar-King. Only one king did Malekith not call upon, and one king alone that had no debt to settle. Aenarion's spirit remained unsummoned, wherever it had departed.

But Malekith did not stop there.

He was Phoenix King, the Lord of Lords, and to him was owed

every oath of fealty and dedication ever sworn upon Ulthuan. With *Asuryath* a storm of white fire, he called forth every hero and heroine that ever laid down his or her life for the cause of the elves, from Eltharion the Grim who had died only a year before trying to rescue Tyrion's daughter, to Yeasir, his lieutenant from ancient Anlec, killed when he had stood up to Malekith's soldiers to protect the heir to Tiranoc before the Sundering had flooded that kingdom.

With these ancient heroes to lead them, the Phoenix King and Everqueen at the forefront of the fight, the army of Malekith surged forwards into Tyrion's host, possessed of a righteousness of spirit that eclipsed the blind blood-thirst of their foes.

Seeing that the battle turned against him Tyrion was at last forced to come forward himself. His sword arm never ceasing in its rise and fall, he cut his way through the throng, heading directly for the Phoenix King.

'Finally,' Malekith said to Seraphon. 'A foe worth fighting.'

A panicked thought intruded upon the Phoenix King's mind and in the moment of distraction he noticed that the vortex was almost free, riding and crashing like a ship on storm-tossed waves that had broken its moorings. The sense of another close at hand announced a message from Teclis.

'Summoning the kings of old has upset the balance of our incantations!' bellowed the mage into Malekith's thoughts. 'Look what your meddling has wrought!'

Malekith glanced towards the lodestones and saw that a handful of the mages were dead, their desiccated corpses propped up against the waystones they had been controlling. Like ribbons in a storm the winds of magic fluttered free and fierce.

The white of Malhandir streaked towards Malekith through the melee, the Dragon of Cothique on the horse's back a vision of destruction.

'I have more pressing matters, nephew. I am playing my part, mage, now play yours!'

Taking to the air, Malekith watched as the Phoenix Kings of old tried to confront Tyrion. Each in turn fell to the Widowmaker, speared and sliced by the shard of icy death in his hand. Tyrion plunged onward, reckless in his haste, trampling friend as well as foe beneath the hooves of his steed.

It was then that Malekith realised his error. Tyrion rode not for him, but for Teclis.

Seraphon swooped at his command and magic rained from Malekith's sword, but Malhandir was swifter even than dragon or bolt or fireball. Cursing himself for his lapse, Malekith strained every nerve to ensnare Tyrion with a spell while Seraphon, urged on by her master, almost tore herself apart in her efforts to catch the blur of white and gold on the ground below.

Teclis was unaware of the doom descending upon him, arms reaching into the air as though he tried to seize hold of the winds of magic like reins. Oblivious to his brother bearing down, the mage howled his enchantments into the vortex.

But there was to be one last turn of allegiance. No mere horse was Malhandir, but descended from the father of horses in the time before the Everqueen. He had borne Tyrion across countless battlefields and almost died a dozen times for his master, but now at the last the Lord of Steeds sensed that it was not Tyrion he carried but a far darker creature.

As Malekith dropped like a comet, Malhandir pranced, tossing Tyrion from his back to fall onto the hard rock of the outcrop where the bases of the lodestones met. The Dragon of Cothique lashed out with the icefang but Malhandir was already galloping away. The Widowmaker in his grasp, Tyrion stalked on, eyes fixed on Teclis.

Malekith smiled as Seraphon flexed her claws. Enslaved to the rage of Khaine, Tyrion had turned his back on the Phoenix King, possessed by the thirst for vengeance against his brother. He was but moments from death.

A piercing shriek cut across the clamour of battle, a warning scream that caused Tyrion to turn when Seraphon was but a heartbeat from snatching up the Dragon of Cothique. Malekith recognised the voice as his mother's but had no time to curse her interference as Tyrion spun with supernatural speed and speared the Widowmaker towards the diving black dragon, rolling beneath the outstretched claws.

Seraphon needed no command and banked fast, pouring forth a billow of noxious vapour from her maw.

Purple lightning erupted around the dragon and her rider, crackling across scales and armour. Screeching agony from Morathi's spell, Seraphon spasmed, wings folding as she fell. Malekith leapt clear a moment before she hit the rock, wings and spine cracking, scales and flesh torn by the jagged stone upthrusts.

Landing lightly, Malekith turned to find Tyrion almost upon him. The Widowmaker flashed for the Phoenix King's throat. *Asuryath* moved as though of its own accord and the two godly blades clashed with a shower of icy sparks and white fire.

So did Malekith and Tyrion, Asuryan and Khaine, finally meet to decide who would prevail.

THIRTY-FIVE

One King to Rule Them

Tyrion's sword was in constant motion, but no slower was Malekith's blade. Ice and fire wreathed the pair, the toll of enchanted steel sounding out with every heartbeat as the two demigods fought.

Malekith was aware that the winds of magic were almost undone, and in this moment stuck true to his task, defending and engaging Tyrion rather than forcing the fight for a kill one way or the other. For Tyrion the duel was a venting of a bloodlust long in the making, his red eyes fixed on his foe, every lick and lash of the Widowmaker intended to maim and kill, only centuries of unthinking instinct moving the Godslayer in defence when Malekith counter-attacked.

Malekith was wounded first, taking a cut to his left arm that bit deep to the bone. Had it not been for Hotek's craft the arm would have been lost altogether, though the limb hanging dead at his side caused the Phoenix King some difficulty. In retaliation Malekith swept his sword towards Tyrion's throat. The avatar of Khaine eluded the blow but at the expense of his jaw as the tip of *Asuryath* raked across his face.

They parted for but a moment and then flew at each other again, their swords a blur to all that watched. Malekith circled, keeping his good side presented to his foe, while Tyrion unleashed a blistering set of strikes both high and low, seeking any gap in the Phoenix King's defences.

Each was cut a dozen times and more from glancing blows, their suits of armour streaming with blood, their blades hissing with magic. Malekith renewed his efforts, sensing that he was tiring, knowing that he had to overwhelm Khaine's incarnation quickly. The vortex was almost freed, and in a few more heartbeats Teclis's spell would be complete.

Tyrion weathered the Phoenix King's offensive with hasty parries and dodges, always just ahead of the next blow. Malekith could not help but remember the result of their earlier encounter and fear crept into his heart as he looked into the unthinking, raging gaze of his foe. The dread crept through his body like ice, seeping from the wounds inflicted by the Widowmaker, sapping his spirit as well as his stamina.

It was then that Malekith knew he could not win.

The efforts of his earlier sorcery and the wounds he had received had taken too much of a toll. He could defend himself for a time more, but not long enough, or he could try to end Tyrion with one last effort.

His first blow took the avatar of Khaine back a step, his second rang against Tyrion's helm, almost shearing through his skull. The armour of Aenarion held against the blow, however, and the impact sent shock tingling up Malekith's weary arm.

As before, Malekith became aware of a presence near at hand – a familiar coiling of Ulgu that he now recognised as the shadow-walking of Alith Anar. Between flurries of sword strokes, he scanned the piles of dead and dying heaped upon the lodestones, searching for the Shadow King.

He finally spied Alith Anar in the shadow of a waystone, calmly watching the fight with the moonbow drawn, an arrow unerringly following Malekith's heart. Distracted, the Phoenix King could manage only a clumsy parry of Tyrion's next attack, and to his horror *Asuryath* shattered from the blow.

Tyrion's backswing caught Malekith across the breastplate, rending through the armour of midnight and slicing open his fire-ravaged chest. Hurled to his back, Malekith gasped for air, sucking in hot lungfuls, hands scrabbling in the blood and mud.

Spitting blood, he pushed himself to his feet, the remnant of *Asuryath* still in his hand.

'I regret nothing!' snarled Malekith, raising the bladeless hilt of his sword in mocking salute.

Tyrion replied with a salute of his own, cross-hilt to his chin, before raising the Widowmaker high above his head for the deathblow. As his arm extended, Tyrion turned, and right before Malekith was revealed a tear in Aenarion's armour where Imrik's lance had wounded the prince.

Alith had seen it also. While Morathi's triumphant laughter echoed over the killing ground, a black shaft sped from the shadows and buried to the fletching in Tyrion's chest. Malekith's strength fled as he fell back, mirroring Tyrion's fall as his last life's blood spurted from the mortal wound.

Morathi's laughter became a drawn-out shriek of despair, but her cries sounded distant, muffled.

Crashing to the ground face-first, Malekith barely felt his fall. There was a pain in his back, but soon all he felt was numbness. Overhead the winds of magic danced and writhed, finally freed from the vortex.

His heart fluttered and then stopped.

A lifetime and a moment later, Malekith felt himself lifted up, elevated into the sky upon Ulgu the Wind of Shadow. It wrapped about him and pierced him, passing through limb and artery, becoming part of him.

* * *

He opened his eyes, still lying on the ground, and felt different. The winds of magic were no more. As though the sun had burned away a morning mist, their presence had been washed from the world. Inside he felt Ulgu writhe, trapped within his immortal flesh, bound to his body as it had once been bound to the waystone.

All had become still, the sounds of fighting washed away by a clear sea breeze. He heard footsteps and though there was no sensation yet in his body, he swivelled his eyes to see Alarielle picking her way through the falling waystones to hasten to the spot where Tyrion and Malekith lay. Her face was distant and unreadable, while around her the eyes of elves who had hovered on the brink of death snapped open as the Everqueen passed, their broken bones reknitting and their agonies receding.

Alarielle stooped briefly at Malekith's side. This close, he could feel the raw Ghyran that filled her. Always she had been a queen of life, and now the bargain was made whole, the wind of magic finding home in her. The Phoenix King realised that there was an arrow in his back and though his memory was dim now recalled that Anar had loosed another shaft as he fell, but even this had not finished Malekith. The Everqueen brushed the arrow-shaft protruding from his back and the wood burst into a fine cloud of seeds. They hung in the air for a moment, gossamer against the light. Then the wind scattered them across the rock. The seeds took root wherever they landed, shoots bursting from the husks to burrow into cracks. Alarielle's presence was all the nourishment the seeds required. Decades of growth occurred in seconds, and soon a thin but glorious glade of oaks stood at the isle's heart.

Malekith's fists clenched and unclenched as the strange forest unfurled about him, but he otherwise made no move. Alarielle paid him no further heed. Without a word, she knelt in the dust beside Tyrion. Malekith watched as a single tear spilled from the Everqueen's cheek, splashing across the prince's brow. In death, all the malice and cruelty had faded from the prince's face, and his aspect was again that which had brought hope to his people.

The ground rumbled and a short distance from where Alarielle knelt, a waystone collapsed, showering the ground with dust and shards of stone. The rock where the vortex had once stood fell away, replaced by a seething cauldron of white water.

Malekith, at last roused, staggered to his feet. No one moved to help and as blood splashed to the wet rocks he noticed that not all of his wounds were healing. The shaft of the arrow had been transmuted by Alarielle's touch, but the tip remained, lodged close to his heart. Every motion was agony, but Malekith was no stranger to pain. He reached out for the Widowmaker, which lay where it had fallen from Tyrion's hands. Malekith's Ulgu-wreathed form blurred as he moved, every motion leaving an afterimage of shadow in its wake.

It was Alarielle who first saw Malekith moving towards the ice-fang. She cried out in alarm and moved to block his path. Others heard the warning and started forward, but were all too late. The shadowy fingers of Malekith's right hand closed around the Widowmaker's hilt, and the Phoenix King gave a snort of triumph.

For a long moment, Malekith stood silhouetted against the billowing sea spray, the Widowmaker outstretched.

'Naught but steel,' he declared, feeling nothing of Khaine's power remaining in the blade. 'Just metal, nothing more.'

The Phoenix King turned and hurled the sword into the frothing waters. For a heartbeat, the Widowmaker glinted darkly. Then it was gone to the depths of the ocean. With its master's passing, the legendary Sword of Khaine could neither command Malekith, nor offer him anything that a dozen other blades could not provide.

As the Widowmaker vanished, another great tremor struck the Isle of the Dead. Jagged spurs of rock burst from the ground, and waystones sank into the whirling waters. Stone by stone, inch by inch, the island began to slip into the sea. It was the same all across Ulthuan. For thousands of years, only the magic of the Great Vortex had kept the continent above the waves. Now, with the magic scattered, the hungry ocean laid claim to a prize long denied.

'You have work to do. Save our people,' Malekith told the Everqueen, sparing a brief glance for dead Tyrion. 'He really is the very image of my father, you know.'

Malekith managed a few more paces before his injuries and weakness proved too much. He stumbled and then collapsed and his unconscious form was carried from the Isle of the Dead by the survivors of the Shadowfire Guard.

EPILOGUE

His every footstep was silent, his movements precise. He had tracked his quarry for hours, and confrontation was at last here. Silently, the hunter entered the glade, approaching the Phoenix King from behind. The hunter's bow was slung upon his shoulder, but his hand was on his sword's pommel.

It was pathetic really. Twice before the Phoenix King had detected the approach of Alith Anar, on the Blighted Isle and the Isle of the Dead. Malekith had become the embodiment of Ulgu, the power of shadow, but the so-called Shadow King still thought that he could sneak up on the former ruler of Nagarythe.

It was strange to Malekith that Alith had survived so long, being nearly as old as he was. Malekith had done so only through the armour of midnight and daemonic pacts, his mother, now swallowed up by the Realm of Chaos trying to prevent Teclis unleashing the power of the vortex, had sustained herself with blood-rites and sorcery, while others like Ariel had been divine embodiments, fragments of the gods on the mortal plane. Alith had spent much time with the raven heralds in his youth, devotees of Morai-heg, so perhaps he was the incarnation not of Drakira the queen of vengeance as some suspected, but of capricious fate itself.

Whatever the source of the Shadow King's longevity, he had not matured at all, and Malekith saw him as the same broken child pretending to be a prince he had confronted and sent running into the darkness before the Sundering had destroyed Nagarythe.

He had advanced to within a dozen paces when Malekith's voice broke the silence.

'I have been expecting you,' the king announced without turning. Clichéd, but Alith Anar seemed to have turned his life into a long cliché in recent years. 'Have you come to finish what you began?'

At last Malekith turned, his gaze falling across the other.

'I do not know,' said Alith Anar, and there was uncertainty in his voice while suspicion vied with hope in his eyes. 'I should kill you, avenge the horrors you have wrought...'

His words faded into the darkness.

'And yet your sword remains sheathed,' Malekith noted, with a faint trace of mockery.

'As does yours,' remarked the Shadow King.

'Perhaps we are neither of us what we used to be.'

'Perhaps,' Alith conceded. 'I wish I could believe that.'

'Then you have come as my assassin.'

'No, but I do come bearing a message.'

Alith Anar took a step closer, his gaze hardening as he stared up at Malekith. The Phoenix King smiled, remembering the same resolute look on the youngster's face moments before Malekith had revealed the fact that he and the tyrannical Witch King of Nagarythe were one and the same, shattering every illusion the boy had held about the world and his former prince.

'My arrow tip rests next to your heart, and you will never be able to remove it. The agony it causes shall suffice as my vengeance for as long as you serve our people. Fail them, and my next shot will take your life.'

'Your threats mean nothing,' Malekith growled.

'Then you have nothing to fear,' Alith Anar replied. The moon passed behind a cloud. The Shadow King departed, leaving Malekith alone with his thoughts.

Not long after Alith had left, another entered the clearing. Alarielle stopped beside her husband and held a hand to his arm.

'It is done?' she asked.

'Yes, he was here just now.'

'It is better this way. If you simply kill him, others will try to avenge him. We are one people again, the aesenar included.'

'He thinks he has me on a leash,' Malekith said quietly.

'Good, it will stop him doing something rash that we would all regret.' Alarielle slipped something into Malekith's metal hand and turned away. 'We will control our own destiny from now on – Morai-heg will tug the strands of fate no more.'

When she was gone Malekith opened his fingers, revealing a notched arrow head of black steel. Perhaps the illusion of fulfilling his ancient oaths of vengeance would mature Alith and make him a useful member of the court. He certainly had deadly skills, and Malekith had an empire to rebuild.

So it was that in Athel Loren the elves made their home again, dwelling in the mystical forest as they had done in the time before the Coming of Chaos. As Lileath had told Teclis, there was sanctuary to be found there, and the perils of the world were kept from them for a time.

The winds of magic unchained by Teclis found resting places in great personalities of many races, across Ulthuan and Elthin Arvan. Nagash and his dead legions still walked abroad and Archaon the self-proclaimed Everchosen of Chaos laid waste to all in his path.

Malekith and Alarielle were wed and he was crowned again as Phoenix King, and they believed the great cycle of the gods and life had started again, rebirth from death, growth from destruction, harmony from discord. Only the future would reveal whether the son of Aenarion could truly overcome so much personal bitterness and strife and become the ruler the elves needed.

Such a pity that neither Malekith nor the elves had any future, for the Rhana Dandra was the End Times and there was to be no new beginning, only more death and misery.

Lileath had lied to them. They had sanctuary, for a while, but all things fall to Chaos.

Eventually.

WARHAMMER®
THE END TIMES

THE RISE OF THE
HORNED RAT

GUY HALEY

An extract from The Rise of the Horned Rat,
Book IV of Warhammer: The End Times
by Guy Haley

The mortal skaven were in full debate. Things were not going well. Shouting and squeaking raised a clamour that shook the room. Many were standing to wave accusing forepaws at one another. Some squeaked privately behind their hands to one another, or shot knowing looks across the table as deals were silently struck and as quickly broken.

Just as Verminking had silenced the Shadow Council, so Kritislik the Seerlord silenced the Council of Thirteen, although nowhere near as majestically. He was white-furred and horned, and that should have ensured him supremacy. He was chief of the grey seers, the wizard lords of the skaven, blessed by the Horned Rat himself, and nominal chief of the Council in his absence. But the others were in rebellious mood. Kritislik was agitated, squeaking rapidly and without authority. He had yet to squirt musk, but the look of fear was on him, in his twitching nose, widened eyes and bristling fur.

'Quiet-quiet! You blame, shout-squeak! All fault here. Great victories we have-were in manlands of Estalia and Tilea.'

'Many slaves, much plunder-spoils,' said Kratch Doomclaw, warlord of Clan Rictus. 'All is going to plan. Soon the man-things will fall. Listen to the white-fur.'

'No!' said one, huge and deep voiced. He was black as night and unconquerable as the mountains. Lord Gnawdwell of Clan Mors. 'You take-steal too much, far beyond your scavenge rights. You test my patience, thief-thief, sneaker. I will not listen to your prattling one heartbeat longer.'

'My clanrats, my victory,' said Kratch, making an effort to keep his voice low and slow. 'Where is Lord Gnawdwell's trophy-prize? I shall squeak you where – still in the hands of the dwarf-things, who you have not yet defeated.'

Squeaking laughter came from several of the others, including, most irksomely for Gnawdwell, Lord Paskrit, the obese warlord-general of all Skavendom.

The lords of the four greater clans scowled at this display of indiscipline among the warlord clans. Lord Morskittar of Clan Skryre, emperor of warlocks and tinkerer in chief, was not impressed.

'Many devices, many weapons, many warptokens' worth of new machines you of the warlord clans were given-granted in aid of the Great Uprising. What have we to show-see for it? Yes-yes, very good. Tilea-place and Estalia-place gone-destroyed.'

General noises of approval interrupted him. Morskittar held his paws up, palms flat, and bared his teeth in disapproval. 'Fools to cheer like stupid slave-meat! The weakest human-lands destroyed only. Frog-things still in their stone temple-homes. Dwarf-things still in the mountains. And Empire-place not yet destroyed!' He shook his head, his tail lashing back and forth behind him. 'Disappointing.'

'What you squeak-say? Where are your armies?' said Lord Griznek Mancarver of Clan Skab. 'Guns no good without paw-fingers to pull triggers.'

More uproar and shouted accusations. All around the room,

the elite Albino Guard of the Council stiffened, ready to intervene on the winning side should open conflict erupt.

'No! No!' said Morskittar. 'I will speak! I will speak!' He slammed a skull carved of pure warpstone down onto the table. It banged like a cannon, the report buying him silence. 'Why point-indicate me with paw of blame?' said Morskittar slyly. 'I say the grey seers are the ones who shoulder responsibility. Clan Scruten are those who bring everything to ruin.' He pointed at Kritislik.

'Yes-yes!' chittered the others immediately, all of whom had their own reasons for loathing the priest-magicians. 'The seers, Clan Scruten!'

'Outrage! Outrage!' squealed Kritislik. 'I have led this council long ages-time! I led great summoning many breedings ago! I speak for the Horned Rat!'

'You speak for yourself,' said Paskrit the Vast, gruffly. Sensing weakness, he heaved his bulk up to face Kritislik on his footpaws. 'You speak for Clan Scruten. Always scheming, always plotting. Always say do this, do that! Why is it Clan Mors find itself fighting Clan Rictus? Why Clan Skurvy lose half of thrall clans the day before sea-battle of Sartosa-place?'

'Grey seer is why, Clan Scruten! Clan Scruten are to blame,' croaked Arch-Plaguelord Nurglitch.

They all shouted then, except for the inscrutable Nightlord Sneek, master of Clan Eshin, who watched it all with hooded eyes half hidden by his mask and no scent to betray his thoughts.

'It is not our fault! Your incompetence and greed-grasping stops the obeying of our rightful orders! We are the horned rats. We are the chosen-best of the Great Horned One! You fight-fight, scrapping like common rat-things on human middens. Listen to us, or suffer,' shouted Kritislik.

'No! Lies-deceit. You pit us against one another when all we wish to do is work in harmony for the betterment of all skavenkind!' said Lord Gnawdwell.

The others nodded solemnly. 'Truth-word!' they said. 'We

would conquer, but for you. Grey seers make us fight-fight!' They would all happily have knifed each other in the back at the least provocation, whether a grey seer was pulling the strings or not. That the grey seers usually *were* pulling the strings complicated matters enormously.

The Council of Thirteen erupted into a cacophony of squeaked accusations. The scent of aggression grew strong.

The Shadow Lords looked on with growing disapproval.

'See-see,' said Verminking. 'Great victories they have, and now they fall to fighting.'

'They are what they are, and no more,' said Vermalanx disinterestedly. 'Children yet, but mastery shall come to them. Then true greatness we shall see-smell in due course. I care not for this – my Nurglitch's plans are well advanced.'

'Yes-yes,' said Throxstraggle, Vermalanx's ally and fellow plaguelord. 'What care we for these pup squeakings?'

'Your grave error to set aside Clan Pestilens from the doing-aims of the others. You are not apart from this, poxlords,' said Verminking. 'You and yours distance yourselves, but Clan Pestilens is nothing alone. You think-remember that.'

Vermalanx chirred angrily.

'No mastery will come. They fail! They fail!' spat Basqueek. 'Fool-things! Squabbling while the world slips from their paws. Always the same, civil war comes again. Skavenblight will ring to the sound of blade on blade. Man-things and dwarf-things will recover, and skaven stay in the shadows. Always the same.'

'Yes-yes,' said Verminking. 'They fail. But watch...'

In the mortal realm, Kritislik stood, waving a fist at the other Lords of Decay, admonishing them for their stupidity. From the look on his face, he thought it was working, for the others suddenly fell silent and shrank back in their seats, eyes wide. A few bared their throats in submission before they could catch themselves. Someone shamefully let spray the musk of fear. It hung heavy over the crowd, an accusation of cowardice.

Kritislik began to crow. The mightiest lords of Skavendom, and he had them in the palm of his paw. Now was his chance to stamp his authority all over this rabble again!

Or maybe not. Kritislik was so taken by his own oratory that he had completely failed to notice the shape growing behind him.

Black smoke jetted from the seat of the Horned Rat. The wisps of shadow built into a cloud that writhed and began to take the form of something huge and malevolent.

'Ah! Now! Order, is good, yes! You listen-hear good, you...' Kritislik stopped mid-sentence. His nose twitched. 'You are not listening to me, are you? You do not hear-smell me good?' he said. He was answered by eleven shaking heads, the owners of which were all trying to look inconspicuous.

He turned around to see a horned head forming from darkness more complete than that found in the deepest places of the world.

Kritislik threw himself to the floor in outright obeisance as the manifested Horned Rat opened eyes that flooded the room with sickly green light. Words of power rumbled from some other place, the voice underpinned by hideous chittering – the death-squeaks of every rat and skaven ever to have drawn breath.

'*Children of the Horned Rat,*' he said, his voice as final as a tunnel collapse, '*how you disappoint your father.*'

'O Great One! O Horned One! Once more I welcome you to the–'

'*No one summon-bids I, Kritislik. I come, I go, wherever I please. I have no master.*'

'I... I...'

'*You squabble pathetically. This will cease now. Your plans are sound, your alliances are not. I will not countenance another failure. Long have Clan Scruten had my blessing. I have given you my mark, great power, and long life.*' The head bore down on Kritislik, lips parting to show teeth made of crackling light. '*You have wasted my favour.*'

Without warning, a hand formed from the smoke, scrabbling as if seeking purchase on an unseen barrier. Fingers and claws pointed forwards. The air warped as the hand pushed against an unseen skin, then burst its way into common reality and reached down.

Kritislik squealed in terror as he was plucked from the floor by his tail. His fine robes dropped down to cover his head. The musk of fear sprayed without restraint, followed by a rich stream of droppings.

'The others are right-correct, little Kritislik.' A second hand reached out from the darkness, where now a muscular torso had also formed. A gentle claw-finger lifted the hem of Kritislik's upended robes to reveal his petrified face, and stroked along his horns. *'So much I have given you, and yet you scheme for more. Greedy, when there is enough for all to feast upon. Your avarice stops now.'*

The mouth of the Horned Rat gaped wide. Kritislik was hoisted high by the tail over a maw swirling with terrible possibilities. Kritislik stared down and gibbered at what he saw there.

'M-mercy! M-mercy, O Great One! We will double our efforts! Triple them! Quadrupl-' His pleas ended in a scream as his tail was released. The grey seer fell into the eternally hungry mouth of his god. The Horned Rat's jaws snapped shut. His eyes closed with pleasure, and when he opened them again they burned with a cold and terrible light.

'Thirteen times thirteen passes of the Chaos moon I will give you. Thirteen times thirteen moons I will wait. Go to your legions and your workshops! Bring me victory. Bring me dominance over this mortal realm! You must be as one, work as one, as single-minded as a swarm pouring from a cracked sewer-pipe – all rats scurry-flood in same direction. Only then will you inherit the ruins of this world, only then will you rule. Thirteen times thirteen moons! Fail, and all will suffer the fate of the seer.'

With a crackle of green lightning and the tolling of a bell so loud the room quaked, the Horned Rat vanished. Kritislik's bones lay black and smoking upon the floor.